New York Times bestselling author **Sarah Mayberry** was born in Melbourne, Australia. Ever since she learned to read and write she has wanted to be an author. She studied professional writing and literature before embarking on various writing-related jobs, working as a magazine editor and in various story-related roles on Australia's longest-running serial drama, *Neighbours*. She inherited a love of romances from both her grandmothers and fulfilled her fondest wish when she was accepted for publication.

New York Times Bestselling Author

Sarah Mayberry
and
Shoma Narayanan

AFTER-HOURS
NEGOTIATION

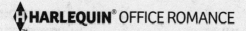

Recycling programs
for this product may
not exist in your area.

ISBN-13: 978-0-373-60128-8

After-Hours Negotiation

Copyright © 2015 by Harlequin Books S.A.

The publisher acknowledges the copyright holders
of the individual works as follows:

Can't Get Enough
Copyright © 2005 by Small Cow Productions PTY Ltd.

An Offer She Can't Refuse
Copyright © 2014 by Shoma Narayanan

Printed in U.S.A.

CONTENTS

CAN'T GET ENOUGH

Sarah Mayberry

Many thanks to the gang at *Neighbours*,
and to my friends and family for
always believing. Special thanks to La-La,
and to Wanda for making my writing better.
Lastly, thanks to Chris, who has taught me
so much about storytelling.
You're my romantic hero, and I love you.

CHAPTER ONE

CLAIRE MARSDEN WAS LATE. She hated being late almost as much as she hated brussels sprouts. And she hated brussels sprouts a lot. Traffic inched forward, and she craned her head out her window, confirming that the entrance to the company parking complex was just five car lengths ahead. Unfortunately, there were five cars occupying those five car lengths, and they were all moving as though they were powered by arthritic turtles. She willed them to move faster, concentrating intently on the shiny bumper of the pickup in front of her.

Nothing. So much for any latent powers of ESP she might have.

Might as well use the time to slap on some lipstick. She flipped her visor mirror down and blinked in horror at the too-close image that reflected back at her: eyes red, nose just beginning to peel thanks to too much sun on the weekend and a hefty gob of what her godchild Oscar rather charmingly called "eye booger" in the corner of one eye.

"Aren't you the belle of the ball," she told her reflection.

A dab of moisturizer, some judicious use of

Kleenex and a swipe of lipstick went a long way to repairing the damage. She was just completing the last curve of pink-brown lipstick across her lips when the car behind her honked. A jagged lipstick smear raced up her cheek before she could control her reflexes.

Realizing the lane was now clear all the way to the coveted car park entrance, she slapped the visor up, deciding to fix her face later. With an apologetic wave for the driver behind her, she accelerated forward and zipped up the entrance ramp with a spurt of speed.

Now it was simply a case of snagging her favorite spot near the stairwell, and she could still make her first meeting of the day....

She frowned as she pulled up in front of *her* spot. A shiny red sports car gleamed smugly there, light reflecting off its sleek curves. Its owner had gone to the trouble of reversing in—obviously a fan of the quick getaway. The frown creasing her forehead deepened. She knew the owner of this car, and, indeed, he was fond of the quick getaway; at least a dozen women at Beck and Wise could vouch for just how fond.

"Stupid slacker," she ground out under her breath as she threw her car into reverse and began trawling for another spot.

Everyone knew that spot was hers. She made a point of parking there every day. Okay, so it didn't actually have her name on it—Beck and Wise only reserved parking spaces for its very senior executives—but it was common knowledge.

And she knew for a fact that Jack Brook was fully aware of her attachment to the spot; she ignored him every time she passed him on her way to or from her car. Just last week she'd glided coolly past him, not acknowledging his presence with so much as the twitch of an eyelid. So he knew. Oh, yes, he knew.

At last she found another spot, a full five rows farther back than her usual one. She turned into it with more verve than necessary, and had to waste precious seconds correcting the error. The contents of her handbag were spread out across her passenger seat after her ad hoc repair mission in the traffic jam, and she scrabbled around until she'd stuffed them all back into her sleek black leather purse. Like much of her life, it looked perfect on the outside, its chaotic contents well hidden from prying eyes.

She broke into a fast trot as she cleared the first row of cars, but realized very quickly that no amount of training or conditioning could prepare someone for a hundred-yard dash in leather pumps. Slowing to a tight-assed scamper, she spared a glance for the gleaming red affront in her parking spot as she pushed open the door to the car park stairwell.

Jack Brook. Just thinking his name made her grind her teeth. From the moment she'd first laid eyes on him two years ago she'd had his number, and everything she'd heard or seen of him since had only confirmed that initial snap judgment.

Too good-looking for his own good—if you liked tall, dark, blue-eyed, broad-shouldered men.

Too smart for his own good, too—if you admired creative, clever, arrogant, witty minds.

And too damn aware of all of the above, as far as she was concerned.

Most of the women at Beck and Wise thought he was dreamy. Most of the men, too, come to think of it. If they weren't admiring his latest magazine article, they were playing racquetball with him after work, or laughing at one of his jokes.

And he just made her want to spit. Call it an instinctive rejection of a type of man she'd always found incredibly unappealing. Call it the opposite of sexual magnetism. Whatever, it made her back go stiff whenever she caught sight of his dark head, it compelled her to press her full lips into a tight, ungenerous line at the mere sound of his voice, and it switched her clever tongue to take-no-prisoners mode. Not that it did her much good. Usually he'd just smirk at anything she said and throw some off-the-cuff smart comment her way—and damn him if nine times out of ten she wasn't left floundering and feeling stupid. Another excellent reason to avoid him as much as possible.

It wasn't that big a deal, usually. Beck and Wise was a huge publishing company, a media giant that produced hundreds of magazines for the Australian marketplace. Jack worked on a whole different floor to her—when he was in the office—on a whole different selection of magazine titles. If she put some effort into it, she could manage things so that she barely ever saw him.

But now he'd slipped his red penis-compensator into her parking spot, and she couldn't simply assign him to his usual category of "necessary evil" and forget about him.

The automatic doors to the impressive thirty-story Beck and Wise building swished open as she entered, and she glanced longingly across at the foyer coffee shop as a hit of freshly ground coffee beans washed over her. No time for coffee today. She spared a thought for her favorite double mocha latte, eyeing the distinctive steaming cup in the hands of one lucky, contented customer. Her eyes automatically lifted to scan the coffee-lover's face, and she felt her lips assume their usual streamlined position as she looked into Jack Brook's deep blue eyes.

Bastard. Now he had her favorite parking spot *and* her favorite coffee.

She forced herself to look away, concentrating instead on the elevator bank ahead. Checking her watch, she stabbed the up button urgently, then sighed with relief as the doors in front of her opened on a cheery chime. Entering, she punched the button for her floor, then looked up to see Jack bearing down on her, his stride lengthening as he sped up to beat the doors. They made eye contact again, and the corners of his ridiculously blue eyes crinkled as he flashed one of his patented engaging grins at her.

"Could you…?" he called, just a few steps away now.

She moved instinctively, her finger reaching for

the button before her conscious mind could approve or disapprove the action. He'd stolen her parking spot, after all. And he had that delicious-looking coffee in his hand…

The doors began to slide shut. Realizing what she'd done, his eyes widened with confusion and then, quickly, annoyance. She tried to despise the little zing of triumph that shot up her spine, but when the doors closed completely she didn't fight the smile that leaped to her lips.

Take that, Smug-boy, she thought.

And then she saw her reflection in the polished steel elevator doors: a huge smear of lipstick raced up her cheek like some bizarre experiment in modern art. Groaning, she closed her eyes. Why did Jack Brook always have the last word?

JACK STOOD STARING at the closed elevator doors for a full twenty seconds. What was it with that uptight cow from the fifteenth floor? Claire Something-or-other, that was her name. Always frowning. Her lips always squished into nothingness. Her chin always high and haughty. And what was with the weird lipstick?

He shook his head, genuinely baffled. To his knowledge, he'd never done a thing to offend her. Yet every time he smiled her way she blew him off. It was as if she'd caught him double-dipping, or cheating on his taxes, or something.

He hated women like that. Women who acted as though every gesture of friendliness, every joke or helpful suggestion was about you trying to crack their defenses and get them into bed. As if he'd be interested in some tightly stitched-up chick who'd probably just lie there and stare at the ceiling anyway. Thanks, but he'd rather fly solo.

He stepped into the next elevator car and punched the button for the seventeenth floor. Claire What's-her-name didn't have anything to worry about where he was concerned. He liked his women young—sub-twenty, if possible—bubbly and full of life. Preferably in a bikini, but a one-piece was also acceptable. He grinned. Okay, so he was exaggerating a little, but if the hat fit…

He took a sip of his latte, then shook his head as the image of Claire's bestriped face disappearing behind the closing elevator doors popped into his mind. God, how petty. How stupid and silly and petty.

And then he got it. He threw back his head and laughed out loud at exactly the same time that the elevator car slid to a smooth stop on the fifteenth floor—someone must have pressed the up button. Heads turned as people looked up from their work, and he saw Claire's head snap around and her eyes narrow as she spotted him from her office doorway. He grinned and fished in his pocket, pulling his car keys out and dangling them suggestively.

Her lips practically disappeared as she glared at him, and he gave her a little finger wave as the doors closed between them for the second time that day.

She was pissed about the parking spot! He practically giggled as he relished the moment. Imagine being that invested in something so mundane. Imagine wanting to take revenge over something so small and insignificant. Admittedly, the thought that the space he'd reversed into this morning was usually filled by her sensible sedan had crossed his mind at the time. And just as quickly exited at the other end. It would do her good to have a bit of variety, he'd thought. She looked as though she was a creature of habit, always in the same sensible boxy suits, always with her dark, curly hair cut sensibly short. So he was practically doing her a favor, forcing her to break her routine. She might even thank him for the new perspective he was offering her.

Or not. He was still smiling as he stepped out onto the seventeenth floor, raising his latte in greeting at his assistant Linda as he passed by.

"Why are you looking particularly naughty this morning? What trouble have you just stirred up?" she demanded as she followed him into his corner office.

He smiled mysteriously and waggled his eyebrows at her, glancing out the window at his fantastic view of the city of Melbourne. The sky was blue, fluffy clouds floated across the sky…and seventeen floors down, if only he had X-ray vision, he could spot his car…in her spot.…

"Jack? What on earth have you done?" Linda asked, real worry in her voice now.

"Relax. It's nothing. Just a stupid…thing that happened. With that Claire girl from Homes and Decorating," he said.

Linda gave him a look.

"Claire Marsden, you mean?"

"Is she the sensible one? With the skinny little mouth?"

"Are we talking about the same woman ? On the short side? Cute as a button?" Linda queried.

He made a dismissive noise, unprepared to think positive things about Claire Marsden right now.

"Well, I think she's very attractive," Linda continued.

"Compared to the Russian women's weight-lifting team, you mean?"

"Whatever did she do to get you so offside?" Linda asked, her eyes wide at his unaccustomed cruelty.

He shrugged, suddenly aware that he'd actually allowed himself to get quite worked up.

"We just had a little…transport dispute this morning."

"I see. Well, she's a nice person. My niece Ronnie spent a week doing work experience with her recently. Claire was very supportive and helpful, and Ronnie is really inspired to have a go at journalism now."

He paused in the act of flipping open the lid on his notebook computer.

"Why didn't you ask me about the work experience? I'd have been happy to have Ronnie up here."

Linda made a noise in the back of her throat. He recognized it as her deeply skeptical grunt and decided he was offended.

"What's that supposed to mean?"

"Oh, come on, Jack. You're hardly the most patient of men. I didn't want you breathing down Ronnie's neck, making her nervous. Besides, you're far too good-looking and Ronnie's far too young and blond for my personal comfort."

He leaned back in his chair, happy for any opportunity to crank his assistant up a little.

"Blond you say? Just how old is she?"

Linda shook her head and slapped his mail down onto his desk.

"Keep your trousers on and read your mail, Mr. Sexy," she said.

He took another big slurp of latte while he waited for his computer to boot up. A dialogue box flashed onto the screen and he typed in his password, flicking idly through the few letters Linda had just given him while the computer logged in to the company network.

Nothing exciting there. In his role as managing editor, he oversaw the production of six monthly magazine titles. It meant he got a lot of mail—most of it dull. Today he had a complaint from one of the tour operators they'd profiled in a recent Travel Time issue, which could go straight in the recycling bin, and a couple of letters to the editor from two of the other titles he managed.

He turned his attention to his e-mail, his eyebrows rising with surprise as he saw he had a message from the Big Kahuna himself, Morgan Beck. He scanned the note quickly, then called Linda in.

"Can you cancel my two o'clock and reschedule it for me? I've been summoned upstairs by God."

"Can do. Anything else?"

He flashed his most disarming smile, turning on the charm shamelessly. To her credit, Linda remained steadfastly unaffected, instead shaking her head ruefully.

"Don't waste your little-boy-lost routine on me. What do you want?"

"Do you think you could also swing past the post office and collect the mail from my personal box? I haven't had a chance to get over there since I flew back into town yesterday."

"Jack, we've been over this. I'm more than happy to collect your personal mail for you every day during my lunch break. Just give me the key to your box and it will be taken care of."

Sliding the small key from his key ring, Jack hesitated before handing it over.

"I feel bad asking you to run personal errands for me," he confessed when Linda made an impatient noise.

"Well, get over it. You're a good boss, you don't treat me like a slave, and I'm happy to help you out however I can."

Overcoming his personal scruples, Jack shrugged and handed the key over. Linda gave him an amused look as she slid it into her hip pocket.

"Don't worry—I'll let you know when you've crossed the line and turned into a heartless corporate shark."

"My deepest, darkest fear. How did you know?" Jack joked.

"I'm psychic. Which is why I suspect it's useless suggesting you tidy yourself up a bit before your appointment with Mr. Beck," Linda said, her tone indicating she already knew his response.

"You *are* psychic, you know. It's uncanny," he said, loving that he could annoy her.

Linda's eyes flicked down to his black, three-quarter-length cargo pants, slip-on sandals and unironed Hawaiian shirt.

"You're lucky Mr. Beck likes you," she said on her way out of his office.

Jack snorted, his mood shifting abruptly as her words triggered a memory.

Luck.

What a concept. What a stupid, random, insane, cruel concept. He was very quiet for a moment as he stared out unseeingly at his view. And then he remembered that big smear of lipstick across Claire Marsden's face and he laughed to himself all over again.

CHAPTER TWO

BUSY. THE THOUGHT registered somewhere between Claire's third impromptu meeting of the day and the fourth phone call from the client she'd been wooing for the past six months. Now that they'd signed the contracts, Hillcrest Hardware were keen to have their new custom magazine in their hot little hands.

Ironic, if you had the time to appreciate such things. She'd spent so long explaining, and illustrating, and cajoling to bring them to the point of saying yes, and now they were more keen than she was. And she was pretty damn keen.

Despite the fact that it was well past midday and she still hadn't read her e-mail, she paused to appreciate the larger-than-life blowup of the front cover for the launch edition of *Welcome Home* magazine that was leaning against her office wall. Gleaming floorboards reflected light from wide, white-framed windows, and a rustic wood dining setting graced the center of the tastefully decorated room. Color Your World read one of the cover lines, while another claimed Bring Your Garden to Life in an Instant. A little bubble of pride blossomed in her belly. After all the hard work, they were finally a go.

Her own magazine. Based on a concept she'd created. Executed just how she thought it should be executed. It simply didn't get better.

She was the one who had seen the opportunity for a custom magazine within the Hillcrest Hardware chain. She'd watched the growth in demand for decorator magazines, and she'd found a progressive hardware retailer in the marketplace who was looking for a new way to create relationships with its customers. It had made sense to her to answer one need with the other, just as it had made sense to the executives at Hillcrest when she'd pitched it to them six months ago.

Now she was about to launch a new magazine title into the Australian marketplace, an important, key part of her five-year plan. Soon, if she played her cards right, the corner office and senior management status she coveted would be hers—it was just a matter of time.

Today was Wednesday; by this time next week, she should have editorial sign-off from her client, and the magazine should be well into production. Another week or so later, and the first edition would be rolling off the printing presses.

A goofy smile still wreathing her lips, Claire clicked the mouse on the e-mail icon on her computer screen and watched as her in-box registered way too many notifications. Sighing, she realized she was going to have to get her assistant to prioritize them for her, alert her to the urgent ones and print the rest off for her to read in bed later that night. Another fascinating evening.

It was just as well there was no man also planning on sharing her bed.

She paused for a moment, annoyed with herself. Where had that thought come from? Parts of her body twitched suggestively, and she shrugged. Okay, it had been a while. And a bit of frustration release was necessary every now and then, but that was what George Clooney movies were for. This was more important. *Welcome Home* was her baby, and it deserved all her attention.

Besides, it wasn't as though there was a battle going on here between the magazine and her personal life; apart from her training regime and the actual triathlon meets themselves, she had no personal life. There was work, and there was the road and the pool and her bike. End of story.

And it was a nice, uncomplicated, successful story. She was fulfilled. Really. And hadn't she made it into the state triathlon semifinals thanks to all that focus?

Okay, maybe she was a little horny. But that could wait. Sex would always be there, but this opportunity wouldn't.

A recent memory volunteered itself suddenly— last time she'd visited her grandmother she'd been astonished to learn that her gran was telling everyone in the old people's home that she was a lesbian.

"Just to take the heat off them all wondering when

you're getting married and having children, dear," her gran had explained.

So Claire wasn't going to be young forever. But this was important, and sometimes other things had to take a backseat to work. In five years' time, she'd be ensconced in that corner office, in charge of a handful of quality magazines. The sacrifices and loneliness were worth it. For the time being.

Having talked her nether regions into submission, she called her assistant, Tom, in and asked him to sort through the rest of her e-mails.

She was just about to plunge into her in-tray when a familiar figure propped itself against her door frame.

"We still on for lunch?"

Claire stared at her friend Katherine in dismay.

"You forgot, didn't you?" Katherine guessed, one hand resting on her slim hip.

"I'm sorry. I've got so much on, I think I should just work through lunch," Claire apologized.

But Katherine wasn't about to take no for an answer. Swinging around, she called in reinforcements.

"Tom! Get over here and help me convince your boss she needs to eat lunch," she called imperatively.

Tom shot up from his seat as though he'd been electrocuted, and Claire had to stifle a laugh as he stared at Katherine slavishly. At nearly six feet tall with legs that seemed to go on forever and a bust that would put a 1950s pinup to shame, Katherine was every man's sexual fantasy. The fact that she was funny, clever and worked as editor of a sports magazine were bonuses that most men didn't seem to mind, either. At a tender twenty years, Tom was like a bunny in the headlights of her attractiveness.

"I tell her all the time she should have a lunch break, but she thinks a protein shake is enough," Tom said, sounding for all the world like a worried Jewish mother.

"Are you listening to what Tom is saying, Claire?" Katherine asked, the glint in her eye signaling that she wasn't unaware of Tom's adoration.

Shaking her head at her friend, Claire checked her watch.

"Twenty minutes," she said.

"Done. Thanks for the backup, Tom," Katherine said, giving him a big smile.

Tom just stood there, apparently stunned by such beneficence.

Claire grabbed her handbag and followed Katherine to the elevator.

"You're cruel," Claire admonished.

"How so? I was perfectly nice to him!"

Claire gave Katherine's close-fitting deep red, short-skirted suit and elegant high heels a once-over.

"You ought to be registered as a deadly weapon. Or given a handicap. How are the rest of us mere mortals supposed to compete?"

"You do okay, from what I've seen," Katherine commented dryly.

"Right. That's why I watched three George Clooney movies this month."

The elevator door opened and they exited into the foyer, heading for the coffee shop.

"The opportunities are there, but you choose not to see them."

Claire rolled her eyes—as if she wouldn't have noticed an eligible guy interested in her! To prove her point, a young courier walked straight into a potted palm because he was too busy tracking Katherine's progress across the foyer to look where he was going.

"You see that? Nobody walks into plants for me, I can tell you."

"You don't believe me? What about Cameron Johnson in layout? And that cute security guard on the night shift?"

Claire had to rack her brain to get even a vague mental image of the men. Needless to say, they hadn't walked into a wall, or any other obstacle, the last time she had been in their vicinity—*that* she would have remembered.

"You're deluded."

They settled at their usual table in the far back corner of the coffee shop and picked up a menu each, even though neither of them ever strayed from their normal order—a chicken club sandwich.

"You don't *want* to see—that's your problem. When was the last time you had a date?" Katherine challenged.

Claire studied the menu intently. Why had she even brought this subject up? Hadn't she just decided that she was happy with her work-oriented world at the moment?

"Forget I said anything. I was only joking, anyway," she hedged.

Katherine shook her head sympathetically.

"That long, huh?"

Desperate for some way to avoid the conversation Claire suspected was in the offing, she scanned the coffee shop looking for a distraction. She twitched as she noted Jack Brook propped at the lunch bar, one leg resting comfortably on the foot rail as he chatted to a woman she didn't recognize. He looked so confident and happy and self-assured that she felt her toes curling in her shoes with annoyance.

"You went out with Jack Brook for a while, didn't you?" she found herself blurting.

Katherine looked surprised and she turned to follow Claire's line of sight, quickly spotting Jack lounging at the bar.

The glance she shot Claire was unreadable.

"Yeah, I did. For a few short, spectacular weeks a couple of years ago."

The waiter stopped by their table, and Claire and Katherine both ordered the chicken club sandwich. Silence fell. Aware that Katherine was now thinking completely the wrong thing, Claire felt honor-bound to correct her.

"He parked in my space this morning," she explained. "He's such an arrogant jerk, I just wondered what you saw in him."

"That's simple—pretty much what every other woman sees in him. He's gorgeous."

Claire pulled a face, her eyes sliding across to contemplate Jack's profile.

"He really does nothing for me," she said airily.

Katherine made a small disbelieving noise.

"Then you're officially the walking dead. Whether or not Jack Brook is gorgeous is not a matter of subjective opinion. He has those amazing eyes, and a body to die for—fantastic skin, great arms. And he's a great lover. Really…gifted, if you get what I mean," Katherine said, wiggling her eyebrows suggestively.

Claire shifted in her seat, but she was unable to stop her gaze from sneaking over to him. He was teasing his lunch companion, reaching out to swipe a bit of frosting off her cake. As Claire watched he slid his chocolate-coated finger into his mouth and licked it, his actions completely unconscious and completely erotic. She flicked her eyes away from the blatant display, but, again, they slid back to him of their own accord. Now he was shoving his hand into his pants pocket as he leaned casually on the bar. The fabric tightened across his thighs and, unbelievably, she felt herself blushing as she considered what Katherine had said. Gifted… *What* exactly did that mean? Was that about the finger-licking thing, or the part of his trousers that was holding her attention right now?

"You know, a fling with someone like Jack could be exactly what you need," Katherine said.

Claire jerked her attention back to her friend.

"Are you insane? I wouldn't sleep with Jack Brook

if you paid me. He's cocky, conceited, smug—and a complete man-slut."

"I see."

Katherine was smiling knowingly, and Claire bristled. Determined to prove her point, she leaned across the table.

"If you gave me the choice of kissing Jack Brook or punching him in the face, I'd choose the punch every time," she said firmly.

"Ah. So you have thought about kissing Jack, then?"

Claire was about to launch into all the reasons why she considered Jack Brook to be subhuman when Katherine's face suddenly lit up as though she'd just thought of something funny. She laughed, nodding her head as though she'd just worked something out. Claire frowned at her, suspicious.

"What?"

"I just remembered something. I was talking about you with Jack once. He wanted to know why we were friends—he thought you were prissy."

Claire sat bolt upright in her seat and glared across at Jack. What a pig! How dare he call her prissy? What a horrible thing to say—as if she was some dried-up spinster aunt or something. She had the urge to go over and give him a piece of her mind....

"Where does he get off talking about me like that?" she snapped, dragging her gaze away from Jack to find Katherine studying her speculatively.

Claire suddenly felt very exposed under her friend's knowing gaze.

"I mean, as if I care what a jerk like him thinks about me."

Katherine simply quirked an eyebrow disbelievingly.

"Can we please talk about something—any-thing—else?" Claire asked, fiddling with her paper napkin and cutlery.

To her everlasting relief, their sandwiches arrived.

"You're lucky I'm really hungry," Katherine said lightly. "You're off the hook—for the moment."

TWENTY MINUTES HAD turned into half an hour by the time they settled their bill and made their way back to the elevator. Claire thought Katherine had let the subject of Jack Brook drop entirely, but just as they were parting ways, Katherine suddenly got serious. Despite Claire's protestations, Katherine insisted on explaining why she and Jack had broken up. Claire listened with arms crossed, determined not to give Katherine any more reasons to jump to ridiculous conclusions about her and Jack Brook. Given that every word her friend said just confirmed her pre-conceived beliefs about the man, it wasn't hard.

"I just want you to go in with your eyes open," Katherine finally concluded.

"Kat, hell will freeze over before I even consider having a polite conversation with that man," Claire said.

"If you say so."

Claire was shaking her head as she returned to her office, bewildered by Katherine's determination to imagine some sort of...*thing* between her and Jack Brook.

"Not in a million years," she muttered to herself as she began packing her briefcase for her afternoon appointment at Hillcrest Hardware.

"Claire! Oh, my God—I'm so glad I've found you!"

It was Tom, sweaty and excited in her doorway.

"I was checking your e-mails while you were at lunch—Morgan Beck wants to see you at two! I went straight down to the coffee shop, but you'd already left..."

Galvanized, Claire checked her watch, then sighed with relief when she saw it was only ten to two. Plenty of time to get up to the thirtieth floor— if she hustled.

She forced herself to suppress the many panicky thoughts that were suddenly clamoring for attention and equal-opportunity worry time in her mind and instead focused on her schedule for the rest of the afternoon. She'd have to push back that appointment with Hillcrest, then... It was no use—all she wanted to do was fret over this unprecedented call from the thirtieth floor. Why would Morgan Beck want to see her out of the blue like this? Surely *Welcome Home* had been well and truly signed, sealed and delivered? They'd praised her, promoted her to editor, handed the whole project over into her capable hands. What more was there to say?

"Tom, I need you to ring Hillcrest Hardware and tell them I'll be approximately twenty minutes late," she said, slinging her handbag over her shoulder and grabbing her briefcase. "I'll head straight out after seeing Mr. Beck."

Tom was taking notes, loving the excitement of the moment.

"I'll ring the traffic report and leave a message on your cell phone if there are any traffic delays," he suggested eagerly.

"That would be great, thanks," she said, hiding a smile at his action-stations demeanor.

Satisfied that she'd covered all bases, she headed for the ladies' room, her mind working overtime trying to find the reason behind this summons. The mirror revealed that hectic color stained her cheeks and the first thing she did was sluice a great handful of cold water over her face. Patting it dry with some hand towel, she took a deep breath and slowly exhaled.

Be calm. Everything is fine. They can't take this off you now—it's your idea, she told herself.

The mantra appeared to work. Her heart climbed down from her throat and back into her chest to resume normal activities, and she quickly dabbed on some mascara and a fresh layer of lipstick. Wetting her fingers under the tap, she spruced up her short curls, ensuring her face was framed nicely. One final check over, the last-minute realization that she had a blouse button undone flashing her belly button, and then she was out of there and heading for the elevator.

Five to two. She pressed the call button. Even if

the elevator stopped on every floor, she'd be on time. Some of the tension eased out of her shoulders and she rotated her left arm a little. It was still sore from last night's workout, but post-exercise soreness was simply the price you paid for getting stronger. And she needed strength if she was going to lift her personal best time and place in the state triathlon finals in two weeks' time.

Claire tried to be objective as she considered her chances of scoring a place in the final three. She'd shaved several seconds off her swim and bike legs over the past few months, but she still needed to build stamina for the long hill runs. She was confident she was getting there, though. Every training session was a gain.

It was one of the things she loved about triathlons—for her, the races were more about beating herself than the other competitors. Each time she went out there, she was competing with her own best times—and success or failure was never a matter of opinion, but objective fact. She liked that, liked knowing that she was getting somewhere, slowly but surely. Becoming the best person she could be. And, of course, it was a great way of burning off all the stress from a hard day in the office.

Despite all the promises she'd made herself, she couldn't stop her mind from thinking about Harry. The closer she got to the finals, the more he crept into her thoughts. Would he come to watch her? She shook her head at her own naïveté—of course he wouldn't. The only reason she continued to invite him to events of interest in her life was out of some bizarre sense of courtesy. It was a little game they played, she and her father, where she pretended he might be interested, and he came up with a palatable excuse for why he wasn't.

The elevator door pinged open in front of her, and she stepped inside and pressed the button for the thirtieth floor, suppressing the little flash of nervousness that usually accompanied any trip in an elevator. The trick was to think about something else, she'd learned over the years.

She was figuring out tonight's training regime when the elevator pinged to a halt just two floors up, and she raised preoccupied eyes and felt her lips instinctively disappearing. She deliberately avoided making eye contact with Jack Brook as he stepped in beside her, but it seemed he wasn't about to let her off so easily.

"Good afternoon," he said cheerily, and there was no mistaking the smug self-satisfaction in his tone.

She tried to manage an acknowledging smile and nod, but she was too busy feeling self-conscious after her lunchtime conversation with Katherine. Suddenly she found herself very aware of how close to him she was standing. She could practically feel the heat coming off his body—was that even possible?—and the woody, tangy scent of his aftershave teased at her. Easing a step away, she searched for something to help restore her usual equilibrium where Jack Brook was concerned. Her gaze fell on his bare toes peeking out from his slip-on sandals, and she found herself seizing on his typically unprofessional office attire as a way to distract herself.

His ridiculous getup had barely registered earlier, but now she gave it her full, disdainful attention. Suits and other acceptable office wear were obviously not cool enough for Jack "The Man" Brook, she noted. He probably thought he was being really cutting edge in those three-quarter cargo pants. And the sandals—how *European* of him. As for the artfully creased shirt…

She smiled minutely, pleased to realize that the strange, self-conscious feeling had evaporated and she was once again in control of the situation and herself. Then he spoke.

"How you doin'?" he asked, lounging against the wall casually, taking up too much space.

Don't respond, don't respond, don't respond, she chanted internally.

"Sleep in this morning?" she asked, eyes flicking over his crumpled shirt.

"Not *sleep* in, no. But I guess I was a little slow rising to the occasion," Jack said provocatively.

She decided she simply would not blush in response to his suggestive comment. That was what he wanted, after all. And there was no way she would satisfy his juvenile baiting. Except, thanks to Katherine's innuendo earlier, a slow wash of heat already was rising up her chest and into her face. She scratched the ear nearest him, trying to cover her embarrassment.

"Warm today," Jack said, knowingness oozing from every pore.

She ignored him, a strategy she should have stuck with from the start. How on earth could Katherine ever imagine that Claire could be attracted to a man like Jack Brook?

The elevator halted on the thirtieth floor, and she suddenly realized Jack was getting out with her. She glanced at him out of the corner of her eye. He must be talking to one of the financial presidents or something. Trying to buddy-buddy himself an even fatter paycheck, no doubt.

She turned toward Morgan Beck's office suite. Again, Jack followed. She shot him a look. What was going on? There was only one man at the end of this plush-carpeted hallway, and he had an appointment with her.

Jack raised his eyebrows at her, one of those innocent, questioning looks that was supposed to be cute. It made her want to growl deep in her chest.

Pasting a smile on her face, she lengthened her stride and made it to Morgan's assistant's desk ahead of Jack.

"Ms. Bell, I've got a two-o'clock with Mr. Beck," she said, being sure to inject just the right amount of friendliness and respect into her tone. Like a lot of high-powered assistants, Jenny Bell had a bit of a chip on her shoulder about being condescended to by some of the company's executives.

"Of course, Claire. Morgan is just on a phone call. Why don't you take a seat?"

Jenny smiled approvingly at her, and Claire turned toward the waiting area, confident she'd aced that particular obstacle course. Offices were like triathlons in many ways, she mused as she sat, automatically pulling her neat black skirt down over her knees. If you trained hard, respected the referees and gave thanks to the support crews, you had a real chance of not only finishing, but placing well.

Picking up one of the many Beck and Wise publications displayed artfully on the coffee table nearby, she waited for Jack to explain his presence.

"Jenny, you are looking finer than ever. When are you going to give in and finally come waterskiing with me up at the cabin? You know you want to," Jack teased, his whole attitude one of casual confidence as he leaned against Jenny's forbidding reception desk.

Oh, boy. Jenny was renowned for being a real stickler for protocol and proper office conduct, and Claire almost winced as she imagined the arctic blast Jack was about to receive. Almost, but not quite. Instead, she leaned forward, just in case she missed a single delicious nuance. It was about time Mr. Cocky got the message that the world was not his personal love pit....

"You'd better be careful, Jack. I might just take you up on that offer one day—we'll see how fast you run then."

Claire blinked. Good grief, Jenny Bell was *flirting* with Jack Brook. Actually batting her eyelids and flicking her thick plait of gray hair over her shoulder.

Claire slumped a little lower in her seat. Was she the only member of the sisterhood who was immune to Jack's flashy charms?

"You say yes, we'll see what happens," Jack warned her. Claire almost gasped with outrage as he reached across and plucked the pencil from Jenny's hands. "I'm going to keep this as a souvenir," he said cheekily, sauntering over to take a seat beside Claire.

A delighted peal of laughter sounded from Jenny Bell.

"For that you get a coffee while you wait—black, one sugar, right?"

It was like James Bond and Ms. Moneypenny, only he was licensed to make her feel ill. Claire could feel her upper lip curling with distaste.

"How about you, Claire? Would you like a coffee, or tea perhaps?"

This came as Jenny was about to exit, an afterthought.

"No, I'm fine, thank you," Claire managed to choke out, even dredging up a smile from somewhere.

Jenny disappeared into the small kitchen behind her desk, and Claire concentrated on the magazine she'd picked up. She should have paid more attention when she'd grabbed it from the pile on the table— *Big Game Fishing* was hardly her bag. Worse, as she flicked through it trying to find something to grab her attention, her eye was caught by the byline on the major story—Jack Brook. She rolled her eyes. Of course he was into big game fishing. What was she thinking? The man was practically Hemingway reincarnate, with his skydiving and racy car and chain of women and travel writing. He'd probably even run with the bulls in Pamplona.

Out of the corner of her eye she saw him stretch out his long legs, his tanned arm resting on the couch between them. He was amusing himself with the pencil he'd taken from Jenny, rolling it back and forth between his long, strong fingers. She found herself fixating on the dexterous movement of his hands for a beat. *He has a body to die for.* Katherine's words slipped insidiously into Claire's mind. Jack Brook would be an amazing lover, of that she had no doubt. The way he looked at women, the glint in his eye, the casual, animal elegance of his walk—the man simply screamed sex. There would be nothing tentative or uncertain about his technique—he looked as though he knew exactly what buttons to push, and when, and how hard, and…

Claire blinked, stunned at the direction her thoughts had taken. She must be stressed out or something. That was the only explanation for her aberrant thoughts.

Mindlessly flipping the pages, she surreptitiously checked her watch. What was it with big bosses and the waiting game? In all her years in publishing, she'd yet to walk straight into a superior's office at the time of her appointment. There was always the standard keep-you-waiting ploy to be played out, just to remind you of your place in the pecking order.

A big male hand suddenly grabbed the page she was staring at blankly, pulling the magazine across so that Jack could see what she was reading.

"Thought I recognized that picture," he said, stabbing a neatly manicured index finger at the photo accompanying his big article. It showed a snow-white, luxuriously appointed yacht bobbing on a brilliant azure sea. "Hell of a boat. Crew of fifteen just to run her. Now that's money."

She gritted her teeth.

"Spent a full week on her. Pretty hard coming back to nine-to-five-dom after that, I can tell you."

"I wasn't aware you worked nine to five," she couldn't resist saying. The man was always off on some stupid assignment somewhere.

He narrowed his eyes at her.

"I was speaking metaphorically. You know what that is, don't you? As in—she was as sour as a lemon," he said, and she sat up straighter. What a jerk!

"Actually, that's a simile. A metaphor is more like—his ego was monumental," she returned sweetly.

He was opening his mouth to respond when the door to Morgan Beck's office swung open. Their heads swiveled as one and she didn't need to look to know that Jack's face wore the same friendly-not-too-sucky smile that hers did.

"Claire, Jack. Come on in," Morgan said.

She stood, the smile almost slipping off her face. Up until this second, she'd been telling herself that

Jack Brook's visit to the thirtieth floor had nothing to do with her. And she'd almost been believing it. Now she gave free rein to the paranoid feminist within and began imagining half a dozen scenarios where she was shafted royally. Her stomach sunk below knee level as she followed Jack into Morgan Beck's inner sanctum.

"Now, Jack, how much do you know about Claire's new project for the Hillcrest Hardware chain?" Morgan asked, toying with an expensive-looking fountain pen as he leaned back in his well-padded executive chair.

"I understand it's a custom magazine job, a monthly decorator title to be sold only in their stores at a cheaper than usual cover price to create customer loyalty," Jack said.

She resisted the urge to stare at him. How did he know all this? She couldn't have named a single title he worked for. Apart from *Big Game Fishing,* of course.

"Sounds like he's got the important bits right, doesn't it, Claire?"

She nodded, too anxious to trust her voice.

"Before we go any further, I want to acknowledge that this project has been yours, Claire, from the word go. But unfortunately, we've hit a bit of a snag. I've had my thinking cap on, though, and I've come to the conclusion that Jack might be the man to help us out."

She swallowed hard and forced air into her lungs.

"This is a problem from Hillcrest, I'm assuming?" she asked, trying to find her feet.

"Yes, but don't go getting too fussed about it. Old Hank Hillcrest is a dyed-in-the-wool sexist and he's got some pretty wacky ideas. One of those is that the magazine's outlook is too feminine."

Claire frowned. Too feminine? Over half of the magazine's content was aimed at offering heavy-duty building projects to experienced DIYers, along with reviews of new hardware and building products. In fact, the only feminine parts of the magazine were the decorator segments, and a small cookery section which was designed to showcase Hillcrest's kitchen products.

She said as much to Morgan, and he nodded his head sympathetically.

"Claire, I know all this. They know all this. Hell, even cranky old Hillcrest knows all this. But he just doesn't have it in him to let this go without putting his sticky fingerprints all over it. So, as I said, I had an idea.

"You probably don't know this, but Jack started out his career with us in the Homes and Decorating division, writing up projects for our DIY titles. Over the years, he's branched out, moved on. But I bet I wouldn't be wrong if I suggested you still keep your hand in with a bit of DIY work here and there, right, Jack?"

She found herself turning to look at Jack, all the words of protest catching at the back of her throat. She was going to be sick. She was truly going to puke her guts up all over Morgan Beck's polished walnut desk.

"Sure, Morgan, I've got a few projects on the go. But it sounds to me like you've got a done deal with Hillcrest already. And by the looks of things, Claire's put in all the hard yards on this project," Jack said.

Underneath the sick feeling and the anger and the dread, she managed to be surprised at this response from Jack. He actually sounded uncomfortable, reluctant.

"Let's not get ahead of ourselves, people. I'm not suggesting for a moment that Claire be cut out of this thing. We would never do that to you, Claire—please be assured of that."

Morgan took a moment to simply make eye contact with her, his faded blue eyes powerfully sincere. She held his gaze, wanting him to see she had what it took to survive this last hiccup.

"What exactly are you suggesting then, Mr. Beck?" she asked carefully.

"I want to assign Jack to *Welcome Home* as an associate editor for a while—six months, tops. Just so he can have a few meetings with old man Hillcrest, shoot the breeze, all that stuff Jack does so well. It'll be purely window dressing. Jack'll write up a few articles, and then we'll just downplay his involvement until he simply disappears altogether."

She tried to get her head around it. They wanted to give half the credit for her magazine, based on her concept, sold to the client by her, to this crinkle-shirted lothario slouching next to her?

"This…this really…" She struggled to find a way to finish her sentence that didn't have the word "sucks" in it.

"I've got to agree with Claire, Morgan. Surely we can just tough this out? Once Hillcrest have the first edition of their new magazine in hand, they'll be so dazzled they'll forget any objections," Jack said.

Morgan nodded, almost as though he was giving Jack's suggestion some thought.

"We've gone over all this, Jack, believe me. What I'm suggesting is painless, simple and foolproof. I think we can all work together to pull this off, don't you?"

There was no mistaking the sudden glint of steel in Morgan's eyes now. She found herself fixating on the small tufts of hair remaining on his otherwise bald head. She'd always thought of them indulgently as pseudo teddy-bear ears, but now she realized he probably cultivated them to cover the scars from where he'd had his twin horns surgically removed.

"I'll leave the details of all this up to you two, and I know I can rely upon you both to be discreet about this…arrangement."

Somehow she managed to find her feet. Her legs felt numb and heavy, and the distance between her chair and the doors leading back to the reception area seemed a mile off. Morgan leaned forward and shook her hand, again going for the meaningful eye contact. He'd probably look that way as he was pushing her out of a lifeboat on the *Titanic*—deeply moved, but completely committed to saving his own backside.

Anger trickled into her frozen limbs. She lifted her chin, aware she must be looking like a stunned mullet. Although it felt as though her face might crack, she forced her lips into a curve that she hoped resembled a smile.

"I'm sure we can smooth this over," she said, and she was amazed at how professional and calm she sounded. As she turned toward the door she glanced just once at Jack Brook, and she saw surprise and something else—respect?—in his deep blue eyes before she fixed her attention on the double doors ahead and concentrated on putting one foot in front of the other.

Just get me out of here, just get me out of here, just get me out of here, she begged herself, already aware that her mask of calm was about to dissolve. To show any weakness in front of these men… She'd rather charge at the plate-glass window behind Morgan's desk and take a dive down to the sidewalk.

Jenny looked up and smiled at Claire as she approached, and again Claire dragged her lips into a smile.

"See you later, Claire," the assistant said.

The rest of the office geography assumed the visual equivalent of white noise as Claire honed in on the ladies' sign at the end of the hall and simply walked.

She had no idea what had happened to Jack Brook, but she had no intention of hanging around to discuss details with him—or worse, to listen to some mealymouthed vote of sympathy.

The veneered surface of the restroom door felt smooth and cool beneath her fingers and at last she was alone. She couldn't even look at herself in the mirror, afraid all of her emotions would be painfully obvious: disgust, disappointment, anger, betrayal.

God, when would enough be enough in this world? When would her achievements measure up for these people? When would her skills and talents be acknowledged?

She threw her handbag and briefcase onto the marble vanity and at last faced her reflection in the mirror. To her surprise she looked calm. Cool. Hard. Determined.

She snorted. The great irony of her life was that a childhood of insecurity and disappointment had helped her build a tough fortress of impenetrability as an adult. So now when she was disappointed, no one ever knew. Except for her.

Angry tears burned at the back of her eyes and she clenched them shut for a moment. She would not cry. She hated that when she became angry one of her first responses was to feel tears coming on. It felt weak, ineffectual—a child's response to being thwarted or hurt. If she were a man, she wouldn't be in here being a big sooky-la-la. If she were a man, she'd be off somewhere kicking a hole in a wall or punching up some innocent bystander in a bar.

Inspired, she took a step toward the wastepaper can and gave it a good, solid kick. It slid across the tiled floor and slammed into the far wall, toppling

SARAH MAYBERRY   47

to one side and spilling out a morning's worth of
scrunched-up paper towel and tissue.

"Hah!" she said out loud.

As an expression of her anger and hurt and dis-
enchantment, it felt woefully inadequate.

And now there was a pile of tissue all over the
floor. Unable to stop herself, she knelt and scooped
the scrunched-up paper back into the bin.

Just like a man, she mocked herself.

The outer door swung open and one of the finance
directors' assistants entered the room. Claire shot to
her feet, smiled awkwardly, then entered a stall as a
way of avoiding explanations.

She waited until the other woman had left, then
emerged to wash her hands. Patting them dry, she
checked her watch: a good five minutes since the
meeting had ended. She could head for the elevators
now and be confident of avoiding Jack. She could
ride the elevator all the way down to the foyer, and
just keep on walking. She'd always planned to come
back to the office after her appointment with Hillcrest and work late, as usual, but now she impulsively
decided to take the rest of the afternoon off. Perhaps
if she went for a really punishing run she could lose
some of the anger coiling in her belly.

And then she could return to Beck and Wise tomorrow and show them that she wasn't going to let
them beat her.

It felt like a plan. If only she didn't still want to
scream at someone.

Her hand shook a little as she reclaimed her bag

and briefcase, and she took a deep breath before exiting. To her relief, the waiting area near the elevator bank was empty, and she pressed the call button stiffly. A car eased its doors open almost immediately, and she stepped in and pressed the foyer button.

The doors had almost slid to a complete close when a tanned arm shot into the narrowing gap. The doors automatically bounced open, and she gritted her teeth as Jack stepped into the car.

She refused to look at him, but she could feel his eyes on her as the elevator gathered momentum and sped downward.

Silence stretched between them. She kept her eyes glued to the floor indicator, just wanting an out from the elevator, this day, her life.

"Look—" he began to say, but she cut him off.

"Spare me. You've never liked me, and I've never liked you, so don't bother mouthing some empty platitude at me, okay? Of all the unpalatable aspects of this deal, you I find the most difficult to swallow."

She'd planned on exiting grandly into the foyer on these cutting and deeply satisfying words, but all of a sudden the lights flashed once, then blackness descended at the same time that the grinding shriek of metal-on-metal filled the car and the elevator shuddered to a halt.

CHAPTER THREE

"WHAT THE—?" Jack exclaimed.

"What's happening?" Claire demanded at almost the same time.

"Probably just a freak glitch," he said into the darkness, wishing he felt as confident as he sounded.

"You're an expert on elevator technology now, are you?" she asked sharply.

He couldn't see her, but he rolled his eyes at the corner he guessed she was occupying.

"No, I'm being optimistic. Would you prefer I start reciting the Lord's Prayer and scribbling my will on the back of an envelope?"

Silence. Good. He was sick of her attitude and misdirected anger. As for that dig she'd made just before the elevator went crazy... It had been a long time since someone had told him to his face that she didn't like him. And he was surprised at how much it annoyed him.

An emergency light flickered to life above them and he moved to the control panel. The pale, inadequate glow allowed him to find the compartment which hid the emergency phone, and he pried it open and reached for the receiver.

"Hello? Is anyone there?" he asked, suddenly aware that his heart was pounding faster than usual.

Okay, so this was a bit scary. And maybe he should forgive Claire for being a tad shrill. He glanced across at her as the continuing silence on the other end of the phone sunk in. Her face was pale, taut. Frightened.

"Nothing," he said.

As if she didn't trust him to know the difference between a live phone and a dead one, she crossed to take a listen herself. He leaned against the side wall, elaborately casual as he waited for her to confirm his initial assessment.

"You're right," she said.

"Wow, that must have really hurt," he couldn't resist saying.

She shot him a look that would have turned lesser men to stone.

"What, didn't expect to have to actually stay and cop the consequences of all that mouthing off?" he asked, for some reason feeling really angry with her now. "I know you probably prefer to just hit and run, but unfortunately we appear to be stuck for the short term."

He watched, fascinated, as the color flooded back into her cheeks and her eyes burned with an angry light. Pretty impressive, a part of his brain acknowledged. She even drew her shoulders back and inhaled sharply, and, for the first time ever, he found his eyes dropping to her suit-encased chest.

"It's easy for you to stand there all smug and confident. Did you just have your idea taken away from you and handed to someone completely undeserving? Did you just get treated like some token office bimbo? No. Because you're a man. A racquetball playing, big-game-fishing, bungee-jumping man with a stupid red sports car and the right equipment between his legs to get ahead in this company."

If he'd been a cartoon, his hair would have been streaming back from his head as if he'd just stepped out of a wind tunnel. Whoa, but this was one angry woman. And he could see her point, really he could. But he didn't like the way she was sighting her feminist crosshairs directly on him.

"Listen, I had nothing to do with what just happened in that meeting. You think I want anything to do with this? And if we're talking about tokenism, I'm the one who's being wheeled in as the token male on this project for appearance's sake. How do you think that makes me feel?"

"Don't you dare mock me!" she warned him.

"Then don't you blame your problems on me," he countered. "I can't see why you'd make me the bad guy in all this. Contrary to your belief, I have never disliked you. I barely know you."

She raised an eyebrow skeptically, her whole attitude one of disbelief.

"I know what you said about me," she shot at him.

"Excuse me?"

"You heard."

Genuinely baffled, Jack raised his hands in the air, palms up. "I have no idea what you're talking about. I have better things to do than spend my spare time hanging around talking about you."

That got her! The color was back in her cheeks, and she glared at him fiercely.

"You called me prissy! So don't you dare stand there pulling that Mr. Innocent act," she hissed at him.

Jack frowned. What the hell was she going on about? He'd been speaking the truth when he said that he didn't spend his time sitting around talking about her.

"Sorry, but I think you've got that wrong, lady," he said bluntly.

"Really? We'll just have to ask my good friend Katherine Kirk when we get out of here then, won't we?"

Although his expression didn't change, Jack felt a moment of doubt. Now that she mentioned it, he could vaguely remember having a beer with Katherine some time ago after work. He'd just had a run-in with Claire in an editorial meeting and come out second best....

He made a mental note to thank Katherine for dumping him in it.

Claire was waiting for his response, hands on her hips.

"Well? What do you have to say to that?"

He shrugged. He'd said it, might as well own it. It wasn't as though it wasn't true. "Prissy might have been overstating it. You can be pretty anal, though."

She made a hissing sound, kind of like a kettle

about to blow its top, then opened her mouth to retaliate just as the phone rang. They both jumped, startled. Praying this was good news, he reached for the receiver with alacrity.

"Hello?" he asked, feeling her eyes on him, sensing her hopes, like his own, beginning to rise at this contact.

"This is Ted Evans from Security. I'm making contact to ascertain the exact number of persons in lift number six," an officious voice asked.

"Well, Ted, there are two of us, and we'd sure as hell love to get out of here."

Claire made an exasperated noise that he guessed was supposed to signal her wholehearted agreement.

"Two. Right. Well, uh— Who am I talking to?"

"Jack. Jack Brook."

"Right. Jack. You're the one with the red Porsche, yeah? Nice little number," Ted said, his tone all male appreciation. "It's an early 2002 model, right? The one with tiptronic transmission? Very nice."

Jack reined in his frustration. This guy didn't seem to have a real tight grasp on the urgency of their situation.

"About the elevator, Ted," he hinted.

He glanced up as Claire shifted restlessly, a frown creasing her forehead as she no doubt wondered what was going on. He could imagine her reaction if he told her Ted wanted to talk cars.

"Well, we've got a bit of a situation here, Jack. There's been a major power blackout across this whole part of town—something about a fire at the power plant—and most of the building's services have shut down. Air-conditioning, security systems, elevators. You know."

Jack rolled his eyes. Claire shook her head with confusion.

"What's going on?" she asked.

He tried to look reassuring as he returned his attention to Ted.

"So there are other people stuck in elevators?"

"Sure are. Only two of the twelve cars were empty. Elevator four has ten people in it," Ted reported with relish.

Jack grimaced. Ten people would make for a cozy lift compartment. Thank God it was just him and Claire. Out of the corner of his eye, he noted her frown deepening. On second thoughts, maybe a cozy, friendly elevator wasn't such a bad option....

"So how long are we talking here? Half an hour? Ten minutes? What?" he asked, deciding it was time to force Ted to the point.

"Can't tell you that just yet. We've contacted the manufacturer, and they're sending a team out."

Jack tried to control the sinking sensation in his gut.

"So...we could be talking hours here," he said reluctantly.

He could feel Claire stiffen even though she was as far from him as she could get.

"That's not good enough," she said, striding across to pull the receiver from his hand.

"Who am I talking to?" she demanded.

He resumed his lounging position against the wall. He was all for making a little noise if it was going to get them rescued sooner, but he wished her the best of luck up against the remarkably prosaic Ted.

Jack inspected his fingernails as Claire quizzed the security guard, trying to suppress the swell of satisfaction he felt when she returned the receiver to its cradle a few minutes later, her shoulders slumped: she hadn't gotten any further than he had.

"Could be worse. Could be ten people in here," he said lightly, taking in her white face.

She was silent as she crossed back to her side of the space, but he could see her hands were shaking as she brushed her hair back from her face.

Damn. He took a deep breath, then let it out. She was scared. Anyone could see that. And as much as she probably deserved for him to simply ignore her, he couldn't turn his back on her distress.

"Listen, I'm sure they'll have us out of here soon. I think I remember reading somewhere that elevators have manual override functions where they can just winch us down."

He kept an eye on her, noticing her chest was heaving a little now.

"Ah, Claire, you wouldn't happen to be a little claustrophobic at all, would you?" he asked.

She was concentrating fiercely on the carpet in front of her toes, completely unresponsive now.

Okay. He tried to think of something to say or do to help her out. Not being afraid of anything himself, he found it difficult to understand this sort of thing.

"I learned this meditation technique once at a temple in India—" he began to say tentatively, but then Claire slumped against the wall and began sliding down it and he realized she'd fainted.

He leaped across the distance between them, catching her before her head hit the ground. Her hair was soft and silky against his hands, and he could smell her shampoo as he gently guided her onto the carpet. Vanilla. Nice.

A quick once-over revealed that her skirt had ridden up a little, and that her legs were skewed awkwardly, but her eyelids were flickering now and he decided he'd rather stick his head in a crocodile's mouth than be caught adjusting Claire Marsden's clothing while she was semiconscious. Still, he couldn't help noticing that the shortened skirt length belied his previous impression of her legs. Not bad. As a rule, he preferred tall, slim, modelesque women, but Claire's legs were really something of a surprise. Almost as though she could read his mind, Claire made a disgusted noise in the back of her throat, and then her eyes popped open.

CLAIRE CAME OUT of the empty darkness and opened her eyes, blinking rapidly as she tried to reorient herself. Where was she? What had happened? She felt the ground under her back. And why was she lying on the carpet? And then Jack's face loomed over her and she found herself staring into his concerned blue eyes.

"You okay?" he asked, and it all came flooding back.

They were trapped in an elevator. With no hope of escape for hours. A dizzying tide of fear rushed back up at her and she clamped down on it fiercely. It had been years since she'd allowed this childish terror of enclosed spaces to master her. But while she could suppress it for the short trip up to the fifteenth floor each day, being stuck in a tiny elevator car for several hours was more than her powers of self-control could manage. She'd been grimly hanging on to her calm ever since they'd ground to a halt, but the news that they were going to have to settle in for a long wait had been too much.

"Claire? You all right?" Jack asked again.

He looked funny upside down, she noted, feeling a little detached as she tried to keep her fear at arm's length. Like an alien, his mouth where his eyes should be…

"Hello? Are you in there?" he asked, waving a hand in front of her face.

At last she snapped her attention back.

"I'm okay," she said. "I think."

"Afraid of small spaces?" he asked simply.

"Since I was a kid," she admitted, hating telling him, of all people.

"Ever fainted before?" he asked, clearly trying to ascertain the extent of her phobia.

"No. But this is the first time I've been stuck in an elevator," she said, managing to dredge up a small smile.

He blinked at her, and she realized that this was probably the first time she'd ever done anything except glare at Jack.

"You have lips."

Her turn to blink. "I beg your pardon?"

He shook his head, made a forget-it gesture in the air with his hand. "Nothing."

She narrowed her eyes. Nothing? She didn't think so. "You said I have lips. What exactly is that supposed to mean?"

He sighed, scanned the roof as though looking for inspiration, then shrugged. All of this upside down, him hovering over her prone body.

"It's just that most of the time when you see me you have no lips," he said.

She stared at him. "I assure you, these are not detachable," she said.

He looked skeptical. "Except when you see me. Then they disappear. Like this." He gave an example, thinning his lips into a prim, ungenerous line.

"I do not do that," she said, even as she felt her mouth assuming the usual tense expression she wore around him.

Damn him.

"You're doing it right now."

She stretched her mouth wide and forced her lips to assume a more relaxed expression.

"Happy?"

"That's better," he said approvingly.

She could feel her lips thinning again at his smug response.

"And there we go again," he observed.

She closed her eyes for a moment. This was insane. She was trapped in an elevator with the company's number-one playboy having a conversation about her lip posture while lying flat on her back.

"Feeling faint again?"

She blinked, recognizing that the fear that had been lapping around her knees had receded to toe-height.

"No. I feel...better."

He looked pleased and a little proud. *He's been distracting me,* she suddenly realized. With that thought came an abrupt awareness that her legs were sprawled out inelegantly and her skirt hiked up on one side. She reached a hand down to rearrange her skirt even as she moved to sit up. A heavy male hand landed in the middle of her chest.

"Take it slow," Jack warned, and even though he'd taken his hand away she could still feel the heat and weight of it as she slowly sat upright.

She glanced around the elevator car. Nothing much had changed since she hit the deck: same brushed metal sides, same industrial carpet base, same small, inadequate light.

She knew he was watching her carefully, and she made an effort to appear calm, biting down on the sensation that there simply wasn't enough room, or air or anything in this tiny little space....

"Okay, this meditation technique I was telling you about," Jack said suddenly, and she suspected that her rising panic might be more than obvious.

"I'll be okay," she said, wishing it were true. Wishing the doors would simply slide open and let her out.

"Humor me. Close your eyes."

She shook her head stubbornly, and he snorted his exasperation.

"For Pete's sake—just let go for a second. That's all I'm asking," he said. "You can stitch yourself back up nice and tight once we're out of here."

She blinked, more stung by his comment than she'd have thought possible. For a moment there she had forgotten what he thought of her, that he was her enemy. Afraid he'd see her reaction, she closed her eyes obediently.

"Great. Now, starting on your next inhalation, I want you to concentrate on your left nostril. Pretend your right nostril is blocked, and concentrate on breathing up your left nostril to the point between your eyes. And then exhale down your right nostril, again concentrating on the sensation. Then, in through the right, and out through the left. Keep repeating it until you feel better."

His voice was slow and calm, and even though most of her mind was busy being annoyed and hurt and scared, she managed to focus on her breathing. A few breaths later, and she was really getting into it, feeling the sensation of air traveling up one nostril and down the other. A few minutes of this, and a lovely calm was starting to build inside her. She popped an eye open to find Jack had moved back to his side of the car, and was sitting down, his back to the wall.

"This is pretty good. Thanks."

"Nothing to do with me—thank the ancient yogis of India."

"I will, next time I see them. But in the meantime, I really appreciate it."

She maintained some serious eye contact when she said it, wanting him to know that she acknowledged his help, that she wasn't the kind of person she suspected he thought she was. He simply nodded, once, letting her know her message had been received and understood.

Silence slipped between them, and for the first time she became aware of how stuffy it was becoming. She unbuttoned her suit jacket and shrugged out of it. She regarded it for a moment—it was an expensive suit, a treat she'd bought herself for her birthday last year. Oh, well. Sacrifices had to be made if they were going to be stuck in here for hours on end. She rolled it up and placed it behind her, making a pad to lean against. And then she sat, alternately studying her hands, or the tips of her shoes.

It was like being stuck at all of the most disastrous parties of her teenage years rolled into one. She knew she should say something. In fact, a dozen conversational gambits suggested themselves to her, but they all felt wrong. For starters, she'd been arguing flat out with Jack not ten minutes ago. Ten minutes before that, he'd been handed half her project on a silver platter. And then there was Katherine's lunchtime exposé about Jack's...talents. If that wasn't enough to stifle conversation, Claire didn't know what was.

How she wished her friend had kept her insider knowledge to herself. The last thing she needed was to develop some stupid awareness of Jack as a man. She was stuck in an elevator with him, for Pete's sake. She didn't want to know that he was great in bed, and had a fantastic body. It was bad enough that she'd been mentally undressing him while they waited for Morgan earlier. She flicked a look across at him, but her glance skittered away again when she saw that his shirt was sticking to his sweat-dampened skin, giving her a very nice idea of just how well muscled and proportioned his chest was. She could even see his dark, flat male nipples through the damp fabric....

This man is your nemesis, she told herself fiercely. *He represents everything you loathe in men.* Determined to get over her stupid preoccupation, she deliberately reminded herself that in addition to having a broad, sexy chest, long, strong fingers and knowing, all-seeing eyes, Jack had stolen her parking spot this morning.

A surge of annoyance raced through her. That was better. Suddenly he was just a man again—an annoying man who regularly operated as a thorn in her professional side. She tapped one shoe toe against the other, then followed with a little heel click as she relived that frustrating moment of finding his car in her space. There was no way he didn't know that was her usual spot. He'd have to be either blind or stupid not to know, and she knew he was neither. So—

"Why did you park in my spot this morning?"

She nearly bit her tongue off as she spoke her thought out loud. Now it was out there, however, and there was nothing for it but to pretend she'd meant to challenge him all along.

"I wasn't aware that we'd been assigned parking spaces. Was there a memo sent around? I must have missed it," he said, and she felt her buttocks clench with annoyance.

A memo. Very funny. Any sexual thoughts she'd had about Mr. Annoying receded at a rapid pace.

"You know exactly what I mean. You usually park over near the pillar in the middle. And I always park near the stairwell. It's a system, a habit. And it works. So why did you take my spot this morning? And don't tell me you didn't know it was mine, because you gave yourself away when you wagged your keys at me this morning."

"You're not serious? You're really all bunged up over a stupid parking spot?"

She sat up straighter at the disbelieving scorn in his voice.

"It's not the spot; it's the principle. Tell me you didn't do it just to annoy me and I'll drop it. But first you have to look me in the eye and say that pissing me off was not on your agenda when you filched my spot this morning."

He rolled his eyes. "Do you know how juvenile

you sound? Let me guess—only child, not used to sharing, right?"

She felt a small, familiar stab of regret, and she pushed it down, back into the place where it belonged.

"Look me in the eye and I'll never mention it again," she dared him.

Jack shook his head as though she'd just suggested he pull his underpants over his head and run around making chicken noises.

She simply raised an eyebrow and waited. Finally he got sick of rolling his eyes and telling her she was unbelievable.

"All right. When I parked my car in that spot this morning, pissing you off did not in any way inform my decision," he said, but at the last minute he broke eye contact and his gaze wandered somewhere over her shoulder.

"Huh! You liar! You big fat liar! You *did* do it to piss me off!" she gasped.

"Okay, you want the truth? You're right—I did do it on purpose. You've parked in that spot every single day for the past year. I thought it was time you had a change."

She nearly swallowed her tongue.

He thought it was time she had a change?

"You thought it was time I had a change? *You*—a man who hasn't yet grasped the basics of ironing— thought it was time for *me* to have a change?"

She realized her mouth was hanging open and she shut it with an audible click.

"Yeah. I did."

His earlier words came flooding back, something about her stitching herself back up nice and tight. Added to his original assessment of her as prissy, it made a pretty unattractive picture. Suddenly she got it—he thought she was some repressed, neurotic career woman. The type of person who had to have routine, made sure she ate all the five major food groups and was never late paying her bills. The idea so outraged her that she couldn't stop the challenge popping out her mouth.

"You think I'm uptight, don't you?"

Her temper increased another few degrees when he simply raised an eyebrow at her.

"Answer me!" she demanded, and even to her own ears she sounded shrill and shrewish. He waited until the echo from her screech had died before spreading his hands as though presenting a fait accompli.

"I rest my case."

She stared at him, very aware of the pulse beating madly at the base of her neck. She hated that she was behaving this way, hated that he could crank her up so easily. Most of all she hated that just five minutes ago she'd been imagining his bare chest, while he was sitting there thinking she was uptight and repressed.

Across the elevator car, Jack yawned ostentatiously, making a show of checking his watch, all of it meant to imply he was waiting for her next "snappy" comeback. Her temper boiled over and without thinking, she slid off one of her imported

Italian leather pumps and slung it across the room at him. Unfortunately, hand-eye coordination had never been her strong suit and it simply bounced harmlessly off the wall next to his head.

It did shock him though, which gave her great satisfaction.

"There's another one where that came from, so keep your stupid male chauvinist generalizations to yourself," she warned him.

She started as her shoe landed in her lap with just enough force behind it to make her realize he was much better at ball sports than her.

"That's how much of a male chauvinist I am. I respect you as an equal so much I know you can take what you dish out," he said, and the complaint about him nearly hurting her died on her lips.

Sneaky bastard.

If her first throw had connected, she could have hurt him, and they both knew it. By giving her back some of what she'd dished out, he was forcing her to acknowledge her own double standards—that it was okay for a woman to hit a man, but not vice versa.

A taut silence stretched between them. She bit her lip to contain the hundred and one explanations, justifications and motivations for the way she lived her life, to prove to him he'd got it wrong, got her wrong. She wanted to tell him that her bedroom at home looked as if a bomb hit it, that she laughed at dirty jokes and that sometimes she even drank her beer straight from the bottle. She wasn't uptight or prissy, she was just very professional at work. And very committed to her training schedule.

Thinking all this through helped take the edge off his words. He was just using some pathetic playboy measuring stick to assess her, and because she didn't match his idea of what a woman should be, he labeled her repressed and uptight. Just because she didn't wear tight miniskirts to work and fall all over herself to giggle at his jokes and wear her cleavage like the latest fashion accessory. Just because she was an achiever, and hardworking, and focused.

The truth was, he was probably scared of her. Threatened. It was typical, really—putting her down so he could build himself up. Almost, she felt better. Almost.

Unbidden, a memory popped up: the dinner she'd had with her old college friends last month. There had been lots of excited chatter as they caught up on the four years since they'd all last hooked up. Sue had been full of her kids' antics, her husband's achievements and her own dream of selling her handmade quilts on the internet. Georgia had been excited about her upcoming wedding to the fabulous Greg, as well as being quietly proud of achieving partner in the law firm where she worked. And Claire had shared her achievements with the magazine, and talked about her chances of winning the upcoming statewide triathlon semifinal. She'd gone home that night feeling contented and replete after a good catch-up with her old friends. Now she remembered a look she'd caught Georgia and Sue exchanging. Was it possible they'd felt sorry for "poor Claire" and her empty life? When she'd apologetically left the table to take a quick cell phone call from someone at Hillcrest Hardware, had they talked in hushed tones about her being uptight and dronelike? About how alone she was—*still single*—and how she was filling her empty hours with meaningless exercise?

Suddenly Georgia's suggestion that Claire should meet her friend Tony—a *really amazing, laid-back guy*—took on a whole new light.

Hell, maybe everyone thought she was uptight. Miserable, she hunched down against the wall.

She racked her brain, trying to think of the last time she'd done something spontaneous and impulsive. There'd been that time when she'd snuck in the back way at the movies with her boyfriend…but that was when she'd been sixteen, and didn't really count anyway as she'd practically wet her pants with terror she was so worried about getting caught.

What about that time she and some triathlete friends had gone skinny-dipping after a late night beach party? Except that she had been one of only a few who'd chosen to swim in their underwear instead of going the full skinny.…

Okay, all right. What about that crazy hat she'd worn to her best friend Jo's party last year? She'd found it in an old magic shop, a top hat with a bunny jumping out of it. She'd won best prize at Jo's party with that hat.

She suppressed a groan and rested her head in her

hands. A hat. She was trying to pin her personality on a stupid novelty hat.

She glared across at the man who'd started all this, focusing all her self-doubt and insecurity on him and his big mouth and insensitive comments. What did he know, anyway? Who was he, sitting there with those stupid sandals and his perfect hair and his designer stubble? Just because all of life's doors had swung open for him as he approached, he wrote her off at a glance. So she wasn't one of the beautiful people, and she wasn't gifted with the sort of charm that had eased his way through life.

She'd always thought those things didn't matter— no, she *knew* they didn't matter. It was who you really were, inside and outside, that counted.

But then she blinked, and she felt a tear run down her cheek. God, she hated Jack Brook.

CHAPTER FOUR

JACK STRETCHED HIS neck to one side and resisted the urge to check his watch, knowing it would only read five minutes past the last time he'd checked. Time dragged as only time could when you were bored out of your mind and stuck in a small, enclosed space with someone who was obviously thirsting for your blood.

He didn't need to be a mind reader to know that Claire Marsden was mentally sticking pins in his voodoo doll doppelganger right now. He'd intercepted one glance from her that was practically dripping with animosity and got the message straight off. Well, she could stew in it, for all he cared. It wasn't his problem.

Except, he couldn't seem to stop glancing across at her every now and then. Just now she looked sad, infinitely sad, as she contemplated the toes of her shoes. He felt a twinge of guilt about what he'd said. Maybe he shouldn't have been so up-front. People had to have their illusions about themselves, after all. And maybe, in her universe, she was a barrel of laughs, the life and soul of the party. Maybe, in her world, with her friends, she was considered a crazy caper merchant in her conservative suits and sensible, safe car. What was it to him, anyway?

A trickle of sweat ran down his back and he became conscious of the increasing stuffiness of the elevator. Without thinking, he slipped open the buttons on his shirt and flapped the two sides to create a breeze. Across the car, Claire glanced at him and then averted her eyes as though he'd just dropped his pants and announced his intention to have group sex with her favorite aunt.

Uptight, that was what he was talking about.

Almost as though she could hear his thoughts, Claire suddenly stood and toed off her shoes. She looked taller from his position on the floor, and he had a mighty fine view as she reached for the hem of her skirt. Instinctively, she must have sensed this and she began turning toward the wall. She hesitated for a moment, an obvious battle going on inside her.

What was she up to? He wasn't sure, but it beat the hell out of not looking at his watch for entertainment.

She glanced across at him, their eyes locking as she wrangled with her better instincts, and then he saw a muscle move in her jaw as she steeled herself. With great deliberation, she hoisted her skirt up in full view of him, reached for the waistband of her panty hose, and tugged them down. He scored a flash of black underwear—lace? He couldn't be sure—before her skirt dropped down discreetly like the curtain at a peep show. Of their own accord, his eyes followed her hands as she rolled each leg of her panty hose down, down, down to the ground where

she stepped out of them daintily. Aware he'd just
been staring like a horny adolescent, he snapped his
gaze away and contemplated the unmoving floor indicator instead.

He simultaneously became conscious of the fact
that his heart rate had just increased and he was
sweating a little more. And he almost did a visual
double take on himself when he realized that another
part of his anatomy hadn't been exactly unmoved by
her actions, either.

Wow, he must be really bored. This was Claire
Marsden, after all, almost the antithesis of everything he considered attractive in a woman: she was
brunette, he preferred blondes; she was serious, he
preferred giggles; she was short, he preferred statu-
esque....

His list of his favorite attributes trickled to a halt
as he glanced across at her and caught a flash of extremely toned, tanned thighs as she settled down
on the floor.

A tan. Claire Marsden had a tan. His mind bog-
gled. He simply couldn't imagine her in a swimsuit.
Another assessing glance at her. Nope, couldn't do it.
Her long-sleeved, high-necked, roomy blouse defied
his attempts to make it disappear, and, for the life
of him, he couldn't come up with a mental image of
what her body might be like. Well, apart from kind
of square and boxy, like her car and her suits. Given
his many years of training and expertise in imagining women naked or in their underwear, he decided
this was another point in favor of his argument for

boredom being the cause of any…interest his body might have displayed over the panty hose incident. Case closed.

Still, her legs were in pretty good shape… He gave himself a mental slap. What, was he in high school again? Could he perhaps think of something that did not pertain to the bare-legged woman sitting opposite him?

He was surprised how much effort it took for him to keep his gaze away from those legs and that tan. Concentrating fiercely, he imagined the next stage in restoring the antique dining table he was working on as a surprise for his mom for Christmas. It would look great in the corner of her living room, and he knew she would love it. Not that he'd be there to see her reaction. His parents were expecting him to fly home to Sydney, but he would send the table instead. He wasn't up for the big family get-together this year. The gruff sadness of his dad, the empty place at the table, the grief in everyone's eyes when they looked at him and saw Robbie. Jack had enough trouble with his own grief without dealing with the weight of theirs.

For starters, there'd be the inevitable kitchen-sink conversation with his mom as she washed the vegetables for dinner. It was her favorite territory for heart-to-hearts, although in a pinch she'd take whatever venue was offered. She'd fix him with her knowing blue eyes and tell him it had been three years now, and he needed to let go. But she didn't know how it felt. None of them did. Then his dad would invite him to tour the garage to check out his latest power tool acquisitions. And in between explaining the clutch on his new hammer drill, he'd make some kind of reference to Robbie and hope that Jack would open up. But that was never going to happen. His grief was like a rock inside him, granite hard and permanent, a part of him now.

No. He wasn't going home for Christmas this year. He'd find somewhere in the Caribbean instead, and go scuba diving and dally with bikini-clad tourists. His parents would understand. They'd have to.

Across the car, Claire shifted and cleared her throat.

"Do you think we should make contact with Ted again, see how things are going?" she asked.

He checked his watch. They'd been stuck in here for an hour now. He shrugged.

"Guess it couldn't hurt."

Standing, he reached for the phone, quickly becoming aware of how much warmer it was in the top half of the car.

"I'll never bitch about air-conditioning again," he murmured as he waited for Ted to pick up.

"What did you say?"

He glanced at her, caught by the arrested expression on her face.

"Air-conditioning. Usually I don't like it—dries everything out. But I'm beginning to understand why it's a necessary evil in a building this size."

She gaped at him, surprise in every line of her body.

"That was true?" she said, something like awe in her voice.

He frowned. What on earth was she talking about? "What?"

She seemed to suddenly realize what she'd said. She shrugged, elaborately casual, dropping her eyes to avoid meeting his. "Nothing. Is Ted not answering?"

He frowned, aware that something had just happened there. He was about to pursue it, but Ted chose that moment to pick up the phone.

"Yes, number six?"

"Ted, we were just wondering how things are going? Rescue team in action yet? Any news on when the power might be back?"

"Negative on the power situation. Not expected to be up and running until O–one hundred. Rescue team is in place, and setting up. Estimated extraction time per car—half an hour to an hour."

Jack suppressed a smile at Ted's military-style reporting. This was probably about as exciting as it got in Ted's line of work.

"Right. So, when can we expect to be, uh, extracted?"

"Car six has only two occupants, and, as such, is a low priority at this stage," Ted said evasively.

"How long, Ted?" Jack insisted.

A pause.

"Let me check on that for you. Hold on."

He rolled his eyes.

"Because I have so many other places I can be right now," he muttered.

"What's he saying?" Claire asked, hope in her voice.

"Don't get excited," he warned her just as Ted picked up the receiver at the other end again.

"Best estimate is between three to five hours, Mr. Brook."

"Thanks, Ted. Don't be a stranger."

Jack put the receiver down and turned to face Claire. She was standing now, and he saw how short she was without her high heels on. Tiny, really—she barely came up to his armpits.

"Three hours is the minimum, I'm afraid."

He watched her closely, worried she might flip out again.

"Relax, I'm not going to freak out again," she assured him. "In fact, this little experience may have cured me for good."

They sank down into their opposing corners again, and he made a special effort to avoid looking at her as she settled. It didn't stop him from *imagining* her thighs again, of course, but it gave him the illusion of self-control....

Silence took over again, and he replayed the small moment before Ted had picked up the phone. What had really happened then?

"Before, when I was talking about the air-conditioning, you said something," he prompted, watching her face carefully.

She was all surprise, widening her eyes innocently as she *tried* to remember. Pity she sucked as an actress.

"Did I? I don't remember," she said.

"Right. And you never inhaled, either."

His challenge hung between them for a moment, then she shrugged.

"Fine. You want it, you got it. When you broke up with Judy Gillespie from Accounts, she told everyone about how you made her turn off her air-conditioning when you stayed the night, even though she got heat rash if it got too warm. I didn't believe it at the time."

He just stared at her, his mind numbed for a moment by this revelation. She raised her eyebrows at him, obviously expecting an answer.

"Nice to know my private life is public property," he finally managed to say.

She laughed, one of those short, sharp mocking laughs that women use to cut men off at the knees.

"And what's that supposed to mean?" he squawked. He sounded more than a little defensive, and he forced his shoulders to relax.

"Come on. You've dated more than half the eligible females in the building. You think they don't talk about you, compare notes? You think they don't warn every new woman who joins the company?"

Compare notes? For a moment he felt exposed and vulnerable, and then he reminded himself that he had nothing to be ashamed or worried about. He prided himself on the fact that no woman left his bed unsatisfied. If half the women's magazine complaints he'd read over the years were true, he was doing okay.

"Yeah? What do they say?"

He could see his cockiness got under her skin, and he felt on firmer ground now.

"You want the truth?" she asked, daring him.

How tough could it be? Maybe a few complaints about him breaking up with some of them, but most of his office flings had been just that—two adults satisfying a mutual curiosity. He was confident he could handle a bit of woman-scorned bitterness.

"Sure. Hit me."

Her expression should have warned him. She actually looked wary, almost as though she was afraid of what she was about to say.

"They say that you're fun and adventurous, but as soon as anything serious develops you run scared. Also, that you're afraid of commitment, afraid of feelings and impossible to talk to. That even though you're good in bed, they never really felt as if you were really there with them. That—"

"Okay, thanks, I think I get the drift," he cut in, holding up a hand to stem the tide.

A profound silence settled between them as his brain whirled round and round trying to process, adjust and justify her words.

"You did ask."

She actually sounded guilty.

"Hey, don't worry about me. I think I know enough about human nature to understand where those kind of comments come from."

She didn't say a word, but she didn't need to. After just an hour of one-on-one with her, he was becoming finely attuned to her body language. A shift of a shoulder, the sniff of her nose, and she might as well have shouted at him.

"What? Fine, then. Where do *you* think those sorts of comments come from?" he demanded.

Her eyes measured him for a moment before she answered. He fought the urge to squirm.

"You think they're just bitter because you broke up with them, don't you? And you're probably right, I'm sure that's some of it. But there are plenty of them who aren't bitter, just sad."

He couldn't let that slide by.

"Because I broke their hearts? Let me tell you, I am never anything but honest with women. They all know the score."

"They're not sad because you rejected them, Jack. They're sad because for a man with so much potential there's so little on offer. Katherine told me that she'd never met a man who was more afraid of his feelings in her life. She said there was no point pursuing anything with someone who was never going to let himself go."

If she'd quoted anyone else, he would have been able to blow it off as sour grapes. But Katherine… He'd thought they'd had a real understanding. A short, hot fling, an absolute meeting of minds—two people who enjoyed each other, looking for nothing more than a bit of companionship and human comfort. No strings, no hassles.

He frowned as he remembered that she'd been the one to drift away, the one to call a halt before the usual awkward time when the relationship should move into the next stage but was never going to, thanks to his own fierce commitment to being uncommitted.

He tried to shake off the strange feeling of oppression that settled over him as he considered that Katherine's assessment was right.

Immediately he thought of Robbie, and he hardened himself. So, maybe they were right, maybe he didn't have anything to offer on that level. That was simply the way it was. He'd given it all to Robbie, and he didn't have anything left to share.

His thoughts snapped back to the woman sitting opposite. He now knew why she judged him the way she did. A spark of anger sprang to life inside him. She *had* judged him, big-time. She'd listened to office gossip and rumor, and she'd formed her own opinions of him, and decided he was lacking. Hence all that talk about him being the action-man about the office. Hence her thinly veiled contempt for him.

Vaguely, he was aware of how quickly his temper had gone from zero to one hundred.

"And let me tell you, that air-conditioning story is bull. Judy never told me she got heat rash. I said I didn't like the air-conditioning, sure, but she never said she'd get a rash if it wasn't on."

He felt small and stupid as soon as he'd said it. What was he defending himself to Claire for, anyway?

"I told you, I didn't believe it at the time."

Now she was being understanding. She even looked like she was regretting what she'd said to him. He didn't like it that she suddenly seemed to have the upper hand. He was much more comfortable with their normal status quo, where he disdained her repression and she expressed her contempt for his freewheeling attitude.

"I'm surprised you haven't got better things to do than sit around gossiping about me all day. Workload must be a bit lighter than I remember it down in Homes," he snipped.

She rolled her eyes at him. "Spare me. You think I want to stand around and talk about the office stud all day? It's impossible not to pick this stuff up. It's like osmosis."

He sat up straight, bristling.

"I'd prefer it if you didn't call me that, thank you," he found himself saying stiffly.

Can you hear yourself? Now who's uptight?

"I beg your pardon?"

Her incredulity was clear. But he'd drawn a line in the sand, and he had to stand by it.

"Office stud. I find it offensive. How would you like it if I called you the town bike?"

She surprised him by laughing out loud. "Go ahead, see if I object."

For a moment he stared at her, taking in the transformation in her face when she laughed. She looked…nice. Approachable. Attractive.

All just a sugarcoating for her inner shrew, he reminded himself. *Don't forget that. Never forget that.*

CLAIRE PLUCKED AT the neck of her heavy silk shirt,
trying to get some air between it and her hot skin.
Why hadn't she picked a cotton shirt this morning?
She pictured the litter of clothes all over her bedroom and declined to comment on the grounds that
she already knew why: she was a pig, and she needed
to do the laundry.

She spared a glance for the office stud opposite.
Now that she knew he hated being called that she'd
make sure to slip it into as many conversations as
possible. See how he liked being pigeonholed.

His face was closed, quiet, but she could feel his
vulnerability. She'd shocked him with her revela-
tions about what his exes and flings thought of him,
there was no question. She felt a vague guilt at having spilled so many beans on him. For the first time,
she questioned some of the stories she'd heard about
him, and some of her value judgments. So, he dated
a lot. Was that so bad? And then she remembered
twenty-three-year-old Fiona from Legal, her heart-
shaped face blotched with tears as she explained how
Jack had made an excuse for not staying the night in
her bed after they'd *done it.* He'd ended their short
romance the next day at lunchtime.

He didn't deserve sympathy. Fiona deserved sympathy—as well as a good kick in the wazoo for letting herself be suckered in by Mr. Silvertongue.

Claire was considering trying to take a nap when

movement caught her eye and she looked up to see
Jack shrugging out of his shirt.

"What?" he asked defensively. "You want me to
ask permission or something?"

What a jerk.

"You can take it all off for all I care," she told
him stiffly.

He raised an eyebrow, obviously doubting her.
"Feel free to take off whatever you want, too," he
said idly, the glint of his eyes giving away the fact
that he was mocking her.

She could feel her lips disappearing again and
she forced them to behave before he noticed. He was
sooooo annoying. She'd truly never met anyone else
who could get her so riled so quickly.

What was it about him that got up her nose so
much? She studied him through her eyelashes, trying to work it out, and found her gaze drawn to the
broad expanse of hairy chest he'd just exposed. All
that huntin'-shootin'-fishin' obviously agreed with
him because he was in pretty good shape, his pecs
nicely defined, his stomach flat, the hint of strong ab-
dominal muscles showing as he breathed. She knew
from experience how tough it was to get lean enough
to see those ab muscles, and she reassessed her notion of his sybaritic lifestyle. Okay, maybe he wasn't
out wining and dining every night. Every second
night, probably. He'd need to, just to fit in all his office romances.

It was nice to see a bit of hair on a chest, she decided idly, feeling drowsy in the stuffy atmosphere.

Most male triathletes made a habit of waxing their chests to gain a little less drag in the water, and it had been a while since she'd seen a nicely haired male chest. He had a good tan, too, and the hairs looked healthy and dark and springy against his brown skin. Her eyes followed the trail of hair as it narrowed over those taut abs of his until it was just a promise as it disappeared altogether beneath the waistband of his pants. She found herself staring at a point just below his waistband, wondering again about exactly how gifted Jack was supposed to be....

"Can I help you with anything?"

She started out of her daze, suddenly realizing she was staring unashamedly at his crotch. Flaming embarrassment swept up her body in a burning wave, and she was powerless to do anything about it.

She was a good blusher, she'd learned to her detriment over the years. Even her ears glowed when she was totally humiliated. Like now. She felt almost incandescent with heat and she resolutely kept her gaze away from his as she fought to control her own body.

But the more she thought about it, the more she seemed to sizzle and glow, and she tried not to think about how guilty and pathetic she must seem to him.

At last the flush seemed to dissipate, but it left her feeling unbearably hot. Her blouse felt sticky, confining and oppressive. Briefly, she flicked an envious gaze across at Jack's bare chest, only to be caught in the knowing beam of his blue eyes.

A small residual flood of color washed her cheeks as she tore her gaze from him. He was laughing at her! Why, oh, why had she stared at him like that? Was she so hard up that the first bit of decent male action to come her way sent her into zombie-drool mode? Even if that male action was attached to the world's most annoying personality?

She flapped her blouse ineffectually, succeeding only in moving around more hot air.

"Take it off."

It was a dare, not a suggestion. A challenge, and the expression on his handsome, smug face told her that he knew she wouldn't take him up on it.

Her hands were on her buttons before she could think. One button, two, three. And he just sat there, his lips quirked to one side, apparently vastly amused by everything she did. She tried to remember which bra she'd put on this morning. *Not the stretched-out one with the pills and the no-nonsense, no-trim elastic. Please, not that one.* She wanted so badly to peek beneath her blouse to check, but then he'd know. The man was psychic. He'd definitely know.

Four buttons, only three to go now. A patch of black bra showed in her peripheral vision. Maybe if she glanced down casually, just as though she wasn't sure where the next button was? She risked it, sighing with relief when she saw her unexciting but presentable plain black bra. It was a simple, smooth cup style that was more about good design and elegance than frills and see-through bits, and she was damn grateful that she'd put it on this morning. More confident now, she slipped the last button loose, tugged her blouse open and began working on the buttons on her cuff.

He was still watching her, she could feel it. Trying to pay her back for gawking at him earlier, obviously. She could handle it. It was just like wearing a crop top during training, and while she wasn't into showing off her body and flashing it around, she was quietly confident that it was in good shape.

She shrugged the damp silk from her shoulders and slid it off her arms as nonchalantly as possible. Determined to prove she was not the uptight prude he thought she was, she sighed loudly.

"You're right, that's much better."

She even circled her shoulders around, as if she was warming up for a swim. His eyes were glued to her, and she was loving it.

"Yep, that's definitely better," she repeated, mostly just to annoy him.

Smiling sweetly at him, she spread her shirt out on the scratchy industrial carpet, then rerolled her jacket into a tighter pillow.

"I'm going to see if I can get some sleep," she told him blithely.

He was still just sitting there, an unreadable expression on his face. Probably didn't know what to say now that she'd proved him wrong. Typical.

CHAPTER FIVE

JACK CONCENTRATED FIERCELY on the idea of puppies frolicking in fresh snow. He conjured up an image of a fresh alpine stream, clear water burbling over mossy rocks. He even resorted to imagining a photograph of his grandmother, the one where she was looking very stern and schoolmarmish. None of it stopped the rest of his body from whooping it up over the sight of Claire Marsden in a bra. Whoever designed her suits and blouses was a master of disguise, that was for sure. The CIA should be talking to that guy. Hollywood should be using him instead of all that computer gimmickry they were all so fond of these days.

Because Claire was hot, and Jack had never even suspected it. From the soft, even tan across her chest and torso to the gentle rise of her breasts from one of the sexiest bras he'd ever seen, she was a revelation.

Hot. Damn hot.

It wasn't just that she was built—although that had a lot to do with it. Her breasts were definitely on the generous side, definitely a very nice handful. And it wasn't just the ripple of highly toned muscles on her stomach—although that was pretty damn good, also. It was more that it all fit together so well. She was small but perfect, and generous in all the areas she should be.

In short, hot.

His body seemed determined to worship that hotness in its own very special way, and no matter what he told himself—*she's a shrew, she hates me, she probably irons her underwear*—he was unable to stop it. Thank God he was sitting with his knees drawn up and his back against the wall. Thank God she'd decided to go to sleep, and that she'd rolled to face the wall. Perhaps with those breasts out of his immediate view he could get a grip on himself. Figuratively speaking.

It was a bit disconcerting, really. Not since the uncertain years of adolescence had his body been so at odds with his mind. Because she just wasn't his type. And they didn't get along, at all. And, if he was being completely honest, she annoyed him. She was bossy, and defensive, and too quick with a smart comeback. Too much trouble, all round. So it was very strange to be annoyed and irritated by her, but also wonder what color her nipples were, and if she tasted as good as she looked.

Very confusing. Disturbing, even.

He checked his watch, then returned to studying her back. Damn if she didn't have a nice back, too—smooth, unblemished skin, nicely shaped vertebrae—

He pulled himself up short. *Nicely shaped vertebrae?* Was he going insane?

A little desperate, he cast a glance around his brushed steel cell and then suddenly got it. Stockholm Syndrome, or whatever it was called. That thing where the people were held hostage and started to identify with, and like, and sympathize with their captors. That's exactly what was happening here— Stockholm Syndrome! She was his captor, and he was starting to sympathize with her. Once he was restored to his normal environment, nature would reassert itself.

Relief washed over him. Good old science—always there with an explanation for everything.

Following her example, he decided to try for some shut-eye. If they were going to be in here for another five or so hours, sleeping some of it off was a really good idea. Of course, he wasn't feeling very snoozy, but if she could sleep, so could he.

He lay down, quickly becoming aware that the carpet was the prickly, unforgiving type that was designed to survive a nuclear holocaust. He sat up and spread out his shirt like a towel at the beach. Once on his back, he stared at the ceiling, his hand automatically sliding down and across his belly and beneath the waistband of his pants to find the long scar that cut low across his stomach and around his side. He couldn't feel the familiar ridge under his fingers without thinking of Robbie, and he made a point of thinking of Robbie every day. It was the least he could do because it was all he had left.

People always talked about feeling as though they'd lost a part of themselves when a loved one dies, but Jack knew with rock-solid certainty that he'd lost the best part of himself when his twin brother succumbed to kidney disease.

Even though it had been three years now, he couldn't think about it without tasting the bitterness and anger again. It should have been him. Robbie had always been smarter, stronger, funnier. Robbie had been the one who'd chosen medicine, while Jack had been just bumming around, trying to find something that held his interest. If fate had to take someone, it should have been him.

"It's so hot in here."

It was almost a relief to be distracted from his own thoughts.

"Not much we can do about it," he replied, knowing it would annoy her. After all, it was what he was good at.

"Imagine if Robinson Crusoe had that attitude. We need to be innovative, think outside the box. Or the elevator, I guess."

His eyes still on the ceiling, he shook his head minutely in exasperation.

"This isn't *Gilligan's Island,* Mary Ann. We can't just bake a batch of coconut cream pies and wait for the Professor to find a way to get us back home."

"Ginger, if you don't mind."

"What?"

"Ginger. I always wanted to be Ginger, not Mary Ann."

That surprised him so much that he turned to look at her and found she was on her back also, and was looking at him. Without his permission, his eyes flickered down to her chest. Her full breasts strained at the fabric of her bra now that she was on her back, and he felt a definite tightening in his groin. What was it with him and those breasts? He'd seen great breasts before. And he'd see them again. Plenty of them, in matched sets. These weren't the only breasts in the world. So why was he suddenly so hot to see them and touch them and taste them?

"Ginger was a redhead," he said, forcing himself to concentrate on the subject at hand.

"So? On the inside, maybe I'm a redhead." Her eyes dared him to contradict her.

"Hey, it's your split personality, not mine."

"Exactly."

Their old friend silence crept back into the elevator. Jack bent his legs and rested one ankle on the opposite knee, for something to do. And to try and distract himself from thinking about her breasts.

He bet they were firm. Firm, and sensitive. He bet if he took her nipple into his mouth, she'd cry out. He had a flash of Claire's eyes clouded with desire, her lids slightly lowered, her mouth open and wet.

"Who would you have been?" she asked suddenly.

"What?" he asked, almost starting with guilt.

"On the island. Who would you have been?" she repeated.

"Mr. Howell."

"You're kidding? Ugh!"

She sounded genuinely disgusted. He had a natural skill in this area, it seemed.

"Come on, think about it. He was rich, he managed to work it so everyone else did everything for him and he still had his main squeeze with him on the island."

She laughed. Another surprise—she had a sense of humor.

"You're the most practical playboy I've ever met," she said.

She was smiling again, her face just an arm's length or so away. It was almost like being in a very large bed, him on one side, her on the other. His body had things to say about the idea of being in bed with this new-improved, friendly, black-bra-wearing Claire Marsden, and he ruthlessly changed the subject. And kept his eyes fixed firmly on her face.

"Okay, Desert Island Top Five," he announced.

"I don't think we need to pretend we're trapped on a desert island, do you?"

She had a point.

"Trapped in an Elevator Top Five, then. All-time favorite movies," he said.

She shot him a look, seemed about to say something, hesitated and then spat it out anyway.

"I thought you were angry with me."

He shrugged. "You want to spend another five hours arguing or sitting here glaring at each other?"

"Good point. Okay. Top five movies. The first one is easy—*The Big Sleep,* definitely."

He couldn't help himself. "Surprise, surprise."

"Excuse me?"

"Everyone picks a black-and-white movie, preferably something with Bogie in it. Gives you street cred."

"But it's my favorite movie!" She sounded outraged.

He made sure there was a heavy dose of doubt in his tone. "Of course it is."

"Wait till it's your turn," she warned him. "Second movie would be *When Harry Met Sally.* I can watch it over and over and it's still clever and funny."

"So predictable, not even worth commenting on."

She threw him an exasperated look.

"You know what's predictable? You not agreeing with a word I say. I swear if I said the sky was blue, you'd disagree with me just for the sake of it."

"Depends."

She snorted with exasperation this time, and he found he was enjoying needling her like this.

"On what, pray tell?"

"If it was nighttime or daytime."

She half laughed at his lame joke, and he tried not to notice how pretty she looked and the way her breasts jiggled invitingly. *Those damn breasts!*

"Okay, third movie. Getting tougher now. Have to have a comedy in there, otherwise it's just way too boring."

She stretched one leg in the air, waggling it around aimlessly as she considered her options. Jack's eyes followed the hem of her skirt as it slid down to reveal more of her thighs. As if her breasts weren't doing him enough damage. But it was impossible to keep his eyes from the sleek, tanned firmness of her legs.

She really had great legs. They looked strong, and flexible. Like they could grip a man hard around the hips as he—

"There's Something About Mary!" she said suddenly, and he threw a mental bucket of cold water on himself.

She was watching for his reaction, so he simply looked thoughtful, although he was really quietly impressed. And not a little surprised. The lady didn't mind a good dose of potty humor. Not what he would have picked from her at all. Great breasts, great thighs and fond of puerile comedy. If they hadn't been stuck in this elevator together, she would have taken those secrets to her grave.

"Hmm."

She shook her head and continued. "Fourth movie… Something I can watch again and again, but is still fun… *Con Air.*"

He nearly sat up he was so shocked. "No way!"

"What?"

"You do not like *Con Air.*"

"I think I do."

"No way."

"Jack, I think I know if I like a movie or not. And I want *Con Air* as my number four."

"But—"

She was lying on her side now, leaning on her elbow. Her hand on her face made her cheek squish up, making her look almost cherubic and more than a little naughty as her eyes sparkled across at him.

"What's your problem?" she demanded.

"I was going to have *Con Air,*" he admitted.

"Really?"

"Yeah."

"Wow. Something in common. Scary," she said.

"You're telling me."

"Don't worry, I'm sure it'll never happen again. And you can have *Con Air* on your list, too."

"But then we'll have two copies of the same movie."

She almost laughed at his little gag, the twisting of her lips giving it away.

"Fifth and last movie…*The Wizard of Oz.*"

"The singing munchkins? The wicked witch of the west? You're not watching that in my elevator, I can tell you."

She was getting better at not reacting to his jibes.

"Your turn."

She sat up, rubbing her hands together with exaggerated anticipation, obviously looking forward to shooting him down in flames. He found himself admiring the dancing light in her eyes, and the way she leaned forward slightly, ready to take him on. The fact that her new position also gave him a great look at her cleavage was irrelevant. Completely irrelevant.

"Number one—*His Girl Friday,* with Cary Grant and Rosalind Russell."

He enjoyed watching her indignation grow.

"But you picked on me for having a black-and-white movie!"

"That's just me, I guess. I'm a contrary bastard."

Her eyes narrowed and she made an encouraging motion with her hand. "Keep 'em coming," she prodded him.

"Number two—*Rocky*. But only the first one. I hate sequels."

She rolled her eyes. "Typical. Macho movie about men being manly."

"You finished?"

She smiled brightly. "Not really. But it'll keep."

Boy, she was pretty cute when she smiled. He caught the thought and gave himself a mental slap. This Stockholm Syndrome thing was getting out of control. It was one thing to admire breasts and thighs, but thinking that someone was cute when she smiled was moving into dangerous territory.

"Three—*Raiders of the Lost Ark*."

"Sad, but predictable. Let me guess—you have a secret craving to travel the world, wear hats and be heroic?"

He made a point of looking very patient and forbearing. "Four—*Blade Runner*. Best sci-fi movie ever made."

His look dared her to disagree, but she just shrugged.

"I didn't mind it," she admitted.

"You didn't *mind* it? I s'pose you think the Colorado River is a nice little stream?"

"Number five, cough it up," she said, wisely ignoring his baiting.

He took his time, making a big show of being very thoughtful. She didn't buy any of it, but sat with a look that very plainly said, "I know you're about to be very annoying, and I'm ready for it."

"It's tough, very tough. A couple of good contenders. But I'm going to have to go with *Porkies*."

She managed to maintain a very creditable poker face. "That surprises me. You don't think you're overlooking some of the excellent work in *Revenge of the Nerds?* And let's not forget that seminal classic, *Bikini Shop*."

He played along. "I did consider *Bikini Shop* briefly, but I decided it was too derivative. Plus there are more boob jokes in *Porkies*."

"Of course. I stand corrected."

The subterranean grumble of his unfed stomach hijacked the rest of the conversation. In the small confines of the lift, it seemed inordinately loud and he found himself staring at his own belly.

"Sorry. I guess I'm hungry."

He hauled himself upright, aware that the waistband on his cargo pants had dropped a little with the movement. He patted his complaining stomach, then watched her eyes follow the motion. A small frown appeared between her eyebrows, just for a second, and when he glanced down he realized his scar was showing. Sighing, he braced himself for the inevitable "Wow, how'd you get that?"

It never came. Instead, she turned to her handbag and started rummaging through it. He watched, perplexed, as her frustration grew until she finally just emptied the whole bag out onto the elevator floor. An enormous array of crap spilled out over the carpeted space between them, successfully distracting him from the increasingly hypnotic power her breasts seemed to hold over him. He surveyed the array of purse-rubble disbelievingly. This jumble of junk belonged to Claire "Crisply Ironed" Marsden?

"Wow. You got a spare Learjet or helicopter in there we could use?" he asked as she began pawing through the debris.

"Trust me, it's all very valuable and necessary," she said, intent on her search.

He leaned forward to pick up a child-size water pistol.

"Very handy with some clients, I'm sure." For an insane moment, he wondered what she would do if he squirted her in the breasts with the gun, and then offered to lick the water off. Before he could so much as tighten his finger on the trigger, she reached up and took the water pistol out of his hand.

"It's my godchild's. Here they are!"

Triumphant, she held aloft a packet of mints as though she'd just found the Holy Grail itself. Very pleased with herself, she offered the pack to him.

"Help yourself," she encouraged him.

She was very proud of her mints, and he didn't have the heart to tell her they wouldn't put a dint in his appetite. So he peeled off a mint, more than a little bemused by this new side to Claire. This godmother-to-someone's-child, lover-of-action-movies, owner-of-a-junk-filled-handbag Claire. It didn't gel with his previous ideas of her at all. If he'd thought about her at all—and he hadn't, thanks to the boxy suits and the efficient way she had of cutting him dead each time she saw him—he'd have imagined her in one of those minimalist white apartments with everything arranged in tidy, geometric patterns. He'd have bet she made her bed with hospital corners, watched worthy historical dramas on public access TV and listened to opera in the original Italian.

Now he knew that at least some of those assumptions were wrong. For starters, those ugly suits of hers had been hiding an Aladdin's cave of earthy delights—exhibit *A* being those spectacular breasts, followed closely by the firm silkiness of her thighs. Plus she had a sense of humor. And she was messy, despite appearances, if her handbag was anything to go by.

Floundering and uncomfortable with this new, far more sexy, human take on Claire Marsden, he tried gamely to cling to his old misconceptions.

"Do you like opera?" he asked, wanting to be able to retreat to familiar, predictable territory. He made a bet with himself that she even knew Italian and had a season's pass.

She poked out her tongue playfully, something he'd never seen her do before. Who was this woman? And what had she done with the real Claire Marsden?

"Hate it. And I know you're going to call me a philistine now and tell me how beautiful and moving it is, but I'm just not into it, okay? So sue me," she said.

She was sucking on a mint, the action puckering her lips a little, and he had to drag his fascinated gaze away from her mouth to respond.

"Bunch of incomprehensible screaming, if you ask me," he said vaguely, beginning to worry again about Stockholm Syndrome.

What if there was no cure? What if he got out of here and this feeling he was beginning to get— this sort of defrosting feeling coupled with a definite physical interest—what if it didn't go away? He didn't want to get to know Claire. He certainly didn't want to *like* her, after all the crap she'd piled on him today. But the niggling thought that perhaps he'd misjudged her kept shouting for attention at the back of his mind. That, and the fact that he had an erection that was becoming increasingly difficult to hide.

HE WAS QUITE entertaining, really. But then, if you were going to be a successful playboy, she guessed you'd have to have a fair line in being charming and entertaining. Stock in trade, really.

The movie talk had been fun. And she'd been surprised by how many movies they'd both liked. Of course, she'd expected him to be prejudiced against *The Wizard of Oz*. Only the truly good and insightful understood how great a movie it was.

She finished stuffing all her bits back into her handbag, and settled once again into her lolling position on the floor. It was getting really warm now. All their talking hadn't helped things any, sucking up all the available air. For a moment, she wondered about how airtight the lift was and imagined running out of oxygen. The walls seemed to frown in over her and all of a sudden she was finding it difficult to breathe again.

"Claire?"

When she didn't answer, he nudged her foot with his, forcing her to look up. He tapped his nose, and she nodded as she remembered to follow his technique.

After a minute or so of nostril breathing, she felt the tension in her chest easing.

"Thanks."

"The nose knows."

She flapped a hand in front of her face, desperate for a bit of fresh air.

"It's just so stuffy in here. Now I know how microwave popcorn feels."

He shot her a look that plainly told her to quit whining.

"I know, talking about it doesn't make it any better. But surely we could pry the doors open a bit, get some fresh air in?" she suggested hopefully.

But he just shook his head.

"Sadly, I left my pry bar at home this morning. Unless you have one in your bag?"

She huffed at him impatiently, already reassessing the good will he'd generated during their movie banter. Amusing he might be, but scratch the surface and he had a solid core of annoying just waiting to be expressed.

Pushing the wet curls back from her forehead, she rolled her head back on her jacket-pillow and stared at the ceiling. This waiting was bringing new meaning to the word *bored*. She remembered seeing some pages from the local paper stuffed in amongst the rubble in her handbag, and she reached for them in desperation. Never had reports on the local school fair or lost dogs seemed so enticing. She unfolded the pages and realized with disappointment that they were from the classifieds section of the paper. She remembered now that she'd grabbed them because she needed to arrange for a plumber to look at her dishwasher.

Still, desperate times bred desperate measures, and she found herself perusing every single ad. Plumbers, gardeners, electricians. She found three spelling mistakes and about a million grammatical errors. But who was counting, right? She was about to flip the page when she saw a small photo ad for a car dealership. The flash of red paintwork caught her eye and she squinted, trying to work out what make of car it was in the tiny photo. A Mustang! And a convertible, if she wasn't mistaken. Excellent. She settled back to enjoy a good ten minutes' worth of fantasizing about owning a red Mustang convertible. By the time she'd killed a quarter of an hour imagining herself cruising around with the roof off, her practical side was beginning to assert itself. The roof probably leaked, parts would be expensive, and there was nothing at all wrong with her late-model sedan. Besides, she wasn't a red convertible kind of girl. Sighing, she rolled the pages back up and put them to one side.

"Could I…?" Jack asked, eyeing the paper greedily.

"It's pretty dull stuff—but you're welcome to it." She flipped the paper over to his side of the elevator and tried to think of something else to occupy herself. She'd seen an interview with a guy who'd been held captive by South American freedom fighters once. He'd been locked up on his own for months and months, and he claimed he held on to his sanity and his purpose by having imaginary conversations with his family, acting out both sides in his cell.

She slid a sideways look at the man lying beside her. She'd never hear the last of it if she had an imaginary conversation with her father. The idea was so absurd, she almost laughed out loud. Not the least because she couldn't begin to imagine what a real conversation with her father might be like. The familiar feeling of anger twined with rejection stole into her belly, and she steeled herself against it. Harry was not a good investment for hopes, emotions and dreams.

The sound of Jack's stomach growling saved her from further naval gazing.

"Have another mint," she said, tossing the roll of candy across to him.

She returned to her mindless study of the elevator's ceiling, her eyes sliding across the familiar configuration of emergency light, utility access and the ubiquitous expanse of brushed steel.

She allowed her heavy eyelids to close, then sat up straight, inspiration energizing her.

"The utility access!" she crowed excitedly, scrambling to her feet.

Jack was staring up at her from his prone position, a shiny scrap of foil from the mint roll curled on his chest.

"Huh?"

"The utility access, in the ceiling. We can open it, let some of this hot air out. Surely there must be cooler air out there in the elevator shaft?" she said.

He liked the idea, she could tell by the way his eyes darkened to a deeper blue.

"Smart thinking, 99," he said in a really appalling Maxwell Smart voice.

"As an impressionist, you make a great elevator mechanic," she told him playfully, then caught herself up short.

Was she *flirting* with Jack Brook? She looked at him out of the corners of her eyes as he eased himself to his feet and brushed himself off.

She had to admit, she'd come a long way from her initial impression of him. He wasn't as big a swine as she'd always imagined. In fact, he was quite kind, she decided, remembering his deft handling of her claustrophobia. Admitting that Jack Brook was not the devil incarnate she'd always classified him as was like opening herself up to the suggestion that the world might not be flat: too much was predicated on all her previous assumptions and judgments. Their whole past relationship was founded on the basis that she didn't like him, he didn't like her and never the twain should meet.

"Hinges at one end, catch at the other. I don't think we'll even need that crowbar of yours," Jack was saying, and she snapped her focus back to the current issue and away from the scary thought that more than just her claustrophobia was getting a work-out in here.

The ceiling was quite high, she suddenly realized.

"Can you reach it?" she wondered out loud, and he gave her a pitying look.

"I think we'll be fine," he said confidently.

But when he reached casually for the catch they both quickly saw that even standing on the very tips of his toes, he could only just get his fingertips on the mechanism. He didn't so much as glance at her once he realized he'd spoken too soon, so she leaned against the side of the lift and watched as he jumped up and down futilely a few times, his hands flailing uselessly against the catch each time he made contact with the roof. He finally gave up and turned to her, a warning expression writ large on his face.

"Don't say a word."

"Did I even open my mouth?" she defended herself.

"You don't need to. Come on, I'll give you a boost."

She hung back a moment, not really sure how to go about this.

"Come on," he said impatiently.

She stepped forward slowly, deeply reluctant to be in physical contact with him. It just didn't seem... right.

"What should I—" she began, but Jack was already bending forward to grab her around the waist and lift her toward the ceiling. At about the same time her feet left the ground she became aware of his face pressed into her cleavage, and she stared down at his dark head, appalled.

CHAPTER SIX

"COME ON, I'M not Atlas, for Pete's sake," Jack grumbled, his words muffled by her breasts.

Oh, boy. A thousand and one sensations skittered along her nerve ends and she closed her eyes against the assault. His stubbled cheeks rasped faintly against her skin, and she could feel his breath, hot and moist, with each impatient word. His arms were two strong bands around her body, his chest against her belly, her legs hanging a foot or two off the ground.

He made an exasperated noise, and she belatedly looked toward the ceiling, but it was miles away.

"This isn't going to work," she told him, and the tension in his arms relaxed abruptly and she dropped back down to earth, sliding along his body all the way.

Her heart was beating out of control, and somewhere deep inside, something long-ignored awoke and lifted its head to look around drowsily. *Desire.* His skin had been hot and smooth and hard, and it had been way, way too long since she'd been held by a man. She didn't need to look down at herself to know that through the mere act of talking into her cleavage, Jack had managed to turn her nipples into two embarrassing declarations of arousal.

And for my next act, I shall implode with humiliation, she thought as she hurriedly crossed her arms to hide her traitorous nipples.

How on earth could her body react to Jack like that? It was as though she was suddenly being held captive by some strange alien force. *Come on,* she told her body, *the guy's a poster boy for everything I dislike in a man. We're complete opposites. We have nothing in common. He doesn't even like me. How can you do this to me?*

But her body wasn't taking any calls. Instead, it was resolutely hanging on to the memory of his flesh against hers, his hands splayed firmly across her back, the prickle of his whiskers on her breasts.

"Okay, I'm sure you've got plenty of smart ideas," Jack said, his own arms crossed over his chest now.

Ideas? Boy, did she have ideas. Instantly, her out-of-control body imagined a dozen X-rated scenarios, all of them involving Jack naked, ready and willing. She fought the urge to cross her legs and squirm.

"Um. Sure. You could…you could go down on all fours and I could stand on your back," she finally managed to say past the lump of misguided lust in her throat.

He uncrossed his arms, and she watched, almost hypnotized, as the muscles along his chest and stomach rippled in reaction. *Cool. Make him do it again,* her body urged.

"I know it would probably satisfy some deep inner

need for you, but you are not standing on my back to reach for the sky," Jack countered.

"Okay, okay." Desperately she searched around for another idea, anything, before he realized she was acting like a crazy woman, her eyes practically falling out of her head ogling him.

"What about a shoulder ride?" she suggested.

He gave it a moment's thought, then shrugged his lack of objection to the idea. She tried not to get too absorbed in following the ripple of muscle this caused down his body. But she must have been staring, because the next thing she noticed he was giving her a really weird look. The kind of look you give a dog when you think it might have rabies. She almost lifted a hand to check she wasn't foaming at the mouth.

"You want to do this now?" he asked warily.

"Sure."

Concentrate, she warned herself. *Concentrate, and we'll write off the last five minutes as some extremely strange reaction to oxygen deprivation.*

He squatted in front of her, and she froze a moment, staring at his well-muscled back. He really was in fine shape. Most guys who had desk jobs as he did would have let themselves go soft and run to fat, but he either had a truly stunning metabolism, or a natural affection for exercise. For the first time, she understood how Fiona from Legal, and Katherine and all those other women were unable to resist him. He was just plain sexy. Tall, and strong, and handsome, and…

"What are you waiting for, an engraved invitation?" he asked.

She blinked. *What is wrong with me?*

"Let's just get this over with," he suggested, impatience oozing from every pore as he swiveled his head around to look at her.

Slapping every inappropriate thought to one side, she hitched her skirt around her waist, stepped toward him, and slung her left leg over his shoulder. She almost jumped when he immediately enclosed her ankle in a warm, firm grip.

"Other leg, come on," he ordered, leaning forward a little so she could find her balance.

She obediently slid her other leg over his shoulder, and before she could brace herself he'd locked her other ankle in place and was surging to his feet. For a scary moment she teetered on his shoulders, and instinctively she grasped at his head for balance.

His hair was thick and wavy, and she ploughed her fingers into it as she searched for a grip.

"Yow!" he howled, and she immediately loosened her death grip.

"Sorry."

"Can you reach it?" he asked, and she tried not to register the rasp of his stubbly cheek against the tender skin of her inner thighs.

Jack Brook with his face against her thighs? She had trouble even processing the thought, let alone the sensation. Forcing herself to focus on the matter at hand, she studied the catch on the cover a moment, then flicked it open. Tentative, she pushed the cover upward, but it gave way readily, flopping open to clang loudly on the elevator car's roof.

"Done!" she said with satisfaction.

Taking advantage of the opportunity, she shoved a hand up into the opening.

"Much cooler out there. Hopefully it'll make a difference in here," she reported.

She was about to suggest he put her down when he slid his hands up her shins and over her knees to grasp her firmly just above each knee. And then he began jiggling from side to side, causing her to renew her death grip on his hair.

"What are you doing?" she squeaked.

She'd instinctively clamped her thighs tighter around his neck as soon as her balance was in jeopardy, and she could actually *feel* him grin.

"Victory dance," he said, and she held her breath as he twirled them both around in a little circle.

What a goof. But she couldn't help smiling: ridiculous as it seemed, opening a stupid utility hatch felt like an achievement. She smiled as she felt the shifting of his strong shoulders beneath her as he danced a few more steps, and even managed a little bongo-drum accompaniment on his head.

She was still smiling when he announced he was going to let her down. He crouched low, and she maneuvered first one then the other leg off his shoulders, hastily pulling her skirt back down where it belonged before he turned around to face her, a jubilant smile on his face.

He's beautiful. She tried to squelch the thought, to pretend it had never entered her mind.

"Feels better already. Way to go, team," he said, holding his hand up in the classic high-five position.

She slapped his open palm, all the while trying to forget the feel of his hands on her thighs. And his hands sliding up her legs. And his face against her breasts.

Stop it, stop it, stop it.

This had to be caused by some weird combination of claustrophobia and lack of oxygen. That's all this hyperawareness of him was. Hell, they probably did laboratory experiments like this all the time. At NASA or something. The Effects of Enforced Intimacy on Hardworking Female Executives. Or something like that.

Find something else to think about. Her frazzled brain sought desperately for a diversion as they both returned to their opposite sides of the elevator. She found her eyes tracking to the scar that slashed across his abdomen, and before she knew it the words had popped out. "That's a pretty decent scar you've got there."

She wished the words back the moment they were uttered. *How rude! How invasive and nosy and rude!* Wondering what sort of a kisser he was was better than being nosy. She could tell by the way his eyes dropped to the floor that he was thinking of some way to palm her off—which she deserved—and she rushed into speech again.

"Ignore me. I didn't mean to say that. I think I'm oxygen deprived," she blathered.

She could feel him watching her, assessing her, and then he shook his head minutely as though shaking something off.

"It's okay. It's pretty noticeable. Someone once told me it looked like a shark had attacked me."

She made a disbelieving noise.

"Hardly. Unless sharks are getting medical training these days."

He smiled a little, just a quirk of one side of his mouth. Then he said, "I donated a kidney to someone. My brother."

She could tell it had cost him a lot to say it. And she could feel the weight of a long and sad story dragging the words down. This was not a story with a happy ending, she sensed.

"That's pretty incredible. And scary. Your brother was lucky you were a match," she offered, deeply uncertain about what to say.

He'd crossed his arms across his chest, the classic "locked off" signal in body language. She didn't need it to know she was deep in territory he normally kept very private.

"Yeah. Well, not really. We were twins. Perfect match."

His face was so carefully blank, but she could tell. There was a lot of anger and pain pent up in this man, and she guessed why.

"He died?" There was no other explanation for Jack referring to his brother in the past tense.

"Yeah."

"What was his name?"

"Robbie. Or Robert, according to Mom."

She was totally at sea. And she just knew she was going to say the wrong thing any second now. But she also knew she was being given a very privileged insight into Jack's life. No one at work had ever gossiped about this stuff, and she knew absolutely that he didn't talk about it. Normally.

But this wasn't a normal situation, as she was beginning to appreciate more and more with each passing moment.

"I don't have any brothers or sisters," she volunteered. "I can't imagine what it would be like to lose someone so close to you. Especially a twin. Was he a writer like you?"

He barked out a bitter little laugh, and she could see so clearly the anger inside him.

I bet you blame the world for Robbie being gone. I bet you blame God, Buddha, modern medicine and anyone else who comes to mind. But most of all, I bet you blame yourself.

"He was a doctor. A pediatrician. He just loved kids, and even though it cut him up when he couldn't help someone, he always stayed in there, fighting away. But them's the breaks, right? Fate, luck, destiny. Whatever. The doctor dies, the writer lives."

The words could have peeled paint. She just let the anger wash over her. It wasn't for her, anyway.

He ran a hand over his face, almost as though he was removing a mask or wiping something away.

"It doesn't matter."

Of course, it did. In fact, it was probably what shaped his life. She cocked her head to one side, considering. All her preconceptions, and observations, and judgments reorganized themselves and settled into a new pattern to accommodate this information, and she suddenly understood why Jack shied away from commitment, and drove a sports car, and skated by on the surface of things: he already had a world of pain to deal with, and he just didn't have the room, or the time, or the inclination to handle any more.

She blinked, and it was as if she was seeing him with new eyes. The lines around his mouth weren't all from smiling and laughing. The spark in those bright blue eyes of his was as much about covering as it was about charming. She felt an enormous desire to cross the space between them and take him in her arms. She actually swallowed at the intensity of it. She wanted to cradle his head on her breast, and soothe him, and tell him that one day he would be reconciled to his brother's death, but first he had to let himself feel it.

It was a bone-deep longing, and it was so powerful she actually sat on her hands, in case they reached out toward him of their own accord. Jack would be horrified if she offered him comfort. In fact, she knew with a crystal-clear prescience that he was going to regret ever having said a word once they were out of this elevator.

And what could she offer him, anyway? They

weren't even friends. They didn't even like each other.

But despite all that, she found herself talking. Perhaps because she couldn't offer him comfort, she instead offered him something of herself so he wouldn't feel so exposed.

"I'm the biggest regret of my father's life. He wanted a boy so badly, but my mom died just after I was born. I was his one chance. So Harry tried to turn me into a boy for a while, but I hated the mountains, and I was too scared of falling when he took me climbing. And then one time he had to turn back from an expedition he'd taken me on because I got sick. And that was it. He just kind of...wrote me off."

They were the most honest and painful words she'd ever spoken. In fact, she wondered if she'd even thought any of this through so clearly before. Even as the words tumbled out, she understood why she never acknowledged this stuff: it was like taking her skin off and letting the world see all her fears and ugly places.

Her mind swung around to that damned unanswered invitation for her father to watch her compete at the finals in just over two weeks' time. Why had she put herself in a position where he could write her off yet again?

Jack was looking at her strangely. "Your dad's not Harry Marsden, the explorer?" he asked, amazed.

She simply nodded.

"I never knew," he said.

"I don't exactly have T-shirts made up."

He studied her face appraisingly. "You look like him."

"Not enough, apparently."

A silence, then Jack said, "Thanks."

He held her eyes, and it was the most open and honest contact they'd ever shared. It felt like a fresh start. She smiled, and he smiled back, and all of a sudden all of her lust rolled over her, but this time it was tinged with a desire to ease his unhappiness, to do something without considering the merits and worrying about the consequences.

Could he read her thoughts? It seemed he could, because his eyes dropped to her breasts. She liked that, liked that he'd noticed her that way. She felt her heart skip into overdrive. Had his eyes darkened? Was she getting the message from him that she thought she was? She wasn't sure. Doubt assailed her. He was so much more experienced than her. For Pete's sake, he'd slept with half the building. What would he want with her?

"Claire."

It was an invitation. Wasn't it? She wanted it to be. Very badly. Because she hadn't been this hot for someone for a long time. But he was just sitting there, opposite her. What was he thinking? Should she…should she make the first move? Tentative, she leaned forward, placing a hand in front of herself so she could lean even farther across the space that separated her from him.

His eyes were locked on hers, and she could see something come to life in them. He looked hungry and sexy and very intent. He leaned forward. There was an excruciating moment, a moment between breaths, where she waited for his lips to touch hers. And then they were kissing, tentatively at first, no other part of their bodies touching. His lips were warm, and he tasted of mints and she felt a shimmering *something* unfolding inside her. By some unspoken agreement, they both broke the kiss to stop and stare at each other for a moment. His eyes were very close to hers, and she felt as though she was drowning in the myriad blues of his irises. And then, as if drawn by gravity or magnetism or some force outside of themselves, they came together again. This time she felt a twist of excitement spiral through her as his tongue darted into her mouth for the first time, and then, all of a sudden, it was as though something had exploded inside her. She couldn't get a enough of him, and she sensed the same greedy hunger in him as he reached for her.

His hands swept up her arms, and a shower of heat followed. She clutched at him, off balance, drunk with lust. His skin was smooth and firm, perfectly sculpted over planes and rounds of muscle. She explored him feverishly, measuring the breadth of his shoulders, racing her fingers through the silky hair on his chest. His hands were tracing her face, running down her neck, brushing across the sensitive skin of her upper chest. She sucked in her breath as his hands slid smoothly down and onto her breasts, his thumbs finding her already-erect nipples through the satin of her bra. He plucked at her breasts with a firm, sure touch, and an answering note sounded deep in her belly and she felt herself tighten. As amazing as it seemed, she wanted him. She wanted him right now.

Jack was nibbling his way down her neck now, and she let out a small, excited moan as he brushed her bra straps down her arms and took one of her taut, aching nipples into his mouth. She bucked instinctively, unable to control the urge to push up into something as a storm of sensation raced through her body. His mouth was so hot, and his tongue so quick and firm…

"Jack, Jack—" she whimpered, unable to tell him exactly what it was she was feeling, or what she wanted.

He simply lifted his head to grin wolfishly at her, his eyes shining with desire, and she found herself grinning back at him, glorying in the absolute need that gripped them both. Bold, she reached for the closure on his pants, even as he pushed her skirt up and pressed a palm against the moist heat between her thighs. She could feel how ready she was, was almost embarrassed by how ready she was, but it only seemed to increase his desire as he helped her push his cargo pants down over his hips. His erection was hard and proud against his belly and she reached for it with sure hands. He was big and beautiful and she wanted him inside her as soon as was humanly possible.

He must have been a mind reader, because no sooner had she wrapped her fingers around his shaft than he was dragging her panties off impatiently. She got lost in space and time for a beat as he swept a knowing hand across her mound, his thumb finding the sensitive nub of her clitoris unerringly. A shaft of pure desire rippled through her, and while she was still recovering, he slid his fingers down to the slippery folds of her inner lips. She clenched in anticipation of his penetration, but he held back as his thumb continued to work her clitoris.

"You want me inside you?" he whispered huskily at her ear, his finger circling her slickness now, teasing.

In answer she raised her hand to her mouth and licked her palm, her eyes holding his as she slid it back between their bodies and slicked her wet hand up and down his shaft, her thumb gliding across the delicate velvet of the head of his penis before sliding down again. As she had before him, he shuddered in response, and she felt a surge of feminine satisfaction as a muscle clenched in his jaw.

"You want to be inside me?" she whispered back, increasing the tempo of her movements, loving the feel of him in her hand.

Suddenly he twisted away from her, grabbing his wallet, finding a condom and putting it on, all before she could protest his leaving. Then she was on her back and he was positioned between her legs, his body weight supported by his formidable arms as he hung above her. There was a split second of thrilling anticipation and then he was plunging inside her, filling her completely, so much so that the base of his shaft ground satisfyingly into her swollen clitoris as he buried his length in her.

She gasped her surprise—it was never, ever this good for her. It was as though he'd been made for her, as though she'd been waiting for this moment for so long that she was on a hair trigger, ready to explode. And then Jack was stroking in and out of her, each sweep driving her crazy. She clutched at his back, his butt, his shoulders, pushed her hips up to him, rocked away, gasped out his name. Straining, wanting all of him, she chased the growing tension inside herself, loving the harsh sound of his breathing as he rode her. Just when she thought it couldn't get any better, he reached a hand between them and found her clitoris again, swollen with need, ready for him. One, two, three passes of his deft thumb and the tension inside her broke in a cascading wave and she was falling apart in his arms, her muscles clenching around him, her hips bucking, his name on her lips.

It was as though he'd been waiting for her, because no sooner had she dissolved around him than he'd stiffened with his own orgasm, shuddering into her, his face pressed against her neck.

For a long time afterward there was nothing but the sound of their harsh breathing. Jack lay on top of her, still inside her, and she tried to pull the fragmented parts of herself back together.

She felt...consumed. There was no other word for it. Utterly, completely consumed by the magic they'd just created together. The best sex she'd ever had. Ever. Hands down. The most amazing sensual experience of her life.

At last Jack raised his head, and their eyes met. He looked as blown away as she felt, his blue eyes incredulous as he looked deeply into hers. A smile softened the curve of his mouth, and he opened his mouth to speak—

The phone rang. They both stiffened. The phone sounded again, and Jack shrugged ruefully.

"I have to get that."

"I know."

He withdrew and rolled away from her in one smooth move, and the sudden loss of skin contact made her feel inexplicably cold and alone. Flushed, she watched as Jack reached for the phone.

"Yeah?" he said, one hand coming up to push the hair back from his forehead. The action hid his face from her momentarily, just when it was very important that she be able to see his face, his reaction. His body seemed tight, defensive. What was he thinking? His hand dropped down at last, and she studied him closely.

He glanced across at her, his eyes flicking down from her face to her still-sprawling body. Suddenly she felt exposed, spread out in front of him with her skirt rucked up, her bra pulled down. With trembling hands she tugged her bra into place and slid her panties on before pushing her skirt down, listening all the while to the cryptic, monosyllabic conversation Jack was having with whomever was on the other end of the phone.

"Great, thanks," Jack said, at last placing the receiver back on the hook.

He reached for his boxers before he spoke.

"Ted estimates about five minutes," he reported, and she nodded her understanding.

It was over. They were about to be rescued, and their enforced encounter was at an end. Neither of them said anything as they shuffled into the rest of their clothes. Claire didn't know what to think or feel. Somewhere, deep in the back of her mind, she was shocked at what had just happened. She felt as though she was swimming in treacle as she tried to analyze her feelings. It had been so good…so intense. She'd never felt anything close to the kind of passion she'd just experienced.

But now it was over, and it was back to the real world, to office politics and maneuvering and executive meetings ad infinitum.

She shot a glance across at Jack, trying to work out what he was thinking. They'd just had the wildest, most uninhibited sex in all the world. Was he feeling as shell-shocked and shaky and amazed as she was?

He glanced across at her, his expression unreadable, and her spirits sagged. Of course he wasn't. She was kidding herself. He was probably thrilled to be getting out of here. As she should be. What had just happened had been an aberration, an insane one-off that would never have happened outside of this very particular set of circumstances. Hell, it probably happened to him every second day—this was the office stud they were talking about, after all.

"They're winching us to the nearest floor," Jack explained belatedly.

They'd pry the doors open there, and then they would go their separate ways. This moment, this incredible, challenging time-out from the normal world, would be gone forever.

Claire found herself reaching into her bag, grabbing one of her business cards and a pen. Urgent, she scribbled her home number on it, not thinking, just feeling. She'd just shared the most extraordinary physical connection with this man. It had been more than great sex—surely she hadn't imagined it? Surely, he, too, must think that there was something undiscovered here—something with so much potential that it would be crazy to walk away from it?

"Here," she said softly, and when he met her eyes she saw Jack's confusion and amazement and she felt a surge of confidence as she slid the card into his hand.

"My home number," she said huskily.

Before he could respond, the elevator lurched up several feet, and the sound of screeching metal filled the car. Slowly the doors slid open to reveal a crowd of onlookers and rescue workers.

She and Jack were swept up by their various assistants and colleagues, and before she knew it, Jack was heading one way down the hall, and she was being ushered another. She glanced over her shoulder once, but he was listening to something his assistant was saying and he didn't see her.

It was almost as though it all had never happened. But she remembered the look in his eyes as she slid the card into his hand.

He'll call, she assured herself fiercely. *He has to after what just happened between us....*

JACK PROPPED CLAIRE'S business card on his hall bureau as soon as he got home, liking the invitation and potential contained in that small piece of card. It was a no-brainer, really. He'd just had the best sex of his life, and she'd told him to call her. What man wouldn't want more of what he'd just tasted?

Still, there was an uneasy feeling in the pit of his stomach, and it wasn't until he was shucking his clothes in the bathroom and stepping into the shower that he realized he couldn't possibly call. Because there'd been that moment afterward, when he'd still been inside her. He'd looked down into her eyes and seen so much vulnerability and surprise and amazement in her face. And he'd felt a weird surge of protectiveness and tenderness that had nothing to do with hot sex or physical chemistry....

Every survival instinct he possessed screamed "Run." And he was used to following those instincts—not for nothing had he remained single all these years.

The bottom line was that Claire Marsden intrigued him and attracted him in a way that made him feel distinctly uncomfortable, and every instinct told him that that was very dangerous to his status quo, hot sex or no hot sex.

Even as he acknowledged this and accepted it, his body protested. How could he walk away from something so hot and intense? His hands curved reflexively as he remembered the weight of her breasts, and he closed his eyes for a brief moment and groaned with frustration as he remembered the taste of her and the smell of her and the feel of her. She'd been pure desire, uninhibited, wild. Tight and wet and so responsive, her body seemingly attuned to his naturally.

He made a disgusted noise as he registered that he was now fully erect and aching for round two with Claire Marsden. Brutal, he switched the shower to cold and stood with gritted teeth under the punishing spray for a full five minutes, trying to purge the memory of her silky skin.

Because it wasn't just about animal attraction. There was more—that wasn't the only thing that drew him. He admired her bravery in holding up under the ridiculous conditions Morgan Beck had imposed on her. He thought she was funny and clever. And for some reason, he'd told her about his brother when he hadn't spoken about Robbie with anyone—family included—for more than a year.

And that was the scary part. Because even now he was wondering if she was okay, wondering what she was thinking. Perhaps she was in the shower, too....

He stepped from the shower and swiped at the water on his chest and arms with a towel. He couldn't call her, it was as simple as that. Claire had to be off-limits. He liked her, and he couldn't raise her expectations. He wasn't a forever kind of guy, and she was a forever kind of woman. It was never a good combination, and he didn't want to hurt her.

And she scares the crap out of you, an honest little voice chimed deep inside him.

That didn't mean he wasn't tempted, however, when he passed that taunting white rectangle an hour later. Fortuitously, he had his portable phone in hand, and he almost dialed her number. Almost.

It was exactly because he wanted to call her so much that he didn't. There was something different about Claire, about the way she made him think and feel. And it was distinctly unsettling.

No, she was best set to one side and avoided. Too much at stake, too hard. Too daunting and demanding. Repressing a small pang, he tossed out her card.

He decided to organize some assignments that would take him out of the office, but then the memory of his recent meeting with Morgan rang in his mind. Damn it, he was expected to be on hand to play macho man for old man Hillcrest. How was he supposed to resist having his way with Claire when he was supposed to be her associate editor?

He ran a frustrated hand through his hair, catching sight of himself in the mirror as he paced. He paused, leaned in to look himself in the eye. Could he trust himself to work side by side with Claire and not give in to the impulse to touch her?

Not a chance. Unless certain parts of his body

came with an off switch he hadn't been aware of previously, the only way to stop himself from making a fatal mistake was to pull back as far as he could go.

It wasn't as if it was a tough decision, anyway. In many respects, getting to see Claire a lot was the only attractive aspect of the whole arrangement Morgan had proposed.

Who in their right mind would want to be the token anything on a project? Not Jack Brook, that was for sure. He'd been too taken by surprise to put up a good fight when Morgan had sprung the idea on him and Claire today, but he wasn't hot to put his hand up for credit on a project he'd had no involvement with. It was unethical, and unfair to Claire.

He padded into the bedroom, his decision made. First thing tomorrow he'd call Beck and make his position clear.

CLAIRE FORCED HERSELF to go for a run, despite the burning urge to sit by the phone and will it to ring. She had an answering machine, and it would take a message if Jack called while she was out. She only had to repeat this to herself five times before she could force herself out the front door of her apartment. All other considerations aside, she had only two more weeks of training until the finals and she hadn't done all this hard work to blow it off because she and Jack Brook had had wild animal sex in the elevator at work. Every time she thought about it she battled a wash of embarrassment, closely followed by a rush of desire. She was going crazy pacing around her apartment, second-guessing herself, staring at the phone.

So now she was ignoring the burning muscles in her thighs and pushing herself harder up the hill. She forced herself to go past the car dealership where she usually turned for home, then stopped in her tracks for a beat as she caught sight of a red Mustang convertible holding a place of pride in the center of the yard. *Well, hello, old friend,* she thought, remembering the ad that had kept her entertained for a full fifteen minutes that afternoon. The car looked much better in real life—shiny and red and fun. Pity she wasn't a convertible kind of girl, she mused a little wistfully as she pushed on up another hill, her mind almost immediately reverting to its default position of wondering what Jack was doing right now, if he'd called, and what would happen next.

For a second she allowed her mind to flash back to the elevator. A surge of heat swept through her. She could almost feel his mouth on her skin again, feel the wet thrill of his tongue on her breasts. Her body tightened at the memory, and she realized that in a split second she'd undone all the good work her nice, mind-numbing run had done. She briefly considered pushing herself to do another few miles in an attempt to regain some control over her wayward body, but she suspected it would be futile. She'd tasted Jack Brook, and she wanted more—it was as simple as that.

How could a few hours change the way she felt about someone so much? How could she go from

thinking someone was incredibly egotistical, cocky
and overly confident to wondering if he lay awake
at night thinking about his brother?

She had no answers, but she knew that something
had shifted forever in that elevator car, and even
though in her more rational moments she regretted
having given in to the crazy urge to make love to
him, and then giving him her home number, she was
also glad.

When she got home and saw that no one had
called she had to quell a wash of disappointment.

Maybe he had something on this evening.

Like a date.

With another woman.

She pushed the thought away all through her quick
post-run shower. There was no way he could turn his
back on what had happened between them in the lift.
It had been so hot, so intense—surely he was aching
to explore what they'd discovered in the same way
that she was? Or even, on a more basic level, come
back for seconds?

Determined to believe, Claire dumped the entire
contents of her underwear drawer onto her bed and
searched through the tangle of silk, satin and cotton
until she found her best set of underwear—a deep au-
bergine lace bra with matching panties, very elegant
but understatedly sexy at the same time.

She pulled them on, sprayed her wrists and cleavage with her favorite perfume, and spent some time
creating a smoky, seductive look with eyeliner and
mascara. Surveying herself in her bathroom mir-

ror, she felt a surge of confidence. She was ready
for him, ready to pick up where they left off, ready
to explore the animal attraction that had sprung to
life between them.

The sound of her doorbell buzzing jolted her out
of her lust-filled musings, and she dragged on a pair
of jeans and a handy T-shirt before padding her way
to the door.

"I'm coming," she called out as she approached
the door, then felt a little kick of adrenaline in her
belly as she wondered if it possibly could be Jack on
the other side of the door.

Her breath caught in her throat as she reached
for the door handle. Maybe he'd looked up her address, and hadn't bothered with phoning because he
just hadn't been able to put her out of his mind, the
way she hadn't been able to put him out of hers….
Between her legs, her muscles tightened and she
clenched her thighs together, reveling in the thrill
of desire that raced through her. If Jack was here, in
a few minutes she'd have him inside her again, the
firm, delicious pressure of his erection satisfying
the ache that had already started at the centre of her.

"Hey there! I've brought champagne and chocolate, and I want to hear all the details," Katherine
said as she breezed past Claire.

Claire tried to ignore the leaden disappointment
that had replaced the buzz in her blood. Forcing a
smile, she went to fetch champagne glasses.

"So, three hours in a lift with Jack Brook. I want
a blow-by-blow account of every minute," Kather-

ine said, rubbing her hands together in mock anticipation.

Claire stared at her friend for a horrified second, praying that she wouldn't blush. The last thing she wanted was to dissect what had happened with Katherine—or anyone, for that matter. This was between Claire and Jack, and she wanted to find out exactly what it was before letting the world know anything at all.

Painfully aware that she probably looked as though she'd just sat on a cactus, Claire attempted to shrug nonchalantly. "Nothing happened. We argued, then we talked, then we got rescued. It was an exercise in boredom more than anything."

Katherine sipped her champagne, her pale blue eyes sharp as they quizzed Claire over the rim of the glass. Claire fought the urge to squirm guiltily.

"You realize that half the building was on fire with jealousy? Stuck in the elevator with Jack—my God, it's a whole new genre of erotic fantasy."

Claire took a huge gulp of champagne and wrenched her eyes away from the damned phone.

"Sorry to disappoint, but it was hot and airless and dull. Very dull."

Unbidden, an image of Jack sliding his pants down his hips popped into her mind, the length of him proud and hard and ready for action. She felt a blush stealing into her cheeks, and she shot a look at her friend. Fortunately, Katherine was studying the lid of the chocolate box, trying to make a selection.

"I like the hard-centered ones—something to

chew on," she muttered as she plucked her selection from the box.

Claire took advantage of Katherine's distraction to broaden the conversation.

"Do you know who else was trapped? Anyone we know?" she asked, sitting back in her chair and pretending she had all the time in the world.

All the while her mind was working overtime—what if Jack called while Katherine was here? What if he wanted to come over, and she couldn't get rid of Katherine?

"One of the lifts had ten women in it. Can you imagine? Apparently they took turns hyperventilating and freaking out."

Claire forced a smile.

"Wow."

Her eyes strayed to the wall clock over Katherine's shoulder. Eight o'clock. When was Jack going to call?

Two and a half hours later, and she knew the answer to that question: never. Katherine was full of champagne and chocolate, and Claire had sore cheek muscles from forcing smiles she didn't believe in.

Moaning about having eaten too much, Katherine finally rubbed her stomach one last time and called it a night. Claire closed the door on her and turned to contemplate her empty apartment.

It was 10:30. So much for her hot night. The empty champagne bottle and almost-empty chocolate box mocked her.

She felt heavy, a bit dazed. Vaguely she realized

she felt humiliated. She dragged off her clothes, and moved into her en suite to prepare for bed. The sight of herself decked out in her very best underwear was a slap in the face.

What had she been thinking, for Pete's sake?

And what on earth had she been thinking when she tore her clothes off and climbed Jack Brook like a cat on a curtain? Had she lost all semblance of self-respect in that tiny, airless space? Suddenly she groaned as she recalled pressing her business card into his hand. She never did stuff like that, ever. All of her life she'd been careful, modest, demure. And now she'd just blotted her copybook spectacularly.

Worst of all, while she'd been sitting here all night, wrapped up in some fantasy world where hot sex equaled spiritual meaning, he'd probably been thinking of the hot blonde he was no doubt taking to dinner.

She stared at her reflection for a beat, forcing herself to face the brutal facts. A sophisticated guy like Jack—he knew the rules. He knew that what had happened in the elevator was a one-off, never to be repeated. He must have been amazed when she gave him her number. She closed her eyes against the wash of humiliation that threatened.

Why, oh, why had she been so stupid?

By the time she'd cleansed and brushed and flossed and crawled into bed, she'd convinced herself it was good riddance to bad rubbish. The man had disaster written all over him. He was a self-confessed commitaphobe with a very short attention span. He was so closed off and protected, she doubted he'd ever let an emotion stronger than pleasure or satisfaction breach his defenses.

Yes, the physical attraction between them had been hot, but that wasn't the only thing in life, right? It certainly wasn't worth humiliating herself over, that was for sure.

Nope, she was very, very lucky he'd never taken her up on her stupid, ill-informed, ill-considered, impulsive, deranged invitation. She thumped her pillow decisively, determined to put the whole experience behind her.

But then she started thinking about work tomorrow. About seeing Jack for the first time. About looking at him, and remembering, and knowing. Her eyes popped open and she stared at the ceiling.

What if he told someone else at work what had happened? What if she walked into the building tomorrow and people stopped talking as she approached? She had a vivid picture of her business card taped up in the men's restroom—*For a good time, call Claire Marsden.*

For a moment she felt sick to her stomach, but then reason returned. She didn't know how she knew, but she knew—absolutely—that Jack wouldn't tell anyone what had happened between them while they were trapped. The realization calmed her. No matter what else she'd managed to misinterpret between them, she knew that she had this right—what happened in the elevator, stayed in the elevator.

And long might it stay that way. Relieved, she

rolled onto her side and willed herself to sleep. She was just drifting off when she remembered that she was supposed to work with Jack for the next few weeks or however long Beck deemed it was necessary to salve old man Hillcrest's ego.

That was something of a stumbling block. An Everest-size stumbling block. She sat bolt-upright in bed. If she was honest, she wanted very badly to tell Morgan Beck to shove his stupid arrangement. But that wasn't the way she worked. What Beck had asked from her was wrong, and unfair, and she was still deeply ashamed about sitting through that initial meeting with Jack and Beck without making her feelings clear.

But innate self-honesty forced her to admit that even if she'd had prior warning about the agenda of the meeting, she wouldn't have kicked up a fuss. Her philosophy in her working life had always been to give her bosses what they asked for. While there were limits to this philosophy—both moral and legal—it had held her in good stead until now.

But did her ethos stretch to swallowing this blatant vote of no confidence without voicing an objection?

She shook her head in her silent apartment.

"No. I don't have to just lie down and take it," she told her darkened bedroom.

Tomorrow she'd let him know in no uncertain terms that she wouldn't accept Jack on her project.

She tried to imagine herself stalking into her

boss's office and laying her cards confidently on the table. And failed. Miserably.

Perhaps if she really talked it through with Beck, they could come up with another solution. As grown adults, seeing eye to eye. Discussing the issues rationally.

This felt much more her style. It still made her feel nervous, but it was doable.

Of course, sticking up for herself would mean that she didn't have to work with Jack anymore, too. How convenient. She could simply ignore him for a few weeks in the car park and editorial meetings and the elevator, just like old times, and pretty soon he'd forget that Claire Marsden had ever torn his clothes off and had sex with him.

And that was absolutely what she wanted.

So, she was decided. First thing tomorrow, she'd make an appointment with Morgan and see if she could regain control of her life. It should have been the last thing she thought of before she drifted off to sleep. But instead, just as she gave herself up to sleep, memories from the elevator came back to haunt her. The firm, knowing pressure of his clever fingers as he circled her swollen wetness; the sweet, addictive tug of desire between her thighs as he suckled on her breasts; the deep satisfaction of having all of him inside her, and his strongly muscled body tense and passionate above hers.

She moaned frustratedly into the pillow and rolled over. But the memories kept on coming: the wet velvet sweep of his tongue on her neck. That first thrill as he pressed the palm of his hand against her damp mound. The rising excitement as they taunted each other with what they really wanted....

Claire thumped a pillow with her fist. "Get out of my head, Jack Brook," she muttered.

But it was no good. She was too turned on to sleep. Despite every rational reason for disliking the man, her body had other ideas.

She rolled over again, her nipples brushing against the cotton of her sheets. They wanted Jack's touch, the heat of his tongue and mouth, and they sat tight and proud, waiting for something that was never going to happen. Claire slid a hand over each breast and pressed them into her chest.

Stop it, she urged her body. *Forget him.*

But instead of calming her overheated body, the pressure triggered a pulse of desire between her legs. Claire's eyes flickered open, and she glared at the ceiling.

"Damn you," she told an absent Jack Brook.

Then she gave in to her desire and slid a hand down the length of her body and between her legs. Closing her eyes as she slicked a finger over her own wetness, she imagined it was Jack touching her, and that any moment now she would feel the warm, velvet nudge of his erection against her outer folds. As her body thrummed tighter and tighter with tension, she remembered the taste of Jack, and the strength of Jack, and the feeling of being filled by him. The way he'd tugged so tightly on her nipples. The way he'd run his hands over her body as though he couldn't get enough. The feel of him beneath her hands, the hard, smooth power of his body.

She gasped out her release, her orgasm an echo of the one she'd shared with him earlier. It should have been the end of it, but she lay awake for a long time afterward, angry with herself for wanting a man who clearly didn't want her.

CHAPTER SEVEN

"He said what?"

Claire stared at Morgan Beck, aware that she'd crouched forward in her chair and placed one hand imperiously on his desk.

"You heard me, Claire. I know this whole arrangement sticks in your craw but I flatter myself that after thirty years in the business I know what I'm doing. I don't care what sort of a disagreement you and Jack have had, but you're just going to have to sort it out."

Morgan was cranky, his voice hard and his posture aggressive as he glared across the desk at her.

"I just don't understand it. Yesterday the two of you seemed to be in perfect accord, and now this," he said.

You have no idea, she thought. And she tried very hard to get the image of her and Jack doing the wild thing on the elevator floor out of her mind as she held her boss's eye. Now was not the time to get turned on by rogue memories. This was her career she was talking about here. Jack and his perfect penis could go hang as far as she was concerned.

"Wait a minute—are you telling me that Jack

Brook has refused to work with me?" she asked, still trying to get a grip on this concept.

"Have I been talking to myself for the last five minutes, Claire?"

She fought back the impulsive urge to tell him to keep his pants on, then blanched that any such urge had even crossed her mind. What was wrong with her? When she'd first entered his office, she'd found him seated with his feet up on his desk. She'd had trouble hiding her smile at his aggressive, I'm-the-boss posture. She'd got control of her unruly mouth, but she'd been appalled at herself—when had she ever felt anything but respect and a faint tinge of fear for Morgan Beck?

"Mr. Beck, this comes as a complete shock to me," she assured him now, neatly sidestepping the fact that she'd come to work this morning with the single-minded intention of finagling her boss into removing Jack from her project. It was one thing for her to reject him...

"Really?"

The single word dripped disbelief. She found herself glaring back at her boss, her temper well and truly firing on all cylinders now. Before she could stop herself, hot and angry words were pouring out.

"Yes, really. Do you truly think I'm so pathetic that I'd get him to do my dirty work for me? I assure you, if I didn't want to work with Jack Brook I'd let you know in no uncertain terms."

Okay, that was a lie, because she'd spent the whole night trying to come up with subtle, nonaggressive ways of suggesting Jack be reassigned. But Morgan didn't seem to understand that she'd spoken out of anger—his eyebrows were rising up, his expression one of pure shock. She tried to remember if she'd ever come close to speaking to him like this before.

No, probably not. Mostly she concentrated on smiling and sounding competent and on top of things when she met with him. Mostly she'd been way too aware of his power and her own desire to win his approval.

But today she was too annoyed to remember any of that. Today she was outraged that not only had Jack left her dangling all night, he'd also pipped her at the post on the work front, too. To top things off, this balding little man in front of her thought she was so wimpy that she'd use someone else as her front man.

"You know, I was prepared to wear all this rubbish about placating Mr. Hillcrest, but I'm beginning to wonder if I wouldn't be better off stepping aside and letting you simply replace me with someone better qualified," she heard herself saying silkily.

Good grief. Give a girl a little rush of power to the head, and suddenly she was the Genghis Khan of office politics!

Morgan had gone pale, but she bit down on the apology that sprang to her lips the moment she uttered her challenge. Instinctively, she understood that much hung in the balance right now.

He needs me, she reminded herself. *It's my project, and he needs me, and he should remember that.*

Except this wasn't her style at all. She was a worker, a quiet achiever. A nonconfronter. And she was going to lose her job. She was going to be escorted from the building by mustached security guards, and she was never going to get another job in publishing. She'd get kicked out of her apartment, and her car would be repossessed, and before she knew it she'd be coming up with catchy names for bad adult movies for a living, titles such as *Ordinary Peepholes* and *Free Willy*. Although, technically, that was no different from the original even if it had a new interpretation. Maybe she'd be no good at this new career, either. Ah—*Three Willy!* Maybe she'd survive, then...

To her surprise, Beck suddenly laughed, pushing himself back from his desk and loosening his tie a little.

"Okay, Claire. Point taken. I apologize."

Her vision of her career in pornography receded and she hoped she wasn't looking as surprised as she felt. *He was apologizing.* Her boss was apologizing. She'd answered back and threatened him and he hadn't had her escorted from the building. A slow feeling of elation bubbled into her blood. She felt... strong. Powerful. Valued.

All these years she'd been toeing the line and working hard and waiting to be acknowledged— and all it took was a bit of mouthing off to get some respect.

"Look, it's a crappy situation we've put you in. I acknowledge that. But if you can swallow your pride for just a few months, I assure you we'll get Jack off your back as soon as we can. And your…flexibility won't be forgotten."

A little drunk with her newly discovered power, she toyed with the idea of making another startling, bold statement. Something such as "I hate that tie," or perhaps, "For God's sake, do something about what's left of your hair," while she was on a roll, but she was wise enough to know when to quit.

"I'm not happy," was what she actually said. "But I'll do it, because I've put too much into *Welcome Home* to walk away."

Her boss nodded.

"Understood. The board knows that magazine is all yours, Claire, don't ever underestimate that. We consider you one of our most talented executives."

She managed to contain the grin that was threatening to stretch her mouth wide. Respect *and* praise, all because she'd lost her temper.

"I trust I can leave it with you to sort things out with Jack?" her boss was saying, shuffling papers around on his desk.

She recognized the meeting was over and she stood quickly.

"I'll take care of it," she assured him.

Once out of Beck's hallowed office, her focus swung around to consider Jack and his sneakery. It was a testament to how angry she was that she didn't even think twice about getting in the elevator and taking it down to Jack's level. She was concentrating instead on what she was going to say to him.

He'd gone behind her back and tried to undermine her on her own project. She conveniently swept to one side the thought that she had been about to do the same to him. And she couldn't even bear to think that while she'd been sitting home all night agonizing over why he hadn't called, he'd been planning to approach Beck and get out of working with her.

She steamed out of the elevator and surveyed the open-plan office space confronting her, quickly spotting Jack's assistant at a desk in the corner. Her eyes narrowed as she considered the fact that Jack enjoyed a corner office. One more reason to find him incredibly annoying.

Linda looked up with a smile when Claire stopped at her desk.

"I need to see Jack," she said baldly.

Linda's smile faded as she registered Claire's mood, and Claire immediately felt like a jerk.

Perhaps she was taking this pushy thing a little too far....

"I mean—how are you?" she tried again, summoning a smile of her own.

"Fine. Jack's not in right now," Linda volunteered.

She shifted her gaze to the closed door over Linda's shoulder.

"Is that a he's-in-but-doesn't-want-to-be-disturbed not in, or a real not in?" she asked, trying to keep the annoyance out of her voice.

"He's in a meeting down in Sports," Linda expanded.

"Right." Claire stood for a moment, tapping her

toe as she considered her options. She could leave a message for him, go back down to her office, get stuck into some work.

She shook her head. She could just imagine him screwing up any message she left him and tossing it in the bin as he headed out to an executive racquetball game.

"I'll wait," she announced suddenly. Then she pointed to Jack's office door. "In there."

Linda opened her mouth to protest, but Claire sailed past and into Jack's inner sanctum. She did a quick survey of the room, aware that Linda had followed her and was standing behind her.

"Can I get you a coffee while you wait?" Linda asked politely, nothing in her tone giving away her true feelings.

"I'm fine, thanks," she said.

Linda gave a small nod and exited, closing the door behind her.

So she can warn him without me overhearing, Claire guessed. Well, tough. He'd have to come back here some time.

She glanced at the two seating options—a hard-looking chair at the front of Jack's desk, or a squishy-looking sofa in the corner. She opted for the squishy sofa, throwing herself into it impatiently. It embraced her like an overly affectionate uncle, its cushions giving way alarmingly so that her butt sank low enough to lift her feet off the carpet.

Only Jack Brook could have a bucket-seat couch, she thought, struggling to lever herself up and out of its tenacious hold. She'd worked herself into a sweat and only managed to wriggle her hips forward, finally getting her high heels on the ground, when the door swung open and Jack entered. His blue gaze swung around like a spotlight and she felt the completeness of his scrutiny, becoming painfully aware of her flushed cheeks, the way her skirt was rucked up and the fact that the buttons at the front of her blouse were strained and gaping open because of the way her arms were levered behind her. This was not the way she'd imagined seeing him for the first time after what had happened between them. Neither had she imagined that her body would instantly go onto high alert, eager for any signal from him. Suddenly her breasts felt tight and sensitized in her bra, and she was aware of the brush of her silk shirt against her skin.

She gritted her teeth against the knowing smile dancing around Jack's lips and pushed herself up and out of the sofa with a surge of power. It was like coming out of quicksand, and she staggered a little before finding her balance.

Jack just watched her all the while, one hip braced against his desk, his arms folded across his chest. She stood panting before him, pushing her skirt back down.

"That's the most stupid couch in all the world," she said, aware that any advantage she'd had was long gone.

"I like it," he said simply.

"You would."

She tried to regain the towering anger and feeling of self-righteousness she'd had when she arrived not two minutes ago. Unfortunately, most of her was too busy remembering what it had felt like to be pressed up against his chest, to have his hands on her skin and his tongue in her mouth. A floodgate of sense memories threatened to engulf her—the look on his face as he slid inside her; the small noise of appreciation he'd made when he'd first seen her bare breasts; the moist heat of his breath against the skin of her neck as he shuddered out his climax. She blinked, overwhelmed for a moment by a surge of desire. Fortunately for her dignity, close on the heels of those searing memories came the painful reminder of how humiliated she'd felt when he didn't call last night.

Snap out of it, she told herself, squaring her shoulders and looking him in the eye. The effect was ruined somewhat when one of her blouse buttons popped off, performing a little somersault in the air between them before tumbling to land at his feet. The cool breeze on her torso told her that once again her underwear was on display, and she was unable to stop the flush of heat that was even now flooding her face.

"We really have to stop meeting like this," he drawled, stooping to pick up her button.

She hated him for his casual nonchalance—if his shirt had popped open she would have been bug-eyed and slathering with lust. But he just stood there, cool as a cucumber, completely unaffected by her near nudity. The bastard.

She crossed her arms in front of her breasts but a glance down revealed that this only made them seem to pop up and out over her bra even more. Yesterday in the elevator, and now this. She wanted to die, and as quickly as possible, please.

She could feel his eyes on her, and she settled for holding the two sides of her blouse together with one clenched fist.

"I've just been up seeing Morgan Beck," she announced, determined to win back the initiative.

Perhaps if she just pretended she hadn't practically forced herself on him, it would just go away.

"Figured as much."

His tone smacked so much of casual expectation that she felt her anger heating up all over again.

"Well, thanks for consulting me first. Thanks a lot. I get hauled up there first thing this morning and he practically accused me of making you ask to be taken off the magazine."

He looked surprised. "Where the hell did he get that from?"

"From you, I take it."

"Well, you're wrong. As usual. All I told him was that I had too much on my plate to take on your project, as well."

She puffed her cheeks out to stop from swearing out loud, almost letting go of her blouse she was so furious.

"Take on my project?" she stuttered. "Are you forgetting that you were only ever going to be the token

male, wheeled out for meetings to keep that Neanderthal at Hillcrest happy? Take on my project my ass!"

He frowned at her, straightening from his lounging position against his desk. Good. Nice to see him abandon his casual observer stance and wade in at last. She hated the idea that everything she did vastly amused him, that he liked poking her with a stick and seeing what she did next.

If only her heart hadn't leaped as he took a step closer to her, she'd feel almost happy with the turn of events.

"Lady, you have rocks in your head if you thought I was ever going to just roll over and play dead. If I'm working on something, I'm working on it. I'm not in the habit of taking credit for something I didn't do."

"Morgan made the terms of your involvement very clear—it's in name only. You are not sticking your oar into my magazine," she declared hotly.

"Which is exactly why I told Beck I didn't have the time for the project. You should be thanking me instead of carrying on like a harpy."

This made her so angry she needed both hands free to gesticulate at him, and she abandoned her blouse to the Fates.

"You are the most arrogant man I have ever met. I can't believe I actually— I can't believe I didn't implode out of self-defense after spending more than five minutes in your company yesterday." She refused to acknowledge what she'd almost said, instead planting her hands on her hips and glaring at him.

"Ditto. Again, another good reason for us not working together."

"Well, get over it. Because I told Morgan we could sort this out," she fired back at him.

He looked so surprised she almost laughed.

"You did?"

"Someone has to be grown-up about this. And I'm not going to see my magazine stall because of your ego."

"*My* ego?"

He stared at her, but then, almost as if some irresistible force drew his gaze downward, his eyes dropped to her chest. She'd been aware that his eyes had strayed below her neckline more than once in the past few minutes. She felt his gaze like heat on her skin, and she swallowed nervously. Or was it excitedly? She was so confused right now, it was hard to tell the difference. In a split second all her thoughts turned from being furious with him to feverishly anticipating the touch of his hands on her breasts again. She wanted to feel the welcome weight of his body on top of hers. She wanted to touch his smooth, firm skin and hold the strength of him in her hands again. In an instant her panties were damp with wet heat, and her breath was coming short and sharp. She wanted him—but he had to make the first move. She couldn't risk making herself vulnerable again.

JACK COULDN'T STOP his gaze from dropping to her breasts. He ordered himself not to look, but it was useless. What man could resist when fate had handed him such a golden opportunity? She was wearing a cream lace bra today, and her breasts curved lovingly into it, rising and falling with each breath she took.

She was so damn hot. How was he supposed to resist her when she was running around taunting him like this? He was trying to do the right thing here, trying to be a nice guy and spare her feelings. Because it would be the easiest thing in the world to just sleep with her again, drink his fill, explore the chemistry between them and then move on. He was doing her a favor, damn it—and now she was showing him exactly what he was missing out on.

All he had to do was reach out and pull her to him. His muscles tensed in anticipation. He'd slide her shirt off, then that bra—pretty as it was, it was nothing compared to her unadorned breasts. The pale pink of her nipples, the way they puckered so responsively under his touch, the taste of her, the heat of her skin, the little hitch she got in her breathing when he sucked her nipples deep into his mouth. He'd back her against the desk, pull up that prim little skirt of hers and slide himself into her. She'd get that look in her eye, that glazed but oddly intent look, and she would tilt her hips and tighten her strong, firm legs around his hips—

He didn't need to look down to know that he was rock hard again, his erection straining against the fly of his jeans. Something had to give—and he had a feeling it was going to be him.

"For Pete's sake, how am I supposed to concentrate? Come here," he said, reaching toward her impatiently.

Before Claire could object she'd been forcibly hauled forward by the lapels of her shirt. His body was hard and warm against hers, and for a beat they stood pressed against each other, neither saying a word, their eyes locked together. Her mind was racing. Was he going to kiss her again? God, she wanted him to—even after the humiliation of last night, she wanted him, bad. A muscle twitched in his jaw, and she inhaled sharply, feeling the fullness of her breasts press against his chest. Then he grabbed something from his desk, jamming it between them. A metallic click sounded, and he pushed her away.

She blinked down at her shirt, staring in growing indignation at the staple now holding her blouse together more modestly. Two messy hunks of fabric stuck out on either side of the staple—a five-year-old with bad eyesight could have done a better job.

"This is a Gucci shirt," she said slowly, enunciating carefully so he understood exactly what he'd done.

"I was doing you a favor. I know how uptight you are about public displays of underwear."

She felt a stress twitch break out below her left eye. She was sure that if she had her lawyers introduce the ruined Gucci shirt as exhibit *A* during her murder trial, she could fully justify turning his stupid desk stapler on him till he died the death of a thousand tiny puncture wounds.

She managed to ignore the fact that once again

she had been putty in his hands, while he remained supremely unaffected. She could bring that realization out later and really soak up the rejection. But for now, there was her favorite shirt to consider....

He seemed to sense the surge of homicidal feeling rising within her, because he wisely moved away until the desk was between them.

"As much as I enjoy having you carp at me, I do have another meeting in five minutes. So if you don't mind...?" he said carelessly.

She stood there, her hands curled into two tight fists by her sides.

"I'm not leaving this office until we've sorted this out. I need a man to talk golf and football with Hillcrest, and you are a man. But that's all I need. I don't want you writing big-game-fishing articles for *Welcome Home,* I don't want you interfering in the design process and I certainly don't want you having any say over editorial content."

He cocked his head to one side as though he was actually considering it. "Gee, you make it sound like such an attractive gig. No."

She glared at him, reading the determination in every line of his body. He was even breathing a little faster, just like her. He was like her in many ways, she realized, remembering all the things they'd found in common yesterday. And before she could stop herself, she was considering how *she'd* react if he came to her with this offer. What if there was some female-oriented magazine he was working on, and

"Give me a project every issue. You've got a fur-
niture-making section, yeah? Give me something
in that, and I'll press the flesh and laugh at old man
Hillcrest's bad jokes. It's that, or nothing. I can't take
credit for something I didn't even touch."

She was aware that her jaw was hanging slackly
and she made an effort to not look too witless and
stunned. She'd been expecting something offensive
at best. This was...well, very reasonable.

"That's it? That's all you want?" she clarified.

"Don't sound so disappointed."

Once again she was on the back foot. Why did that always happen with this man?

"I just...I thought you would... Look, it doesn't matter. The project idea is good. Actually, it'll be helpful. I'm sort of breaking in a project guy, and he's a bit nervous about taking on the full workload," she stumbled, trying hard to regain some kind of professional footing.

A hard task when your most prominent fashion accessory is a stapled cleavage.

"Fine. Can I have my office back now?"

He sounded bored. Her back went up again like clockwork.

"Of course. Just say the word," she said, aware her voice came out hard and tight.

"I thought I did," he drawled.

She blinked at him, aware that his casualness had caught her on the raw. Just when she thought he was a decent human being, he had to go and be like this.

She heard a heavy sigh from him behind her as she headed for the door.

"Claire, hang on a minute. About last night—" he began to say, and she realized with horror that he was about to offer her some sop for not calling.

"It's fine, Jack. Already forgotten," she said briskly.

"I want to explain. I just think that you're—" he tried again.

She spun around, desperate to stop him from saying something about how mistaken she was, how she'd misunderstood him. "Forget it. Okay? I wish the whole thing had never happened. Enough said."

He held her gaze for a moment, and she hoped she looked suitably indifferent. If humiliation resembled indifference in any way, she figured she had a chance.

"Your call," he said, and she shot him a look. Had he meant to choose those words, exactly?

Impossible to tell. She attempted to reassemble a little dignity and self-respect around herself.

"I've got a meeting scheduled with Hillcrest tomorrow at ten," she said coolly, already turning toward the door.

"Fine. I'll be there."

She paused on the threshold of his office.

"And please wear a tie. Hillcrest is a traditional man."

"Hillcrest will have to learn to loosen up a little. Do him good." He had a dangerous, indolent air, along with a definite "give it your best shot" glint in his eye.

She took a deep breath and reached for some patience. "Jack. Please. Just once. Is it so painful to be conventional, even for just five minutes?"

He shrugged, oozing innocence from every pore. "Hey—I don't even own a tie. So it's irrelevant."

She made an exasperated noise in the back of her throat. He was laughing at her again, leaning against his desk, his broad shoulders silhouetted against his stunning corner-office view.

"Fine. Come in your best holey T-shirt and grass-stained jeans, forget to shave, stink of beer and scratch your furry face through the whole meeting. See if I care."

With that, she wheeled out of his office, slamming the door behind her. Or at least trying to. Except it had one of those nifty pneumatic door closers on it, and all she got was a bit of kick-back when she tried to force the mechanism.

She could still hear his laughter when the elevator doors closed on her. She headed straight for the ladies' room on her floor, and once she was in the safe confines of a private cubicle, she leaned against the wall and threw her head back, closing her eyes against the cocktail of emotions waiting to swamp her.

She felt so weak. Hadn't last night taught her anything? Intellectually she knew that Jack was a disaster area, a no-go zone, even though she'd already been there. But her body could not resist him. Just thinking about how he'd smelled, and the heat of his body against hers when he hauled her close to staple her cleavage—it was enough to get her hot all over again. Claire glanced down and saw that her nipples were stiff and aroused, jutting out against the silk of her shirt proudly. Between her legs, a dull ache throbbed, and she pressed her hand against her mound through the fabric of her skirt.

I don't want this, she ordered her body. *I don't want to feel this way about Jack Brook! Stop it immediately!*

After five minutes of strong self-talk, she emerged

from the cubicle. The hectic-cheeked woman who greeted her in the mirror was a stranger, and she shook her head at the gleam of desire that still shone in her eyes.

After a few minutes of wrangling, she managed to extract the staples, but her shirt was ruined. Toying with the idea of sending him the bill, she headed to the nearby shopping mall to find a replacement so she'd be presentable for her afternoon meetings. If only her pride could be salvaged so easily. She had only to remember the way Jack had calmly stapled her to decency to feel a rush of humiliation. She'd spent the bulk of a sleepless night inventing conversations where he explained why he hadn't called, great excuses that meant she could still indulge the fantasy that she hadn't behaved like a total wanton in the elevator. Boy, was she deluded. She'd built up this whole...*thing* between them, imagining a whole lot of stuff she had no business imagining. And all he'd been concerned about was extracting himself from Morgan Beck's assignment.

They'd been stuck in an airless space for several hours. He'd been bored. They'd shared things they hadn't told anyone else, and he'd taken what she'd so willingly offered.

Big deal. She was sure that's what he was thinking. It must have been what he was thinking when he went to tell Beck he wouldn't work with her. And when he decided not to call her last night, despite what had happened.

Bottom line: in the real world, out of claustrophobic elevators where people were forced to strip down to their underwear, men like Jack Brook did not look twice at women like her.

If only she'd known that *before* she'd let him slide her bra off and slide himself into her, before she'd had the best damn sex of her life.

Why had she given him the opportunity to reject her?

She had a sudden flash of Jack sitting on high— Zeus on his mountain—laughing at her as she scampered around at his feet like all the other women in his life.

She was walking past a display in the men's section of a department store, and she almost ran into the young salesman setting it up. She stared down at the colorful array of ties the guy was finessing, and she remembered Jack's refusal to wear a tie to her meeting with Hillcrest.

Suddenly she saw red. It was her meeting, and her client, and her magazine. And he was working with her. The least he could do was respect her reading of her client's sensibilities.

Determined now, she turned to the salesman.

"Excuse me. Which would you say is the most conservative tie you stock? The sort of tie a retired banker might wear, for example?" she asked silkily.

"Definitely something with stripes. Or a royal insignia. That always seems to go over well with our older customers." The salesman helpfully displayed two or three ties for her.

"I'll take that one," she said, pointing to the tie that combined stripes with a royal insignia.

And Jack Brook would wear it if it killed her.

CHAPTER EIGHT

JACK WALKED BACK into his office after his last meeting of the day and groaned at the pile of paperwork Linda had left on his desk: afternoon mail, letters to sign, blah, blah, blah. He sighed heavily and dropped into his chair, swinging his feet up onto his desk as he reached for the pile of mail. His feet knocked something to the floor, and he leaned sideways in his chair to peer around the edge and make sure he hadn't broken anything.

His stapler lay on its side on the plush carpet, and he stared at it a moment. Unbidden, unwanted, unwise, a Technicolor image of Claire Marsden's lacy bra popped into his mind. Complete with a memory of how she'd smelled and how she'd felt when he'd pulled her close to remedy the temptation. Because—really—how was a man supposed to have a good, solid argument with a woman when all he could think about was burying his face in her cleavage? And, after that, burying other parts of his body in her, also. He'd been so close to giving in to the need to touch her. If he closed his eyes for more than a heartbeat, images of their time in the elevator flashed back at him. It was the only thing he seemed able to think about. That, and all the other things he wanted to do to her. Once was not enough, he was fast discovering, where Claire Marsden was concerned. At least, that was what his body believed. Intellectually—well, that was a whole other ball game.

Because it was impossible to remember Claire's spectacular body without remembering her spectacular temper. The spark of remembered lust faded as he recalled her insulting insinuation—that he'd told Beck she wanted him off the magazine. Man, he'd busted his ass being diplomatic with Beck that morning, explaining how he was loathe to work on something he wasn't truly contributing to, pointing out his work schedule was already very hectic, stressing that Claire was very good and very likely to be able to soothe savage-beast-Hillcrest all on her own.

And she reads that as him setting her up! Which was the problem with her, when he got right down to it. She was always ready and willing to read an ulterior motive into everything he did. More trouble than she was worth.

Insidious and undeniable, the memory of her simple but sincere sympathy for him snuck into his mind. She'd said exactly the right thing, and she'd even anted up with a confession of her own so he wouldn't feel like a complete dick when the doors opened. So she wasn't an absolute lost cause....

And then there was the sex. He kept coming back to that. Had he ever been that hot for a woman? Surely in his teens he'd had encounters that were that hot...but he couldn't quite remember with whom or when. In fact, all past encounters paled into insignificance beside what had happened yesterday. It was even beginning to worry him a little, the way his mind would automatically drift to those few precious memories of the smell of her skin, and the sound of her excited breath in his ear, whenever he let his guard down. He'd nearly embarrassed himself several times in meetings today. One moment he was discussing deadlines and feature stores, and the next he was fighting off sense memories of tanned skin and the wet, voluptuous slide of his body in hers. And as for how his body had reacted when her shirt had popped open... It had been a close-run thing, and he'd been forced to seek refuge behind his desk to hide his desire. The last thing he needed was for little Miss Uptight to know the potential hold she had over him....

He started as Linda stuck her head into his office doorway.

"I'm going now. See you tomorrow," she said.

He grunted a goodbye, deliberately pulling his attention back to his pile of mail.

Stop thinking about Claire, he ordered himself. He'd already laid her ghost to rest last night, when he'd decided not to call her. So why did she keep rising to the surface of his mind?

Here he was again, reverting to thinking about her as soon as all other distractions were gone! He'd already walked down this road, and it was a dead end. Time to move on. With a real force of will, he focused on his mail, sorting through more than half of it until he came to an internal mail envelope. Like most internal mail envelopes, the previous recipient had crossed their name out before reusing the envelope for another message. He stared at Claire's crossed-out name for a second, then squeezed the bag, frowning. It felt bulky, not like paperwork. Mystified, he broke the sticky-tape seal and pulled out a small shopping bag. The cool slither of silk on his hands clued him into the bag's contents before he'd pulled the tie out. It was striped, with some sort of lion and crown etched into it. The sort of tie his grandfather had always been fond of. He stared at it, genuinely dumbstruck for a moment.

She was a real piece of work. Not content to have the last word, she'd gone out and bought him the perfect response to his claim not to own a tie.

Well, she could whistle Dixie as far as he was concerned—there was no way he was wearing a stupid tie. Especially not this particular stupid tie.

Thank God he hadn't called her last night. He'd regretted it earlier today, even after their fight he'd found it in himself to regret it, because there was something about her that drew him… But after this? No way. He and she were chalk and cheese. She'd drive him crazy. He tossed the tie negligently to one side.

He actually snorted his exasperation and disbelief out loud as he reached for the folder Linda had filled with his personal mail from his post office box. There were a handful of bills, but one envelope caught his attention. That was his Mom's handwriting scrawled across the front of the pale lavender rectangle. A dead, dull weight settled on his chest as he lifted the flap on the envelope, knowing full well what was inside: a birthday card.

Just like his Mom. She never forgot birthdays, even though he'd made his feelings clear on the subject. He almost laughed out loud. He'd been mostly successful in ignoring the march of time this year. He'd figured that if he was very careful and skimmed along through November, he could skip over his and Robbie's birthday.

But he'd still known that it was coming up, just the same—otherwise he wouldn't have felt that instant weight upon seeing his mother's card. Otherwise he wouldn't have this well of grief opening up inside him so readily and easily.

Liquid heat threatened at the back of his eyes, and he pushed himself to his feet, dropping the card onto his desk, ignoring all that needed to be signed for tomorrow. He had to get out of there, right now.

THERE WAS A CALL waiting on her answering machine when Claire got home from work that evening, and she despised herself for the little thrill of anticipation she felt as she noted the flashing message light. Maybe Jack had called after all. Maybe he'd felt as angry and frustrated and disappointed as she had after their argument.

Then she gave herself a mental slap. There was no way Jack would have called after the fight they'd had in his office. Or, if he called her at all, it would only be to give her hell for having foisted a tie on him, despite his insistence that he wouldn't wear one.

But it was her father's voice on the answering machine. She stared at the small black appliance as he told her that he was in town unexpectedly. Would she like to catch up for dinner?

She hadn't spoken to her father in months. She sent him e-mails on a regular basis, mostly because she was determined to do all that she could to have some kind of relationship with him. Occasionally he replied, but he rarely commented on her news. Instead he concentrated on his latest expedition or project, his letters reading more like press releases than missives from a father to his only child.

Warily pleased, she called the hotel number Harry had left. His voice sounded unfamiliar and distant when he answered the phone.

"Dad, it's me, Claire," she said.

"Oh, hello, Claire. I take it you got my message?"

As usual, the cool matter-of-factness of his manner stopped her from saying any of the things she instinctively wanted to say—that it had been a long time, that she'd been thinking about him. That she was hoping he could make it to her triathlon final.

They quickly arranged for her to meet him at his hotel for dinner—he was disinclined to let her take him out to any of her favorite Melbourne restaurants. In a city that was well-known for its food and wine culture, Harry preferred to chance the hotel dining room, and she felt unequal to the task of convincing him otherwise.

She settled for a scaled-down version of her training session for the evening, and it was only as she was discarding the third top she'd tried on in ten minutes that she acknowledged she was nervous.

Ridiculous, really—but he was her father, and their relationship was uneasy at best. Still, he'd made the effort to get in contact while he was in town. That was something, a change. She allowed herself to hope that maybe all her hard work in maintaining contact had perhaps gotten through to him on some level.

She was surprised at how old he looked when they met up in the foyer of his hotel. At sixty, he was very active and still organized expeditions, even if he didn't lead them himself anymore. But his hair had thinned, and was now completely white, and his eyes seemed faded somehow. She had to fight a surge of emotion as she realized that time was running out for them to reconcile.

"Claire. Good to see you," he said, leaning forward stiffly to kiss her cheek.

Ignoring his formality, she hugged him, pressing her cheek close to his.

"How are you?" she asked warmly.

"Good, good. A little annoyed at having to make this extraneous trip to Melbourne when we're so close to heading off, but these things happen."

Unsure of what he was talking about, Claire followed him into the dining room and waited till they had been seated before venturing further.

"You're organizing another expedition, I take it?" she asked.

Obviously her father was unaware that he hadn't communicated with her for some time.

"Yes. It's a joint Australian-Swiss assault on Everest. We were supposed to leave next month…but I don't want to bore you with the details. How is work? And your marathon thingy?"

She blinked with surprise. Her father never tired of talking about his work, and he never enquired after her life. She struggled to pull her thoughts together. "Work is good. Busy, but good. We're very close to launching our first edition of the magazine. And my triathlon training is coming along well. Just two weeks to go now."

He made the appropriate noises as he studied the wine list, while she studied his face. Was this truly the breakthrough she'd been hoping for all her life? Or, if not that, exactly, perhaps the beginning of a thaw?

"This is the magazine that you devised, the hardware thing?"

Another surprise—he'd read her e-mails, actually remembered their content.

"Yes. It's more home renovation and decoration than hardware, really. But you've got the basic idea."

He shot her an assessing look, then indicated her menu. "Better hurry up and decide—I can't stand waiting around for my meal," he said, already signaling for the waiter to come over.

There was a momentary hiatus in their conversation as Claire hurriedly decided on a salad as entrée and fish for her main, and the wine waiter poured some wine into her glass—a red, her father's choice.

"So, I guess this Beck character who runs all those magazines of yours must be pretty pleased with you, then."

"Well, he's certainly happy to have landed a new client."

She took a mouthful of her wine, wondering that her father even remembered what company she worked for.

"But you know him, yes? You've spoken with him?"

For the first time she registered that this was more than just polite interest from Harry. What was going on here?

"I've had several meetings with him, of course. Have you met him somewhere?"

Her father shook his head vigorously, tearing his dinner roll apart. "No, but I will tomorrow. Just trying to get a bit of a feel for the man. What do you know of him? Is he a sports man?"

Claire sat back in her chair, baffled and bemused. Why would her father care what she thought of her boss, or what he thought of her? And why on earth would her father, renowned explorer, be having a meeting with Morgan Beck, millionaire publisher?

And then she got it.

"Is he thinking of funding one of your expeditions?" she asked flatly. She watched her father's face closely, feeling that this moment was pivotal somehow. It was possible she was wrong, that her father truly had found some smidgen of sentiment in himself as the years rolled by and was genuinely interested in his daughter's life.

"As a matter of fact, yes. It's a bit of a difficult situation, actually. This Beck character was interested in getting involved right from the get-go, but then we had a better offer from the Swiss side of things. Now our Swiss guy has dropped his bundle, and I'm hoping to talk Beck into renewing his offer."

Harry was animated and enthusiastic as he explained his situation to her, describing the details of the assault, the makeup of the team, the differing experience levels, the problems he'd had and overcome.

And she sat there, watching his face light up with passion for his subject, for the only thing he'd ever really loved, the bitter taste of disappointment in her mouth.

Who had she been kidding, really, when she thought that her father had suddenly become all Brady Bunch?

Harry seemed to sense her preoccupation, and he broke off his recital to consider her. "Is something wrong, Claire? Don't you like the wine?"

She stared at him for a beat, tempted to just let things slide like she always had. But suddenly she couldn't bear the thought of pushing her own thoughts and feelings down again. Yesterday she'd admitted to Jack that she was the disappointment of her father's life. But it didn't have to be that way. She wasn't a bad person—she was just different from what he'd wanted in a child. But did that mean she had to accept the crumbs from his table for the rest of her life?

"You know, I thought you'd asked me here to spend time with *me,* because you wanted to see *me,*" she said.

"Yes, of course, and that's exactly what we're doing," her father said, the picture of surprise.

"No, it's not. We're having dinner because you want something from my boss. You're not really interested in my magazine or my triathlon or anything else in my life."

She tried hard to keep the tears out of her voice, but they were lurking there, giving her a husky vibrato. Her father was pulling an exasperated face, and shaking his head.

"I don't know where you're getting all this from, Claire. I was in town, I asked you to dinner—it was as simple as that."

"Really? Fine, then tell me when my triathlon final is. I told you earlier, when you asked, because you were so interested in my life, so it shouldn't be any big stretch for you to remember what I said."

She held her father's eye, challenging him.

"I can't recall the exact details, but I know it's soon…" her father began, and Claire pushed her chair back and stood up.

"I am your daughter, and I love you, but I am not going to be the only one participating in this relationship. I call you and e-mail you and offer to fly to visit

you for Christmas every year, and you can't even remember a conversation we had five minutes ago."

Slinging her handbag over her shoulder, Claire
turned to leave.

"You let me know if you're prepared to put a bit of
effort in, because I'm not going to make it easy for
you anymore," she said over her shoulder.

She walked straight out and didn't look back.

She was proud of herself all the way home in the
car. Then reaction set in. He would be so angry with
her, she probably wouldn't hear from him for months
and months. She never, ever caused a fuss with him,
because she knew how he hated having to deal with
emotional messes. She understood, deep in her heart
of hearts, that if she didn't keep up the contact with
her father, she would never hear from him. Whatever
faint connection that existed between them would
fade and shrivel, and she'd be utterly alone.

It was a scary thought, but she refused to take
it to bed with her. She was a grown, adult woman.
She had an exciting, vibrant life of her own. She
was about to launch a new magazine. She had a real
chance at winning the state triathlon finals. And
she'd had dirty, wild elevator sex with the office
playboy not twenty-four hours ago.

Never did she think that she would turn to those
stolen, wanton moments with Jack as a source of
comfort, but the world was a strange and amazing
placc. For some reason, thinking of him, going over
their argument today, and the discussions they'd had

in the elevator, made her feel a whole lot better.
She had stuff going on in her life. She didn't need
her dad.

Inevitably her thoughts turned from what she and
Jack had talked and argued about in the elevator to
what they'd done, and before long she was imagining what might have happened in Jack's office today
if he'd kissed her again instead of stapling her shirt
shut. What if he'd slid her shirt off, and then her bra?
She would have reached for his jeans, because she'd
been thinking about having him inside her ever since
he'd withdrawn from her. Maybe she would have
sunk to her knees and taken him in her mouth, loving the look on his face as she laved him with her
tongue. And maybe he wouldn't have been able to
stand it for long, and he'd have pushed her onto that
stupid, squishy couch in the corner and reached down
between her legs to push her panties aside—too impatient to remove them entirely—then he'd be inside
her again and—

Claire was panting into her pillow. Very resolute,
she got out of bed and rummaged through her drawers until she found a pair of pajamas. She always
slept naked, but these were desperate times. Pulling on underwear, and then the pajamas, she slid
back into bed.

No more fantasies about Jack Brook, she warned
herself.

Armored in cotton and determination, she finally
drifted off to sleep.

THE NEXT MORNING she was feeling distinctly jittery about having cut off communication with her father and about seeing Jack again. First, there was that irritating thing her heart did whenever Jack was in the room—it was almost as though it missed a beat now and then, lurching around inside her chest like a drunken sailor. Then there was the powerful physical awareness she seemed to have developed for him ever since they'd gotten down and dirty. You'd think that jumping on each other would have put an end to any sexual tension, but, if anything, it was worse. Now when she looked at his strong thighs and long fingers and broad shoulders she knew exactly how devastating they could be. And, to her shame, she wanted to be devastated. Badly. Hence the fact that he suddenly had top billing in all her sexual fantasies. Slowly but surely, he was driving her crazy.

Combine that with the fact that she was almost one hundred percent certain that he wouldn't be happy about her gift tie, and she had plenty of justification for the butterflies winging their way around her midsection.

Then there was her father. Why had she laid down the gauntlet like that? Why couldn't she have just eaten her dinner like a good girl and maintained the status quo? Really, it was getting to the point where she shouldn't be allowed out without a keeper.

She spent the time before her first meeting with Jack and Hillcrest Hardware looking up whenever anyone walked near her office, and jumping every time her phone rang. She felt like a sitting duck, waiting to be ambushed by Jack from one side, or her father on the other.

By a quarter to ten, she had talked herself around to a reasonable state of calm. If her father was going to make contact with her, it wouldn't be for some time. He'd want to leave a nice long buffer between her angry words and any future conversation to ensure she was calm and over whatever madness had had her in its grip. As for Jack— Well, she had no choice but to be ready to face him, tie or no tie.

Except he didn't come. As the time drew closer to 10:00 and her appointment with Hillcrest, she had to use stronger and stronger arguments for not reaching for the phone to confirm Jack's presence. She had to trust him; he was a successful, experienced executive; he wouldn't bail on her. On the last count she couldn't be so confident, however. They'd fought almost every time they'd been alone together for more than five minutes. There was a chance he'd see this as an extension of their battle of wills.

At 10:00 on the dot her assistant Tom told her that the Hillcrest executives were in the foyer. Caving at last, she reached for the phone and called Jack's office. The moment Linda picked up the call she knew Jack had hung her out to dry.

"Jack, is that you?" Linda demanded anxiously.

Claire took a moment to remind herself not to shoot the messenger. "No, Linda, this is Claire Marsden. I have a ten o'clock with Jack and Hillcrest Hardware, but I'm guessing that I'm going to be handling this alone…?"

There was a slight pause on the other end of the phone, then, "I'm sorry, Claire, but your appointment isn't in Jack's diary. I guess you made it with him directly. Otherwise I would have called you earlier to let you know…he seems to be running a little late today…."

The usually competent and professional Linda sounded extremely rattled, but Claire didn't have time to deal with the other woman's concern for her no-good, lazy, sneaky boss. The big rat was probably relaxing somewhere, lazing around enjoying his self-appointed long weekend.

Ending the call as nicely as possible, she headed in to take on Hillcrest and his honchos.

It wasn't a pleasant meeting, mostly because Hank Hillcrest managed to convey his deep skepticism about the appointment of Jack Brook to the magazine. The old man's repeated references to the "so-called Jack Brook," as though she and Morgan had made him up, became almost more than she could bear during the one-hour torture session. Somehow she managed to placate her client, spinning a yarn about Jack flying back in from a big-game safari in Africa and his flight being delayed. By the time she'd finished, Hank Hillcrest was so intrigued she began to suspect she'd have to cough up a genuine lion's head trophy just to shut the man up.

At last she shook hands with the now-cheerful Hillcrest executives and saw them out into the foyer amid assurances that she would bring Jack out to meet them at their head office next week.

No sooner had the elevator doors closed on them than she let her smile drop. She couldn't remember ever being so furious with anyone. She was so angry, in fact, that she was a little scared of herself, and she deliberately took the stairs to Jack's floor in order to give herself some time to calm down. Her shirt was already clinging to her thanks to the tense meeting, and she slung her jacket over her arm as she exited the stairwell and made her way purposefully to Linda's desk.

Linda was looking harried, and she glanced up at Claire distractedly. Almost as though she was talking to herself, Linda explained that she'd managed to reschedule all but one of Jack's meetings, but she still hadn't heard from him.

"Probably too scared to turn up now," Claire suggested coolly.

Linda gave her an impatient look.

"You don't understand. Jack has never ever done anything like this before. I know he looks casual and laid-back, but he's always punctual, he always meets his deadlines and he always lets me know what's going on. I've worked for him for two years now, and this has never happened, ever. I'm worried."

Which made two of them, because as Linda spoke an awful image of Jack's stupid red sports car wrapped around a tree popped into Claire's brain.

"I take it he's not answering his home line or his cell phone?" she ventured reluctantly.

"His home line just rings out, and his cell phone goes straight through to his voice mail."

She saw the worry in Linda's eyes and patted the other woman's arm reassuringly.

"Have you checked his office? Maybe he left a note or something in there and forgot to put it on your desk."

"I had a quick scout around, but nothing struck me," Linda said doubtfully.

As one they turned toward Jack's closed office door, and, at Linda's nod, Claire stepped forward and pushed it open. Jack's desk was a mess, which didn't seem too unusual, but she couldn't fail to see the tie she'd sent him strewn on the floor like an old sock.

She automatically bent to pick it up, smoothing the silk through her fingers as she continued surveying Jack's desk. Linda frowned at the tie, curious.

"What's a tie doing in Jack's office? He never wears a tie. I wonder if…?" Linda's startled eyes connected with Claire's, and Claire could see the other woman was busy constructing an Agatha Christie plot.

"It's okay. I bought it for him," she explained.

Linda's eyes went round with surprise, then her hand snuck up to cover her mouth. She was laughing, Claire realized.

"I'm sorry. I was imagining his face. It's just… Jack never wears a tie. I don't think he even owns one."

"I know. That's why I bought him one. For the Hillcrest meeting."

Linda shot her a speculative look, and Claire guessed what the other woman was thinking. "Oh, no—it's nothing like that. I was just trying to annoy him," she hastily explained.

Linda looked unconvinced. "Right."

"No, really. I wanted him to wear a tie to the Hillcrest meeting, he said he didn't have one… It was just a joke, really."

Linda nodded, but Claire got the distinct impression that the other woman didn't believe her. Unwilling to dig a bigger hole for herself, she began surveying the desk again. Linda joined in straight away, but Claire was aware of her lingering scrutiny and she kept her face carefully blank.

"I don't see anything, do you?" Linda said after a futile few minutes.

Claire was shaking her head, about to agree with Linda, when she spotted the discarded birthday card.

Frowning, she plucked it from amongst the mess and flipped it open.

Dearest Jack, thinking of you on this special day. Please be kind to yourself—our love is with you. Don't feel as though you have to go it alone. Lots of love, Mom and Dad.

She turned to Linda, urgent now. "Did this come yesterday?"

Linda shrugged. "How could I know? He may have had it for weeks. Except— Hang on a minute."

Linda scuffled through the papers until she found the torn lavender envelope. Matching it to the card, she nodded once. "Yes. This definitely came yesterday, because I remember the purple envelope. It was in the mail I collected from Jack's personal mailbox. Claire, what's going on? What's this about?"

Claire closed her eyes briefly. This had to be it. Jack's birthday was Robbie's birthday. She opened her eyes, even more worried now than she was before.

Because what on earth happened to a man when all the grief he'd stuffed down deep inside threatened to escape?

She grabbed Linda's arm, imperative. "I need Jack's home address, pronto."

HE LIVED IN A HOUSE. Another surprise. A big old rambling house with a yard and trees and a white picket fence. Parking her car in front, she felt a moment of shame for all the clichés she'd ascribed to Jack. She'd always imagined him in a penthouse apartment, with lots of gleaming chrome and black leather furniture and mood lighting.

Girding her loins, she made her way up the path to the front door and leaned on the doorbell. Nothing. She waited, then tried again. Still nothing. She tried knocking next, and when this was still ineffective, she stepped back and surveyed the house. It was possible he wasn't here at all, of course. Lord, he could be anywhere. But his car gleamed redly at the end of the drive, and she had a gut instinct about this—Jack was very private, and she doubted he'd take his grief to a public place.

She tried the front door, but it was solidly locked, so she headed boldly up the drive, emerging into a beautifully landscaped backyard. Fruit trees and roses, climbing jasmine on the fence and a rustic outdoor setting created a little oasis of calm and tranquility. She smiled at the laughing Buddha statue half-hidden in amongst some irises, then frowned as she saw the back door open and swinging in the breeze.

Well, at least she wasn't breaking and entering....

Feeling a little more tentative now, she stuck her head in the darkened doorway and glanced up and down the hallway. In front of her, old floorboards gleamed all the way down the central hallway to the front door.

"Jack? Jack, are you here?" she called out.

Nothing. Sighing, she stepped properly into the house. The kitchen was on her right. It was old but serviceable, and Jack was obviously in the process of renovating it, with half the tiles removed and the wallpaper stripped down to bare plaster.

Two empty tequila bottles lay on their sides on the kitchen table. *Oh, goody.* Nothing like a tequila hangover.

She found him in the living room, slumped on the couch, his posture defeated and closed. At first she thought he was asleep, but he lifted his head when she put her hand on his shoulder, giving her a minor heart attack.

"Jack!" she said, startled, and he blinked up at her owlishly.

"What are you doing here?" he slurred, and she

pulled back from the truly impressive haze of alcohol he was exuding.

Amazingly, he still managed to look dangerously attractive, despite his bleary-eyed, bestubbled, incoherent state.

"I was worried about you," she said, not bothering to edit herself. She'd be stunned if he remembered any of this.

"Were you? That's nice."

His head sank back down, and she allowed herself a small moment to simply rest her hand on his head, feeling for him. He held too much to himself, blocked himself off too much....

"Jack, I think we should make you some coffee. And some food. You feel like some food?" she suggested, forcing herself to take her hand off his silky, springy hair.

"Don't want anything," he said, childishly.

"I'm sure you don't. But I promise you'll feel better if you eat some food."

"Don't want to feel better."

I bet you don't. She stared down at his still-bowed head, then made a decision. "Why don't we get you in the shower?"

He didn't respond to this, and she crouched down to peer up into his face. "Jack? Jack?"

Slowly he opened his eyes again.

"Don't want shower."

She nodded as though she was agreeing with him. "Sure. But you trust me, don't you? And I think you should have a shower," she said.

He just stared at her, and she leaned forward and slid her arm around his shoulders, bracing herself and ensuring a strong grip on his well-muscled side.

"Come on, now. Let's stand."

It took a few more minutes of coaxing and some serious counterweight balancing to get him to his feet. She cursed herself immediately for not having done a bit of recon and worked out where the shower was before she got him standing, but he was swaying on his feet so much that there was no way she could trust him to stay upright if she went for a quick scout.

So they staggered up the hallway, and she found the bathroom behind the second door she tried. She tried to make him understand she wanted him to sit on the edge of the tub while she took off his boots, but he just stared at her blankly.

"Jack, how much have you had to drink?" she asked suddenly, beginning to wonder if he'd had the whole two bottles of tequila. How much did it take before a person got alcohol poisoning? She didn't have a head for drink herself, and the thought of so much strong spirit made her wince.

He shrugged, clearly disinterested, and she was forced to get down on her knees and lift his feet up one at a time to drag off his expensive-looking boots. The rest of him could go in the shower as is, but the boots just looked too good to ruin, and she knew he wouldn't thank her if she destroyed them. Hell, he was unlikely to thank her anyway, but she was here now....

She'd just tugged his last boot off when Jack

swayed alarmingly and staggered backward. There wasn't far for him to go in the small space; his legs kicked forward, catching the heel of the boot she held and flicking it toward her face, and he slammed against the tiled wall and slid down until his butt was in the tub and his legs were dangling over the edge.

White light exploded behind her eyes as the boot connected with her right cheekbone, and she reeled backward from her crouching position, connecting with the wall behind her.

Claire just breathed through the pain for a moment, then pressed a hand to her face, probing her cheekbone tentatively. Nothing felt broken or wrong, and she guessed she'd be looking at a bruise and nothing more. Still, it hurt like hell, and she took a couple more deep breaths.

"Claire? You okay?"

She looked up quickly to find Jack staring at her, his eyes more lucid now; perhaps the impact had knocked a bit of sense into him, sent some adrenaline into his system to counteract all that alcohol.

"I'm fine."

She pushed off the wall behind her and stood up.

"Come on, let's get you into the shower," she said.

She had to brace herself to help drag him up out of the tub, but he seemed much more aware of things as he sank down onto the edge of the bath and cradled his head in his hands.

"Did you knock your head?" she asked him, worried about concussion now. She leaned over him, reaching behind his head to probe the back of his skull for any bumps or blood.

Suddenly Jack's hand shot out and grabbed hers, and she found herself being pulled down so that she was kneeling in front of him.

"Let me see," he was murmuring. "I hurt you."

He was determined and way too heavy for her to move around without his cooperation, so she let him have his way when he tilted her face up to examine the throbbing mark left by his boot. She tried not to look into his intent but bleary eyes, focusing instead on the tiled wall behind him.

"I hurt you," he repeated, one large hand cradling her chin as the other brushed delicately at her cheek.

She had to swallow against the rush of feeling and memory his tender touch evoked, and she took herself to task firmly—the man was five parts drunk, incoherent and morose, and she was more hard up than she'd ever imagined if this was all it took to move her these days.

"It's okay, Jack. It's just a bruise. You didn't mean it. It was an accident," she reassured him, trying to turn her face away from his probing scrutiny.

"I still hurt you. I'm sorry, Claire, I'm so sorry," Jack said, his voice very low and gruff now.

She froze as both Jack's hands cupped her face and held it steady as he stared intently into her eyes, his own face just a foot away.

"I'm really, really sorry," he said, and she watched as tears welled up in his amazing eyes and spilled over his stubbly cheeks.

"I didn't mean to hurt you," he repeated, the tears still falling.

"Jack, it's okay," she said, tears welling in her own eyes at his misery.

His hands slipped from her face and dropped lifelessly into his lap. His shoulders shuddered, and then he seemed to crumple in on himself and she caught him in her arms as he leaned forward. A cry of anguish that seemed to seep out of his very bones echoed through him, and then he was gripping her back with a terrifying strength as he cried and cried and cried.

His weight pulled him forward off the edge of the tub and onto his knees on the floor, and she knelt with him, her heart aching for him as he wept in her arms.

She soothed a hand down his back and up again, making encouraging noises and wincing a little because he was holding her so tightly.

They stayed like that a while, until well past what her knees were happy with, but she waited until his sobbing had tapered off before soothing a hand down his back one last time and pushing him back from her.

"How about that shower now, Jack?" she suggested.

His eyes were swollen, and he needed to blow his nose, and she had to look away from the raw vulnerability in his face. *This is why men don't let women see them cry,* she realized. Suddenly Jack seemed infinitely fragile.

She got him to his feet and into the shower, and was about to turn on the taps when he caught her hand again.

"Hang on."

With one shoulder wedged against the wall, Jack reached for the waistband on his jeans and she found herself following the movements of his hands with an unnatural fascination as he slipped the stud from its buttonhole and unzipped his fly. He hooked his thumbs into the waistband of his jeans next, and with a smooth motion he shucked them down. She gulped as she realized he'd taken his underwear with the jeans, hastily averting her eyes.

Because to do anything else would be an invasion of privacy, right? But Jack was really, really out of it, and the odds of him remembering any of this with great clarity were pretty damn slim. Almost against her will, her eyes lifted above his ankles where he was even now stepping clumsily out of his jeans and boxers, past his knees, up his well-muscled, nicely haired thighs, until she hit the money shot and swallowed a sudden lump in her throat.

Whoa!

The sight of him was enough to make her thighs tighten instinctively. It had been so hot and intense in the elevator, a lot of the details sort of blurred into one blood-stirring memory. But the sight of him made her remember what it had felt like to be completely, achingly filled by a man. She swallowed, aware that her breathing was a little shallow.

But even though she knew it was rude to stare,

and that she shouldn't be indulging these sorts of fantasies, especially with Jack Brook, she couldn't seem to stop her eyes traveling back down to where all the action was, even as she accepted the T-shirt he'd shucked, and pulled his jeans out from around his feet.

Of its own accord, heat pooled low in her belly, and her heart thrummed against her ribs. She really wanted to touch him. She really wanted to get her hands on the solid, thick length of him, to feel him against her body, *in* her body.

It would be so easy just to step into the shower beside him. To peel off her clothes off and press herself against him and let herself have more of what she'd tasted.

She gave herself a shake at this last salacious thought. The man was not in his right mind. And they had been down this road before, and that way lay rejection and embarrassment.

"Right," she said, more for herself than for Jack, who was leaning against the tiled wall, his eyes closed. "It's going to be cold, okay?" she warned him, shooting one last wistful look downstairs—not even Jack Brook, with all his apparent talents, could withstand the rigors of an ice-cold shower.

She twisted the cold tap on full and leaped back as Jack reacted like a scalded cat despite his drunkenness.

"What the hell?" he demanded, suddenly standing tall and angry and naked, glaring belligerently at her.

"It's for your own good," she squeaked, shutting

the shower door between them with a slam and pressing her palms against the glass. "You really need to sober up."

Jack seemed to take in what she said, but she noted that he reached for the hot tap just the same. The wary glance he shot her made her realize the cold had shocked him far closer to sobriety than she'd imagined, and she suddenly felt very uncomfortable.

"Um, I'm going to make you some food," she mumbled.

He just stared at her through the water-beaded glass, then turned his back on her and reached for the soap.

CHAPTER NINE

SHE MADE HER way back into the kitchen and pulled out a chair, sinking into it gratefully.

Maybe she shouldn't have come. But then she touched her shoulder where not even half an hour ago he'd been clinging desperately as his grief poured out, and she couldn't regret a thing. In her opinion, that crying jag had been a long time coming, and if she'd helped him open up some of his pain, then it didn't matter that he was probably going to hate her for it once he sobered up.

Because while she might not be the most amazingly perspicacious reader of men, she knew enough to know that Jack would rather throw her off a cliff than bump into her every day in the office knowing that she'd seen him so vulnerable.

Well, tough. He'd seen her passed out from some stupid, babyish fear of small spaces. If she could hack it, he could, too.

Now that she'd bolstered her own courage somewhat, she felt free to register the throbbing ache of her cheekbone. Before she did anything else, she needed ice.

She could still hear the shower running as she

wrapped a handful of ice cubes in a clean dish towel, pressing the impromptu ice pack to her cheekbone with a sigh of relief.

"Much better," she told the empty kitchen.

Now—something to eat for a man who'd been drinking all night. She opened cabinet doors randomly until she found a stash of groceries. Here, at last, Jack Brook conformed to her idea of a bachelor—salt, pepper, a packet of noodles and some bottled sauces. Otherwise, that was it.

While she considered herself a decent cook, these kind of ingredients were beyond her. She tried the fridge, and found a package of sausages, some potatoes in the crisper, milk, butter and an onion that looked just about to sprout.

"Okay, now we're talking."

It was twenty minutes later, and she had the onions on the back burner, the sausages already cooked and put to one side, and the potato masher in hand when she registered the fact that she couldn't hear the shower running anymore.

For some reason, this made her feel nervous, and she took her feelings out on the innocent potatoes awaiting her in the saucepan. She added butter, milk, salt and pepper, and concentrated very hard on making the mash lump-free, rather than giving in to the urge to grab her car keys and leave Jack to it now that he was up and about.

You're just feeling guilty because you had a look in the candy shop without permission, she told herself, but it didn't stop her heart from picking up a little.

"This is a surprise."

She swung around to find Jack in the doorway, one shoulder propped against the door frame, a towel slung low around his waist, his eyes clear and dangerous-looking.

Water glistened on his skin, and the hair on his chest was coiled in tight, dark circles. He looked good enough to eat, damn him.

She tried to find a smile, but managed only a nervous grimace.

"You didn't turn up for the Hillcrest meeting. Linda was worried…and I saw the card from your mom," she explained hastily.

He frowned suddenly.

"What happened to your eye?" he asked, starting forward.

She stared at him. Was it possible he'd really forgotten everything so quickly? Then her gaze slid to the two empty bottles of tequila. Despite appearances, it would be stupid to assume he was anywhere near sober now.

"I had an accident. It was nothing," she said, edging away from him. The last thing she needed was for him to know how much his near-nudity was affecting her. She'd already given him more than enough opportunities to laugh in her face.

"So you came over to play nursemaid to me, did you?" Jack asked as he pulled out a chair and sat down.

Her eyes slid down the tanned planes of his chest, and she took in the apparently loosely cinched towel around his waist nervously. Why didn't he go dress? And why did she find it so hard to keep her eyes off his chest?

"I thought you might need a friend," she said.

His eyes narrowed, and she smiled weakly. He was making her feel very nervous. Something about the way he was looking at her. As if he was hungry.

"I made you something to eat," she squeaked, desperately wanting to distract him. "Sausages and mash."

"I'm not hungry."

"But you should eat. You've had a lot to drink—"

"But I'm not hungry," he repeated, and the way he was looking at her made all other protests die in her throat.

He shifted, and the towel moved a little, and she found herself staring a little breathlessly at the hard-muscled thigh now on display. Okay, this was bad. The chest she could handle, but that thigh was well nigh irresistible. She was only flesh and blood, after all. Trying to get a grip, she fought a serious, no-holds-barred battle of wills with her baser self, and finally managed to wrench her eyes away. Only to discover Jack was well aware of her preoccupation.

"See anything you like?" he asked.

She swallowed, turned back to the stove.

"This'll get cold. If I serve it up now, you can eat it later. Just heat it in the microwave…" She trailed off as she heard his chair scrape against the floor, and she spun around to find him approaching her.

She felt like a bunny in headlights. Here was the man she'd been fantasizing about for a solid forty-eight hours, walking almost-naked toward her. She only had to close her eyes to remember the feel of his body under her hands. They'd been on fire in the elevator—and now, here he was, looming over her, obviously thinking the same kinds of things she was....

"I tried to stop thinking about you, but I can't get you out of my head. And now you're here and even if it's a stupid mistake and work sucks afterward, who cares? I want you right now," he said.

She stared at him wide-eyed, conscious of the rush of heat that whooshed down into her thighs at the phrase *I want you.*

He's drunk, you're an idiot, and this should not be happening, she warned herself.

He was in front of her now, not a foot away. She could feel the heat radiating off his body. Or maybe that was her own heat. She had to get a grip. She should get out of here, walk away from this disaster-in-the-making.

Remember what happened afterward, she told herself. But all she could remember was how much her body had ached, how bereft she'd felt when he'd pulled away from her to answer that damned phone.

"I've been thinking about your breasts... I have to taste them again. Take your shirt off," Jack murmured, one hand reaching for the opening of her blouse.

Oh, boy. She watched his hand come closer and closer, and knew that, more than anything, she wanted to give in and let herself have this moment. There was no one to stop them, no earthly reason why they couldn't have at each other and end all the wondering and the lust and the wanting.

But she'd been sensible for too long to be able to ignore all the voices of reason clamoring for attention in the back of her skull. He was too drunk to know what he was really doing, and she didn't go in for casual sex, and he wasn't offering anything else, and they were work colleagues, and he hadn't even bothered to call after what happened between them in the elevator, and he was hurt and looking for something to make himself feel better....

She made herself step backward, no matter how much she wanted to just stay put and have it all. The stove was behind her and she felt the saucepan handle digging into her back.

"This is probably a really bad idea," she said faintly, aware that she'd sound a lot more convincing if her voice wasn't thin and breathy.

"Who cares?" he said, and then he ducked his head and his mouth was on her neck.

A shudder rippled through her from heel to crown as his tongue laved her neck.

Oh-boy-oh-boy-oh-boy. Her thighs felt as though they were going to explode and she could feel her breasts swelling within the confines of her bra.

He's going to regret this in the morning, she thought, and then her flailing hand connected with something and she grabbed it and pushed him away with all her strength, brandishing the object at him.

"Just keep your distance, buddy, okay, or I'll—". She paused a moment to contemplate her weapon of choice: the potato masher.

"Just...don't move," she corrected herself.

"Come on, Claire, live a little," he tempted her.

She couldn't prevent her eyes from dropping below his waist to where the evidence of his arousal was making a very respectable tent beneath his towel.

Oh, please, let's go camping! her wanton half begged, but it was hard to give up the habits of a lifetime.

"I think we need to be calm and rational about this. You've had too much to drink, and I think that you're just channeling your grief into some sort of sex thing with me. You don't really want me. I'm not your type. Plus, I'm really not into this kind of thing. I know after what happened the other day you might think I am, but, honestly, that was a one-off, and—"

She froze as his finger descended on her lips.

"Just, for once, shut up," he said huskily, then he smiled, an I'm-going-to-eat-you-up smile that made bits of her jump up and down with excitement.

She dropped the potato-encrusted masher as he closed the gap between them and then he was up against her, one hand reaching around her back to pull her close, the other sliding down over her butt to lift her against him.

She gasped as his mouth descended on hers, which was just as well because she forgot to breathe as he kissed her with a thoroughness that made her realize that, as spectacular as her recollection of the other day had been, her memory had done him a serious disservice—this man could kiss!

His other hand was doing something tricky behind her back, and then she felt a slight give around her torso and knew he'd released her bra catch through the fabric of her shirt. Wow, what a professional.

If she hadn't been so busy reacquainting herself with the curves and dips of his chest and back, she'd have been worried about just how professional he was. Instead she was grunting with satisfaction as he lifted her off the ground and turned to prop her on the edge of the kitchen sink. One impatient, very male hand swept her skirt up, and then his hips were between her knees and she found herself spreading her thighs and urging him forward so that all of his hardness could press up against her where she needed it the most.

It felt so good—especially because she'd effectively been waiting for this moment for more than two days now. Two days of tortured, argumentative foreplay. But what a payoff.

She had no idea how he got her shirt undone, she just blessed the gods that he did because then his mouth and tongue and hands were on her breasts and she threw back her head and bit her lip and tried not to explode.

His stubble scraping against her skin, his hot tongue teasing her nipple, the firm pressure as he ground his hips into the heart of her…it was almost enough to stop her noticing the tinge of alcohol on his breath. Almost, but not quite.

She managed to think for just a second as he switched his attention from her left breast to her right.

This was wrong. This was folly of the most enormous order. She would regret this if she let it go any further. Worse, she'd be like those other women in the office, the ones who took what little Jack offered, but secretly wanted it all. She knew he wasn't going to call after this. She knew exactly how this encounter was going to end, how bad and stupid she'd feel afterward, and how much she'd regret it.

"No!"

It took great determination to utter that single word and push him away from her. It took even more determination when his towel chose that exact moment to loosen completely and slide to the floor. The very impressive evidence of his arousal tempted her even as she tried to catch her breath. His blue eyes were dilated, his breath coming fast, a frown forming between his eyebrows as he registered that his toy had been taken away from him. She saw him tense to start forward again, and she held up a hand.

"I'm sorry, Jack, I should never have let this get started. But let's stop things before we do something we'll both regret."

She grasped the edges of her shirt and pulled it shut over her still-aching breasts, sliding off the edge of the sink and back down to earth. He seemed to register the finality of her actions, and he ducked to pick up his towel.

"Why'd you come, then?"

She could hear the frustration and rejection in his voice, and paused in the act of buttoning her blouse, aware her heart was still racing out of control and that her hands were shaking.

"Not for this, if that's what you're thinking."

"Really? Could have fooled me." He was almost sneering at her, and she resumed buttoning her blouse, her fingers shaking from hurt and anger now, not lust and frustration.

"You're drunk," she told him quietly, smoothing both palms down her skirt.

"And you're uptight. And scared."

She stared at him. He was like a schoolboy who'd been banned from watching TV for a week.

"Eat something. And try not to choke on it," she told him, sweeping up her purse and car keys on her way out the door.

She stumbled on a crack in the concrete driveway as she half ran to her car. Her bra was hanging loosely around her ribs, and she kept her arms wrapped around her body until she got into the car.

Once locked inside safely, she slammed a hand against the steering wheel and swore loudly. She was a complete idiot. She could not believe she had almost had dirty drunk sex with Jack Brook, the office lothario. Hadn't her bout of dirty elevator sex taught her anything?

His demand rang in her ears. *Why'd you come, then?*

Because I knew you were hurting.

But she could have left him in the shower. She *should* have left him in the shower. And she wasn't ready to consider why she hadn't.

WOODY WOODPECKER HAD taken up residence in his skull and was working on an extension to the facilities. It was the first thought that staggered across Jack's mind as his eyes flickered open early Saturday morning. He lay still and stared at the ceiling for a moment, aware that a headache roughly the size of a small planet was waiting to descend on him. He forced himself to sit up, and the headache descended like a banshee. Cradling his aching forehead in his hands, Jack took his tongue on a tour around his mouth. Not good. If he didn't know better, he'd suspect some poor woodland creature had crawled in there and died last night.

Slowly he stood and made his way to the kitchen, wondering vaguely along the way why he was naked. The kitchen faucet drew him like a magnet and he stuck his mouth beneath it and simply drank until he could hear water sloshing around inside himself.

Then he turned and leaned against the sink, trying to hazily recollect where he kept the aspirin these days. His eyes fell on the two empty bottles of tequila on the kitchen table, and he grimaced. Why on earth had he chosen such a lethal poison?

His gaze tracked to the left and he found himself contemplating a mess of saucepans on the stove. Frowning, he stared at the congealed food: mash, sausages, onions. And then memory flooded back and he closed his eyes in sheer self-defense.

Claire. She came over because...that bit he couldn't quite grasp. But he remembered her being hurt, remembered touching her face... Hell, he'd hurt her. The memory of overbalancing in the bathroom was vague, but he got the gist of it.

Great. He was such an asshole.

Hard on the heels of this revelation came another: he'd cried. He'd cried like a baby, like a little boy who'd lost his puppy.

Like a man who'd never grieved for his dead twin.

His first impulse was to writhe with humiliation. Of all the people to witness his self-indulgence, Claire Marsden was almost the worst he could imagine. Perhaps only Mike Tyson rated higher.

But the memory of being held and soothed in her arms washed over him then, and he could almost feel her empathy and calm as she waited him out.

Maybe she hadn't been such a bad choice, after all. It didn't escape his attention that after a long time of not daring to say Robbie's name out loud, he'd chosen to tell her about his brother the other day in the elevator. And now he'd blubbered all over her....

But try as he might, he couldn't find a way to reconcile himself to such a display of emotion and helplessness. Way too revealing. Way too emasculating. And he never cried. Never. Not at Robbie's bedside. Not at Robbie's graveside.

Yet all it took was a few gallons of tequila and Claire Marsden and he was howling like a pro.

In case he'd forgotten, his headache stepped things up a notch and he groaned. Before anything else, aspirin was required. In large, industrial doses.

He headed to the far cabinet, but the feel of something soft and mushy underfoot stopped him in his tracks. A dozen suggestions flitted across his mind, none of them pretty, before he steeled himself to glance down.

Mashed potato? He laughed with relief, and then sobered suddenly as the last jigsaw puzzle piece of memory slotted into place.

Claire Marsden, sans bra, sans attitude, all hot, wanton woman, on his kitchen sink. It was enough to make parts of him salute with respect.

How in hell had that happened?

And—more importantly—why had it stopped? Because it had been good. Very good. Even his tequila-soaked memory of it was good, very good. He'd been determined to keep his distance after their last intimate encounter, sure that he'd made the right decision. But, for some reason, he'd abandoned his game plan and succumbed again. It was becoming something of a habit, in fact. A scary, addictive habit.

An accusation leaped to mind out of the blue. *You're drunk.*

Only Claire Marsden could be responsible for the inflection he was recalling so vividly. And, indeed, he had been drunk. Really, stinking, rotten, putrid drunk. That probably explained his lack of impulse control. And the dismal quality of his memory of the whole thing. He cursed himself—at least if he wasn't able to repeat the experience in reality, he should be able to repeat it in the privacy of his own mind. His own messed-up, confused mind.

He downed a couple of aspirin and visited the kitchen faucet for one last monumental watering before staggering back to his bedroom. Throwing himself on the bed, he slung a protective arm across his eyes and began regretting the last twenty-four hours in earnest.

He'd been feeling...well, he'd been *feeling,* bottom line. So he'd tried to drown it in a tequila bath. Or vat, more likely, given the way his head was throbbing.

Hell, when was the aspirin going to kick in? He groaned a little, just to compound his self-inflicted misery.

His eyes felt gritty, dry. *That would be from all the crying, you big girl,* he told himself in disgust. Why had he bawled in front of Claire? His toes curled at the very idea of revealing himself so completely to a woman who had already judged him and found him wanting, and he groaned out loud again.

If he was given the moment all over again, he might actually choose Mike Tyson to witness his breakdown over Claire—that's how much he regretted it.

Hard to regret the other part of her visit, however. He'd wanted to touch her and taste her again so badly. She'd been the elusive star of his erotic dreams. And now the faint memory of the press of her body against his teased at him. She'd been up for it. He could still feel her hands gripping his shoulders, pulling him closer.

How had they leaped from mutual antagonism to mutual lust in the space it took a drunken man to traverse his kitchen? And why did it keep happening? First in the elevator, then the near miss with the stapler and now this. When was he going to learn to stop playing with fire?

Even now, lying here hungover and messed up, he only had to think of her to send blood rushing south of the border. It was as though he had no control over his own carnal desires where Claire was concerned. He didn't want to want her every logical, rational brain cell argued that she represented nothing but trouble. Yet his penis had very definite views on the subject. He lifted his head and glared at the offending organ.

"Down, boy. You have no idea what you're asking for."

One thing was for sure—Claire had regretted what had happened between them almost instantly. If he closed his eyes, he could actually relive her pulling her blouse closed across her bared breasts. He tried to freeze-frame it on that bit of the memory, but it inevitably tipped over into revealing the hurt and disappointment on her face as she gathered herself together and headed for the door. And she was already pissed at him for not calling her after their last encounter.…

More bad behavior such as this, and he'd be on every feminist hit list in the country—and he could guarantee that Claire would never even glance his way again. And that was a good thing, a really good thing. Wasn't it?

CLAIRE STEPPED OUT of the shower, toweling her body roughly. It was useless, however. No matter what she did, anything that touched her skin reminded her of Jack's hands on her body.

And it wasn't as if she needed prompting to remember her ill-fated visit to Jack's home. For starters, she had a huge, shiny black eye to mark the occasion. And whisker rash on her neck from where he had... Well, it didn't really matter what he'd done. It was more that she wished it all undone. Please.

She dropped the towel abruptly, padding out into the living room. For a moment she simply stood there, aware that her back and most of her legs were still wet. And that if she looked down, she'd see her nipples were erect.

Damn Jack Brook!

And damn herself. She'd had a long, uninterrupted, sleepless night to consider just how delusional she'd become over the past few days. She'd come to the only sane conclusion: she'd put her hand into the wolf's mouth, and he'd tried to bite it off. Twice. She shouldn't be surprised that the wolf had acted according to instinct—that was what wolves did, after all. But she had to wonder why she was traipsing around offering herself up at every possible opportunity like an almost-out-of-date platter of hors d'oeuvres.

That bit she hadn't been able to work out. She didn't know what was going on inside her convoluted, messed-up mind at the moment. If someone had asked her what she thought of her life and herself a few days ago, she would have been able to say confidently that she was happy, satisfied, settled. But today, at this moment, standing naked in her apartment, she would respond very differently.

Now she felt like every certainty in her life was up for grabs. Hell, she wondered if she even wanted to keep doing *Welcome Home*. But she couldn't for the life of her work out if that was because it seemed now to be inextricably entwined with Jack, or because Morgan had taken all of the glow and shine out of it for her. Or perhaps it was both…

She also wasn't talking to her father, and probably wouldn't be for the near future.

Truly, her life sucked.

She tugged her swimsuit crop top on, grimacing as the lycra clung to her damp skin. This was her second-last weekend before the triathlon final, and she had to focus. She hadn't trained for all these months for nothing. She wanted to win. Jack and her messed-up feelings for him didn't matter. Her father and the fact that he'd probably removed her number from his Rolodex didn't matter.

What she needed was some punishing exercise, and that flashy memory-wiping thing Will Smith and Tommy Lee Jones used in *Men in Black*. Then she could forget all the nice things she'd learned about

Jack over the past few days and consign the memory of his hands on her skin to the dustbin of time.

Nice idea. Shame about the reality.

CHAPTER TEN

HE HAD TO APOLOGIZE. SOMEHOW Jack had to stand in front of Claire and apologize for crying on her then nearly molesting her. It was a conclusion that was waiting for him, fully formed and unavoidable, when he woke up for the second time that Saturday morning.

It wasn't going to be easy. Or pretty. But it had to be done.

He managed to push the consideration to the back of his mind during the rest of the day, what with nursing the mother of all hangovers and then catching up on all the work he'd let slide while he had his meltdown. By the time night was falling, he'd come up with a raft of reasons for putting it off, any time it swam to the front of his consciousness. For starters, he didn't have her phone number. And, really, that sort of thing should be handled face-to-face.

By midmorning on Sunday he admitted to himself that he wasn't going to call her. He didn't know what to say. He hadn't asked her to come over to his place. He hadn't asked to be trapped in the elevator with her. And she had something on him now. She'd seen him cry, for Pete's sake. Even his mother hadn't seen him cry since he was seven—and that was only because he broke his leg in two places jumping off the roof of the shed.

And—deep, dark honesty here—he felt too raw to face her just yet. He wasn't quite sure why he'd let rip with all his grief for Robbie the other night, but he was still sorting through it all in the back of his mind somewhere. Maybe when he understood what had happened he would know why he'd confessed all to a woman he'd barely known a week ago, but who now held sway over most of his subconscious. Damn her and her silky breasts. And damn the raging hard-on that kept rearing its persistent head whenever he so much as thought her name.

Then it was Monday, and he couldn't put off the apology any longer. He rehearsed a couple of very rational, mature explanations in his head as he showered. Somehow, every scenario kept sliding to the same conclusion—Claire, sans clothing, assuring him that one night of unbridled, no-strings-attached sex with him was the only recompense she could possibly accept for his shabby behavior.

Like magic, the die-hard boner that had haunted him all weekend was back. Jack groaned out loud. He had to get this woman out of his system. The way he was going, he'd walk into her office to apologize and Mr. Stiffy would want to join in. No, it was time to deal with his body's stupid fascination with Claire. Reaching down between his legs, he very deliberately pictured a sexy blond woman he'd dated a few months ago. She'd had small, high breasts and long legs….

But try as he might, the only face and body he could summon up out of his subconscious was Claire's. A couple of hot encounters, and he was turning into a stalker. Great. Especially when the chances of actually achieving any kind of satisfaction again on that front were extremely slim. She and he were about as compatible as…as chilies and ice cream.

Clenching his eyes shut, he tried to imagine anyone else—Angelina Jolie, Halle Berry, Naomi Campbell…but no dice. Claire Marsden remained centre stage in his brain. With a despairing groan he surrendered himself to the demands of his body, giving himself up to the heat of the shower and his dangerous fantasies. Undressing Claire again in his mind's eye, he watched her face transform with desire, reveling in the little hiccup in her breathing when he bit gently on her nipples. He could almost feel the weight of her breasts in his hands, and the smooth curve of her butt as he lifted her and plunged into her wetness. He imagined the feel of her skin beneath his hands, and the slick, tight heat of her wrapped around him…

Too quickly he shuddered out his release, then sagged against the tiled shower wall.

"That's it," he told his rebellious body. "Now leave me alone."

In a feeble attempt to ease his way into an apology, he decided to go to the trouble of dressing well.

The iron was dragged out of its dusty hidey-hole, and he even toyed with the idea—briefly, just briefly—of wearing the tie she'd given him. But a man had his principles, after all.

Now he stood in front of his bathroom mirror and practiced a smile. The man smiling back at him looked sick and insincere.

Great. He couldn't even fool himself.

He had planned on going straight to her office to apologize the moment he got into work, kind of like swallowing his medicine really fast and pretending he couldn't taste it. But he found himself diverting instead to the foyer coffee shop. A good dose of caffeine, and then he'd be ready. And he was not avoiding the situation. Not at all.

But somehow, when he got in the elevator he found himself punching the button for his floor, not hers. He'd just check his e-mails, and make sure there were no urgent phone calls. And then he'd do it. Definitely.

MONDAY MORNING. CLAIRE sat in her car and tried to pretend it was like any other Monday for a full ten minutes, but she still couldn't force herself to get out and face the working week. She didn't ever want to see Jack again. She certainly didn't want to see him while she was sporting this lurid black eye. Apart from purely aesthetic reasons—and she didn't care about him thinking she was ugly, she really didn't—it made pretending that last Friday never happened impossible.

Why had she let him kiss her? A whole weekend of pounding the pavement, swimming lap after lap and riding her bike till her backside felt like it would never be the same again, had not even put a dint in her regret and self-recrimination. She'd spent nearly two years ignoring the man and telling herself she was superior to the other women in the office who fell all over him, then he'd barely glanced at her and she was ripping her clothes off in an elevator for him, and writhing around all over his kitchen sink. Just the thought of it made her flush with humiliation. And remembered desire. Which only made the humiliation more humiliating. Did she have no self-respect whatsoever?

Which brought her back to how to handle the current situation. She was still discarding options when the elevator pinged to a halt on her floor. She adjusted the enormous Jackie-O-esque sunglasses she'd bought on the weekend, then began weaving her way through the warren of workstations on the way to her office.

She was braced to cope with stares and shock when people saw the shiner—she'd dealt with it all weekend—but most people were too busy to notice her, and Tom wasn't at his desk. She slipped virtually unnoticed into her office and for a cowardly second toyed with the idea of keeping on the glasses all day. But she knew that it would just add fuel to the fire if she tried to hide her eye. The trick to pulling this off with the minimum of fuss and bother was to brazen it out.

She'd decided on a nice, innocuous explanation for her eye—she'd had an accident while training. No connection between her and Jack. No need for either of them to bring it up, even if he remembered. And he might not, right? He'd had a lot to drink....

She grunted with self-disgust.

Like he didn't remember. As if she could get that lucky. How on earth was she going to look at him? And why had she felt it was her responsibility to save him from himself in the first place? Lastly, why had Beck foisted Jack, of all people, onto her project?

Feeling ridiculously exposed and vulnerable, she turned on her computer, then carefully slid off the sunglasses. Her in-tray was groaning with mail and memos, and she dragged it toward herself gratefully—anything to stop her mind from running in circles like a mouse in a wheel.

She was engrossed in paperwork when Tom entered loaded up with muffins and take-out coffees from downstairs.

"Now, I knew you wouldn't have had time to have breakfast, as usual," he said brightly.

She lifted her head to thank him, and he almost lost his grip on the coffees as he registered her damaged eye.

"Good golly, Miss Molly! What on earth happened to you?" he squeaked.

For a second there she'd forgotten about the eye.

"Bit of an accident out training. Looks worse than it is," she said, hoping she sounded dismissive but instead sounding nervous.

She tried to smile calmly as Tom came closer, his face screwed up with a mixture of fascination and disgust as he studied her bruise.

"Man, that is *sooooo* bad. I have never seen a worse shiner in my life. Does it hurt? It looks like it hurts."

She felt her smile slip a little. If she couldn't even cope with Tom, how was she going to face Jack?

"It's fine. Really. And it'll be gone in a few days' time."

"Are you kidding? That thing is going to go yellow and brown and purple and green—you just wait."

Her smile felt as though it was set in concrete, and she reached for the muffin bag Tom had dumped unceremoniously on the desk.

"Don't suppose there are any blueberry in here?" she asked, desperate to divert him.

But Tom was still hyped about her eye. He leaned out of her office doorway.

"Hey, Kirsty, Helen, Roy—come check out Claire's shiner! It's unreal!" he hollered.

It was going to be a long day.

As Tom herded his colleagues into her office so he could show her off like a sideshow freak, she was vaguely aware of a stir on the other side of the floor. A hushed quiet, closely followed by lots of feminine discussion. But Tom was pointing out the many different colors of purple in her bruise to Kirsty, and she didn't see the human bouquet until it appeared in her doorway.

Jack was holding the largest bunch of flowers

Claire had ever seen. A veritable riot of color, so large that only his head and legs were visible at either end of the damn thing. Tom and Kirsty and Helen and Roy all looked from her to Jack and back again, then smiled knowingly.

She didn't need to be a rocket scientist to work out what they were thinking. Or to understand why her heart was suddenly racing. Damn him.

A sudden memory of how his stubbled cheek had felt against the soft skin of her neck flashed across her brain, and a wave of heat followed quickly in its wake. She felt dizzy, and unbearably transparent. He could probably read every thought crossing her mind. She could just imagine him laughing with his buddies over the uptight chick at work who'd turned to butter the moment he'd crooked his little finger.

"Um, did you want to see me, Jack?" she managed to say finally. Her voice came out squeaky and breathy, and Kirsty and Helen nudged each other meaningfully.

Jack was staring at her face, a small frown creasing his brow.

"Jack?"

He blinked, then looked from her to the flowers to the interested spectators crowded around her desk.

"Yes. Yes, that would be good," he said awkwardly.

She waited for her uninvited guests to slowly, reluctantly ease from the room. Tom lingered the longest, shooting one last speculative look over his shoulder as he exited.

She waited till they were all gone before crossing to the door and closing it. Taking a deep breath, she turned to face Jack.

HE'D GIVEN HER a black eye. Jack couldn't believe it. He'd given women a lot of things over the years—flowers, chocolates, orgasms. But never a black eye.

He didn't know what to do. He'd come down here with a game plan—hand over the flowers, apologize for leaving her high and dry with Hillcrest and manfully skirt around the topic of having sobbed his heart out on her shoulder. But now she was sporting a painful-looking shiner and all bets were off. Guilt and regret swamped him. He'd hurt her—she'd come around to be his friend and he'd hurt her.

"This is really awkward. I've never given a woman a black eye before," he heard himself say.

Very smooth. She was staring at him as if he was a few chromosomes short of being fully human.

"What I mean is…I'm really sorry. I didn't realize. These flowers were for bailing on the Hillcrest meeting, and for, you know, the other…thing. But that eye…I'm really sorry."

She'd gone pale. She broke eye contact with him, her gaze shifting over his shoulder. Why couldn't he just say what he meant? Why couldn't he say that he wouldn't hurt her for all the world? That seeing her like this, knowing he'd done this to her, made him feel sick to the stomach?

"It's fine, it was an accident. There's no need to talk about it. Really," she said.

Of their own accord, his eyes found her breasts. She was wearing a high-necked, dark red blouse, but he knew what lay beneath her librarian's wardrobe now. It was amazing that he'd never noticed before, really. She was a very attractive woman. And passionate. He couldn't forget the way she'd responded to his touch.

He wrenched his eyes away from her chest. What was he doing? This was a woman he'd blubbered all over like an idiot. A woman who'd made her feelings about him pretty clear. A woman who was sporting a glowing shiner thanks to his drunken grief. He shouldn't be thinking about pushing her up against the desk and lifting her neat little skirt. It was too late, however—the erection he'd thought he'd tamed that morning was back with a vengeance.

Confused and angry with himself, he thrust the flowers into her arms.

"Here. I'm sorry," he said, ready to make a run for it.

But she just stared at the bouquet, her eyes shifting over his shoulder again.

"I can't take them," she said, thrusting the flowers back at him.

This wasn't how it was supposed to go. She had to take the flowers. She had to accept his apology, because he was not having this hanging over him. She already had enough on him, she wasn't having this. It was bad enough that he couldn't get her out of his head, that she peopled his dreams and haunted his subconscious.

"But they're yours," he insisted, shoving them back at her.

"But I don't want them."

Back to him.

"You have to take them."

Back at her.

"Do you have any idea how this looks?" she pointed out, thrusting the flowers back at him one last time and then retreating behind her desk.

"It looks like I'm giving you flowers. Or it would, if you could stop being so damned uptight for ten seconds," he snapped.

She sucked in a breath and her hands found her hips. He willed himself to not look at her breasts, and had to be content with snatching a quick look before glancing away.

"Take a look over your shoulder," she snapped at him.

Frowning, he turned and saw that half the floor was standing watching their little interplay through the glass wall of Claire's office. Did these people have no lives of their own?

"Think for a minute, Jack. You, the office play-boy, bringing *me* flowers. And I have a black eye. What do you think people are going to make of that?"

He tossed the flowers on her desk, his temper really firing now. Did she have to sound so disgusted by the prospect that people might think there was something going on between them?

"I don't care what people think. And I thought

we'd agreed I don't like being called the office play-boy."

"Maybe you should have thought about that before you did all those laps of the typing pool."

He made an exasperated noise. She didn't like that. Her lips went all thin, and her nostrils flared.

"I'm serious, Jack. I don't want to be another notch in your bedpost. Now the whole office thinks we're sleeping with each other, thanks to these stupid flowers."

"Sweetheart, I never make the same mistake twice, so don't get your hopes up."

It was out before he could think, a jibe straight from the school yard, and he'd have to be blind to miss the flash of hurt in her eyes before she put on her game face.

"Don't flatter yourself. I prefer my men a little more sophisticated, not to mention sober."

He'd deserved that, but it still made him see red.

"For a moment there I forgot who I was dealing with, but thank you for the reminder, Little Miss Hospital Corners."

Before she could say anything else he'd flung her office door open.

"Excuse me, your attention please."

He waited until the whole floor had stopped what it was doing and turned to face him. For a split second his impulse control kicked in, but by then his mouth was fully engaged.

"For the record, Claire Marsden and I are not having sex."

He heard her horrified intake of breath and spun around to face her.

"Happy now?"

She could only stare at him. He managed to make it all the way to the elevator before the remorse and guilt hit him. But by then it was too late to do anything except keep going.

SHE STOOD FROZEN in place for a full minute after he'd gone. It was only when Tom came and knocked awkwardly on her door that she found her spine.

"Can I get you anything? Coffee? An aspirin?" he asked helpfully.

She groaned and dropped into her chair.

"Do I look that pitiful?"

Tom just smiled weakly, obviously not wanting to lie.

"Should I…should I get a vase for these?" he asked, gesturing toward the flowers Jack had all but thrown at her.

"Hell, no. Take them away. Give them to the assistants, or your girlfriend, or whoever. I never want to see them again," she said.

Tom eased them out from under her nose, and she made a show of getting on with business so that the rest of the prying eyes in the office would have nothing to feed off. She made a phone call, checked her e-mail, opened some letters. All the while, her mind was a careful blank. Somewhere, deep inside, was a tsunami of humiliation just waiting to swamp her. But she was damned if she would give Jack Brook the satisfaction of giving in to it with half the office watching.

"Okay, let's go."

She looked up to find Katherine in her doorway, a determined look on her face.

"Sorry, what?"

"Claire, I've just had no less than three phone calls from people on your floor telling me that Jack Brook just brought you flowers and told the whole building that you're not having sex. Come on, we're heading out."

It didn't feel like a request, more like a demand, and because she was still reeling from Jack's very public display, Claire meekly collected her purse and followed Katherine to the stairwell. A few heads turned and someone sniggered. Katherine sniffed haughtily and lifted her chin high, true friend that she was, but, despite all her determination, a hot tide washed up Claire's chest and into her face.

Katherine led her down a floor before stopping and sitting on a step. Claire obediently followed suit, feeling completely out of her depth in this undiscovered world of office romances.

"Okay, what's going on between you and Jack?" Katherine asked bluntly.

"Nothing. I mean, we've been forced to work together, but that's all."

"Right. Which is why he's just told the world that he's not sleeping with you. Where there's smoke, Claire..."

Katherine was regarding her intently, and Claire couldn't quite meet her eye.

"Something might have happened the other day in the elevator. And again the other day at his place."

"Did he do that to your face?" Katherine asked, her expression tight.

Claire guessed what her friend was thinking and hastened to reassure her.

"It was an accident, he was drunk—"

"Right!" Katherine stood, six feet of pure, angry woman. Realizing she had the wrong end of the stick, Claire grabbed her ankle before she could barge up to Jack's office and give him what for.

"It wasn't like that. I was helping him take his boots off, and he tripped. It was my fault as much as his," she explained.

Katherine froze, then some of the tension dropped out of her and she sat beside Claire on the step. Silence stretched between them for a beat. Then, "So you're seeing him, huh?" Katherine asked, her expression unreadable.

Claire shook her head, then winced when it made her eye hurt.

"Uh-uh. Things just got out of control. We don't even like each other."

Although, that wasn't quite as true as it used to be. Even humiliated and angry, she had to admit that there were aspects of Jack that she liked and admired.

"I keep hearing this from you a lot lately. Love

and hate are just opposite ends of the same spectrum. You know that, don't you?"

Claire stared at her, genuinely horrified. "Are you kidding? There is no way I feel anything close to… *that* for Jack Brook. We just got stuck with each other, and we were bored. It's kind of a power thing. That's all."

She almost convinced herself. Katherine sighed and stood, brushing her skirt down.

"Well, good luck. He's a hard nut to crack," she said ruefully.

Claire looked at her sharply. "Did you—did you love him?" she asked hesitantly, picking up on something in Katherine's voice.

"Of course not, we barely lasted more than a week or two. I just think he's a good guy, underneath it all. Kind of the one that got away, you know."

Claire nodded her understanding, and Katherine squeezed her shoulder briefly before heading down the stairs to her own floor.

"Oh, and forget about the gossip. That time I got busted with the Xerox guy in the photocopier room? A five-day wonder. Something else will come up, and you and Jack will be old news, I promise."

Claire smiled weakly, but as soon as her friend was gone she dropped her head into her hands and sighed heavily. She could honestly say she'd never been more humiliated in all her life. She'd worked so hard to project a certain image at Beck and Wise. She had a reputation for being hardworking and serious, and she liked that. It was important to her to get ahead, to secure her own future. She'd learned the hard way that the only person you could rely on in life was yourself.

And she'd stupidly dropped her guard and allowed herself to feel something for Jack. After just a few brief hours in an elevator, she had written off a lifetime of caution and carefulness and given in to her baser instincts. And look where it had got her—the whole building was talking about her.

Perhaps this was why she'd always kept Jack at arm's length—because she'd known, deep down inside, that he was her nemesis, romantically speaking. A force with the power to scramble her thoughts, hijack her libido and drag her focus from the things she truly considered important, like her sport and her career.

Katherine was a good friend, but she was wrong about Claire and Jack—there was no love-hate thing going on here. For some strange reason, they had discovered a sexual chemistry. That was it, pure and simple. And Claire wasn't about to let it ruin her life. A lot of things that were really important to her were coming to fruition in the next few weeks. She wasn't about to let Jack distract her from her dreams.

She sat up, then stood. Goodbye, easy-to-bait, slightly infatuated Claire.

She smoothed her skirt, adjusted her cuffs. Hello, cool, polished professional who could cut through Jack's flirting and bravado like a hot knife through butter. From now on, she gave him nothing. And if that meant it was back to the cold-war status that had existed before they were trapped in the elevator, fine. Because she wasn't letting him get the better of her again.

HE'D GONE TOO FAR. That much was obvious. He'd gone down there intending to apologize, and he'd wound up being nasty. All because she'd gotten all prim and proper about people thinking they were sleeping together.

It wasn't as if it was a big deal that a man and a woman might want to have sex with each other. It had happened before in the history of time. Sure, it was unlikely that it would ever happen again between him and Claire, but it was nothing for her to be getting her knickers in a knot over. Boy, was she uptight.

And probably mad as hell with him. Beck had had no idea what he was doing when he'd forced the two of them to work together.

Jack groaned and spun around in his chair. Clouds scudded across the bright blue sky in the world outside, and he wished he was out there instead of stuck inside having to deal with the repercussions of his actions.

Why had he given in to the impulse to humiliate her? A little voice whispered something deep inside, but Jack stomped on it mercilessly. He didn't want to think about how mad he'd gotten when it became clear that Claire was embarrassed about having had sex with him. That she *regretted* their encounters. While he'd been tossing and turning and fighting to retain control of his subconscious all weekend, she'd been cleaning him out of her memory and her life. For some reason, it rankled very deeply that she could dismiss him so easily. So he'd lashed out. And the rest would go down in office history, no doubt.

Of course, they were beyond apology now. You couldn't apologize for an apology that had gone wrong.

All that was left now was retreat. Which was no bad thing, when push came to shove. Because he was spending way too much of his day thinking about Claire. Ever since their time in the elevator she hadn't been far from his thoughts. And that was not on.

He knew what he wanted out of life. Uncomplicated friendships with women. A successful career. Travel. Excitement. Freedom.

And the absolute guarantee that he would never again feel as bereft as he'd felt the day his brother died.

So, it was decided, then. No more enjoying himself teasing Claire. Definitely no more checking out her butt or her breasts, or imagining what it would be like to make love to her again, no holds barred, in the privacy of a bedroom. Long and slow, hard and fast and lots of ways in between. And forget trying to make her laugh. No, it was back to basics—work, work and more work. He'd just grit his teeth and get through this stupid alliance Beck had manipulated, and that would be that. From now on, professionalism was the name of the day. Coolheaded professionalism and self-control.

CLAIRE CHECKED her watch and resisted the urge to drum her fingers. Jack was late. Again. It was Thursday, three days since the Flowers Incident. Three days of calm and focus as she got back on track with work and training. Her event times were good, the magazine was coming along nicely and she'd managed to live down the sniggers and gossip generated by Jack's impromptu announcement. She was even coming to terms with the fact that there had been nothing but a very speaking silence from her father. She was in the zone. Cool as a cucumber.

Sure, she hadn't actually come face-to-face with Jack yet. She'd organized this meeting between him and Hank Hillcrest through the nice, safe mechanism of e-mail—but she'd done it. It had only taken her an hour or so to compose a suitably terse, chill note explaining about the store tour that Hank Hillcrest wanted to take them on today. But that was all part of the new attitude—terse and chill. A lean, mean business machine. With a central oasis of cool confidence.

Except now Jack was late, and her confidence and cool were beginning to curl at the edges. If he didn't show a second time, if he left her standing outside the building waiting…she would seriously have to suppress murderous urges if he let her down again.

The low, throaty burble of a sports engine cut across her thoughts and she turned to find Jack cruising to a halt beside her in his red Porsche. Her stomach contracted nervously and she told herself it was because he'd startled her. No other reason.

Don't give him an inch. She had to remember that.

"You're late."

"There was a pileup on the freeway."

She inclined her head minutely to indicate she was willing to accept this.

"We'd better get a move on if we don't want to be late getting out to Hillcrest headquarters," she said, all brisk business.

"Not a problem," he said, leaning across to open his car door.

It took a moment for her to realize that he wanted her to get in.

"I think we should take my car," she said, balking at the idea of being stuck in such close confines with him for the better part of an hour.

"Sure. If that's what you want. Except my car's all ready to go."

She gave him a sharp look. He sounded very... cooperative. Not a characteristic she associated with him at all.

And, of course, now she couldn't insist on taking her car without looking like a royal pain.

Businesslike. Professional. She had to take her personal reactions out of the equation. What would she do if he was any other business colleague?

Damn it. She'd really wanted to have her own car, to feel in control of this outing.

She pulled the car door open a little wider.

"If you're sure you don't mind driving...?" she asked hopefully.

"Not a problem."

She slid into the low bucket seat, dragging her hem over her knees. His aftershave wrapped itself around her and she stiffened, suddenly unbearably aware of everything about him. The crisp curls on the back of his hands. The way his faded jeans hugged his thighs as he changed gears. The faint stubble darkening his cheeks.

"Take the southeastern out of town," she instructed, riveting her gaze on the hood and refusing to acknowledge all the little messages her body was sending her.

He nodded, and a tense silence fell.

She should have insisted on separate cars. Definitely.

IF HE HAD to mouth one more polite, bland, nothing-burger phrase, Jack truly was going to scream. When had small talk become so excruciating? It was like being stuck in a car with a robot. She looked like Claire Marsden, she smelled like Claire Marsden. She had Claire Marsden's softly curling hair and cute turned-up nose. But all other human qualities had been stripped away to leave nothing but a polite business machine.

Which was how he wanted it, of course. It suited his own agenda absolutely. Except...

He couldn't help remembering the sound of her laughter when they'd discussed their favorite movies. Or the soft curve of her mouth just before he kissed her. And the way her eyes dilated with desire when he touched her just so....

Which was truly disturbing, and enough to renew his determination to keep her at arm's length. He didn't want her haunting his dreams. He didn't even know where to begin negotiating a place for her in his world.

"Just turn left here," she said, indicating a street up ahead.

He turned the corner, immediately spotting the enormous Hillcrest building. Easing the car over a speed bump, he slid into a parking spot and pulled on the hand brake. Silence filled the car as he switched the ignition off.

"Any last-minute things I ought to know before we go in?" he asked.

Anything to fill the void.

She was gathering her things, checking her papers in her briefcase.

"I don't think so."

She was cool, dismissive. He matched her.

"Let's go then."

They got out of the car and began walking toward the front entrance of the huge glass-and-steel building. He stood aside to let her precede him into the building, and just for a second he let his eyes drop down to caress her butt as she passed him. He could remember what that butt felt like in his hands, could remember how he'd held her to him and she'd rubbed herself—

He had to remember. Today was about business. Strictly business.

CHAPTER ELEVEN

CLAIRE STARED AT the polished timber tabletop in front of her and tried to stave off the urge to yawn. Boring did not begin to do justice to the tedium of a day spent talking hardware retailing with Hank Hillcrest. And it was still going, even though the store tour was well over. They'd long since returned from admiring paint departments and lumber yards, and for the past hour they'd been ensconced in Hank's private meeting room enjoying what he referred to as a "good old chin wag."

The entire day had been a unique form of torture for her. Despite her determination to ignore Jack and her traitorous body's reaction to him, she'd had to give herself a severe private talking to several times. Once Jack had stepped backward in the warehouse to make way for a forklift, accidentally walking into her. She'd been seriously incapable of coherent thought for a full ten minutes afterward. And then they'd been forced to sit next to each other in the back of a company car while one of the Hillcrest executives drove them to a store so Jack could "get a feel for the business." His thigh had been pressed against hers the entire time, and she'd been unable to stop the thoughts and sensations that had flooded her. Every inch of her body had felt highly sensitized by the time they'd stepped out of car, and when Jack had put his hand on the small of her back to guide her into the store, a rush of damp heat had pooled between her thighs. This, just from a hand on the small of her back! If things kept up like this, she was going to have to carry a spare pair of panties around with her in simple self-defense.

She'd spent the rest of the afternoon going to insane lengths to keep as many people between them as possible.

Giving up on the intricate wood grain of the table's surface, she tuned back into the conversation Jack and Hank were having. Something about advances in electric drill technology. She studied Jack as he talked. She had to hand it to him, he'd been fantastic today. Patient, intelligent, funny. With Hank and his executives, that was. With her, he'd been cool, brisk, businesslike. Exactly what the doctor ordered, of course. Except she couldn't help feeling a bit piqued when she saw him being funny and charming with everyone but her. All she got was dry business chat and polite observations about the weather. Not that it had made any difference to her body's reaction to him, of course, but it added a nice fillip to her humiliation when he didn't spare her so much as a glance while she was turning to goo at the very sight of him.

A sudden stiffening in Jack's posture alerted her

that something was up and she tuned back into the conversation again.

"...was wondering how you found the elephant populations in Kenya when you were on safari? Last time I was over there they were very positive about herd numbers."

She froze. Jack was staring blank-faced at Hillcrest. As well he might, given that she'd failed to fill him in on her cover story for his absence from last week's meeting. Probably because she'd forgotten it herself. Fortunately, Hank Hillcrest hadn't. Lucky her.

A frown wrinkled Hillcrest's formidable forehead as he waited for Jack's response. She felt sweat break out on her own brow. She should say something. Something witty and clever that would save the day. But her mind was a complete blank. And any second now she knew that Jack was going to open his mouth and deny any knowledge of Africa or safaris and she was going to look like the world's biggest liar.

The silence stretched. Jack's eyes flickered across to her, and she tried to signal him with her eyes. Unfortunately, she hadn't quite mastered the art of eyebrow semaphore. He probably thought she was having a facial spasm.

Then he turned back to Hillcrest and smiled. A big, confident, broad smile. "I think they're pretty happy with the herd populations at the moment," he said carefully. His eyes flickered across to her and she nodded encouragingly to show him he was on the right track.

"Claire was telling me that you like to stay with the local tribes rather than in the tourist facilities...?"

She closed her eyes for a brief moment. She'd been under pressure last week, and the most enormous crock of rubbish had come pouring out her mouth. God only knew what gem Hillcrest was going to re-member next.

When she opened her eyes again Jack was giving her a very pointed look.

"Claire told you that, did she?"

She smiled weakly. Jack settled back into his chair, slipping easily into raconteur mode as he began regaling Hillcrest with tales from his African adventures. Such as the time he drank fresh cow's blood with the Masai tribe he was staying with. And how he'd gone on a hunting party looking for a rogue lion that had been attacking the tribe's herds.

She sat on the edge of her seat throughout, barely believing that he was pulling this off, torn between admiration and disgust at what a good liar he was. And terribly, terribly aware that she now owed him. Big-time.

Finally the meeting was over. Now that he and Jack had the whole African continent in common, Hillcrest was filled with bonhomie and he escorted them all the way down to the foyer. A last round of handshakes and back pats for the men, a restrained handshake for her, and then she and Jack were an-gling across the lot toward his car.

There was silence between them for a beat as they

settled into Jack's low-slung Porsche. She held her breath, waiting. Then Jack turned to her.

"Safari? That was the best excuse you could come up with for me not being at a meeting?"

She winced apologetically. "I'm sorry. I'm a terrible liar."

"What was wrong with simple sickness? A nice, normal bout of food poisoning?"

"He was in a bad mood. I kind of got carried away," she admitted.

"Boy, are you lucky I watched *Tarzan* so much as a kid."

And suddenly they were both laughing. All the tension of the meeting poured out of them as they howled for a good five minutes. The car resounded with their wheezy breathing as they both tried to regain control, but she only had to make eye contact with him and she was off again, and the sight of her crumpled face seemed to have the same effect on him.

Finally they managed to calm down.

"Oh, man," he breathed, rubbing his face. "My face hurts."

Still giggling a little, she fumbled in her handbag to find a tissue, and dabbed at her wet cheeks.

"That was almost better than sex," she said without thinking, and Jack shot her a look.

Why did she say that? To *him,* of all people? She gave herself a mental kick. He probably thought she was obsessed with sex. It was too humiliating.

"I mean—I mean, you know, kind of a release," she found herself blathering.

Great. Sooo much better.

She risked a glance across at him and he was watching her broodingly, all trace of laughter gone from his face.

"Last week—" he began, but she rushed to cut him off.

"Is best forgotten, don't you think?"

He was still watching her. Steeling herself, she pretended a calm she didn't feel and met his gaze square on, even managing a little questioning quirk of the eyebrow. She couldn't read his expression, but she got lost in his eyes. They were so blue, the exact, amazing blue of the sky on a perfect summer's day. When he was like this, laughing and open, she forgot all the reasons why she shouldn't like him. She remembered the intimacy of the elevator, and the feel of his arms tight around her as he cried out his pain. And what it was like to have his skin against hers…

Desire blossomed in her belly. She wanted to kiss him again. She didn't care about the flowers, or the regret that had been plaguing her for days. Suddenly she wanted to throw the rule book out the window and wing it.

His eyes dropped down from hers. Was he looking at her lips? Did he want to kiss her as much as she was aching to kiss him? He had to make the first move this time. She'd put herself on the line and been rejected by him too many times before. She held her breath, hoping, waiting.

"You've got some stuff on your cheek," he finally said, gesturing vaguely toward her face.

She blinked, trying to shake off the fog of lust she'd sunk into. "What?"

"On your cheek. Some, you know—stuff. From your nose. From when we were laughing."

She groped in her handbag and found her compact. Flipping it open hastily, she stared at the reflected image of herself, complete with something that was definitely not tears. She wiped it off with a trembling hand, and blew her nose for good measure.

Great.

Another round to Jack Brook.

A WEEK LATER, Jack leaned back in his chair and tried to restrain the impulse to look at his watch. He was tired. His eyes were gritty, his patience was wearing thin, and he was seriously considering punching Morgan Beck in the face. That, or dragging Claire off her prim little ass and having his way with her, damn the consequences.

He'd been stuck in this meeting with Beck and Claire for four hours now as they discussed a last-minute advertising problem with the magazine. It was a common enough occurrence to have advertisers drop out just prior to the cut-off date, but usually the client didn't get involved. Hank Hillcrest was a law unto himself, however. He'd heard about the advertiser's change of heart, and waded in, and now they had offended advertisers on all sides.

And every time they got close to hammering out

a solution, Hillcrest came up with another objection. Jack was beginning to think the first edition of *Welcome Home* would never even get out of the starting gate.

It wasn't so much the frustration and annoyance of dealing with crusty old Hank that was getting to him. Sure, that was irritating, but it didn't crank up his stress levels anywhere near as much as the fact that he was fast developing an obsession with Claire.

It had been a long week since their visit to Hillcrest headquarters. A week of working together, of cozy chats and working lunches and brainstorming as they cobbled together the last few magazine departments before putting the first edition to bed. A week of staring into Claire's wide brown eyes, of laughing at her quick one-liners, of breathing in her spicy-sweet perfume.

What had started out as a sort of reluctant attraction had fast become a raging fascination. She was such an enigma, with her high-necked blouses and her sexy, toned thighs. Not that he got to see anything of the latter, of course. But he could remember them. Oh, how he remembered them....

He'd tried sticking to his game plan of remaining distant and professional. But he couldn't work with someone every day and not warm to her. Or come to like her. Even admire her.

He lifted his attention from the doodles he'd been scrawling across his notepad, his eyes narrowing as he studied Claire. She was discussing something earnestly with Morgan and she leaned forward slightly in her chair, her hands gesticulating fluidly. There was a slight flush on her cheekbones, and a determined glint in her eye. And the way she was sitting made her skirt ride up, just a little. Not enough for his liking, but enough that he was going to embarrass himself if he had to stand in a hurry.

It made him angry and desperate in equal measures that apparently he had no control over himself where she was concerned. He didn't want to want her. Hell, he didn't even want to like her. Life had been far, far easier before he'd been stuck in the elevator with her and seen beneath her defenses.

If only he hadn't kissed her and touched her. Perhaps then it wouldn't be so bad. Because now he knew, and, knowing, he wanted more. He knew he shouldn't, that it was the worst idea in the world—but it didn't stop him wanting.

She glanced up, and caught him staring. For a moment their eyes locked, and he realized that she knew exactly what he was thinking. Well, not exactly, because she probably would have run screaming from the building. But she had some idea that he was thinking about her, and him, with as little clothing between them as possible.

She blushed and looked away. And then looked back at him, as if seeking confirmation of what she'd just seen. There was a question in her eyes, and he was so frustrated and angry and aroused that he didn't bother trying to hide his desire. He was sick of it. He'd had a week of pure torture, sitting opposite her, playing nice, keeping his distance.

They both started as Morgan suddenly stood.

"I've got to call my wife, tell her I'll be late home," he said, heading for the door.

Then they were alone in the big executive board-room. Jack's gaze swung to Claire. She was making notes on her files, apparently engrossed in work. He stared at her, willing her to look up, but she kept her head down.

He returned his attention to his notepad. Probably just as well. Every other time he'd given in to his lust for Claire he'd just wound up in trouble.

CLAIRE STARED AT the incoherent jumble of words she'd written. What was wrong with her? It had taken a single week of Jack's company to reduce her to a gibbering wreck. She couldn't concentrate, her analytical skills were a joke and only by sheer dint of will alone had she managed to sound remotely coherent for the past four hours. If Morgan had any idea of the thoughts that were chasing themselves around her head, she'd be pursuing that career in pornography sooner rather than later.

Given the direction and tone of her thoughts, it was probably just as well. Because she could not stop thinking about sex. More specifically, sex with Jack. She thought about him at home. While she was out running. During gym workouts. And now.

Oh, boy, was she thinking about him right now. About how he'd looked in the shower—before she'd turned the cold water on. About the hard plane of his belly. And the firmness of his muscled, male butt. And the way he—

She gave herself a mental slap. This was ridiculous. She had to stop doing this to herself. Especially at work. At home she'd virtually given up on trying to stop thoughts of Jack creeping into her mind. But at work, it was just wrong to be sitting opposite Morgan and have nothing in her head except visions of herself tearing Jack's clothes off.

Except, of course, Morgan wasn't sitting opposite her. He'd just gone to phone his wife. Which meant she was alone with Jack.

She flickered a look across at him. He was making notes. Of course he was, because he was a professional. While she was sitting here marinating in lust, he was applying his mind to the matter at hand. Damn him.

She'd hoped she'd learned her lesson after that moment in the car. But where Jack was concerned, it appeared she was a glutton for punishment. She simply could not stop herself wanting him.

For a beat she wished she were like Katherine, who seemed to be able to throw herself at a short-term fling, take her passion where she found it and move on unscathed.

But she wasn't. She was Claire Marsden. And, if the past few weeks had taught her anything, they'd taught her that she definitely wasn't Jack's type.

She stood abruptly. Jack lifted his head, and she found herself staring into his mesmerizing blue eyes.

"Coffee," she blurted, which was a miracle, really, because the only words in her mind were "Take me."

"I'll get it," he said, standing in one powerful movement. She tore her eyes away from his thighs.

"It's fine, I'll do it," she insisted, moving toward the coffee station at the far end of the room. Out of the corner of her eye she could see he was walking down his side of the table. They met at the coffee machine.

"Really, I'm happy to get you a coffee," she assured him.

"You made the last one," he insisted.

She reached for the coffee can, but he got there ahead of her. A spark of annoyance burned its way through the lust clouding her brain.

"No one's keeping count," she said, reaching out to take the can from his hands.

He twitched it out of her reach.

"Fine, so I'll make it, then," he returned infuriatingly.

Suddenly she found she was really, really angry. She wanted to rip the coffee can from his hands and then beat him about the head with it.

"Look," she said, trying to sound rational and calm, "just hand over the coffee."

"No."

She glared at him, and he glared back. She felt like a thwarted five-year-old. Before she could stop herself, she lunged forward to try and snatch the coffee from him. He was gripping it with both hands now, holding it tight against his body, and they swayed back and forth for a beat, both clutching at the small silver can.

She could smell his deodorant and aftershave, and his fingers were warm on hers as they both scrabbled for purchase on the coffee can. And then, all of a sudden, her fury twisted inside her and she realized her nipples were hard and that she was so turned on it was a wonder there weren't dogs howling at the moon all over town.

She broke away from Jack, confused, hot for it, panting with desire and the exertion of their tug-of-war. They stared at each other for a beat, Jack's own breathing harsh, his face tense. Then he seemed to make a decision.

"To hell with it," he said suddenly, tossing the coffee can to one side and lunging toward her.

Then he was kissing her, his tongue demanding in her mouth, his hands sliding under her jacket and onto her breasts.

She wanted to touch all of him at once. She returned his kisses greedily, her hands roaming across his back, dipping down to grab his butt, then racing back up again to traverse the width of his shoulders.

This was so good—so much better than her memory of that day at Jack's place, better even than in the elevator since she'd had all this time in between to anticipate his touch. Better even than the many fantasies she'd concocted.

He ducked his head to kiss her neck, working his way down into her cleavage. She writhed with pleasure, then snaked a hand between their bodies, feeling a deep and intense satisfaction as she found the rigid length of him, hard and straining against the faded denim of his jeans.

Jack groaned into her mouth, and suddenly he broke away from her, picking her up and turning to place her on the boardroom table before moving to assume a position between her parted thighs. They stared at each other briefly, panting, hot.

His eyes locked with hers, Jack slid a hand under her skirt, and she bit her lip as his fingers stole up her silk-covered legs. The shock as his hand found her naked thigh made her gasp, and he seemed startled, too, that he was suddenly touching bare skin.

"Garters?" he guessed.

"Stay-ups," she clarified, and Jack pushed her skirt up roughly so that he could see her unencumbered. His breathing quickened as he studied her, legs spread, black stockings in stark contrast to the tanned expanse of her upper thighs.

His eyes glinting dangerously, he ducked his head to her breasts again, suckling at her nipples through the thin silk of her shirt, the hunger in him almost frightening. As her head dropped back helplessly, his hand completed its journey, gliding up her thighs to land unerringly on the part of her that needed him the most.

"Yes," she breathed as he rubbed her already swollen mound through the silk of her panties.

And then he was hooking a finger into the elastic, sliding her panties down over her hips. She felt mindless with need, the thought of being one with him again driving out every other consideration. She reached for the stud on his jeans, but Jack simply shook his head at her. Before she could protest, her panties were off and Jack was ducking down to blaze a trail of kisses across her lower belly. But she was aching for him now. She needed him inside her, and she was struggling to tell him just that when he dropped lower still and silenced her with one lightning sweep of his tongue.

"Oh!" she moaned, reaching for the edge of the boardroom table and hanging on for dear life.

His tongue was hard and hot and firm, and she felt overwhelmed by the spiraling desire that was drawing tighter and tighter inside her. She forgot to breathe as he lapped at her, delicate then rough, slippery and deft as he tongued her clitoris again and again. She could feel the faint friction of Jack's stubbly cheeks against her sensitive inner thighs, and the firm, delicious pressure as he parted her slickness and slid a single finger inside.

"Oh, yes!" she cried, writhing, uncontrolled. She was so close, so close—

Then a faint, foreign sound intruded—a phone ringing in the next room. Vaguely Claire registered the rumble of someone talking on the phone through the wall. And suddenly she recalled exactly where she was, and what she and Jack were doing and just who was likely to walk through the boardroom door any second now.

Was she insane? Had she lost it completely?

She stiffened and Jack's head lifted at the same

time that they both heard the distinct sound of Morgan talking to Jenny just outside the door. Claire's heart leaped into her throat, and she pushed Jack away and slid off the table in one clumsy move. Breathless, disoriented, she tucked her shirt in and pushed her skirt down. The feel of the silk lining of her skirt against her bare butt reminded her that her panties were lying around here somewhere, and she spotted them on the floor at the same time that the door began to swing open. Jack had been busying himself with buttoning his own buttons and tucking his shirt in, but he spotted her panties at exactly the same moment and suddenly lunged forward.

Claire held her breath as he scooped up the offending triangle of black silk and stuffed it into his jeans pocket just as Morgan stepped into the room, his attention still on Jenny, unseen outside the room.

"...that should be fine. Make the booking for eleven," he was saying.

Her heart pounding, Claire ran a shaky hand through her hair and shot a look at Jack. To her horror, she saw he had her lipstick smeared across his face, and she gestured urgently for him to wipe it off. He, in turn, gestured for her to pull her jacket closed, and she looked down to see twin wet patches on her shirt where he had been sucking her nipples through the silk.

Fingers fumbling, she tugged her jacket closed just as Morgan turned to face them properly. Attempting to be casual, Claire smiled brightly. Out of the corner of her eye, she could see Jack doing

the same. There was a fraught, stretched moment as
Morgan stared from one of them to the other. Then
he frowned.

"Is everything okay in here?" he asked.

Claire didn't dare look at Jack.

"Sure. Absolutely. We were just having a coffee
break," she said, only then realizing that the coffee
can she and Jack had been arguing over was lying
abandoned on the carpet in front of them. All three
of them stared at the can, then Jack laughed.

"To be honest, Claire and I were having a bit of
a wrangle over whose turn it was to make the coffee," he said lightly.

The frown creasing Morgan's forehead deepened,
but he turned back to the other end of the table.

"I see. Perhaps we should finalize these last matters and call it a night."

Claire forced herself to walk back to her place at
the table, horribly aware of how hot and flustered
she felt and no doubt looked. If that phone hadn't
rung in the next room... She felt sick to her stomach as she listened to Morgan drone on for the next
five minutes. Jack was very quiet, also, and eventually it became clear that nothing of great value was
going to be achieved this evening.

Shooting each of them an exasperated look, Morgan slotted his expensive pen back into his expensive
folder and closed it decisively.

"Well, I have to say I'm very disappointed," he
said heavily.

Claire twitched. Out of the corner of her eye she saw Jack stiffen.

"The Hillcrest account is very important to our client-based magazine division. I had hoped that I would have the undivided attention of two of my top editors on this project."

He looked from one to the other, and Claire just resisted the urge to toe the carpet and hang her head.

"Was I wrong in thinking you were the right people for the job?"

"No, Mr. Beck," she said.

"No, Morgan," Jack said.

Morgan eyed them both for another beat or two.

"Well, perhaps we should call it a night."

Claire nodded her acceptance of his decision, and concentrated on shuffling her papers into her briefcase. Issuing them both a curt good-night, Morgan exited. Silence stretched as Claire finished sorting out her briefcase. Then she cleared her throat.

"Could I have my panties, please?" she asked tightly.

She couldn't look at him, but out of the corner of her eye she saw Jack tug her panties from his pocket. He slid them across the table to her, and she scrunched them into a ball and stuffed them into her briefcase.

Then, horribly aware of the cool breeze on her bare derriere, she headed for the door. She couldn't bear the thought of waiting for the elevator, so she bolted for the stairwell. Once the plush-carpeted halls of the thirtieth floor were behind her, she let

out a strangled moan of despair, the sound of it echo-
ing up and down the stairs. When was she going to
learn to stay away from Jack Brook?

CHAPTER TWELVE

THE NEXT DAY was a Friday, and the triathlon final. Claire awoke with a single image burned into her mind's eye: her, sprawled across the Beck and Wise boardroom table, Jack Brook between her thighs, her self-respect and dignity nowhere to be seen.

It was enough to make a girl dye her hair, change her name and emigrate. How was she ever going to look Jack in the eye again? And as for Morgan Beck... Lord knows what he thought had been going on. Something, obviously, hence his little lecture.

Although, really, she should thank her lucky stars that he'd come back when he had. Anything could have happened. Another few minutes, and she and Jack would have been on the floor, oblivious to anything and everything.

Deep down inside, a tiny, forbidden, depraved part of her wished that they'd had those few extra minutes. She'd been craving Jack's hands on her body for days. Was it wrong that she couldn't find it in herself to truly regret what had happened, no matter how humiliating the circumstances?

She rolled over and buried her face in her pillow. She couldn't think about any of this now. She was supposed to be building herself up for the challenge of the race, not reliving each second of her humiliation in psychological Technicolor.

She rolled out of bed and trotted into the bathroom, amusing herself by mentally reviewing her résumé. She could resign by e-mail and never actually have to see Jack Brook or Morgan Beck ever again. Tom could clear out her desk. For five blissful milliseconds, it felt like an option. Then she passed by the answering machine and her eye was caught by the blinking light. She'd been so overwhelmed with shame last night that she hadn't noticed she'd missed a call. She backtracked to press the play button, then froze as an awful thought occurred. *Please don't let it be Beck. Or Jack. Or Katherine. Definitely not Katherine—she'd be able to tell what happened in the boardroom just from the sound of my voice.*

"Claire, it's Harry. I just wanted to let you know it looks like I will be in town for the final tomorrow. I'm assuming you'll have an early start, so I'll make contact with you at the race."

She stared at the machine, all thoughts of Jack and finding another job pushed to one side. Her father was coming. She'd given up on him, really she had. But he was coming, he was coming to watch her race.

Almost two weeks of silence, and now this!

A little flare of hope sprang to life inside her, and she immediately told herself not to be naive. This was her father, after all. Even if he was coming, it didn't necessarily mean anything. She shouldn't get her hopes up.

But would it be completely self-delusional to think this might be a step in the right direction? That she'd told him how she felt, and he'd been moved to take action after her outburst?

As she turned on the shower, she told herself to stop speculating. But it was no use. She'd been worrying about this for too long to set it to one side. She dressed quickly in her competition swimsuit, smoothing suntan lotion into her arms and legs, and putting sunblock on her nose. And all the while her mind was working overtime, hoping that this contact from Harry might signal a change for the good.

She grabbed up her backpack, water bottles and bike helmet and headed out the door, aware that there was a new thread of excitement burbling through her veins, not just the usual prerace jitters or the normal adrenaline buzz that came from anticipating competition.

She realized that she really wanted to win this race.

Of course, she really wanted to win every race—that was the point of competing, right? But this race…she really, really wanted to win this race.

She paused on the next to last step down into the underground garage.

Because of her father?

An image of herself streaking across the finish line, her father watching, flashed into her mind. Yes, because of her father. Because she wanted to prove to him that he'd been wrong about her, to show him that she was a success in her own right and that his approval didn't matter to her at all.

She'd put the bike rack on last night, and her competition bike was already suspended above the tailgate. She threw her helmet and other gear onto the passenger seat, and swung herself into the car.

Her father was coming, and she wanted to win for him. She wanted him to see her win, more correctly.

And she wanted to pretend that she'd never kissed Jack, that they hadn't almost been busted by her boss and that she didn't remember every second of their encounter in the finest detail.

Great mindset to take into a race you've been aiming for all year. Just great.

JACK SPENT A sleepless night going over and over those few heady moments when he'd had Claire in his arms. And his mouth. Those black thigh-high stockings—he'd almost exploded when he saw them. And the way she'd given herself over to the moment. The noise she made as he touched her—that, alone, was enough to make him hard.

Of course, he quickly realized that that way lay torture, and a long, long cold shower later he was finally able to drop off to sleep.

She took over his dreams, too, however. But his subconscious surprised him—his dream wasn't hot and heavy. Instead, he kept seeing the embarrassed color in her cheeks as she made her hasty exit from the boardroom. In his dream he followed her, making her stop and listen to him as he explained—

He awoke with the alarm sounding in his ear and the sense that he'd just missed out on learning something profound.

Maybe it was the dream that made him detour via her office on the way into his own the next morning. He told himself he simply wanted to offer her the sense of solidarity—after all, it had taken two to tango. Or whatever dance it was they'd been considering before Morgan so rudely interrupted them. The S.O.B.

To his surprise, she wasn't there. He didn't examine the surge of disappointment in his gut too closely—that was what his subconscious and those dreams were for, after all. Instead, he stood staring at her empty chair, aware of all the noise and bustle of a normal business day going on behind him. Maybe he should wait for her....

"Can I help you?"

He spun around to find a small, nervous-looking young guy staring at him. The stare was a tad belligerent, and he realized he was standing fully inside Claire's unattended office, hovering over her paper-strewn desk. Bad office etiquette.

Smiling engagingly, he took a step forward until he could lean against the door frame, and some of the alertness in the other guy's face eased.

Territorial little devil.

"Yeah, I'm looking for Claire," he said.

Intense brown eyes flickered up and down his body. "I see." His tone implied that he didn't like what he saw.

Jack gave the little guy back some of his own attitude. "You want to tell me where she's at?"

"I'm not sure I should."

Jack blinked with surprise. "Unless Claire's on a mission for the FBI, I think I'm a pretty low security risk."

To his further surprise, Mr. Intense suddenly moved forward, ushering him back into Claire's office and shutting the door.

Jack frowned. Who was this guy? Surely not Claire's *boyfriend*?

"I just think you should know that I know about your reputation. Everyone does."

Jack stared at the earnest young man quivering in front of him. "Yeah? And what's it to you?"

"Claire's a really nice person. One of the best."

Okay, not a boyfriend. Anyone who'd spent any time with Claire would not describe her as *nice*. Hot, maybe. Damn sexy. But not nice—nice was for hand-knit socks Granny made for you at Christmas.

"And?"

"And she doesn't deserve to be chewed up and spat out by a guy like you."

He actually blinked with surprise. For a brief second he considered grabbing the little guy by the ankles and hanging him upside down out of a window for a while. Then he remembered the feeling he'd had in his chest when he'd woken from that dream this morning.

It was kind of nice that Claire had people looking out for her.

"We're working together. End of story, okay, pal?" he found himself saying.

There was a tense moment as the little guy seemed to consider this. Then he said, "She's competing today." He opened the door, moving toward the desk stationed outside Claire's office.

Suddenly Jack twigged—Claire had a male assistant. He tried not to smile—*of course* she had a male assistant!

A male assistant who'd gone to the trouble of having his name engraved on a little plate to sit on his desk.

"Listen, um, Tom, you want to help me out here? Where exactly is Claire competing? Some magazine thing somewhere? What?"

Tom threw him a you're-weird look.

"No. Why would she be doing that? She's got the semifinal for her triathlon. They had to make it a Friday because it's impossible to shut the beach down on a weekend. If Claire places in this, she gets into the national final and has a chance to go to Hawaii for the Pros," Tom said proudly.

He just stared. Triathlon? Claire was a triathlete?

"This is at St. Kilda beach?"

Tom nodded as though he was dealing with an idiot. Which was quite possible, Jack reflected.

"That's right, near the pier."

"Thanks."

Jack headed for the elevators, completely preoccupied. How had this not come up in all their time in the elevator or all the time they'd spent working together over the past two weeks? It explained why Claire looked nothing short of sensational in her underwear, of course, but it didn't explain why they hadn't discussed what was apparently a major part of her life.

He pulled his cell phone out of his back pocket as he headed toward the car park.

"Linda? Hey, it's me. What have I got on today?"

"No appointments until three, and that's just my yearly review."

"Cool. I'm out of the office for the day, then. By the way, did you know Claire Marsden is a triathlete? Am I the only person in the office who didn't know this?"

Linda's sharp intake of breath gave away her annoyance, and he braced himself for a lecture.

"We'll do your review on Monday, I promise," he offered, trying to head her off at the pass.

"Forget the review, Jack. Just be kind to Claire, okay? She's a really sweet girl, you remember that."

He stared at his handset for a moment. Okay, this was getting ridiculous. Did he have a biohazard warning label painted on his back or something?

"What's this all about?" he asked, annoyed.

"Look, I know you, Jack. Claire's a really nice person."

Again with the nice. He felt his frown deepen.

"That's the second time someone's said that to me today. Am I not a nice person, is that it? And what exactly do you imagine I'm going to do to Claire, anyway, Linda?"

"Don't go getting all snippy on me. It's not that you're a bad person, Jack. It's just you're a… Well, you treat women like they're disposable napkins. One use and they're gone. I've seen you work your way through the office, and that's totally your business, but I get the feeling Claire isn't the kind of woman you do that with."

"Do what with?" he found himself asking, his back well and truly up.

"Take what you want and to hell with the consequences. Now, I'm only telling you this because you have to realize that when you go to work on a woman, you're pretty much irresistible. You know this, Jack, so get that sulky look off your face."

He shook his head over his assistant's uncanny abilities: he had been looking and feeling like a spoiled schoolboy.

"I just want you to think about tomorrow with Claire, that's all. Don't forget how she's going to feel when you're not there whispering sweet nothings in her ear anymore," Linda concluded.

"What about how I'm going to feel? Does anyone ever consider that?" He threw the words back at her.

"Well, if you'd ever let anyone close enough to find out, I'm sure they would," Linda said primly before ending the call.

He stared at his handset before slipping it back into his pocket.

Great, now he was copping lectures from his assistant-cum-second-mother. It seemed the whole office viewed him as some sort of female-targeted

Terminator, his only mission being to seek out women and destroy their emotional lives.

And it wasn't as though he had any designs on Claire, anyway. If you didn't count the near miss in the boardroom last night.

He simply was going to pop down to the shore, see if he could catch some of her race. If he bumped into her, he'd wish her luck. End of story, end of drama.

He could just imagine Linda's face if he'd told her his plans: big-time disapproval.

He shook his head. Hell, he was going to watch a stupid race for a few minutes, that was all. Claire was as safe as houses, and his secretary and the rest of the world could just keep their pants on.

THE SHORE WAS packed with bodies, and he had to shoulder his way through the crowd to gain a spot with a decent vantage point. He'd come just in time to catch the bulk of the male triathletes wading out of the water and racing toward their individual stations to towel off and shove on their running shoes.

He was contemplating what a crazy, rigorous, exhausting sport this was when an added roar from the crowd alerted him to the fact that the first of the female competitors had finished the swim leg and were landing on the beach. Two women he didn't recognize surged out of the water and leaped over the last shallow waves and onto the sand. Then he saw Claire, her face intent as she followed in their wake.

His spontaneous whoop of encouragement took even himself by surprise, as did the flash of pride he felt. She looked amazing, her tanned body taut and strong as she raced up the beach toward her station. Even at this distance he could see the water dripping down her body, and he watched intently as she carefully dried her feet before tying her track shoes on. She looked up once, scanning the crowd. He waved, wanting to let her know he was there, then felt a twinge of disappointment when she didn't spot him.

Then she was off, her body falling into what was obviously a familiar rhythm as she hit the running leg of the race. He craned his neck and body to watch her for as long as he could.

The rest of the crowd pushed around him. He realized he was grinning like an idiot, and he sobered for a moment. Maybe Linda was right, maybe he should just go back to work.

But somehow he found himself working his way through the crowd, trying to locate someone official-looking who could tell him where the race would end.

CLAIRE KEPT HER head down and her mind on nothing but breathing and the fact that the bike leg was just minutes off. She'd managed to maintain her position in the field, and she was confident she could hold her own on the bike. She couldn't stop herself from glancing at the faces alongside the route as she ran, always searching for her father. It was ridiculous to expect to spot him, and just as ridiculous to feel disappointed that she couldn't find him. She'd hoped to see him before the race, had kept an eye out even as she set up her station and limbered up for the swim, but he hadn't come to find her.

The feel of concrete beneath her feet gave way to grass as she ran between the barriers and funneled down toward her station. She pulled her bike away from its stand, then stuffed her feet into her locking pedals. She glanced just once along the rows of faces lined up behind the fences before she took off. Impossible to know if Harry was there or not....

The secret to the bike leg for her was to always take the hills hard. A lot of other competitors conserved their energy on the hills, but she knew she had the stamina to grab a lead there and hold it. She might not be tall like some of the other women competitors, but she had strength and determination on her side, and if she could grab herself an advantage on the hills, she'd go for it. For a moment, she allowed herself to imagine winning. She wanted it so badly, but she found it disturbing that when she pictured herself racing across the finish line, it was her father she imagined coming forward to congratulate her, not some faceless official.

JACK STOOD ON his tiptoes to try and get a better view, apologizing yet again for jostling the backpack of the young blonde standing on his left. She gave him a smile, then looked away flirtatiously, and he recognized that she was giving him all the right signals. He also recognized that he couldn't be less interested. She was attractive—all right, very attractive—in her brightly colored bikini top and short-shorts, but for the life of him he couldn't scrape up anything bar a sort of general approval of her appearance. She was hot, but he was not. Not for her, anyway. Now if it were Claire standing next to him...

This disturbing thought was swept to one side as he spotted the lead cyclist coming around the corner. He'd already memorized Claire's number—twenty-three—and he saw with disappointment that it wasn't her. But the second cyclist wasn't far behind, and he saw Claire's lime-green cycle helmet with a thrill of excitement.

Hell, she could win this thing! He found himself yelling out her name as she bent low over the handlebars of her bike, his own legs unconsciously tensing, his own breath coming faster as he willed her forward.

"Come on, come on! You can do it, baby!" he hollered, punching the air with his fist.

They were in the home stretch now, and Claire was nipping at the other woman's heels, each powerful stroke of her thighs pulling her closer and closer to the lead.

God, he wanted her to win. He felt all her anxiety and desire and drive, and he wanted her to have this moment.

"Come on!" he yelled, vaguely aware that the blonde was covering her ears now.

Only half a bike length between them now. Both women were out of their saddles, leaning hard over their handlebars as they sprinted toward the finish line. He could see the look of anguished effort on Claire's face, and he held his breath.

Could she do it?

With a surge of power, Claire shot into the lead, racing over the finish line a full bike length ahead of the other competitor. He whooped with joy, standing on several people's toes behind him, smiling and apologizing even as he began elbowing his way to the finishing line.

It took him about ten minutes to get there, but he was still smiling like a crazy man, reliving the moment again and again. She'd won! What an effort! She was amazing, really amazing.

He could see Claire stretching out her calves as one of the officials spoke to her. She looked oddly flat as she nodded, obviously responding to the man's questions, her eyes constantly scanning the crowd.

He gave little thought to anything except congratulating her, but a potbellied man laid a hand on his chest as he moved to duck under the barrier separating the crowd from the finishing area.

"Sorry, buddy, officials and support crew only through here," he said.

He frowned, unprepared to accept this when Claire was just a few steps away. He wanted to see her.

"I'm support crew. I'm with number twenty-three, Claire Marsden," he said.

Mr. Potbelly looked him up and down, obviously skeptical. Jack adopted his best man-to-man tone.

"Look, I'm actually her boyfriend, and she's not

expecting me to be in town—I got held up at a conference," he lied.

Mr. Potbelly seemed to have a core of pure schmaltz because he bought it and Jack found himself being eased through a gap in the barriers and patted on the shoulder.

Claire's back was to him, and without thinking he stepped forward and scooped her up in his arms, spinning her around with a whoop.

"You were fantastic! That was completely amazing!" he told her, looking down into her surprised face.

The surprise didn't last for long, however. A moment of brief, gratifying illumination as she recognized him, and then she stiffened and pushed away from him.

"Jack. What are you doing here?" she asked, and he noticed that her eyes slid off him almost instantly, returning to their constant scanning of the crowd.

Suddenly he was hit by a bolt from the blue—she was expecting someone else.

He felt as if he'd been poleaxed. Why hadn't he thought of that before? Why had he always assumed that Claire was single? He felt like the arrogant fool she was always accusing him of being. Why had he just assumed that she was his for the taking—if he chose to take her?

"I was just…kind of in the area," he heard himself say.

Wow, really snappy. And *soooo* convincing. He tried again:

"I actually wanted to apologize. For yesterday. With Beck. I figure that was kind of my fault...." he finished lamely.

He had her full attention now.

"You're sorry about what happened?" she asked, and he felt as though a lot hung in the balance.

"Of course I am," he said.

Her gaze was oddly intent, and he found himself wishing for the first time in his life that he could read another person's mind. What was she thinking?

"Ms. Marsden?"

They both turned to face the race official approaching behind them.

"This was delivered to our office earlier. I'm afraid we didn't get a chance to get it to you before the race," he said.

Claire accepted the folded note with a faint smile and an assurance that all was okay. Jack watched her face closely as she flipped the note open and read it quickly.

He almost missed the faint tightening of her mouth, the quick swallow in her throat. She blinked quickly a few times, and then she smiled brightly at him.

"Well, thanks for coming down. I really have to get to the showers. I guess...I guess I'll see you at work next week," she said, nothing in her demeanor indicating that something important had just happened.

But he knew it had. He could feel the hurt in her,

and he found himself in the unusual position of wanting to help.

"Claire—" He tried to speak, but she was already moving away.

The truth was, he had no idea what to say. Normally, he was the one trying to ease his way out of these kinds of conversations, and he was far more skilled at avoiding talking about feelings and whatnot than he was at inviting confidences.

So he let her walk away and just stood there feeling like a big dummy.

CHAPTER THIRTEEN

HOPE SPRINGS ETERNAL. It was a phrase that might have been coined to describe Claire's relationship with her absentee father. When was she going to learn that she didn't need him, and that what he thought, or felt, didn't matter?

Claire closed her eyes and lifted her face so that the spray from the shower hit her full-on, enduring the sting from the little needles of water because it felt better than giving in to the urge to cry.

"Yo, Claire, congratulations!" one of the other competitors yelled out to her as she passed the communal shower. Claire forced a smile and responded to the rest of the lighthearted ribbing.

She'd qualified for the Hawaii Pro Series now, and she could feel the envy of some of the other women as she toweled off and they discussed the field of likely competitors.

Truth was, at this moment, she wondered if she'd miss it if she never competed again.

She was aware that a dark cloud of disappointment had settled over her with the delivery of her father's belated note of apology, and she knew she was hardly reacting the way she should be. She'd trained so hard for this win. She'd run her best time, and equaled her best bike leg to date. She should be popping champagne and screaming the rafters down with joy. Instead, she was busy manufacturing a party she was attending with friends as an excuse to avoid celebrating with the other competitors.

Yet another disappointment awaited her when she opened her backpack—she'd been so distracted this morning that she'd failed to pack a full change of clothing for after the race, and she sat staring at the lone T-shirt and bra in her kit bag.

"Damn it," she said under her breath, about to reach for her damp swimming bottoms. She'd have to wear the T-shirt home with the towel around her waist....

"What's up, Claire?"

It was Sally, one of the women who she trained with occasionally.

"Just me being stupid. Forgot to pack a change of clothes." She shrugged.

Sally's face cleared.

"Easily fixed. Here, have this," Sally offered, tossing a black bundle toward her. "Give it back to me next week at the gym."

Claire smiled her gratitude, and even managed to keep the smile on her lips as she unrolled the bundle and revealed a halter-neck black cheesecloth sundress, all low back and short-looking flouncy skirt. It was a no-bra kind of a dress, the kind she never, ever wore.

"It'll look great on you, with your dark hair," Sally enthused.

Claire shrugged—she was only going home, after all. She tugged the dress on over her head and let her towel drop. Thankfully it fell to just above her knees, and made her feel less decadent when she decided to forgo the torture of rolling on her wet swimsuit bottoms. Who would ever know, after all? Of course, if she got caught over one of those subway vents à la Ms. Monroe… Or if she got hit by a car… Claire shook off her anxieties, almost laughing at herself. Given that she'd sat through part of an executive meeting sans underpants just yesterday, she could survive a trip home, no problems.

"Sall, you're a lifesaver," she thanked her friend, shoving the rest of her gear into her backpack and padding out into the beach club. She had to make her way through a crowd of folk intent on congratulating her and inviting her to various parties as she headed outside to where her bike was waiting, but she managed to keep smiling as she made her by now well-rehearsed excuse about "another party."

She'd just shaken off the last of her well-wishers when she spotted Jack lounging by her bike. Her step faltered. What was he still doing here? Suddenly she was acutely conscious of the air circulating unhindered around her nethers, and she felt her knees clench together as if they could somehow hold that flimsy, flirty skirt down if a chance wind happened along. The thought of just such a wind had her looking around nervously as she crossed the distance between them.

"Jack."

"Claire."

His response mocked her, but his eyes were serious.

"Did you forget something?" she asked, genuinely confused.

"Yeah. I forgot to ask what was wrong. Back there, when you got that note, something happened. So…here I am."

He said it as though he'd memorized it or rehearsed it a few times. She stared at him, baffled.

"Jack, are you feeling okay?" she asked.

He looked determined.

"I'm fine. But you're not. Let's talk about it."

She couldn't help herself. He sounded so earnest and looked so tortured that the smile was curving her lips before she could stop it.

"What's so funny?"

She shook her head, trying to control her unruly mouth.

"Nothing. You just sounded very…Oprah. Or like one of those self-help books. 'I'm okay, you're okay.' You know."

He looked exasperated. "Give me a break here, this is new territory for me."

She narrowed her eyes at him, wondering. What exactly was going on? And then she realized. He felt sorry for her! Steel stiffened her spine and she found herself talking coolly. "Well, you don't need to worry yourself over me. I'm just fine, thanks."

She concentrated on unlocking her bike and adding her repair kit and water bottles to her backpack.

"Could have fooled me."

"I wish I *had* fooled you," she shot back, and she looked up to find a triumphant smile on his face. She rolled her eyes, aware that she'd responded to his baiting like a laboratory rat at the feeder bar.

"Look. I appreciate the gesture. Let's just leave it at that, okay?"

She shrugged her pack onto one shoulder and began wheeling her bike toward the parking lot, hoping he would take the not-so-subtle hint and let her go. Of course, she should have known better. She glanced at him out of the corner of her eye as he kept pace with her. The man had the hide of a rhino.

"So, you're in the finals now?" he ventured after they'd been dodging through people for a few minutes.

"Yep." She wasn't going to encourage him. For starters, she was somewhat lacking in the underwear department, and when Jack Brook was around, she figured she needed all the protection she could get from her own baser instincts. Last time she'd been pantyless with this man, she'd lost all self-respect and self-control.

"Pretty cool. Big party tonight? Guess you triathlete guys must all hang together?"

"There are a few parties on," she replied evasively,

aware that she wasn't the best liar in the world where Jack was concerned.

But, as usual, he managed to hone in on her weakness.

"And you're going to one?" he pushed.

She resisted the urge to sigh out her frustration.

"I have other plans," she prevaricated.

They'd reached her car now, and she started to bend down to fix her pedals for the drive home, remembering in the nick of time that she should probably crouch—very carefully—rather than tempt fate. Knees clenched together, she did just that, concentrating on pinning her pedals into a stationary position.

"Do those other plans involve anyone else? Like a boyfriend, for example?"

She looked up at him, confused again about why he was here. "I'm not seeing anyone at the moment," she admitted grudgingly.

He looked smug. The bastard.

"So you're just going home to mope?" Jack asked shrewdly.

She shot to her feet.

"Do I look like a moper?" she asked him defiantly, hands on hips.

She was aware of his gaze flickering up and down her body, and she fought the desire to cross her arms over her braless chest.

"Frankly—yes. You look like you just want to go home and crawl under a rock," he said brutally.

She gasped, staring at him openmouthed for a

moment. How did he know? How on earth could he know that was exactly how she felt?

"Takes one to know one," he answered her unspoken question.

"Well, then, from one moper to another, how about a little respect?" she suggested. "How about you let me get on with it."

Jack looked as though he might be considering her suggestion, but then he shook his head.

"Can't do that. Look where my moping got me." He reached out and touched the faded bruise that still marked her cheek. "Or, more correctly, look where it got us. So, no moping."

"Fine. I promise to go home and dance a jig and giggle myself silly. Happy?" she demanded, beginning to feel well and truly cornered.

"Or…you could let me take you out to celebrate. Hell, you just won the state final. One of the guys at the beach club said you almost equaled the record for the running leg. I say that deserves a little champagne, an expensive dinner and a lot of attention."

It was so close to what she'd imagined doing with her father that she had to duck her head to hide the ridiculous tears in her eyes. A strong hand grasped her chin and tipped her face up. She found herself staring into Jack's very blue eyes.

"You don't want to talk, fine. I'm the master of not talking, remember? But at least let me treat you to a nice meal."

She stalled for time, finding his eyes very compelling, aware that her body was clamoring once more for his touch and that that was a very bad and dangerous thing.

"Not a fancy restaurant. Just something nearby," she negotiated.

"Your choice, absolutely."

"And then you let me go home, no questions asked."

He shrugged, oozing confidence now. "Sure. If that's what you want."

His tone suggested she might feel otherwise, and she shot him a wary look. What was really going on here? Was Jack laying a line on her? He stared back at her, apparently guileless.

"I need to take my bike home," she added, hoping that all of her conditions would wear out his good intentions.

"Fine. I'll follow you home."

No such luck.

CHAPTER FOURTEEN

CLAIRE KEPT ONE eye on his red monstrosity in her rearview mirror all the way back to her apartment. It lurked behind her, stalking her through every turn and traffic light. Just like its owner. Why on earth had she agreed to have dinner with Jack?

It was an unanswerable question, but all of her speculation made her nervous and she could barely meet his eyes when she approached him in front of her place.

"I'll just duck in and change. I'll be down in a tick," she said lightly, already turning toward the entrance.

His hand on her arm stopped her.

"Don't. You look fine—great—like that," he said.

She smiled weakly, her mind fixated on the contents of her underwear drawer.

"But I'm not dressed for—" she began to say, but strong hands were on her shoulders, turning her toward his car.

"Relax. We'll go to this place I know near the river—lots of patio space and a great view. You'll fit right in."

It was on the tip of her tongue to ask if all the

other patrons would be sans underwear, too, but instead she just ducked her head and slid into the all-encompassing embrace of his leather upholstered seats.

"I know the owner of this place," Jack enthused as he started the engine. Its low, subterranean hum reverberated throughout the car.

She was aware of his gaze flickering across to her before he pulled out from the curb, and she made a futile attempt to tug the dress hem closer to her knees. Pointless. Sally was a party girl, and this was a party dress.

"They just started up about six months ago, so I try to go there as often as possible. Figure if I'm giving my money to anyone, it might as well be to friends."

He grinned across at her, and she found herself smiling back.

That was a nice thing to do, helping friends out with their fledgling business.

She sat up straighter, giving herself a mental slap about the head. She had to be on her guard tonight. She already knew that she was attracted to Jack. The last thing she wanted was for him to realize that. She could just imagine his amusement if he knew that his pity-assignment was lusting after him this very minute. No, she had to be on the alert. Keep her guard up. One glass of wine, no dessert, straight home. Absolutely.

"MORE CHAMPAGNE?" Jack asked, and Claire found herself nodding blithely, watching the straw-colored fluid rise up toward the top of her tall glass.

A warm haze had settled over her, the result of fantastic food, Jack's witty conversation and two—no, three, counting this one—glasses of champagne. Real French champagne, too, full of yeasty bubbles that tickled her nose.

"This is so nice," she said, raising her glass to her lips.

"Come on, you said you were going to eat half of this," Jack prompted, and she stared at the spoonful of sticky date pudding he was holding under her nose.

"I don't—" she started to stay, but he leaned forward and the spoon with its delicious mouthful was on her lips. Unthinking, she opened her mouth to accept his offering, and she caught a glint of something in his eyes.

Triumph? It confused her, and she snatched up her own spoon when Jack indicated he was ready with another mouthful for her.

"So…the Pro Series. How long have you got to train?" he asked idly, chasing the melting ice cream across the plate with his spoon now.

She answered without thinking.

"Might not go. Who knows?"

He looked startled, and she had to think back over the past few minutes to remember what she'd said.

"Really? You'd just call it quits?"

She shrugged, searching for a way to end this conversational tangent but knowing he was tenacious when he thought she was lying.

"Maybe I got what I wanted out of it," she said, concentrating on scooping up another mouthful of pudding.

He made a grunting noise of disbelief, and she glared at him. Reaching for her champagne glass, she took a big swig before speaking again.

After all, why not? Why not reveal all her petty inadequacies to this man? He'd already seen her passed out from fear, so it couldn't get much worse.

"Maybe I just realized I've been doing it for all the wrong reasons."

She could feel his attention focusing fully on her, and it made her tremble with awareness. What must it be like to have all of that blue-eyed intentness beside you in bed, no interruptions, no hesitations? To have him thinking of nothing but you and him together?

She shoved her champagne glass away from her. Boy, was she a two-glass screamer or what.

"What are the wrong reasons, Claire?" he asked.

She reminded herself that she'd started this. "That note earlier. It was from Harry. I mean, my dad. He phoned yesterday, left a message that he was going to be here for the finals. We had a…discussion, I guess you could call it, a few weeks ago. I told him I wasn't going to be the only one doing any work to stay in contact from now on."

"But he didn't turn up?" Jack prompted.

"No. And the whole race, I was looking for him

in the crowd, wondering where he was. I had it all worked out beforehand, too. I was going to win and show him that I was a success, that he'd missed out by not being around. But you know what? When he didn't turn up, I realized it was really all about wanting him to be proud of me, not about me sticking it to him. I have told myself over and over again that it doesn't matter what he thinks or does, but here I am. Ridiculous, huh?"

She couldn't look up. It sounded so small and sad saying it out loud.

"Everyone wants their parents to be proud of them. It must be tough having a father who's not involved. I can't even imagine it."

"But I thought I'd beaten this. When I hadn't heard from him after my little outburst, I thought that was it. That we'd both just do our own things, that any pretence was over and done with. And then he goes and does this, and I jump at the chance to prove I'm worthy of the great explorer. 'Hey, Dad, look at me! Just because I can't climb a mountain doesn't mean I'm useless.' All these years of training—just so I can prove I'm good enough for him, force him to be proud of me."

"What was his excuse?"

"Oh, some sponsorship opportunity or something. It doesn't matter. Harry is a closed book. I should never have tried to open him. He's been seized shut ever since my mom died."

She shook herself suddenly and sat up straighter.

"Well, that's enough navel gazing from me. Next

you'll have me confessing I never had a date for the
school dance," she joked, aware that she'd just revealed a great deal about herself.

Jack half smiled, but she had a feeling he wasn't
ready to let her off the hook yet. She was right.

"You think you won only because you thought
your dad was there, don't you?" he asked.

That made her look up, straight into his eyes. How
did he know this stuff?

"It's obvious, isn't it? All this training. Pretty
much everything I do at Beck and Wise—it's all
because I want him to sit up and take notice of me."

There, it was out. She reached for her champagne
glass, but Jack was there ahead of her and he slid it
out of her reach. She glared at him, but he just shook
his head.

"Let's go crazy and have a discussion where both
of us are in our right minds," he said, his smile self-
deprecating.

"Maybe I don't want to be," she mumbled, acutely
aware of how exposed she was feeling right now.

"Reckless talk," he said lightly.

"Sure. I mean, why not? All my life I've done
the right thing, toed the line, took what was offered.
I've flossed and eaten oat bran and stayed within
the speed limit. And where has it got me? When we
were in the elevator, you said I was uptight. At the
time, I wanted to mess you up, bad. But you're right.
I am uptight. I'm so worried about what other people think—what my dad will think—that I don't do
anything unless I'm sure it's safe."

She stopped, aware that she had just spewed her innermost thoughts onto the table in front of a man who probably was wishing a trap door would appear at his feet and save him. Then she realized that she was doing what she always did—worrying about what other people thought, allowing herself to be paralyzed by it.

"Are we remembering the same elevator? The one where we jumped each other like crazy people? Doesn't sound like someone who's uptight or plays it safe to me," Jack said.

Claire blushed, mortified that he'd brought up their encounter in the elevator just when she thought they'd both agreed to pretend it had never happened.

"That was different," she mumbled, eyeing her champagne flute with longing. If she had to be embarrassed, she could at least be drunk.

"You're the sort of person who's always going to strive to achieve, no matter what anyone else thinks or wants," Jack continued. "It's in your nature. That's why you're about to start up a brand-new magazine. That's why people respect you. That's why you won today."

She shook her head, intent on exposing all her dark places tonight, for good or bad. He'd said it earlier: reckless talk. She *was* feeling reckless. She'd won today, but she felt like a loser and she didn't like it at all. She hated her life, hated what she'd become in trying to please her father.

She leaned across the table confidentially.

"You want to know how uptight I am? Even now,

I'm sitting here regretting having said a word to you about any of this. Worse, I'm sitting here worried about the fact that I'm not wearing any underwear, terrified of every breath of breeze that comes our way. And I'm scared spitless of what would happen if I told you that I wished Morgan had never interrupted us last night. How pathetic is that?"

She raised an eyebrow at him, waiting for him to laugh or mumble an excuse about having to go home and wash the cat or take a violin lesson. But he just stared at her for a moment, his expression unreadable. Then she noticed a muscle in his jaw flexing, and she realized his eyes had darkened to almost navy.

"No underwear, huh?" he asked, his voice husky.

Jack Brook was turned on by the fact that she, Claire Marsden, wasn't wearing any panties.

"Forgot to pack a change of clothes," she said vaguely, absolutely fascinated by the intent look in his eyes.

"Right. You forgot," he repeated.

Suddenly she felt powerful. This man wanted her. He wanted her right now. And she wanted him. And they could do something about that, because they were both grown-ups with no strings attached. Lots of skeletons in the closet, of course, and monkeys on their backs, but no strings. If she could just find the courage to ignore a lifetime of coloring within the lines…

"Take me home."

Her invitation hung between them. Jack licked his lips, took a deep breath, then nodded.

The instant he said yes, all of her newfound courage disappeared down some invisible sinkhole at her feet. Oh, boy, what had she just done?

You want this, she reminded herself. *You've been fantasizing about this for the past two weeks.* Then why was she feeling as if she'd just put her head in the lion's mouth?

She almost jumped when Jack's hand slid around her hip and onto the small of her back as he guided her toward his car. Could he sense the turmoil within her? Was that why he was being so...circumspect? Because she'd kind of expected him to kiss her once they were alone in the parking lot. At the very least. She'd just offered him an incredibly blatant invitation. Shouldn't he be all fired up by now?

She snuck a look at him as he opened the car door for her. What was he thinking? She slid into the car, trying very hard to keep a neutral expression on her face.

JACK CIRCLED AROUND to his side of the car, aware that his heart was beating a little too fast in his chest. Could he make it all the way to her place before he jumped her? It was going to be a close-run thing, but he dearly wanted to ensure complete and utter privacy before he got Claire naked, because he planned to keep her that way for a long time.

She intrigued him. She excited him. And she touched him. While he had supportive parents who erred more on the side of too much attention than not enough, he understood what it was like to yearn for something unattainable. And it must be so much worse when the person you want to connect with should have every reason in the world for wanting exactly the same thing, but didn't.

And just because Claire understood that there were all kinds of fathers in the world didn't make it any easier to accept the facts. Did a person ever fully resign herself to something like that?

And was he a predatory rat for taking her up on her invitation when she was obviously feeling vulnerable tonight? Shouldn't he just drop her off at her place and keep driving? Was he that much of a gentleman?

He glanced across at her, noticing that she was playing with the hem of her skirt. And, inevitably, his thoughts turned to what was beneath that skirt. Those smooth, toned thighs of hers...and no underwear. He'd tasted her once, briefly—too briefly. He wanted more, a whole lot more. He shifted to ease the sudden tightening in his jeans.

So, no, he wasn't that much of a gentleman.

But he would give her the opportunity to back out, if that was what she wanted. That was the best he could offer, because he wanted her so bad that he was half-inclined to simply pull over and make love to her in his car. Only the thought that there wasn't nearly enough room to do everything he wanted kept his hands on the wheel and his foot on the gas. He knew that once he started touching her, nothing short of a biblical event was going to stop him from drinking his fill of her.

But if they got to her place and she wanted to back out, then he'd let her go, he told himself virtuously. This time. Maybe.

CHAPTER FIFTEEN

CLAIRE TWISTED THE hem of her skirt around and around, longing for some sign from Jack that he wanted her as much as she wanted him.

Then she remembered exactly what she'd said back at the restaurant: *take me home*.

She closed her eyes briefly. She was such a doofus.

What on earth did *take me home* mean, when you got right down to it? She'd meant "Take me home and make love to me till I forget my own name." But what had he heard? "Please return me to my place of residence now that I've revealed I am lacking in the panty department"? Or, "I'm so desperate and sad and pathetic, please would you consider throwing a bit of casual sex my way to alleviate my pain"?

Writhing internally over her patent lack of skills in the pickup department, she turned her head to stare out the window and saw they were passing the car dealership near her apartment. As the red Mustang slid by her window, she stiffened—they were almost home. Even as she was thinking the thought the car slowed down, then stopped altogether.

She tried to swallow the enormous lump of nervousness lodged in her throat as he exited the car and walked around to open her door. She attempted to smile up at him, but suspected she just looked constipated.

She managed to climb out of the car without revealing more than she already had, and they stood for a moment, poised on the edge of a decision.

Is he coming up? Or is he trying to find a way to break it to me gently?

She flickered a look at him, but it was difficult to see his expression properly in the dark. Maybe she should be glad he wasn't making any moves, maybe she should just write this off as a bad experience and slink to her bed alone.

But he was standing there, tall and strong and sexy, and she wanted him. She didn't really know how to make it more obvious that she wanted him. The problem was, if he hadn't understood what she said back at the restaurant, she didn't think she had it in her to throw herself at his feet again.

Perhaps if she just…kind of headed upstairs? Then, if he followed her, she'd know he was coming up. Good plan, very good plan. She turned slowly toward the entrance to her building, every sense attuned to him, and felt him following her.

Okay. Right. So he was coming up. He was coming upstairs, to her place. To make love. Or, more accurately, to have sex. A thrill of relief that she wasn't as hopeless at this blatant-sexual-invitation-thing as she'd thought, closely followed by a wave of anticipation, made her knees go weak.

The automatic doors to the lobby opened as they approached, and she headed toward the stairwell, then stopped.

"Um, I usually take the stairs rather than the elevator. It's only on the second floor, but if you prefer...?" She hesitated.

Jack shrugged, gestured toward the stairs.

"Stairs are fine."

She nodded, let out some of the breath she'd been holding and moved across to the first flight of stairs. She was acutely aware of him behind her, and of Sally's stupid flirty dress brushing against the back of her thighs with each step she took.

She was also acutely aware of the fact that he'd yet to make a move on her. It all felt very...businesslike. Was that the way these things were done? Maybe he was just very private?

He waited until they were almost at the top of the first flight of stairs before he spoke.

"Claire?"

She froze with one foot on the stair tread ahead, one below, and glanced over her shoulder at him.

"You know your problem? Sometimes you think too much."

Jack's voice was gentle, low. She managed a real smile, somewhat reassured by the sexy look in his eyes.

Maybe this was going to be all right.

When his hand brushed against her hip as she continued up the stairs, she realized "all right" might be a gross underestimation. Instantly it felt as though every inch of her skin was hypersensitized. When his hand smoothed over her hip all the way to where the dress skimmed her bare thighs, she felt her heart kick up a gear.

And when his hand began stroking her thigh ever so lightly as she continued up the next flight of stairs, she thought she was going to turn into a boneless, quivering mess and slither down to the lobby between his legs.

His touch was light, delicate, searching, and she slowed down, barely moving now, biting her bottom lip to stop herself from groaning out loud as his hand smoothed farther up her thigh, sliding under the dress now and swooping up to just touch the lowest curve of her butt before sweeping down again.

A small animal sound escaped her despite her precautionary measures, and Jack's hand slid up again, venturing closer to her butt this time, then smoothing forward to reach around and just brush against her lower belly. She shivered, aware of the dull ache of desire that was beginning to throb between her legs.

"You like that?" he said huskily, and she noticed that she'd stopped climbing the stairs altogether now, and that he was standing right behind her, his breath tickling her ear. He was so tall that the fact he was standing a step down put them on an even footing.

She opened her mouth to respond, but any thoughts she had were swept away when Jack's hand slid up for another pass, this time reaching around across her hip and smoothing down over her stomach until he was dipping between her legs with firm, knowing fingers.

She gasped, wanting everything, all of it. A collage of ideas and shapes and sensations danced across her closed eyelids, and she wanted them all. Suddenly, she needed to feel Jack inside her, and she turned abruptly to face him, pushing his unresisting body against the wall.

"I want you right now," she whispered, a little surprised by her own audacity.

Jack smiled, a wicked wolf's smile, and she stood on tiptoes and kissed him, wanting to taste his wickedness, wanting to borrow some of his confidence and sexiness. He pulled her close, deepening the kiss, his tongue dancing with hers as one hand swept up under her dress to smooth over her butt again, while the other slid up her torso to take possession of her breast. It felt heavy with need, and when he ducked his head to tongue her nipples through the halter top, she had to lean against the wall to stay upright.

The sound of her gasps of desire echoed around them in the stairwell, and then they heard the scrape of a shoe on cement. Someone else was coming.

It was enough to bring them marginally to their senses, and Jack lifted his head slowly and nibbled at her ear for a moment before reluctantly relinquishing her breasts.

"I want you on a bed. Or at least something that's not concrete," he said, and she nodded dumbly.

She thrilled to the fact that he kept his hand possessively on her hip all the way up to the hallway outside her apartment. Then he took the key from her shaking hand and opened the door, pushing her ahead of him into her living room.

A moment of stillness passed as they stood there facing each other, alone at last, only the sound of their heavy breathing breaking the silence. After all this time of sniping at each other, it came down to this.

"Take it off," he said finally, indicating her dress.

She hesitated a moment, but there was no denying the demand in his eyes. She loosened the tie around her neck and released the halter top. His eyes seemed to flare as her breasts were revealed, and that feeling of power came back to her. Slowly, she reached for the zipper at the base of her spine to undo the skirt of the dress, aware that Jack's eyes followed every swaying movement of her breasts.

The dress slid down her thighs and he crossed the distance between them in a flash.

"Where's the bedroom?" he asked breathlessly, but she could only pant. He just shook his head then, and the next thing she knew she was on the carpet and he was on top of her, his mouth ducking to lick and suck at her breasts, his hands smoothing over her hips and thighs.

She wanted him to touch her *there* so much, but he seemed intent on teasing her, his fingers sweeping tantalizingly close to where all her heat awaited him, and then moving away again. She whimpered with the need for his touch, arching up under him.

"Now!" she demanded, and she felt him smiling against her breast.

He nipped her breast playfully, and she arched her back again.

"Jack!" she asked again, but he continued to tease her with his almost-caresses, and finally she'd had enough.

With a surge of strength, she pushed him away and began tearing at the buttons on his shirt. He kept trying to distract her, his hands plucking at her nipples, but she gritted her teeth and ignored his laughing to tear his shirt apart. Then she reached for his waistband.

"Help me get these off!" she ordered him breathlessly, and he obliged her by lifting his hips so she could pull his jeans over his butt and down his legs. He kicked them away as she ate him up hungrily with her eyes.

He was so beautiful. She splayed her fingers through the hair on his chest, but it was impossible to ignore the part of him that was demanding the most attention. Greatly daring, she slid her body against his, reveling in the spread of her breasts against his hairy chest, capturing his mouth for a brief but intense kiss before sliding back down his body. He tried to distract her as she moved lower and lower, her tongue chasing a hot trail down his chest and belly. His knee came up between her thighs, and she pressed herself against him, wanting so much more, but getting great pleasure from the pressure. Then she slid off his knee and continued down farther still, reaching for his erection and shooting him a challenging look before taking him in her mouth.

"Claire!" he cried out, and she loved the lack of control in his voice.

He tasted good, sweet and hard and she could feel his body tensing beneath her hands as she raced her tongue across the velvety head of his penis, her hand firmly stroking his shaft. A strong hand came down to still her movements.

"Quit while you're ahead, lady," he warned her. He broke away to grab a condom from his wallet, put it on, and then he was on her like a wild thing, his mouth almost too demanding on her breasts, his hands at last finding the centre of her, one finger plunging inside her where she was so, so ready for him. He made an approving noise as he found her clitoris and she bucked under his hand, and while she was still gasping her approval, she felt his hardness nudging at her thighs and she spread her legs wide, rising up to meet him.

It was like coming home. She forgot everything— her name, the rasp of the carpet against her back, the fact that her neighbors could probably hear her ec- static groans and pleadings. Jack's face was intense and hard above hers, his eyes boring into hers as he thrust time and time again inside her. So deep. So hard and sure and perfect. She felt a pressure grow- ing inside her, at first faint but then increasingly strong and she felt her face contort with the want- ing. She closed her eyes, but Jack's voice whispered in her ear.

"Look at me. I want to see you," he said, and she opened her eyes just as she lost her grip on the world and became nothing but pulsating feeling and release.

He seemed to feed off her, and she felt his body tense and shudder as he surged into her one last time.

And then they were once again two bodies instead of one, their chests heaving against each other, eyes rueful as they regretted how quickly it had all gone. Jack kissed her face, slid a tongue along her neck, nibbled her earlobe. She sighed, smoothed her hands down his back, grasped his rounded, muscular butt.

"Give me a few moments, and we'll see if we can break another record," Jack whispered in her ear.

She laughed, then made a little regretful sound as he withdrew from her.

"Shower?" he suggested, one hand trailing down her body, stopping to explore dips and peaks along the way.

"Mmm," she agreed, allowing him to pull her to her feet.

She led the way into her bathroom, loving it when he slapped her behind gently, then cupped it with his big hands as he followed her into the shower.

"I worship this butt," he said, nuzzling her neck from behind.

"Really?" she blurted, surprised.

Jack turned her round, kissed her.

"You have the sexiest, most desirable little body. Don't tell me you don't know that?" he asked.

She shrugged, concentrating on turning on the water and getting the temperature right.

"Claire." He sounded so serious she stopped what she was doing and turned to him.

"Believe this now. I have wanted you since the moment I realized what those boxy suits of yours have been hiding. Okay?"

He was absolutely convincing, and she allowed herself to believe him, even if it was just for tonight.

"Okay."

He didn't look convinced.

"Repeat after me. 'I am very sexy,'" he instructed lightly, reaching for the soap.

"Jack!" she protested, but he had worked up a lather in his hands now and he reached for her breasts.

"Come on. 'I am very sexy.'"

She squirmed beneath his expert touch. "All right, all right. You're very sexy," she laughed.

Jack seemed inclined to force the issue, but other parts of him had recovered quite nicely and she took the matter firmly in hand, so to speak.

"Don't mess with me when I'm holding the remote control," she mock-warned him.

The rest of the shower passed in a haze of murmurs and groans and impatient noises. At last Jack shut off the water, his face hard with desire, and hauled her out of the shower and threw her, still wet, onto the bed.

He climbed on beside her, stalking toward her like a very large, very hungry jungle cat.

"This time, we go slow," he promised her.

He was true to his word. Sliding his body along hers, he pulled her close and kissed and caressed her until she was breathless. It was all so good—his hands, his mouth, the way he fit against her. She felt overwhelmed by desire. It was all too much, she felt out of control and Jack seemed to sense it. Soothing, he toyed almost absently with her breasts, circling her nipples gently with teasing fingers, pressing the occasional kiss into her cleavage. Just as she was beginning to relax into his touch, he picked things up, dancing his fingers across her nipples, then plucking at them more firmly, and finally drawing each straining tip into his mouth one at a time.

Liquid heat throbbed powerfully between her thighs. Once again she ached with need for him, and she reached for his erection with greedy hands. Jack tensed as she slicked her hand up and down his hard shaft and lifted her hips toward him, straining.

"All in good time, baby," he teased, brushing her hand away.

Claire liked the way he took control, the way he seemed to know so surely what she wanted.

But two could play at that game.

As Jack lifted his head from one breast and made to move to the other, she rolled out from under him and shoved him down on the bed. Before he could stop her, she was astride him, the swollen head of his penis pressing against her slick lips, but not quite penetrating her. She slid her hands along his arms until she held his wrists down on either side of his head. He could shake her off with barely a flex of his muscles, but they both indulged the fiction that she held him captive.

"Now I'm in charge," she threatened mockingly, gyrating suggestively against him.

Jack's eyes were navy dark as he watched her, his teeth just showing through his slightly parted lips. Greatly daring, she rubbed herself against him and felt the giveaway tension in his body. Watching him closely, she tilted her hips and guided his hardness into her. His eyes were almost closed now, but she could just see the glint of his eyes as she paused briefly before plunging onto him, taking him deep inside.

He filled her completely and utterly, and she threw back her head and reveled in the ride. Excitement built within her as Jack's hands caressed her breasts more and more firmly, and then suddenly, out of nowhere, she was throbbing around him again, gasping his name. In the aftermath, Jack moved like lightning, flipping her back onto the bed so that he was again on top. In charge once more, he continued the ride, reaching a hand between their bodies and searching for her clitoris. She cried out as he found it, squirming beneath him, sure that she was too sensitive, too stimulated. But Jack knew better, and in seconds she felt the excitement beginning to build again. He leaned over her now, shifting higher so that every thrust provided the maximum stimulation. And before she knew it she was lost, but he was with her this time, shuddering into her, holding her close.

They broke apart at last, panting. She could feel her heart pounding, and she closed her eyes. Had she ever felt this fulfilled, this amazing?

A foot nudged her calf, and she opened her eyes to find Jack watching her. He smiled saucily.

"Don't even think about going to sleep," he warned, and to her astonishment she felt an answering tightness in her body.

She had a feeling it was going to be a long, hot, breathless night.

JACK WOKE BEFORE HER, and he simply watched her, resisting the urge to tuck an errant curl behind her ear. Her mouth was open a little, and every now and then she screwed up her eyes and made unintelligible noises in her sleep. She'd be mortified if she knew. He found himself smiling, enjoying the small moment.

Then he frowned, realizing something felt different.

He rolled onto his back and blinked up at the ceiling. Maybe it was because he'd stayed the whole night. That was probably it. Because normally he wasn't keen on doing that. There was all that morning-after awkwardness. But for some reason, he'd stayed last night.

His mind tripped over the incredible evening they'd shared. He hadn't seemed to be able to get enough of her, and she'd equaled his passion time and time again. He smiled, remembering how they'd argued like teenagers in the elevator just a few weeks ago. Who'd have thought they would wind up like this?

And then he realized what was different—it wasn't just that he'd stayed the night, it was that he wanted to stay this morning. He wasn't thinking about getting up and finding his clothes, or concocting a legitimate excuse for hightailing it out of there. He wanted to stay, to talk, to have breakfast. Hopefully to make love again. Whatever. Whatever it was people did when one of them didn't run for the hills the next morning.

He found his heart rate picking up as Claire stirred beside him, her eyelids flickering before she at last opened her eyes and locked gazes with him for the first time in the light of day. And then he registered the look in her eyes, and all his pleasant imaginings withered to nothing. She looked panicked, shocked.

Unwelcoming.

Damn.

He could feel her body stiffen next to his and he froze, unsure what to do. A minute ago he'd been trying to decide if they'd breakfast here or go find somewhere down by the bay. But now she looked as though she was ready to throw a sheet out the window and try to shimmy her way down if that was what it was going to take to escape him.

It seemed he may have miscalculated somewhat. Perhaps she needed a little time to relax and get used to things? He tried a smile, but she stared at him as if he were some oversize cockroach she'd found on the sheets.

"Hi," he said, for lack of anything else.

"Hi."

She'd got more of a grip on herself, he could see. Or more accurately, he couldn't see, because she'd disappeared behind an impenetrable mask of politeness.

"Would you—would you like breakfast?" she asked, and he watched her wriggle away from him to the edge of the bed, being very careful all the while to keep the sheet clutched to her chest.

So it was going to be like this.

He fought back a bitter laugh. All these years he'd been the one to long for a quick escape the morning after. And the one time he wanted to stay, he was being herded toward the door. Perhaps she was worried about what happened next? He honestly hadn't given it much thought, but maybe she wanted to talk about it. Women, in his experience, could never get enough talk.

"Claire—" he began to say, but she cut him off.

"I know, I understand, believe me, it's exactly what I was thinking. We have to work together, and it's awkward, but, hey, it's got to be out of our systems now, right?"

She'd spotted a silky dressing gown on the bedroom floor, and he watched as she stretched out one leg, clenched her toes into the silky fabric, and dragged it toward herself, all the while ensuring the sheet continued to cover all her vital areas. He was so fascinated by it all that he answered honestly.

"Well, in a word—no," he said, and she snapped her head around to stare at him.

"No?" she repeated, her eyes wide.

He fought the urge to lean forward and kiss her. She was just so...kissable.

"No. I don't honestly think I've gotten it out of my system," he elaborated.

She stared at him for a moment, then shook her head decisively. Standing abruptly, she forsook the safety of her modesty sheet and shrugged into the dressing gown. He was treated to a tantalizing glimpse of curvy hip and swelling breast before she pulled the wrap tight around herself and cinched it with a tie-belt.

He found himself facing Professional Claire, the competent, on-the-ball, matter-of-fact woman who strode the halls of Beck and Wise every Monday to Friday.

"Look, Jack, I'm going to be straight with you. I'm not really up for one of your flings. I mean, I know we've sort of had one, a mini one, anyway, but I'm not up for any more than this," she said, sounding very brisk and businesslike.

He could feel himself getting a little annoyed at all the assumptions she was making. Feeling at a disadvantage lying on the bed, he stood and approached her. Her eyes dropped rather gratifyingly below his waistline, but she looked away very quickly.

"What if I don't want a fling, mini or otherwise? What if I want more than that?"

Where had that come from? He'd even surprised

himself with that one. Surely he didn't want a…well, a *relationship* with Claire? The idea seemed very strange and alien, but it didn't stop him from feeling deeply offended when she attempted to smother the smile that leaped to her lips. He frowned.

"Are you laughing at me?"

She shook her head, her lips pressed together primly now. But he'd seen it.

"You did, you just laughed at me!" he accused.

Claire at last looked him in the eye, and he saw that any trace of laughter was gone from her face now.

"Jack. Come on, listen to yourself. This is you, consummate playboy, and me, uptight chick from the office. We have nothing in common except for some physical…curiosity, which we fully explored last night."

Jack opened his mouth to tell her that she was wrong, then shut it again, the words unspoken. He didn't know what to say. Worse, he didn't know what to do except to get dressed and go. He didn't even know what his own feelings were, so how could he question hers when she was basically drawing a line under what had happened between them?

"I guess I should go, then," he suggested dully.

She nodded, stooping to detangle the sheets.

"That's probably the most sensible thing."

Jack padded into the living room, blinking at the sight of his clothes strewn all over the floor. There was only one button intact on his shirt—she'd ripped the rest off—and he found his jeans rucked up in the corner near the television. He stood staring at them for a moment, almost driven to turn around and try to talk to her, sort things out. Because it felt wrong to end things this way. He didn't know what else there was to explore, but he felt as though this was incomplete, wrong. But then he remembered the look that had crept into her eyes the moment she'd seen him this morning. That was not the look of a woman who wanted to "explore" things.

CLAIRE FELT AS though she was holding her breath as she waited for Jack to finish dressing in the living room. She scooted over to her chest of drawers and grabbed a pair of panties, pulling them on hastily beneath her robe, feeling somehow safer with a bit of satin and cotton between her and Jack's all-knowing gaze. After all, it was the lack of panties that had got her into this situation in the first place.

She could hear the clink of his belt buckle, and she guessed he was probably mostly decent by now. God, she wanted him gone. She needed him gone before she broke down and begged him to stay. Even for just a few more hours. Or—her heart leaped—another night. Whatever he was willing to give her.

Which was why he had to go, of course. She relived the bolt of fear that had ripped through her when she opened her eyes and found him staring at her. She knew from past relationships that she sometimes talked in her sleep, and she had a sudden moment of panic as she imagined what she might have said.

What if she'd said something about him, about her feelings for him?

Oh, anything but that!

Jack would run a mile if she so much as hinted at feeling anything deeper than lust for him. She was so sure of it, so sure that he would reject her, that she quivered at the very thought of it. He had the power to destroy her, she knew, and she didn't have the strength to face him down.

"Claire."

She turned to find him standing in her bedroom door, his shirt held shut with just one dangling button. She blushed, remembering that she'd popped the buttons last night, tearing his clothes off him.

"I'm going now."

She nodded, staring at his back for a moment as he turned toward the front door. She forced herself to follow him out, to smile in a friendly-but-not-too-friendly way at him as he opened the exterior door and then turned to look at her one last time.

"Claire, I really… Look, maybe this is a bad time…"

He seemed lost for words, his face uncertain. For the first time, she doubted her rock-solid instincts where he was concerned. Was it possible that he…?

He seemed to make a decision, his shoulders squaring and his gaze becoming clearer as he looked down at her. She bit her tongue, resisting the urge to throw herself at his feet. He was probably just feeling guilty, trying to find a way to say goodbye nicely.

"I'm going to call you tonight, okay? When

you've had time to settle down a little. Get some sleep, maybe."

The ghost of a smile came from him. She'd been right—he felt sorry for her!

"If you want to, that's fine, Jack. But it's not necessary, really," she told him coolly.

She felt proud of that coolness. If she could keep this up, she might be able to salvage a little bit of dignity. Jack stared at her for a moment, and then he turned on his heel and was gone. She stared at the closed door for a long time, telling herself she was relieved.

And she was. She was very relieved that Jack hadn't guessed the full extent of her feelings. That would have been the ultimate humiliation, of course. Here he was, throwing lonely Claire a bone, and she'd fallen head over heels in love with him.

She snorted out loud at her own stupidity. Of all the men on the planet, she had to pick Jack Brook to fall in love with. Hell, she'd probably been in love with him subconsciously for years. All her posturing about his dating and his demeanor, all her contempt for him—a paper-thin veil to hide the truth from herself. She'd fallen in love with Jack. She adored him. She thought he was witty, kind, intelligent, funny. She wanted to make love to him until it was medically advisable to take a break.

Thank God he'd gone.

Feeling strangely empty, she padded into her bathroom and shed her robe. The sight of her shower brought back a rush of hot, sticky memories from last night, and she found herself overwhelmed by emotion as she stepped under the stream of hot water.

She wanted...she just *wanted*. She felt as though she'd spent her lifetime *just wanting* a whole bunch of things that were never going to come her way. And she was sick of it, worn out from it, over it. Slowly she slid down the tiled wall until she was huddled on the shower base, the water pummeling her head from on high.

She loved Jack, and there was no way he was ever going to love her back. She'd invested her most precious asset in a man who was too scared to let love into his life. She'd watched him avoid relationships with so many women over the past two years. He'd said it himself when they were trapped in the elevator—he made sure that women always knew the score where he was concerned. No strings, no hassles. She suspected a lot of his commitment phobia came from what had happened with his brother, from not being able to deal with his loss. But that didn't make much difference at the end of the day. Jack was the one who had to decide to take the risk of loving someone—and it sure as hell wouldn't be her. They'd fought like cat and dog most of the time they'd known each other, and, even if they'd discovered an intense sexual chemistry more recently, she wasn't the kind of woman he'd change his life for. Katherine, now she was the kind of woman men changed their lives for. And even she hadn't lured Jack over from the dark side.

By the time Claire emerged from the shower, her

fingers and toes were prunish and she felt well and truly waterlogged. She made herself a bowl of muesli with skim milk and sat in her kitchen eating it like a zombie, her mind mulling over and over the problem of how to reassemble her life and peace of mind.

Work was the big thing. She was stuck with Jack on the stupid Hillcrest project, and there was no way to get out of it. So she was going to have to suck it up. She was going to have to wear her best poker face and laugh at Jack's jokes and try not to claw out his eyes when she heard he was dating someone else from the office.

Suddenly her muesli tasted like small pieces of cardboard, and she pushed the bowl away.

CHAPTER SIXTEEN

JACK WAITED FOR Monday like a man in the desert thirsts for water. He couldn't stop thinking about Claire. In fact, he picked up the phone at least ten times to call her, but each time he put it back again when he realized he had nothing to offer beyond "Hi." What was he going to say to her, after all? "For some reason I can't stop thinking about you, but please don't take that the wrong way as I'm scared to death of commitment"? Yeah, that'd go over real well.

It had been a long time since he'd felt so confused and uncertain, and he found his thoughts turning to Robbie. That was the thing about having a twin—whenever he'd been down, he'd always known that Robbie would understand. Jack had never had to wax poetic or dig deep to explain himself—Robbie had just known. It had been reciprocal, of course. He smiled as he remembered the times he'd found himself drawn to Robbie's place on a Sunday night, a taste for beer in his mouth, only to find his twin with a six-pack waiting and a problem to share.

Robbie would have liked Claire. In fact, Robbie probably would have seen her for what she was the first time he met her, and Jack would have had a fight on his hands to keep her for himself.

Somehow, Jack wound up in his garage, pulling the dust sheets off the Triumph Triple R motorbikes that he and Robbie had bought each other for their last shared birthday. They'd planned to tour Australia on them. But Robbie had gotten sick before they'd had a chance to do more than a few week-long runs up and down the coast.

Now Jack contemplated his bike, sorrow for Robbie and all the dreams that had died with him welling up inside. Tears rolled down his face, but he remembered their first day out on the bikes. Robbie had insisted on wearing an open-faced helmet with old-fashioned motorcycle goggles, despite the fact that Jack had told him over and over that he looked like a mad-ass version of the Red Baron. They'd stopped at a country general store to get drinks, and Robbie had smiled a big, glad-to-be-alive smile at him—revealing the host of small insects that he'd collected in his teeth as they rode. Even now the memory made him laugh, and Jack wiped the last of his tears away with his shirtsleeve.

Decisive, he threw the dust sheet over his own bike. Wheeling Robbie's out into the sun, he checked the gauges and the spark plugs, and flicked the ignition on. The bike hummed to life with barely a hiccup. Grabbing his leathers and his helmet, Jack climbed on.

The ride had cleared his head on many counts, but he was no closer to solving the problem of Claire by

Monday morning. Somehow, though, he still found himself bounding out of bed, taking time over his clothes, making sure he flossed as well as brushed. When he drove past her sedate sedan in its usual spot in the car park, he even felt a smile curving his mouth.

And when she stuck her head into his office first thing, he found himself studying every detail of her appearance, from her curly-topped head to her high-heeled feet. His imagination efficiently whisked away her neat suit and shirt and he enjoyed a full Technicolor image of her naked and willing, panting for him like she had been last Friday night. He dragged his chair closer to his desk to ensure the inevitable side effect of thinking about Claire naked was well hidden beneath several layers of timber and paperwork, and tried to concentrate on what she was saying.

"…called to Sydney for an emergency meeting, so Hillcrest has asked to bring the sign-off meeting forward to this afternoon. He'll be on his way to the airport, so he's offered to swing by here again. How's your schedule looking around two?"

Jack wrenched his fascinated gaze from her full-lipped mouth and tried to remember that English was his first language.

"Fine. Great. Whatever."

She gave him a look that clearly questioned his sanity. As it was a concern he also shared, he tried to focus his attention on something other than the need to kiss her.

"Right. I've booked the meeting room on my floor. I'll see you down there at two, then."

He snapped out of his self-induced stupor as he realized she was about to leave. And that he didn't want that.

"Claire!"

She turned toward him, her face carefully blank and professional.

He stared at her, trying to think of something to say, something that would mean she would stay in his office and he could keep looking at her and smelling her and being with her.

"Um…how was your weekend?" he finally offered.

She flushed, then focused on the wall behind his head as she delivered a little speech that she'd obviously put quite a bit of thought into.

"Look, Jack, I know that things are bound to be awkward after Friday night…but we're both professionals and grown-ups. It happened, let's move on. I'm sure you agree."

No, he didn't. He wasn't sure why he didn't agree, but he didn't. And she was heading for the door again. And this time he couldn't think of a single thing to say to stop her.

He just sat and blinked and breathed for a while after she'd gone. What the hell was going on? Why was his heart still pounding out of control, and why was he battling the desire to either throw Claire Marsden to the ground and lick her until she screamed the building down, or cradle her in his arms and assure her that everything in the world had purpose and meaning?

It took five minutes closeted in a cubicle in the ladies' room before she felt able to face the office again. God, she loved him. Seeing him again, sitting opposite her, within reach—it was a new form of torture.

How was she going to get through this? The future seemed to stretch out ahead of her, bleak and comfortless.

She dragged herself back to her desk. She couldn't focus on work, so she spent an hour playing a numbing game of solitaire on her computer, just so she'd look busy if anyone passed by. Tom kept shooting her concerned looks, and he eventually ventured into her office.

"Are you okay?" he asked hesitantly.

She blinked up at him. *No, Tom, I'm not okay,* she wanted to say. *I've fallen for a man who is afraid of love, and, even if he wasn't, would never pick me to love anyway. I'm boring and square and not sexy enough. I annoy him, I know I do. The only reason he spent the night with me was because he felt sorry for me. And, Tom, here's the worst bit—I can't stop thinking about him. I honestly don't know how I'm going to get through our meeting this afternoon without throwing myself at his feet or just plain throwing up.*

"I'm fine, Tom. But thanks for asking."

He nodded and retreated to his desk, but she could see he wasn't happy. That made two of them.

JACK ENTERED THE meeting room on Claire's floor with a certain degree of trepidation. She was alone in there, waiting for the Hillcrest people to arrive. And, sure enough, his heart went into overdrive the moment he saw her. Before he could give it much more thought, Hillcrest and his cronies arrived.

It wasn't until the meeting was well under way that it hit him. Claire was handling the cranky old baboon with consummate skill, and he was so closely attuned to her she had only to glance his way and Jack knew exactly what she wanted him to do and say. But, really, apart from the occasional reference to giraffes and rhinos, precious little was expected of him because Claire was so damned good. She knew her stuff, and she was funny, and she was flexible, and she knew when to be a bit cheeky and when to give in. She was amazing. Really, truly amazing.

And then he had his revelation. He was watching Claire talk to Hank, her lips curving into a smile and then a laugh as she responded to something the old guy said. It felt as if something tight and controlled had snapped in Jack's chest and then he felt a warm, unfolding sensation as he stared at her.

He loved her. He loved Claire Marsden. It was like being hit by a tsunami, and he actually reached for the table to steady himself.

Everything slotted into place, and the world froze

in its orbit as he examined this new knowledge from every angle. *He loved her.*

Cautiously, he tested the bounds of this new discovery. How would he feel about Claire moving into his house, for example? He remembered all the discarded clothes on her bedroom floor. She was messy—they'd have to deal with that. But she could have her own room for her clothes, like a big walk-in closet. His smile widened into a grin as he realized he actually liked the idea of waking up beside her every day, that he didn't mind if she left her stuff everywhere, as long as he got to laugh with her and hold her and make love to her every day for the rest of his life.

Man, did he have it bad, or what? All these years of being the artful dodger when it came to affairs of the heart, and the one woman who'd always steered clear of him had him in the palm of her hand without even trying.

Vaguely he became aware of Hillcrest saying something: the old guy's lips were moving, but Jack had no idea what was coming out. He must have responded appropriately, however, because Hillcrest smiled and clapped him heartily on the back and shuffled toward the door.

Jack couldn't take his eyes off Claire.

His mom was going to be over the moon. He imagined introducing Claire to his family, and felt a warm glow of pride in his belly. She was so clever and brave and funny. Prickly, of course, and there'd always be arguments. But then there'd always be the mind-blowing sex to make up with, too.

They were good for each other. The way he saw it, they completed each other—she'd made him realize he had to open up and let himself care again, and he'd helped her to relax and live a little. Remembering the hurt in her eyes as she discussed her father's no-show, he made a fierce commitment to himself: he'd make it his life's mission to ensure she never felt unimportant or overlooked again.

He felt as if a load had been lifted from his shoulders and he turned to Claire once the Hillcrest people were gone, ready to spill his guts and offer himself up to her.

"Claire," he said, and she paused in the act of shuffling her paperwork together.

He loved the little frown line that appeared between her eyebrows as she tried to work out what he wanted. He loved the fact that she looked at her watch, her mind obviously elsewhere. It was so *Claire*.

He crossed to the door and closed it to ensure privacy, then turned to face her.

"We need to talk," he said firmly, feeling his way forward into the darkness of this brand-new territory.

She was facing him, her face carefully polite, but he could tell by the set of her shoulders that she was tense, cautious.

He couldn't just come right out with it, could he? No, that would scare her off. He had to be subtle, build up to it. Explain himself.

"I love you."

Of course, straight to the point was also an effective strategy.

He held his breath, his eyes intent on her face as she registered what he'd said. He noted the way her eyes dilated briefly, the way her mouth formed a tiny little shocked O, and the slight flush that washed up her neck and face.

"What did you just say?"

He moved toward her, but Claire put her hand out like a cop stopping traffic.

Okay. Give her time. Let her adjust.

"I love you. I have fallen in love with you," he enunciated carefully.

She still looked shocked. Maybe even scared.

"I don't understand," she stammered.

She'd dropped her papers onto the table now, and was wrapping her arms protectively around her torso.

"What's to understand? I think you're amazing. I know now that all that snapping and sniping between us was just because of *this*," he said, gesturing back and forth between them to indicate their connection. "*This* is very strong, and I'm sick of fighting it, I don't know about you."

"Jack, you don't mean it," she said in a small, distant voice.

He blinked. She didn't sound overjoyed. She didn't sound even slightly joyed.

"Claire—"

"No, Jack. Wait."

Suddenly she was scrambling to collect all her

paperwork, scooping it toward herself in a frenzy. She stood with papers bristling out in every direction and confronted him.

"This was all a mistake. We should never have done the sex thing. It messed everything up. I want you to understand that I totally appreciate what you're trying to do right now, but it's not necessary. Okay. So let's just leave it."

She was making no sense, and he didn't believe a word of it, anyway. There was no way she could feel nothing after the night they'd shared together.

"Claire, just stay and talk for a minute," he said, stepping to block her path to the door.

But she was determined, and she dodged to one side and ducked around him.

"It was a mistake, Jack, believe me. You don't love me. You'll realize that and you'll be glad in a few days. And don't worry, it'll be like this conversation never happened. I promise."

He considered stopping her as she flung the door open and shot out into the corridor, but she was determined, and a sudden leaden feeling had stolen into his limbs.

Maybe he'd gotten it all wrong. Was it possible that all the magic he'd been feeling had been one-sided? He forced himself to be brutal as he examined what he knew of relationships. And he remembered a handful of women who'd been demonstrably head over heels with him with very little encouragement at all. Women who'd declared their love at the drop of a hat, while he'd felt only a vague fondness or attraction for them.

He felt sick. Somewhere, deep inside, he recognized that this was the ultimate irony: the guy who always runs from commitment falling in love at last, but with a woman who doesn't love him back.

He laughed, but it came out as more of a groan.

He loved Claire Marsden and she didn't want a bit of him.

CLAIRE SCURRIED TO her office and shut the door and drew the venetian blinds down and sat in the semi-dark staring at nothing. Her heart was pounding, and she felt there was definite potential to lose her lunch.

One sentence kept circling round and around in her head. *I love you.*

Jack Brook had said he loved her. And for a glorious moment she'd seen this vision of the future, a golden, hazy, perfect vision filled with love and happiness and togetherness. And then reality had snapped back into focus.

Jack Brook did not love her. He felt sorry for her, at best. Maybe she *had* talked in her sleep. Maybe he had figured out how much this had all meant to her. Maybe he even realized that the reason she was looking all puffy and just plain wrong today was because she'd been tortured by visions of him every time she tried to get some sleep over the weekend. So, being a nice, kind guy, he'd decided to do the right thing. It was the only explanation she could come up with.

She sat frozen in her chair, alternating between the desire to charge down to Jack's office and make him prove what he'd just said, and the powerful need to hide beneath her desk and pretend none of it had happened.

A rap at the door started her out of her reverie, and she turned wary eyes to the door, dreading to see Jack as it opened. How could she resist the invitation implicit in his declaration again? She wanted so much to believe him, but she was too scared of what would happen if her love proved to be stronger than his. She couldn't survive being the one who was left caring again. Not after a lifetime of it.

"You *are* in! Tom wasn't sure if you were here or not."

It was Katherine. The other woman hesitated on the threshold, obviously sensing something was wrong.

"I was just..." Claire made a helpless gesture, not sure what to say.

Katherine gave her a searching look, then strode into the room and shut the door behind her. She flicked the light switch on and Claire blinked in the sudden glare.

"This is about Jack, isn't it?" Katherine asked boldly.

Claire could only nod, miserable.

"I did warn you. I know he's damned irresistible, but there's just something holding him back—"

"He said he loved me."

Katherine looked stunned. "He did?"

"Yes."

Katherine's face began to transform, a smile creeping across it as she digested Claire's news. "But that's terrific. Amazing!"

Claire stared at her friend. "Are you mad? Jack Brook doesn't really love me. It's not possible."

Katherine looked confused. "But you just said that he told you he did."

"Yes. But he doesn't know what he's saying. He feels sorry for me. Or he's confused."

Katherine was staring at her strangely. "Claire, Jack wouldn't say something if he didn't mean it. And he certainly wouldn't say something like that because he felt sorry for someone. Trust me, I've been there, done that. Not once did Jack ever say anything just to make me feel good."

"You don't understand. It's because Jack knows how I feel. We— He— Well, we shared a pretty intense time on Friday night and I had a bit of a crisis and I'm sure he just feels sort of…responsible for me. That's all."

"Right. He said all this to you, did he?" Katherine demanded, skeptical.

"Not as such. But I know that's what it is."

Katherine just stood there for a moment studying her, and Claire fought the urge to twitch.

"So, how do you know he thinks all this stuff, then, if he didn't say it? You psychic or something?"

Claire stared at Katherine, startled. "Of course not."

Katherine made a harrumphing noise as though

she'd just decided something. "You know what I think? You're afraid."

Claire stared at her, affronted.

"I hardly think—" she began to say, but Katherine was nodding knowingly, her expression grim.

"Afraid. Scared rigid, if I have any guess. Aren't you two just the pair, then?"

There was judgment in Katherine's tone, and Claire sat up a little straighter.

"You don't know what you're talking about," she said icily.

"Really? Seeing as I know you and Jack pretty well, I think I'm informed enough to have an opinion on the subject."

"Well, you don't know how I feel. Or how Jack feels, for that matter," Claire said stubbornly.

Katherine sighed heavily. "Claire, if Jack had told me he loved me, I would have jumped at the offer and hung on for dear life. What more do you want from the guy?"

Claire narrowed her eyes at her friend, hating the way Katherine was pushing her.

"You know what, I think you're the one who's in love with Jack. You're always asking me about him, giving advice."

"I was trying to be your friend, Claire. Sometimes outsiders can see things more clearly."

"I know exactly what you mean," Claire said pointedly.

Katherine stared at her. "I hope you don't regret

what you're doing. Guys like Jack come along once in a lifetime."

And with that she left, and Claire sank lower in her seat and hung her head in her hands. Why had she been so awful to Katherine?

Because her friend had challenged her, that was why.

You're afraid.

It was ridiculous, of course. Katherine didn't understand. The phone rang, and she leaped on it like it was a lifeline. She didn't have time to sit around contemplating her navel. She had a magazine to launch.

She tried very hard to push Katherine's words and the hurt look on her face out of her mind for the rest of the afternoon, but for the first time in Claire's life, work failed her. She kept remembering the expression on Jack's face when he'd said he loved her, and hope would spring to life in her chest and she'd think *maybe.* Then reality would intrude and she'd stomp all over her stupid, forlorn hope with hobnailed boots of pragmatism. Of course Jack didn't really love her. He couldn't.

Finally her circling thoughts and the churning in her belly got too much for her and she grabbed her bag and headed home early. What she needed was a run—a really hard, punishing run that would wipe all other thought from her mind.

She entered her apartment, slapped on her running gear and was out the door, hitting the pavement as though the hounds of hell were following her.

With each footfall, she pushed Katherine's words away.

"I am not afraid, I am not afraid," she whispered under her breath as she climbed a hill.

But with each mile it became more and more obvious that there was no denying the hard lump of emotion that had been sitting rock-heavy in her stomach from the moment she realized she loved Jack Brook.

Fear. Pure and simple.

Katherine was right—she *was* afraid.

The moment Claire admitted her cowardice, she started justifying it to herself with an avalanche of logic and rationalization. Even if Jack Brook really did love her—and it was a big if—she couldn't risk exposing herself to him. He was tall and perfect and handsome and clever, and she was just Claire. He could have his pick of women—exciting, dynamic, sexy women.

And he'd picked her.

It was such a revolutionary thought that it stopped her in her tracks. Out of all the women he'd dated over the years—including peerless, bombshell Katherine—*he'd picked Claire.*

Hope took advantage of the lull in her defenses to leap to the fore. What if he really did love her? What if he loved her the way she loved him and she'd just pushed him away because she was too scared to even try? What kind of a person did that make her?

She couldn't help remembering the image she'd had of herself when she'd been stuck in the elevator with Jack—a workaholic who buried her lack of life under a training schedule. A dry, humorless shrew who didn't know how to have fun.

It wasn't true. The past few weeks had proven that to her, if nothing else. But if she walked away from Jack's declaration, wasn't she going to become that woman, that beige-suited, hospital-cornered woman who never took risks?

"No!"

She said it so loudly that the man walking his dog nearby turned and stared. She stared back, for the first time registering where her desperate run had led her. She was standing outside the car dealership near her apartment, right in front of the shiny red Mustang convertible that she'd convinced herself she didn't want.

She didn't allow herself to think. Thinking was what stopped her from doing so many things, she realized. This was about taking action, doing what felt right.

"Hey, you," she called out to the car salesman who was buffing a bumper near the back of the lot. "How much for the Mustang?"

He trotted over, welcoming smile in place.

"It's a lovely car, just two owners, both women. Superb leather trim, with—"

She didn't have time for any of this, and she silenced him with an impatient shake of her head.

"How much? That's all I need to know."

"Ten thousand. But don't you want to hear about the—"

No, she didn't. She didn't want to waste any time,

because somewhere in the back of her mind she knew she was about to behave recklessly, and that if she paid too much attention to the fact, nothing would happen and this small window of brave, audacious daring might close over and never appear again.

"I'll take it. I just have to go home and get my checkbook," she said, cutting across his sales patter.

He looked bewildered. "Don't you want to haggle?"

"No," she said.

"Not even a little bit?"

"No. This is what I want."

It felt so refreshing to say those words out loud. *This is what I want.* Not what she thought someone else might want her to want. Not what she thought might project a certain image. Not what her father, or Morgan, or even Jack might think was right.

She insisted that he put a sold sign on it before she left him to jog home and get her checkbook. Her blood was fizzing with expectation. She had a sexy car. She wasn't a stick in the mud. She was exciting and adventurous. The sort of woman that Jack Brook was attracted to. The sort of woman that Jack Brook...loved?

It was so hard, making that last leap of faith. As she brushed her teeth and sprayed on perfume and picked out her sexiest, most exciting summer dress, she skirted around the edges of admitting to herself what she had to do next. Like buying the car, if she examined it too closely she was afraid she'd be paralyzed by old fears. So she told herself she was just sprucing herself up for her new car, so that when she drove it off the lot she'd feel the part. But she knew where she was going, what she was going to do.

She was going to see Jack, and she was going to tell him that she loved him.

In a state of suspended panic that occasionally crossed over into exhilaration, she drove her sensible sedan to the car lot and signed over a large chunk of her savings. The salesman was effervescent with goodwill, throwing in a set of car mats and a key ring. Then she drove out of the lot with the radio on, the top down and her heart in her mouth.

She almost turned around several times on the way to Jack's place. She was too good at protecting herself for that part of herself to give up without a fight. She started by making excuses for why Jack wouldn't be home. Then she told herself that buying the car, becoming a convertible-type-of-girl, was more than enough for one day. Baby steps, that's what were required. Perhaps, in a year or two, she could make her way to Jack's place to serve up her soul on a silver platter.

But the memory of what it had felt like to make love to Jack kept her going. The excitement, the belonging, the sheer magic of it. It had to be right. If she didn't take a chance on this, she'd regret it for the rest of her life.

Perhaps if she hadn't been so preoccupied with taming her own terror, she would have registered the familiar car parked in front of Jack's house as she pulled up. But she didn't. She was too busy forcing one leg after the other up the walk, her courage tightly held in both hands as she took a deep breath and rang the doorbell.

There was a long silence, and then Jack opened the front door, dressed in nothing but a towel, his skin still glistening from the shower. She stared at him, struck once again by how damn perfect and beautiful and sexy he was. She loved the faint curl in his dark hair. She loved the little crinkly lines at the corners of his eyes. And the way his mouth always looked as though he was about to laugh. The depth and breadth of his chest. The strength of his thighs. The way he—

She realized that she was staring at him, and she cleared her throat. "Jack, I have something I need to tell you," she said boldly.

"Okay."

He looked wary, and a bit hopeful. Her courage surged. This was going to work out, it really was.

"I just wanted to say, I'm sorry about this afternoon. I'm an idiot. Actually, I'm more of a coward. Or at least I was," she began, warming up to things.

Jack was smiling now, and she found herself smiling back. It really was going to be okay.

Then she heard the voice—the very feminine voice—calling from the back of the house.

"Jack, I thought you said it was going to be a quick shower."

And then she saw Katherine padding up Jack's hallway, barefoot and in shorts, a half-empty beer glass in her hand.

"Claire!" she said, sounding startled.

But Claire was too busy controlling her gag reflex to respond. All the time she'd been standing on Jack's doorstep, preparing to pour her heart out to him, he'd had another woman warming up out back. Not just any woman—Katherine, her so-called friend, the woman she'd accused of having an unrequited crush on Jack just hours ago.

So much for him loving her.

It felt like a slap in the face. It felt as if she'd closed her eyes and leaped, expecting to land safely in someone's arms, only to find that she'd stepped into a chasm. If only she hadn't allowed herself to hope. For years she'd survived without love, but she'd let herself hope, and now this....

She felt frozen to the spot as she desperately called on all those years of not looking disappointed when she hurt like hell inside. As long as he didn't know what she'd come here for, she might just escape with a little bit of dignity intact. Suddenly that seemed very important. As long as Jack didn't know how close she'd come to making a fool of herself, perhaps her pain wouldn't be quite so all-encompassing.

But it was too late. She felt her face crumpling, felt her world crashing down around her.

This was why she never stuck her neck out. This was why she played it safe.

"Claire, let me explain," Katherine said, heading toward her.

"I have to go," Claire managed to choke out as she backed away from the door.

Jack stepped forward, trying to catch her arm. "Claire, wait!"

Any hope of retaining a shred of pride evaporated as the tears hit. She turned toward her car, already blubbering messy, undignified tears, aware that inside she hurt. She hurt so much she wanted to sink to the ground and howl.

She wrenched the car door open and stabbed the keys into the ignition. Where had all these tears come from? Did she even have this much fluid in her body?

She had to get out of here.

"Claire, will you please just stop and listen?"

He'd stopped to pull on a pair of shorts, but Jack was beside the car now, hovering over her. She panicked, pumping the accelerator madly and turning the key, but the starter motor just whined at her, leaving the engine dead. Furious, blinded by tears, she pumped the accelerator again and twisted the key viciously. Again, nothing. When she moved to try a third time, Jack's large hand reached down to tug the key from her death grip.

"You've flooded it. It's not like your little automatic," he said calmly. "Now, will you please listen to me?"

She glanced up at him through the veil of her tears, registering his concerned face. She felt like such an idiot. She was going to have to quit her job. She'd been fooling herself when she thought she could bear to work with Jack, knowing he was with someone else.

"Just leave me alone, I just want to be alone," she

SARAH MAYBERRY   331

said when Jack tried to open the car door. She hit
the lock, and wound the window up. Since the roof
was down, it was a fairly pointless exercise, but she
was so upset she was beyond caring.

Jack reached over the window, and suddenly the
car door was unlocked and swinging open, and she
was being dragged out into his arms.

"Put me down!" she sobbed, but he just held her
tighter.

"Not until you listen to me, goddamn you," Jack
said.

It felt so good to be in his arms, yet knowing that
she couldn't have him, that he wasn't hers after all,
only made things worse. But he wouldn't let go of
her, so in the end she just gave up and rested her
head on his shoulder and cried. His hands soothed
her back, and he whispered reassurances in her ear.
After a few minutes of steady sobbing she was reduced to snuffling against his damp shoulder, dread
building inside her with every passing second. He
knew, now. He had to know. He knew she loved him,
and now her rejection would be complete.

"Now, just listen for a second," he said, obviously
judging her to be in a somewhat calmer state. "Katherine came around to talk to me because I asked her
to. I know you two are friends, and I needed some
advice. Because I'd just told you I loved you, and
you blew me off."

His words managed to somehow seep past the
mist of tears and pain fogging her brain. Katherine was here for *advice?* Not wild, animal sex?

Claire considered this for a few seconds, decided she might be prepared to believe it. Which meant... which meant...

"Claire, I love you. Why can't you believe that?"

She needed to see him. She pulled back from his shoulder, wiping a hand across her face to try and clear away some of the tears. His blue eyes were deeply sincere, his hands gentle as he cradled her face.

"Really? You're sure? Because I don't think I could handle it if you got to know me and you realized..."

She found herself trailing off. She stared into Jack's eyes as the domino pieces of the past flipped over into each other in her mind.

What had she been about to say? That once Jack really knew her he wouldn't—couldn't—love her?

She blinked at him.

"My father—" she began to say, and then she put her hand over her mouth to stop the words from pouring out.

She couldn't stop herself from thinking as easily, however. As Jack waited patiently, she followed her thought through to its conclusion.

How could Jack love her when her own father wouldn't even give her the time of day? And Harry was honor-bound to love her—it was supposed to be genetic, he was her father. If he couldn't dredge up a shred of feeling, what hope was there that the golden Jack Brook could truly love her in the same, all-encompassing way she loved him?

It was as though something large and monstrous had suddenly stepped out of the shadows and assumed life-size proportions. Like confessing to Jack her fear that she'd only won because she'd "done it for Daddy," it was hard acknowledging this last and final truth. She felt rejected by her father, and she lived her life in fear of being rejected by anyone else.

She stared up at Jack, not even knowing where to begin.

But he did.

"I am not your father, Claire. I love you, and nothing is going to change that. I love your laugh, I love your tears, I love the way you think, the way you get that little wrinkle between your brows when you're confused. I love making love to you, holding you in my arms, touching you. I love your passion and your commitment and your sense of what's fair. I love it that you're honest, even if it means admitting that you're wrong sometimes...."

He kissed her gently.

"Oh, Jack," she managed to whisper, moved to tears again, but good tears this time. She threw herself into his arms, squeezing him as hard as she could, proving to herself that he was real. He squeezed her back, and they stood holding each other, loving each other, for a long time.

"Um, is there something you'd like to say to me?" he asked super-casually.

She pulled back from their embrace to stare at him quizzically. He gave her a sad puppy-dog look, obviously expecting something.

"What?"

And then she realized she still hadn't told him she loved him! Here she was, blubbering all over his front lawn, exposing her most painful fears, and she still hadn't told the man how she felt.

She felt blinded by her love as she beamed up at him. Where to begin? She reached up and cupped his precious face in her hands.

"You are the most wonderful, amazing, clever, sexy man. And I love you. I love you so much that it scares me."

Jack leaned down to kiss her, and she felt the familiar excitement beginning to sweep her up. She moved closer, pressed herself against him. He murmured his appreciation, trailing a hand down her back to find her butt and pull her closer still.

The sound of an engine starting broke the moment, and they looked up to see Katherine's car pulling out from the curb. Katherine shook her head at them ruefully and smiled, then made a phone gesture with her hand and mouthed "Call me" to Claire before driving away.

"I'd forgotten all about her," she admitted guiltily. "I was horrible. I was so jealous, I said some awful things."

Jack started nuzzling her neck again. "Sorry, who are we talking about?"

Claire let her head fall back as he nibbled his way around her earlobe.

"Katherine."

"Oh, Katherine. She's fine. She's just been telling me to keep persevering. She said that anyone who reacted the way you did this afternoon had to be in love."

Claire still owed Katherine some serious chocolate and champagne therapy, but Jack's kisses were becoming more and more insistent and for a while the rest of the world faded into oblivion.

"By the way, what's with the car?" Jack murmured a few minutes later as she sagged in his arms, limp and overcome by lust.

"Car? What car?"

She looked hazily over his shoulder, registering the red Mustang with a frown.

"Oh, right. That's mine," she explained as she drew his head back down for another kiss.

A few minutes later, Jack spoke again.

"So you just went out and bought a new car?"

It was hard to concentrate when she had six feet two inches of sexy, loving man pressed up against her, but she made an effort.

"Yes. That's exactly what I did."

He sounded really surprised, which got her thinking. And suddenly it hit her what she'd done. Had she been on drugs an hour ago? Stunned, she looked up at him.

"I didn't even take it for a test drive. I have no idea how many miles it has. I have no idea if it even has an engine!"

He started laughing, then he bent down and scooped her up into his arms.

"That sounds more like the Claire Marsden I

know and love," he said as he carried her into his house, then into his bedroom. The sight of his large, welcoming bed went a long way to alleviating her buyer's remorse.

"What am I going to do?" she asked vaguely as he dropped her on the bed and started tearing her clothes off.

"We'll work it out," he promised.

And looking up at him leaning over her with love and lust in his eyes, she realized they always would.

* * * * *

Shoma Narayanan started reading Mills and Boon®
romances at the age of eleven, borrowing them
from neighbours so that her parents didn't find
out. At that time, the thought of writing one herself
never entered her head. But a couple of years ago
Shoma took up writing and was amazed at how
much she enjoyed it. Now she works at her banking
job through the week, and tries to balance writing
with household chores during weekends. Her
family has been unfailingly supportive of her
latest hobby.

AN OFFER SHE CAN'T REFUSE

Shoma Narayanan

CHAPTER ONE

DARIUS MISTRY WAS not used to taking orders from anyone. And especially not orders that came from a woman he was supposed to be interviewing. The fact that the woman had turned out to be surprisingly attractive was neither here nor there—this was strictly work, and her behaviour right now seemed more than a little strange.

'Hold my hand,' she was saying. 'Come on, she's almost here.'

Her current boss had just walked into the coffee shop, and Mallika was reacting as if it was a massive disaster. Granted, being caught by your boss while you were being interviewed for another job wasn't the best start to an interview, but it wasn't the end of the world. Mallika's expression suggested a catastrophe on a life-threatening scale—like the *Titanic* hitting the iceberg or Godzilla stomping into town.

'Please, Darius?' she said, and when he didn't react immediately she reached across the table and took his hand. 'Look into my eyes,' she pleaded.

He complied, trying not to notice how soft her skin was, and how her slim and capable-looking hand fitted perfectly into his.

'At least try to *pretend* you're my date,' she begged despairingly.

He laughed. 'You're not doing a great job, either,' he pointed out. 'The whole "deer caught in head-lights" look doesn't suggest you're crazy about me.'

She managed to chuckle at that, and her expression was so appealing that he sighed and put on what he hoped was a suitably infatuated look. Actually, after a second he found he was quite enjoying himself. He had a keen sense of humour, and despite his attempts to remain professional when faced with such an attractive interviewee, the situation was so completely ridiculous it was funny.

He was supposed to be evaluating Mallika for an important role in his company, and instead here he was, holding her hand and gazing deeply into her eyes. Rather beautiful eyes, actually—the momentarily helpless Bambi look was gone now, replaced with an apprehensive but intriguingly mischievous little sparkle.

'My goodness, Mallika, what a surprise!'

The woman who'd stopped by their table was middle-aged and plump and terribly overdressed. Purple silk, loads of fussy jewellery, and make-up that would have put a Bollywood item girl to shame.

'Hi, Vaishali,' Mallika looked up with a suitably friendly smile, but she didn't let go of Darius's hand.

'So this was your "urgent personal meeting", was it?' Vaishali leaned closer to Darius. 'Mallika's kept *you* a pretty closely guarded secret, I must say.'

'We…um…met recently,' Darius said, trying not

to gag at the cloud of cloying perfume. It was like being smothered to death by lilies—the woman must have poured an entire bottle of perfume over herself.

'Ah, well, you deserve to have some fun,' the woman was saying to Mallika, patting her hand in a surprisingly motherly way. 'I'll leave you with your young man, shall I? See you at work tomorrow!'

Her husband had been waiting patiently by her side, and Vaishali tucked her hand in his arm and trotted off with a final wave.

Mallika sighed in relief. 'Close shave,' she said as she released Darius's hand.

Clearly it was no longer of any use to her, but Darius felt absurdly bereft. When he'd first seen her he'd thought Mallika strikingly good-looking, in a natural, outdoorsy kind of way—not his type at all. Now, however, he found himself wishing that she'd held on to his hand just a little bit longer, and the feeling surprised him.

He wasn't entirely sure how he had lost control of the situation, and why he had not asserted himself in his usual role. He usually went for graceful, ultra-feminine women—the kind who'd learnt ballet when they were young and who dabbled in poetry in their spare time. While she was conservatively dressed, in a business suit, Mallika looked as if she'd spent her youth playing cricket with boys and beating them in every game.

Writing off his reaction to her as a momentary aberration, Darius tried to make sense of what had just happened.

'Is she that scary?' Darius asked, and when Mallika didn't answer, he prompted, 'Your boss?'

She bit her lip. 'No, she isn't,' she said after a brief pause. 'She's actually rather nice.'

He was about to ask her why she'd been so nervous, then, but he held the words back. This was a business meeting, and the fewer personal questions he asked the better. Only he didn't feel very businesslike right now. When she'd bitten down on her lower lip his eyes had been automatically attracted to her mouth, and now he couldn't look away. Her lips were full and soft-looking and utterly feminine, and completely in contrast to her direct gaze and the firm lines of her chiselled face...

Okay, this was crazy—sitting and staring at a woman he'd met fifteen minutes ago. One whom he was supposed to be interviewing for a directorship.

'We didn't get very far with our discussion,' he said, trying to sound as if his interest in her was limited to her suitability for the role he'd been telling her about. 'There's a decent restaurant on the twenty-first floor. Would you prefer going there? Less chance your boss might pop up again.'

Mallika hesitated. It had seemed so glamorous when someone from the Nidas Group had head-hunted her to discuss a director level role. Nidas was big—it had been set up by a bunch of young dotcom entrepreneurs a decade ago, and they'd struck gold in almost every business they'd tried their hand at.

They'd started off with online share trading and investments, but later branched off into venture capital and real estate and done much better than players who'd been in the market for thrice the time. Being considered for a directorship in the firm at the age of twenty-nine was a huge ego-boost—it wouldn't have been possible in any other firm, but at Nidas the directors were quite young, and they didn't hold her age against her.

Her first few meetings with Nidas had been preliminary ones, screening her for this final interview with Darius Mistry. For a few days she'd actually thought she could do it—be like any of the other women she'd gone to business school with, take charge of her career, interview with other employers, pretend that she had a *normal* life like everyone else. Reality was sinking in only now.

She glanced across at Darius. When she'd heard the name she'd imagined a paunchy, cheerful, white-haired man—she'd had a Parsi drama teacher at school who'd also been called Darius, and he'd looked just like Santa Claus minus the beard. Darius Mistry had come as a bit of a surprise.

True, his Persian ancestry showed in his pale colouring and hawklike features, but he was in his early thirties, tall and broad-shouldered, and as unlike her former drama teacher as an eagle from a turkey. Not good-looking in the traditional sense, more disturbingly attractive, and he emanated a quiet power and control that had Mallika caught in its glow.

He was still waiting for her to answer, she realised. 'No, I'm fine here,' she said. 'Actually, I just made up my mind. I don't think I want to take the interview any further. I'm sorry—I should have thought this through properly.'

Darius frowned. This afternoon really was *not* going to plan. Mallika had been interviewed by his HR team, as well as by one of his colleagues, and everyone who'd met her had been very impressed. Apparently she'd come across as being sharply intelligent and very, very good at what she did. He'd also looked at the performance of the real estate fund she managed. It had done extremely well, even in a volatile and completely unpredictable market, and before he'd met Mallika he'd built up an image of a hard-nosed, practical businesswoman.

The reality was different enough to be intriguing.

For a few seconds he wondered if she was playing hard to get. People used all kinds of techniques to drive up the benefits package they were offered, but very few started so early in the process. And Mallika looked troubled, a little upset—whatever the reason for her sudden decision to stop the interview process, it definitely wasn't a hard-nosed or practical one.

'You've spent almost five years with your current firm,' he said. 'I know the thought of switching jobs can be a bit overwhelming, but there's no harm going through with the interview process, is there? Once you hear what we're offering you can always say no.'

'I guess…' she said slowly. 'I just don't want to waste your time.'

'My whole night is dedicated to you,' he said.

Promptly Mallika thought of all the things they could get up to together. Her cheeks flushed a little and she took a hasty sip of water, hoping he hadn't noticed her confusion.

'So, how much has Venkat told you about the job?' Darius asked.

'He told me about how you and he set up the share trading division,' she said. 'And how you got a real estate fund going, and that you now want to concentrate on the venture capital side and hire someone to manage the fund for you.'

'That's right,' Darius said. 'The fund was an offshoot of our investments business and it's been doing well—we've consistently outperformed the market.'

She seemed interested, Darius noted as he began telling her more about the role. She was frowning in concentration, and the few questions she asked were focussed and showed that she'd done a good deal of research on the firm and on the job. He asked a few questions in turn, and it was clear that Venkat hadn't been wrong. Mallika knew pretty much everything there was to know about running a real estate fund.

'Does it sound like something you'd like to do?' he asked finally.

It was as if he'd shaken her out of a daydream— her vibrantly alive expression dulled, and her shoulders slumped just a little.

'I love the sound of the job,' she said, almost unwillingly. 'But the timing's not right for me. I have a lot going on right now, and I think maybe it's best I stay where I am.'

'Do you want to take a day to think it over?'

Mallika shook her head. 'No, I...I think I'm pretty

clear that it won't work out. I'm so sorry—I know you have a busy schedule, and I should have thought this through properly before agreeing to meet you.'

She looked so genuinely contrite that he impulsively leaned across the table to cover her hand with his, making her look up in surprise.

'Don't worry about it,' he said, masking his disappointment. 'I'm meeting other people as well, but if you do change your mind let me know.'

Mallika blinked at him, uncharacteristically at a loss for words. It was like being hit by a train, she thought, confused. She'd been so focussed on what he was saying, on trying to stay professional, that she'd forgotten quite how attractive he was. Then he'd smiled and taken her hand, and the feel of his warm skin against hers had sent her long-dormant hormones into overdrive.

We like this man, they were saying excitedly. *Where did you find him? Can we keep him? Please?*

So much for a dispassionate admiration of his looks, she thought, trying to quell the seriously crazy thoughts racing through her brain. There was good-looking, and there was scorching hot—and Darius definitely fell into the second category. The first time she'd grabbed his hand she'd been too worked up to notice—this time a simple touch had sent her hormones into overdrive.

Gingerly, she slid her hand out from under his and gave him what she hoped was a sufficiently cool and professional smile.

'I'll tell you if I change my mind,' she managed as she pulled together her scattered thoughts.

'The salary is negotiable,' he added.

She shook her head. 'It's not about the money,' she assured him. 'But thanks for letting me know.'

Darius knew when not to push—and he also knew he wasn't going to give up so easily.

Mallika looked as if she was all set to leave, and he glanced at his watch. 'It's almost eight-thirty,' he said. 'I'm starving, and I'm sure you are too. D'you have time for a quick bite?'

Perhaps he could get to the bottom of her sudden withdrawal and convince her otherwise.

He was almost sure she was going to say yes, but then her phone pinged and she gave the display a harassed look.

'I need to go,' she said, her attention clearly torn between him and whoever had just messaged her. Her expression was distracted as she stood up hurriedly, her short curls swinging around her cheeks. 'Thanks for being so nice about everything.'

She put her hand out, and Darius got to his feet as he took it. 'Nice' wasn't the impression he wanted to leave her with. 'Nice' suggested she'd forget him the minute she stepped out of the hotel. And he wasn't going to let *that* happen.

'I'll be in touch,' he said, keeping her hand in his a fraction longer than strictly necessary.

She didn't reply, but she blinked once, and he re-alised that she wasn't quite as unaffected by him as she was pretending to be. It was a cheering thought, and he smiled as she walked away.

He'd found her intriguing—an unusual mix of the ultra-competent and the overcautious. And the attraction between them had been hot and instantaneous—if it hadn't been a work meeting he would definitely have taken things further. As it was, he was forced to let her walk away with only a tepid assurance of being in touch later.

The smell of freshly baked bread wafted past, reminding Darius of how hungry he was. He glanced around. Eating alone had never appealed to him, and if he stayed Mallika's boss might see him and come across to ask where Mallika was. He felt strangely protective of the intriguing woman he had only known for a couple of hours.

Mentally he ran through his options. Going home and ordering in. Calling up a friend and heading to a restaurant. Turning up at the excruciatingly boring corporate event he'd earlier declined.

The corporate event was the least appealing, but it would give him an opportunity to network with a bunch of people who could be useful to Nidas in the future. It wasn't too far away, either, and if he left now he'd be able to get there, hang around for an hour or so and still get home in time to catch the last bulletin on his favourite news channel.

He was handing the attendant his valet parking ticket when he spotted Mallika getting into an expensive-looking chauffeur-driven car. She was talking on the phone, and he caught a few words before the doorman closed the door for her and the car zoomed off.

'I'll be home in twenty minutes,' she was saying. 'I *told* you I had a meeting, Aryan. No, I haven't decided. I'll talk to you later...'

Whoever Aryan was, he sounded like a possessive control freak. Darius frowned. He hadn't asked Mallika, but he could have sworn she wasn't married. No *mangalsutra* necklace or rings—but lots of married women didn't wear those. And the way she'd looked at him for that one instant...

Darius shook himself. He was rarely wrong about these things, but meeting Mallika seemed to have seriously addled his brains. He was missing the obvious. She'd hardly have asked him to pretend to be her date if her boss knew that she had a husband.

Restored to his normal confidence once he'd figured that out, he tipped the valet parking attendant lavishly as he got into his car. Not married, and probably not in a serious relationship either. Hopefully this Aryan was her interior decorator, or her tax advisor, or someone equally inconsequential.

'WHAT D'YOU MEAN, she wasn't interested?'

'She doesn't want to change jobs,' Darius explained patiently.

He and Venkat had joined the Nidas Group on the same day, and had spent the last decade setting up the businesses they now headed. Darius was the stable, intelligent one—the brains behind most of what they'd achieved together. Venkat was a typical sales guy—competitive, pushy and notoriously impatient. Outside of work he and Darius were close personal friends, but right now Venkat's expression was that of a bulldog being asked to let go of a particularly juicy bone.

'*Why* does she not want to change jobs? Did you tell her how much we're willing to pay?'

'I did,' Darius said. 'She said she doesn't need the money.'

'You need to meet her again,' Venkat said flatly. 'I have absolutely no clue about this fund management stuff, and if you're leaving we'll go under before you know it. This girl's really good, and she seemed keen until she met you. I'd have thought it would be the exact opposite—girls usually fall for you on first sight. What in heaven's name did you do to put her off?'

'Told her that she'd be working with a bunch of total scumbags,' Darius said, deadpan. 'Look, I'm not prepared to let her go, either, but it will be better to give her some time to think things over and change her mind. I'll make it happen. But in the meantime I've got a bunch of other CVs from HR. Some of them with equally impressive track records.'

Venkat grunted. 'I'll go through the CVs, but you need to work your magic with this girl. Otherwise you can jolly well put your exciting plans on hold and stay here until you can find someone to replace you. I'm terrible at all this HR sort of stuff—you're the one who gets everyone eating out of your hand. Make this Mallika an offer she can't refuse.'

Darius bit back a sigh. Once Venkat decided he wanted something he was like an unstoppable force of nature.

'I'm a businessman, not a Mafia don,' he said drily. 'Let me do it my way. I have an idea on how to win her...'

CHAPTER TWO

THE FLAT WAS dark when Mallika let herself in, and she felt a familiar pang of loss as she put the lights on and surveyed the empty living room. Nothing was the same without her parents, and having a brother who'd completely retreated into his shell emphasised her loneliness rather than reduced it.

It had been a gruelling week. Her job involved meeting builders and visiting construction sites and then spending hours hunched over her computer, calculating the possible return she'd get from each investment she made for her fund.

The Mumbai property market had been at its volatile best these last few months, and investors were wary. Which meant that there was a risk of projects stalling—which in turn meant that buyers who'd already invested found themselves with large amounts of capital locked up and no hope of returns in the short term. And the fund that Mallika worked for was seriously considering stopping investment in properties that were under construction.

The kitchen was dark as well. The cook would have gone home some hours ago, leaving dinner out in microwaveable dishes for Mallika and Aryan. She wasn't particularly hungry, but dinner was the only meal she could make sure her brother actually ate.

The lights in his room were on, and she knocked before entering.

'Aryan? Dinner?' she asked, her heart twisting as she watched him hunch over his laptop. It was as if he didn't see the world around him any more, finding reality in the flickering screen of his computer instead.

'In a minute,' he said, not even looking up.

'Did you have lunch?' she asked, and he shrugged.

'Lalita gave me something,' he said. 'You go ahead and eat—you must be tired.'

It was a measure of how little she expected from him that she actually felt pleased he'd realised how exhausted she was. Leaving him to his computer, she went back to the kitchen—she'd make sure he had something to eat later.

For the last couple of days she'd not been able to get Darius out of her head. The way he'd looked at her, his smile, his voice—it felt as if she'd spent hours with him rather than just a few minutes.

He'd said he'd be in touch, but two days had gone by and he hadn't called. Maybe he'd found someone else more suitable for the role. Someone who *didn't* spot their boss and freak out halfway through a discussion, or run out on him without warning.

Idly she opened the contact list in her phone and started scrolling down it. Darius Mistry. She had his mobile number and his email ID, and the temptation to drop him a text or a short email was huge. She could apologise once again for running out on him. Or tell him that she'd changed her mind about the job.

When it came to professional communications she was confident and practical, but somehow with Darius she found herself prevaricating. Her shyness prevented her from getting in touch for anything other than strictly business reasons.

She was still mulling things over when her phone rang, and she almost dropped it in surprise.

'I was just thinking about you,' she blurted out, and then blushed furiously. Darius was probably already convinced of her weirdness—she didn't need to make it worse. 'I mean…I was just thinking over what you said about this being the right stage in my career to change jobs…'

'Reconsidering, I hope?' he said smoothly, and went on without waiting for her to answer. 'Look, I know you've said you're not interested, but I've interviewed around a dozen completely unsuitable people and I'd really like a chance to pitch the job to you again. Preferably in a place where your boss isn't likely to land up and ruin my sales pitch.'

One part of her felt disappointed that he hadn't called just to speak to her, but she shook herself crossly. *Of course* his interest in her was purely professional. What had got into her?

'I'm really not interested in changing jobs, Darius,' she said, firmly suppressing the little voice in her head that told her to go and meet him anyway. 'And I've wasted your time once already—I wouldn't want to do it again.'

Darius briefly considered telling Mallika that time spent with her would definitely not be wasted, but he bit the words back. This wasn't a seduction, and he'd already made it clear that when it came to business he was as determined as she to get what he wanted.

'It's part of my job,' he said lightly. 'Even if you don't want to join us now, at least I'll get to tell you about the company—and who knows? Maybe you'll want to join at some later time.'

'All right, then,' Mallika conceded. 'When shall I meet you?'

'Tomorrow,' he said decisively. 'Lunch at one of the restaurants in Lower Parel? That's nearer my office than yours, and hopefully we won't run into anyone you know.'

DARIUS WAS BEGINNING to wonder if he'd been stood up when Mallika finally walked into the restaurant. The first thing that struck him was that there was a strained expression in her lovely eyes. The second was that she looked anything but tomboyish now.

Granted, her hair was still styled for convenience rather than glamour, and her make-up was kept to the bare minimum. But she was wearing a sari today— a dark blue silk affair, with a muted print—and her figure was spectacular in it. And her spontaneous smile when she saw him was the best welcome he could ever have hoped for.

He stood as she walked up to him, and Mallika began to feel ridiculously nervous. It was a Friday and he was dressed casually, in a white open-necked cotton shirt over jeans. His thick hair looked slightly damp from the shower, and she had a second's insane urge to reach up and run her fingers through it.

To cover her confusion she held out her hand, and he took it, briefly clasping it between both his hands before he let go.

'Hi,' she said. 'I'm not too late, am I?'

He shook his head. That smile had lit up her face, but now the worried expression was back in her eyes.

'Is everything okay?' he asked quietly once they were both seated and the waiter had put their menu cards in front of them and retired to a safe distance.

Her eyes flew up to his. 'Yes, of course,' she said, sounding just a little defensive.

Aryan was going through a particularly problematic phase, and in the normal course of things she wouldn't have left him alone at home. But she'd promised Darius, and there were meetings in the office that she couldn't avoid. Just this once Aryan would have to manage on his own, with just Lalita the cook to check on him.

'You look tense,' he said. 'Like you're trying to remember whether you locked your front door when you left. Don't worry about it—burglars are usually deeply suspicious of open doors. If it's unlocked, there's absolutely no chance of a break-in.'

She laughed at that. 'What if I did lock it?'

'Ah, then I hope you have a good security system.'

'A simple lock, and a brother who won't notice if someone puts every single thing in the house into packing cases and carries them away under his nose. As long as they don't touch his computer.'

He smiled, his eyes crinkling up at the corners in a maddeningly attractive way. 'Sounds like my kind of guy. Younger brother?'

Mallika nodded. She hardly ever mentioned Aryan in casual conversation, and the ease with which the reference had slipped out surprised her. Darius was beguilingly easy to talk to—she'd need to be on her guard a little.

The waiter was hovering behind her, and she turned her attention to the menu.

'The fish is good,' Darius said.

'It looks delicious,' Mallika said, glancing at the next table, where another waiter had just deposited two plates of grilled fish. 'I'm vegetarian, though.'

'Then the gnocchi?' he said. 'Or the spaghetti in pesto sauce?'

Mallika finally chose the spaghetti, and a glass of wine to go with it—Darius, who'd never paid good money for a vegetarian meal before in his life, found himself ordering grilled vegetables and pasta. A lot of strict vegetarians were put off by someone eating meat at the same table, and he definitely didn't want to risk that. He was on a charm offensive today, and determined to win her over.

'How's your boss?' he asked.

'She's miffed I didn't tell her I was dating someone,' Mallika said with a sigh. Vaishali was a lovely person, but the concept of personal space was completely alien to her. 'She wanted to invite both of us to her house for dinner—I had a devil of a time wriggling out of that one.'

'What did you say to her?' Darius asked, unable to keep a glint out of his eye.

'That I'd been wrong about you and you were actually really self-centred,' Mallika said, delighted she'd managed to keep a poker face. 'And possessive—and controlling.'

She sounded remarkably cheerful about it, and Darius's lips twitched.

'So we aren't dating any longer?'

'We are,' Mallika said. 'You have a few redeeming qualities, but I'm not as sure about you as I was. We're dating, but I'm not introducing you to friends and family just yet.'

'Wouldn't it have been easier to remove me from the scene altogether?'

'If I'd written you off she'd have tried setting me up with a perfectly horrible second cousin of hers. She's spent the last two years trying to palm him off on every unmarried woman she knows.'

'Maybe he's not so bad?' Darius suggested carefully. 'You should meet him—keep your options open.'

Mallika shuddered. 'No, thanks. I've met him once, and that was once too often. He spent forty-five minutes telling me how rich he is, and how he made his money. And he breathes really heavily.'

'Hmm…'

Darius's eyes were dancing wickedly, and Mallika felt a little jolt of awareness go through her. It had been so long since she'd spent any time with an attractive man that she was ridiculously susceptible.

'Can I ask you something?'

She gave him a wary look. 'Yes.'

'Are you atoning for the sins of a past life by working for Vaishali?'

'She's been very good to me,' Mallika said stilt-edly, and when he raised an eyebrow she went on in a rush. 'No, really. She can be a bit overpowering at times, but I owe her a lot. I didn't mean to make her sound like a nightmare boss.'

She sounded as if it really mattered, and Darius nodded.

'If you say so.' He was silent for a few seconds as the waiter put their drinks in front of them. 'So, should I tell you a bit more about the job and the company? You can make up your mind then.'

She nodded, and listened carefully as he explained again about the company structure and the role that he was offering. Unlike her current company, which invested solely in real estate, the Nidas Group had evolved into a conglomerate of companies that included a brokering house, a consumer lending company and the fund where Darius was offering her a job. Darius himself was moving on—he didn't give her any details, but she assumed it was to head up a new division—and he didn't have enough capacity to manage the fund as well.

'I have a question,' she said, once he'd finished telling her about the job. 'Why do you think I'm right for the position?'

'You have a superb track record,' Darius said. 'And Venkat was very impressed after he interviewed you.'

'But *you* haven't interviewed me,' she pointed out. 'Or do you trust Venkat that much?'

'I have every intention of interviewing you,' Darius said, his brows quirking. 'The second you tell me that you're actually interested in the job I'll start firing questions at you.'

Mallika stared at him for a few seconds, and then burst out laughing.

'You have a point,' she said. 'So—the job sounds perfect. It's the logical next step in my career and like you said, I've been in my current job for five years and I'm beginning to stagnate.'

'I can see a "but" coming,' he murmured.

'Yes... I mean...'

'It's not convenient from a personal point of view?' Darius supplied when she hesitated.

Mallika nodded. 'That's it. I can't tell you the details, but...'

'I don't need to know the details,' Darius said. 'But if you tell me what exactly it is that your current company is doing to help you maybe I can see if we can work something out.'

Darius could smell victory, and he wasn't about to let this one go.

'I don't have fixed hours,' she said in a rush. 'Some days I reach work at eight, and some days I go in only in the afternoon. And I do site visits on my own when it's convenient to me. Sometimes I work from home, and there are days when I'm not able to work at all.'

She ground to a halt, her eyes wide and a little apprehensive. Clearly whatever was happening on the personal front was very important to her. He wondered what it was. The kind of flexibility she needed was normally required only if an employee had to care for a sick child or an elderly parent. Mallika wasn't married, and from what she'd said her younger brother sounded responsible. A parent, then, he decided.

The unwelcome thought that she might be going through a messy divorce came to mind, but he pushed it away. A divorce might need her to take time off work, but it wouldn't need her to work from home. It was far more likely that one of her parents needed to be cared for.

He thought for a while. 'We might be able to let you do the same,' he said slowly. 'Can I work this out and get back to you?'

'But when I asked Venkat he said you don't have a flexible working policy!' she said.

'It hasn't been formally approved yet,' Darius said. 'We're still working on it. Yours could be a test case.'

Their food had arrived, and Mallika took a bite of her spaghetti before answering. 'You know,' she said conversationally, 'the job market's really bad nowadays.'

'It is,' Darius agreed, frowning a little.

'And bonuses are dropping and people are getting fired every day.'

'Yes.'

'So you could probably hire anyone you wanted, right? With just as much experience and no complicated conditions. Why are you still trying to convince *me* to take the job?'

When it came to work, Mallika was sharp and to the point. She was intelligent—obviously she was, or Venkat wouldn't have considered hiring her. But Darius found himself wondering why exactly he *was* trying so hard to convince her. He'd never tried to recruit an unwilling candidate before—he'd never had to. And while she was definitely his first choice for the job, there were at least two others who could do the job equally well.

Had this just become about winning? Or perhaps he hadn't been thinking clearly since taking her hand in that coffee shop several days ago. What was going on?

'Venkat's interviewed pretty much everyone in the industry,' he said. 'You're the best fit for the role.'

'But the second best might end up doing a better job,' she said. 'He or she'd be more inclined to take the offer to begin with.'

'It's not just about technical skills,' Darius said. 'We think you'd adjust well to the organisation's culture. And we also need to improve the firm's diversity ratio, now that we're likely to get some foreign investment into the company. That's one of the things investors are likely to look at. There are a lot of women at junior levels, but very few at middle or senior management. There weren't too many CVs that fitted the bill *and* belonged to women—and other than you none of them made a decent showing at interview.'

'But I'm sure you have male candidates who're suitable,' she said, her brow wrinkling. 'Surely this diversity thing isn't so important that you've not interviewed men at all?'

'Venkat's interviewed quite a few,' Darius said. 'Apparently you did better than them as well. Diversity's not more important than talent—it's just that now we've found you we don't want to let you go.'

His gaze was direct and unwavering, and Mallika felt herself melting under it. The attraction she'd felt the first time she'd met him was back in full force—if he told her that he wanted her to join a cult that ate nuts and lived in trees she'd probably consider it seriously. Shifting jobs was a no-brainer in comparison—especially when he was guaranteeing a higher salary and no change to her timings.

She was about to tell him that she'd join when a shadow fell across their table.

'Darius!' a delighted male voice said. 'It's been years, my boy—how are you?'

The speaker was a stalwart-looking man in his early forties, who beamed all over his face as he clapped Darius on his shoulder. The blow would have pitched a weaker man face-down into his grilled vegetables, but Darius hardly winced.

'Gautam,' he said, standing up and taking the

man's hand in a firm grip. 'Long while… I didn't know you were back in Mumbai.'

'Just here for a visit. And…? You're married and everything now? Is this the new Mrs Mistry?'

He looked as if he was about to clap Mallika on the shoulder as well, and Darius intervened hastily.

'No, Mallika is…a friend.'

'Aha! A Miss Mystery, then, not a Mrs Mistry—is that right?' Clearly delighted at his own wit, Gautam smiled even more broadly. 'I'll leave you to it, then. Catch you online later—I'm in Mumbai for a week more…we should try and meet.'

'Yes, I'll look forward to that.'

Darius waited till the man had moved away before sitting down, shaking his head.

'It's fate,' he said solemnly. 'Last time it was your boss—this time it was Gautam. We can't meet without running into someone we know.'

Mallika chuckled. 'He seemed a cheerful guy. He reminds me of a story I read as a kid—there was a man who smiled so wide that the smile met at the back of his face and the top of his head fell off.'

'That's such an awful story,' Darius said. 'Were you a bloodthirsty kind of kid?'

'I was a bit of a tomboy,' she said, confirming Darius's first opinion of her. 'Not bloodthirsty, though.'

She frowned at her plate as she chased the last strand of spaghetti around it. Finally managing to nab it, she raised her fork to her mouth. The spaghetti promptly slithered off and landed on her lap.

'And *that's* why my good clothes never last,' she said, giving the mark on her sari a resigned look as she picked up the pasta and deposited it back on her plate. 'I'm as clumsy as a hippopotamus.'

Anything less hippopotamus-like would be hard to find, Darius thought as he watched her dab ineffectually at the stain with a starched table napkin. Her curly hair fell forward to obscure her face, and her *pallu* slipped off her slim shoulder to reveal a low-cut blouse and more than a hint of cleavage.

Darius averted his eyes hastily—looking down a girl's blouse was something he should have outgrown in high school. The one glimpse he'd got, however, was enough to make him shift uncomfortably in his chair. Really, Darius was so off-kilter he could hardly understand the effect she was having on him.

'Here, let me help with that,' he said, after Mallika had dropped the napkin twice and narrowly missed tipping her plate over. He got up and, taking a handkerchief out of his pocket, wet the corner in a glass of water and came to her side of the table to attend to the sari.

Mallika went very still. He wasn't touching her— he was holding the stained section of sari away from her body and efficiently getting rid of the stain with the damp handkerchief. But he was close enough for her to inhale the scent of clean male skin and she had to fold her hands tightly in her lap to stop herself from involuntarily reaching out and touching him.

'Thanks,' she said stiltedly once he was done.

'You're welcome.' Darius inclined his head

slightly as he went back to his side of the table. 'Dessert?'

'I should choose something that matches the sari,' she said ruefully as she recovered her poise. 'I love chocolate, but I'm not sure I dare!'

'Blueberry cheesecake?' he asked, his eyes dancing with amusement again. 'Or should we live life dangerously and order the sizzling brownie with ice cream?'

'The brownie, I think…' she started to say, but just then her phone rang, and her face went tense as she looked at the display. 'I'm sorry—I'll need to take this call,' she said.

'Haan mausiji,' he heard her say, and then, *'Ji. Ji. Nahin,* I had some work so I had to go out. Calm down…don't panic. I can get home in ten minutes— fifteen at the most, depending on the traffic.'

Her face was a picture of guilt and worry as she closed the call, and his heart went out to her.

'I'm sorry,' she said. 'I need to go. It was a lovely lunch, and thank you so much for putting up with me. I'm really sorry about rushing off again…'

'Don't worry about it,' he said gently. 'Do you need a lift anywhere?'

She shook her head. 'I have a car. Is it okay if I go now? I hate leaving you like this, but I really do need to get home as soon as possible.'

'It's not a problem at all,' he said. 'Take care, and we'll talk soon.'

He put enough money on the table to cover the bill plus a hefty tip, and walked her to the door of the restaurant. Her driver took a couple of minutes to bring the car round, and Mallika was clearly on tenterhooks until he arrived.

'Bye,' she said as the car pulled up and she slid into the back seat. 'I'm really, really sorry about this.'

She clasped his hand impulsively before she closed the car door, and Darius was left with the feel of soft, smooth skin on his. The subtle fragrance of her perfume hung in the air for a few seconds after she left.

He gave himself a shake before turning away to walk back to his office. This was not the way he'd planned to end their meal. He'd sensed she was on the point of accepting the role when they'd been interrupted and he could not be more frustrated with his lack of success so far. But it wasn't over—not when he was this close to getting what he wanted.

CHAPTER THREE

'WELCOME TO NIDAS,' Venkat said, giving Mallika a broad smile. 'I'm so happy you finally decided to join.'

'Same here,' Mallika said cautiously as she shook his outstretched hand.

All the old doubts about changing jobs had come flooding back now that she'd actually done the deed. She'd told Vaishali about the job the day after she'd met Darius, feeling like a complete traitor. But Vaishali had been surprisingly nice about the whole thing. Apparently she had been toying with the idea of taking a sabbatical herself, and she wasn't sure if Mallika's flexible working hours would be acceptable to her replacement.

Feeling a bit like a fledgling, shoved out of its nest before it could fly, Mallika had emailed Darius, confirming that she'd be able to join Nidas in a month. He'd been travelling, and someone from his HR team had got in touch to figure out her salary structure and joining date. Darius hadn't even called her, and Mallika couldn't help feeling a little upset about it. And now that she was actually part of Nidas and about to start work, she was very nervous.

The sight of Venkat wasn't exactly inspiring either. Short and squat and rather belligerent-looking, Venkat was as different from her previous boss as possible.

'We've set up an orientation for you with the team,' he was saying now as he ushered her into his room.

'Darius told me—' Mallika began, but Venkat interrupted before she could complete her sentence.

'Oh, Darius is a busy chap—he won't be able to take you through everything himself.' He peered at her owlishly. 'You do know he's moving out of the firm, right?'

Mallika drew in a sharp breath. A lot of things were suddenly falling into place. Darius's insistence that she join as soon as she possibly could. His asking Venkat to set up her induction plan instead of doing it himself. The lengthy meetings with the other directors, ostensibly to help her get to know them before she joined.

A black curl of disappointment started up in the pit of her stomach. He'd had multiple opportunities to tell her and he'd consciously decided not to. It felt like a betrayal, unreasonable though that was. Unconsciously, a large part of her decision to take the job had been based on the assumption that Darius would be around and that she'd be working closely with him.

Serve her right—trusting a man she hardly knew, she thought, squaring her shoulders and doing her best to keep Venkat from noticing how upset she was.

'He didn't tell me that he was moving out alto-gether,' she said crisply. 'Though I did get the im-pression that he'd be cutting off from this part of the business in a month or so.' She was determined to cover her disappointment with cool professionalism.

'Even less, if he has his way,' Venkat said, and an expression of bewildered loss crossed his face for an instant. 'It was a shock when he told me. We've worked together for years—we set up this business together—and out of the blue he tells me he's quit-ting. I still don't understand why he's doing it.'

Strongly tempted to find out more, Mallika bit down on her questions. It shouldn't matter to her where Darius was going or why.

'When you interviewed me *you* didn't mention that Darius was leaving the firm,' she reminded Ven-kat. 'Why did you assume I'd know now?'

He had the grace to look embarrassed. 'I couldn't tell you before you joined,' he said. 'Darius is a pretty big shareholder, and the news of his leav-ing isn't public yet. I thought he might have told you since—I got the impression you guys are pretty friendly.'

He took in Mallika's suddenly stormy expression and changed the subject in a hurry. 'Now, I thought I'd first introduce you to some of the key people in your team, and then you can start going through our current investment strategies. The team's brilliant—I've been working with them pretty closely for the last few months. I've put them on to a few good things as well. Of course now you're here you'll be in full control, but you can reach out to me whenever you want.'

As THE DAY went by Mallika found herself feeling more and more confident. Venkat evidently valued her input, and his style of working wasn't as different from hers as she had feared.

She was packing up for the day when there was a knock on the door of her room. Assuming that it was the overzealous tea boy, who'd been popping up every half an hour, she said, 'Come in!' and continued stuffing files into her laptop bag.

It was a few seconds before she realised that the man in the room was about twice as large as the tea boy.

'Darius!' she said, her brows coming together in an involuntary frown as she saw him. 'I was wondering if I'd see you today.'

'I meant to come over in the morning, but I had one meeting after another. How was your day?'

'Good,' she said. 'I think I'm going to like working here.'

'Did Venkat manage to spend any time with you?'

'A lot,' she said drily.

Darius laughed. 'He believes in throwing people in at the deep end,' he said. 'But he's a great guy to work with. If you're done for the day d'you want to catch up over coffee? There's a decent café nearby.'

Mallika hesitated. She really wanted to confront

Darius about him leaving, but her upbringing made her shy away from any kind of direct conflict.

Some of her indecision must have shown in her face, because he was beginning to look puzzled.

'Or some other day if you need to leave,' he said easily.

Mallika made up her mind.

'I need to get home, but I have time for a coffee from the machine down the hall,' she said.

Compromise—that was one thing she'd learnt early in life. And also that attacking issues head-on sometimes made them worse. She got to her feet and Darius followed her down the hall.

'On second thoughts, I'll have a soft drink,' she said, taking a can from the fridge next to the coffee dispenser. 'You can have that coffee if you want,' she said, gesturing at the mug Darius had just filled for her.

She picked up a second mug and half filled it with warm water from the machine before putting her un-opened can into it.

'It's too cold,' she explained as Darius raised his eyebrows. 'I'll leave it in the mug for a bit and then it'll be just right and I'll drink it.'

Darius's lips curved into a smile as he followed Mallika back to her room. She was wearing black trousers, a no-nonsense blue shirt, and extremely sensible shoes. The whole outfit looked as if it had been chosen to downplay her looks, but the most boring clothes in the world couldn't conceal the narrowness of her waist and the athletic grace of her walk.

Quite contrary to the intended effect, the clothes made her *more* appealing—at least to him.

'Is Venkat involved in the day-to-day running of the fund?' she asked, perching herself on the edge of her desk and swinging her legs idly.

'Not really…' he said cautiously, and she gave him a quizzical look, 'Okay, he's *very* involved in it—but his area of expertise is sales. You won't be reporting to him, if that's your worry—all the directors report straight to the board.'

'Hmm…no, that isn't what was bothering me.'

She smiled at him, and Darius felt his heartbeat quicken in response.

'But tell me—is it true that he's interfered in some of the investment decisions the team have made in the past?'

It was very likely to be true. Darius had heard rumblings from his team, but he hadn't paid much attention up till now. Mallika's pointing it out after being exactly one day in the job, however, hit him on the raw.

'He's talked to them about a few deals,' he said. 'I wouldn't go so far as to call it interference.'

'Maybe it wasn't brought to your attention, then,' she said, clearly unfazed by the sudden chilliness in his tone. 'But he's made some bad calls, and the fund's asset value has dropped. It'll take me a while to undo the damage.'

It was her air of knowing exactly what to do that got to him.

'I'd suggest you take a few days to understand the

business properly first,' he said firmly, though he was feeling uncharacteristically defensive. 'Before you jump in with both feet and start undoing things.'

Mallika frowned. 'I thought the whole point of my being here was that I already know the business,' she said. 'I researched the fund before I even started interviewing with you guys, and it's obvious that you have problems. Logically, it makes no sense to wait to fix them.'

'There's a lot of stuff you wouldn't know from the outside,' Darius insisted. 'Venkat might have his… quirks, but not all the decisions he's made have been bad.'

She shrugged. 'Statistically speaking, even if you made decisions by rolling dice you would end up making some decent ones. But from what I can make out Venkat is superstitious, and his judgement is coloured.'

It had taken Darius months to realise that Venkat's superstitious side sometimes overruled his normally sharp business brain. Mallika had taken exactly one day to figure it out. She was extraordinarily perceptive and he felt slightly wrong-footed. *Again.*

What was this woman doing to him?

Mallika was leaning forward a little. 'Look, you hired me to run this fund,' she said. 'Not because you liked my face. So let me get on with my work. If I mess up you can play the hero and come in and rescue me.'

For a second Darius was tempted to tell her exactly how much he liked her face, but hard as it was he bit back the words. Being her colleague meant that he had to keep a certain professional distance. Speaking of which… Darius realised just how close he was to Mallika, and rolled his chair a few paces back. Unfortunately as soon he started to speak again Mallika scooted her shapely butt closer to him once more, robbing him of his train of thought.

'You're right about Venkat,' he said, trying to sound as detached as possible. 'The whole super-stition thing….' He hesitated a little while trying to find the right words. 'It's a little…'

'Kooky?' she supplied, putting her head to one side. 'Eccentric? Odd?'

'Unconventional,' he said. 'But it's not uncom-mon.'

'And it's unimportant too, I assume?' she said before she could stop herself. 'As far as you're con-cerned anyway. Because you're not planning to be around when the problems kick in.'

If she'd expected him to look guilty she was disappointed, because he threw his head back and laughed. 'I mightn't be around, but the fund's perfor-mance is still pretty damn important to me. I have a fair bit of my own money invested in it, and I don't fancy seeing it go down the tube.'

'I suppose I should be flattered,' she said drily. 'Here I was, thinking you'd given me the fund to run because you didn't care what happened to it.'

'And now you know I've put my life's savings in your hands,' he said. 'Who told you I was moving out? Venkat?'

'Yes,' she said.

'It's not supposed to be public knowledge yet,' he said. 'The board has asked me to stay on for a few months, and they felt it best that the rest of the firm be told I'm leaving only when it's a lot closer to my last day here.'

'Funny...Venkat assumed you'd already told me,' she said. 'Perhaps he thought it was only fair—given that you recruited me and everything.'

Darius leaned a little closer, his brow creasing. 'Are you annoyed that I didn't tell you?' he demanded, putting a hand under her chin to tip her face upwards. 'Even after what I just said?'

Mallika jerked her head away, trying to ignore the little thrill that went through her at his touch.

'Not annoyed...just a little...concerned,' she said, hoping her words would hide how much she longed to work alongside this charismatic man. 'There might be other things you omitted to mention. I pretty much took everything you said at face value.'

'Now, wait a minute,' he said incredulously. 'Are you suggesting I *lied* to you about the job? What makes you think that?'

'You weren't open at all,' she said. 'All this while you've let me think that you'd be around—that you were simply taking on something within the firm. If I'd known you were leaving...'

'You wouldn't have joined?' He looked quite genuinely puzzled. 'Why not? You seem like you have a handle on things already. My being here or not doesn't make a difference, surely?'

Darius was struggling to keep a smug smile off his face—he wasn't the only one who felt what was between them then.

Oh, but it does, Mallika almost said. The thought of working at Nidas without Darius was unsettling in a not very nice way, and she had to scramble to think of a logical explanation for her anxiety.

'I'm just wondering why you're leaving,' she said. 'If something's going wrong with the company… And I did discuss my working hours with you…'

His brow cleared immediately. 'Oh, the flexi-time thing?' he said. 'Don't worry about that at all—I've cleared it with the board. And give Venkat some time—he's a great guy to work with once you get past his superstitious streak.'

He was probably right—he'd worked with Venkat for years, after all, and she'd only met the man today. And she hadn't known Darius for very long either—there was absolutely no reason for the sinking feeling in the pit of her stomach when she thought about him leaving Nidas.

'Hmm….' she said. 'I think I'll get along well with Venkat—I'll have to. I'll need a lot of help from him for the first few months.'

'Will you?' he asked, feeling oddly jealous.

If Mallika needed help *he'd* have liked to be the one to provide it. For a few seconds before his rational side had kicked in he'd actually thought that she was upset because she'd miss him. Now he was left with an absurd feeling of being sidelined—just another stepping stone in Mallika's life.

Their timing was completely off, he thought rue-fully. If he'd met her either a couple of years earlier or later he'd have tried to get to know her better—per-haps even acted on the growing attraction between the two of them. Right now it was completely out of the question. By the time they were no longer col-leagues he'd be long gone.

'You still haven't told me why you're leaving,' Mallika said, and he blinked.

'Personal reasons,' he said, standing up to leave. 'Don't worry—the company's not about to go under.'

Mallika laughed at that. She had a particularly ap-pealing laugh, Darius thought. It was as happy and uncomplicated as a child's, but it had a woman's ma-turity as well, and a sexy little undertone that was irresistible.

'That's reassuring,' she said, slipping off the desk to land on her feet right next to him.

Darius looked into her eyes and there was an instant of absolute connection that made his earlier thoughts irrelevant. A small part of his brain recognised how clichéd the moment was, and he was even amused. The rest of him was completely overwhelmed, and he kept on looking at her stupidly until she blinked and looked away.

'Goodness, look at the time!' she said, her voice slightly more high-pitched than normal. 'I really need to get going.'

'You haven't touched your drink,' he said, and she blinked at the can as if it had just materialised on her desk. 'I'll...um...carry it with me,' she said. 'What about your coffee?'

'I hate that stuff from the machine,' he said. 'Next time we'll go to a proper café.'

The way he said it made it sound like a promise he couldn't wait to keep.

'See you around, Darius,' she managed to squeak, before making a hasty exit.

THE NEXT TIME he saw her was a few days later, with over fifty other people in the same room. Venkat had called for an investor conference, and Mallika was the main presenter.

Darius came in late, slipping into the back of the room. He very rarely attended investor events, but Venkat had been unusually insistent, and he hadn't been able to resist the thought of seeing Mallika in top professional mode.

She was an impressive speaker—economical with words, but leaving her listeners with no doubt of her grasp over the subject. Slim and graceful in a raw silk printed sari, she exuded an aura of confidence and authority that was strangely attractive. Some people would probably think that it detracted from her femininity but, standing at the back of the room, Darius had to work hard to maintain a professional veneer.

She was quite something.

'She's brilliant, isn't she?' Venkat said, materialising next to Darius.

Mallika was answering a question raised by a

grizzled investor old enough to be her father—and by the way the rest of the audience was nodding they were as impressed as Venkat was.

'It's been a while since we've held an event of this sort—it's bloody expensive, paying for the dinner and the booze, but it's worth it if we get the monies to come in. And people *are* interested—the market's looking up. We'll get a couple of hundred crores of investment after this event.'

'So does that mean you guys are doing perfectly well without me?' Darius asked, giving Venkat an amused look.

'We are,' Venkat said. 'Mallika's probably the best person you could have hired to replace you—in spite of all that flexible working rubbish. But, man, this place isn't going to be the same without you.'

The event wound to a close, and Mallika stepped off the dais to mingle with the guests. Venkat had been called back for the vote of thanks, and Darius stood alone at the back of the room, watching Mallika as she moved from one group of middle-aged men to the next, her smile firmly in place.

There were only a handful of women in the audience, and Darius noted that she spent longer with them, explaining something at length to one group and patiently allowing a much older woman to peer at the necklace of semi-precious stones she was wearing.

It was a while before the audience dispersed, most of them heading towards the buffet dinner.

Mallika's shoulders sagged a tiny bit, and the

smile left her face as she walked towards the exit. It
was as if she'd turned off a switch, changing from a
confident, sparkling professional to a young woman
who was just a little tired with life.

Darius waved to her, and she came across to him.

'I didn't see you come in,' she said. 'Did you just
get here?'

'A while ago,' he said. 'I'm impressed, Mallika.
You had everyone eating out of your hands.'

She shrugged. 'I've done this kind of event many
times before,' she said. 'They're exhausting, but it's
part of my job.'

'What do you find exhausting?' Darius asked.

'Talking to people,' she said. 'It's a strain. Everyone asks the same questions, and by the end of it I
get so sick I could scream. Don't tell Venkat,' she
added, looking up with a quick smile that lit up her
face. 'He's planning a whole series of these events.'

'I was about to tell you that,' Darius said, a smile
tugging at his lips. 'He's thrilled with the way you
handled this one.' She made a little grimace, and a
spurt of chivalry made Darius ask, 'Should I talk to
him? He can handle the events himself—or one of
the other fund managers could speak in your place.'

'The other fund managers aren't lucky for Venkat,' she said drily. 'I doubt he'll agree. Anyway, it's
part of why you hired me, right?'

Darius nodded. It had been unprofessional of him
to suggest he intervene, and he couldn't help admire
Mallika's determination to do every part of her job

well. Even when she obviously hated what she was doing.

It was intriguing, the way her ultra-professional mask slipped at times to betray her vulnerability. He had a feeling she didn't let it happen often, and all his protective instincts surged to the forefront whenever it did.

'Aren't you having dinner?' Venkat asked, popping up next to them. 'Or a drink? Mallika?'

She shook her head. 'I need to leave,' she said. 'My driver's taken the day off, so I've called a cab. The cabbie's been waiting for half an hour already.'

'Wouldn't it have been simpler to drive yourself?'

'I don't drive,' she said. 'I've tried learning a few times, but it's been an unmitigated disaster.'

'And you don't drink either! What a waste,' Venkat said sorrowfully. In his opinion, the best part of an event of this sort was the company-sponsored alcohol. 'Darius?'

Darius shook his head. 'I need to leave as well,' he said. 'Got some people coming over. And I'm driving, so I can't have a drink either.'

Venkat looked ridiculously disappointed, and Darius laughed, clapping him on the shoulder.

'I'll take you out for a drink this Friday,' he promised. 'Come on, Mallika—I'll walk you to the lobby.'

Their event had been held in a rather exclusive midtown hotel, and there were several other corporate events in full swing there. The banquet hall next to theirs was hosting an annual party, and the waiting area outside the banquet hall was dotted with entertainers. Jugglers in clown costumes, living statues, and even a magician or two.

Mallika paused next to a gigantic plastic sphere with a girl playing the violin inside it, and stared at it critically.

'What's the idea?' she asked. 'Why's the girl in the bubble?'

Darius shrugged. 'It's supposed to add a touch of the exotic,' he said. 'In the last party I went to of this sort they'd flown in a belly dancer from Turkey to dance for about ten minutes.'

'Ugh, what an awful job,' Mallika said, wondering which was worse—the few men who were openly leering at the blonde violinist in her low-cut green Tinker Bell dress, or the people who were walking past without even acknowledging her as a human being. 'I'm suddenly feeling a lot better about my own work.'

'No plastic bubbles?' Darius said solemnly as they went down the stairs that led to the hotel lobby. 'That *is* a significant upside, I agree. And wonderful colleagues to work with, perhaps?'

She giggled. 'Like Venkat?'

'Like *me*, I was going to say.' Darius held the door open for her as they went out into the night air. 'But clearly I've not done enough to impress you yet.'

Mallika looked up at him. In the warm light pouring out from the lobby he looked incredible. His hair was slightly mussed, and a few strands fell over his forehead in sexy disarray. He'd come from work, but he'd taken off his tie and undone the top button of his

shirt, and it was difficult to take her eyes off the triangle of exposed skin. And when she did it was only
to lose herself in *his* eyes—dark and amused, with
a hint of something that was disturbingly exciting.

'Consider me impressed,' she said lightly, and
turned away to dig for her phone in her bag, ignoring the sudden movement he made towards her.

'What d'you mean, you've *left*?' she demanded
a few minutes later, having finally got through to
the cabbie.

She listened to what sounded like an incredibly
complicated explanation, and sighed.

'He got another fare and went off,' she said. 'I'll
have to ask the hotel to get me a cab.'

'Or I could drop you home?' Darius suggested.

'Isn't it out of your way?'

'Not terribly,' Darius lied. 'We'll take the sea
link.' Dropping Mallika home would add forty-five
minutes to his drive, but it was worth it.

'If you're sure, then,' Mallika said, heaving a sigh
of relief.

It wouldn't be difficult getting another cab back,
but the thought of the lonely drive home was singu-
larly depressing. And, whether she admitted it to
herself or not, the prospect of spending more time
with Darius held a lot of appeal.

Darius handed his valet parking token to an attendant and put a hand under Mallika's elbow as
he steered her to one side. By Mumbai standards it
was unusually chilly, and there was a strong breeze

blowing. He felt Mallika shiver a little, and gave her a concerned look.

'Do you have a wrap or something?' he asked, and she shook her head, drawing the *pallu* of her sari around her shoulders.

'No, I didn't think it would be cold,' she said.

'And I've left my jacket in my car,' Darius said. 'All my life I've wanted to be chivalrous like in movies—put my jacket around a shivering girl's shoulders—and when I get the perfect opportunity...'

'You find you've forgotten the jacket?' she said, laughing up at him. 'Don't worry about it—I'm not likely to die of frostbite.'

'You could catch a cold, though,' he said, sounding quite serious. 'I'll take you back inside till the car comes up.'

Or you could put your arm around me, Mallika almost said. That would be another favourite Hollywood moment, copied faithfully by Bollywood in multiple movies. Even suggesting it was out of the question, of course, but oh, how she wished she could!

Before she could turn around, a slim woman with waist-length hair came up to them and tapped Darius lightly on the shoulder. A man followed her, a long-suffering look on his face.

'It's Tubby Mistry, isn't it?' she asked, after hesitating a little.

Darius looked around, his face breaking into a smile. 'Nivi! How are you doing?'

'It *is* you!' the woman said, giving a little squeal of delight before throwing herself into his arms.

The man, presumably her husband, gave Mallika a resigned look. Mallika smiled at him, though inwardly she was feeling absurdly jealous of the woman. It was particularly ironic, her turning up and flinging herself into Darius's arms just when Mallika had been wishing she could do exactly that.

'My goodness, I almost didn't recognise you,' Nivi said, stepping back after giving Darius several exuberant hugs and leaving a lipstick mark on his cheek. 'I spotted you when you were walking out of the hotel. You looked so familiar, but I just couldn't place you.'

'She thought you were a TV celeb,' her husband interjected, earning himself a reproachful look.

'You can't blame me for that—he's turned out so utterly gorgeous!' she said. 'You should have seen him in school! He was overweight and gawky and he wore a perfectly hideous pair of glasses. No girl would have turned to look at him twice.'

Her husband cleared his throat, jerking his head towards Mallika.

'Oh, I'm so sorry,' Nivi said, looking genuinely contrite. 'You don't mind, do you? I'm Nivedita. I knew Darius in school, and we've not met in years. I moved back to Kolkata, and I've lived there ever since. We only got here today, and he's the first person I've met from my old life.'

'You must send me some of his school pictures,' Mallika said promptly, and Darius groaned.

'Nivi, if you do anything of that sort I'll have to break that solemn blood oath you made me swear in school.'

'Blackmailer!' she said, giving him another affectionate hug. 'Don't you dare, Darius. Remember all the help I gave you for your Hindi exams?'

'Yes, well, I passed the exams, but I still can't speak a sentence without making mistakes,' he said, and Nivedita laughed.

'You'll learn the language some day,' she said. 'Okay, I'm off now—I can see the two of you are dying to be alone. I'll get in touch with you soon, Tubby.'

'It's our *karma*,' Darius said sadly once Nivedita and her long-suffering husband were out of earshot. 'Faces from the past popping up wherever we go.'

'It's happened exactly once for me—and that time it was a face from the present,' Mallika retorted. 'And Vaishali didn't start drawing up a list of my most embarrassing moments for the whole world to hear.'

'What can I say? Your past isn't as chequered as mine,' Darius said as he took his car keys from the valet parking attendant. 'Come on, let's go.'

'You said Nivedita swore you to a blood oath when you were in school,' Mallika said curiously after she got into the car. 'What was that about?'

'I caught her kissing our house captain,' Darius said as he manoeuvred the car out of a particularly complicated set of barricades at the hotel exit.

'Would that matter now? I'm sure her husband wouldn't be particularly shocked.'

'The house captain was a girl,' Darius said, grinning as Mallika's jaw dropped. 'Nivi was going through an experimental phase.'

'I suppose she finally decided that she preferred men,' Mallika said. 'Bit of a loudmouth isn't she? Were you really that hideous, or was she exaggerating?'

Darius sighed. 'I was a blimp,' he said. 'I weighed almost a hundred kilos and I wore glasses. My mother loved baking, and I loved eating. Luckily I managed to get into my school football team, and the coach made me run twenty rounds of the field every day before the others even turned up for practice. I was down to skin and bone in three months.'

'That explains a lot,' she said, and as he gave her a quizzical look went on, 'You're not vain about your looks. Most good-looking men act like they're doing you a favour by allowing you to breathe the same air as them.'

Darius, who hardly ever thought about his looks at all, felt absurdly flattered. He knew he was a lot more attractive now than he'd been in his schooldays, but he hadn't realised that Mallika liked the way he looked.

'So what happened to the spectacles?' Mallika asked. 'Contact lenses?'

'Laser correction,' Darius said. 'D'you realise you sound like you're interviewing me for a reality show?'

'Serves you right for having become so good-looking,' Mallika said.

They were heading onto the highway that connected North Mumbai to South, and she groaned as she caught sight of a sea of cars.

'We'll be here for ever!' she said. 'There's a new flyover being built, and three of the six lanes are blocked off.'

'If you'd told me just a little earlier I'd have taken a different route,' Darius murmured, edging the car into the least sluggish lane.

'They're all as bad,' she said, sighing. 'Anyway, at least we have each other for company.' There was a short pause after which Mallika said, 'Darius, can I ask you something?'

'Yes,' he said, though his eyes were still on the road. 'Ask away.'

'Where are you going to be working after you leave Nidas?'

She'd expected him to say that he'd got a better offer from a competitor, or perhaps that he was working on a new start-up. What he actually said came as a complete surprise.

'Nowhere,' he said, as casually as if it was the most obvious answer.

Mallika waited a bit, but when he didn't qualify his answer she said tentatively, 'What are you planning to do, then?'

He turned to give her a quick smile.

'Travel,' he said. 'And some volunteer work—but only after a year or so. For the first year I'm planning on Europe and Africa, perhaps a few months in China and Russia. I've made enough money to last me for several years—if it runs out I'm sure I'll find some way of making some more.'

'You're serious?' Mallika asked. 'I mean, I know people do that kind of thing in the West, but I've never heard of anyone in India quitting their job just to...*travel*.'

The way she said 'travel' was impossibly cute, as if it was a strange, slightly dangerous word that she was trying out for the first time—Darius found his lips curving automatically into a smile.

'I'm serious,' he said. 'Not planning to work for the next five years at least. After that... Well, I'll figure it out when I need to.'

Mallika sat silent for a few minutes, trying to digest what she'd just heard. Darius had struck her as a responsible, steady sort of a man—the last kind of man she'd have expected to leave his job and go wandering around the world on a whim. Showed how bad she was at reading people, she thought. Her own father had been careless to the point of being irresponsible, but this was the first time she'd met someone who was consciously and collectedly plunging into uncertainty.

'You don't approve?' Darius asked wryly as the silence stretched on.

She shook her head in confusion, 'It's not that,' she said. 'It's not my place to approve or disapprove—it just seems like such a drastic thing to do. I guess I don't understand why. I mean, you can travel on holidays, can't you? And what about your family?'

'My family understands,' he said. 'They're as crazy as I am, and they won't let a small thing like my being on a different continent affect the way they feel about me. And travelling on holiday isn't the same thing as being completely free, exploring and having adventures. Setting up Nidas was great, and I've loved that part of my life. But now that it's a success it's slowly becoming like any other large company. I don't find it as fulfilling as I did in the days when we were struggling to make a mark. I wasn't born to be a corporate suit.'

'Unlike me,' Mallika said with a little smile. 'I love the structure and safety of working for a large company.'

Her mother had set up a successful business of her own, but she'd hated the uncertainty and the ups and downs, and she'd taught Mallika to hate them as well.

Before he could reply her phone rang, and she frowned as she took the call.

'Hi, Aryan... Yes, I'm on my way back... No, I'm not coming that way. I'm taking the sea link... No, I can't, Aryan. I've taken a lift from someone, it's completely out of our way, and I'm exhausted.' There was a brief pause, and then she said wearily, 'Aryan, can't this wait till Saturday?'

Evidently it couldn't.

'Look, I'll do my best, but I'm not promising anything. Message me the specs.'

She stared out of the window unseeingly, and Darius hesitated a little before asking quietly, 'Everything okay?'

Mallika turned towards him. 'Yes,' she said with a sigh. 'My brother wants a new memory card for his camera. Actually for my camera—he's sort of taken it over, because I don't have time for photography any longer. I just got a little upset with him because he wants me to stop and buy it for him right now.'

'We can stop if you like,' Darius said, wondering why Aryan didn't go and buy the memory card himself. Maybe he was a little spoilt, and used to his sister running errands for him.

'No, it's fine,' Mallika said. 'I'll try calling a few stores and if they have it I'll get off at the nearest point and take a cab.'

'Assuming they're still open by the time we get to South Mumbai,' Darius said, indicating the traffic outside. 'It's already past nine.'

'So it is,' Mallika said.

Her phone pinged and she glanced down, laughing in spite of herself.

'He's figured out there's a shop that sells memory cards and is open till ten-thirty,' she said. 'And he's told the guy who owns it to wait until I get there.'

'Is it on the way?' Darius asked.

Mallika shook her head. 'No, it's in Worli. You can drop me where the sea link ends and then you can go home. It'll save you some time. I can grab a cab.'

'I'll come with you,' Darius said, feeling unreasonably irritated with Mallika as well as with Aryan.

'I'm not sure how safe it is, you traipsing around on your own in the middle of the night.'

'It's perfectly safe,' Mallika said crisply. 'But if you're sure it's not inconvenient…' Here, her lips curved into a disarmingly lovely smile. 'I'd love it if you came along.'

'It's not inconvenient,' Darius said, and it took all his self-control not to lean across and kiss her.

Clearly Mallika didn't believe in the fine art of dissembling—if she wanted him around she came right out and said so, instead of pretending that she'd just feel safer if he came with her. It was an unusual and refreshing trait in a woman, and Darius felt himself fall just a little bit in love with her as he smiled back.

'Aryan isn't as spoilt as he seems,' Mallika said suddenly. 'He's got a bit of an issue with stepping out of the house.'

'His health?' Darius asked.

She shook her head. 'No, it's more of a mental thing. He was pretty badly affected when our parents died, but he didn't show it for a while. And then he started going out less and less, and now he doesn't step out at all. And he doesn't like people coming over, though he's usually okay talking on the phone. That time we went out for lunch and I had to leave— my aunt had come over to look after him and he refused to answer the doorbell. She thought something had happened to him, and she was so upset when she found out that he was perfectly okay—just not in the mood to open the door.'

She ground to a halt, wondering why she'd said so much. Aryan and his peculiarities weren't a good subject for casual conversation.

'So that's why you need a flexible working arrangement,' Darius said slowly, a lot of things he'd found odd about Mallika clicking into place. 'I'm so sorry. I didn't realise that your parents....'

'They died in an accident,' she said hurriedly. 'It was more than two years ago. I don't talk about it much, but it gets more awkward the later I leave it.'

'I get that,' he said, and he looked as if he truly did.

Most people she told either looked awkward or felt terribly sorry for her and gushed over her—both reactions made holding on to her temper tough. Darius looked sympathetic, but not pitying.

'Car accident?' he asked, and she shook her head.

'Gas cylinder explosion,' she said, and he winced.

'That sucks,' he said. 'I'm sorry. Come on, the traffic's finally moving—let's go and get that memory card.'

He kept the conversation light until they'd picked up the memory card—the shop was in an unsavoury little lane, and his lips tightened a little as he thought of Mallika going there alone. He didn't say anything, however, answering her questions on his travel plans instead, and listening to her stories of a holiday in Switzerland that she'd taken with her mother.

It was the first time that Mallika had really opened up and talked, and Darius found his respect for her growing as he listened. She had obviously been very close to her mother, but she was handling her loss with dignity and restraint. Darius had been through his share of family problems, and he could catch the undertone of strain in her voice when she mentioned Aryan. But she didn't complain, and Aryan's name only came up in the context of a hilarious scrap she'd got into with an online clothing store when they'd delivered a set of women's underwear instead of the shirt Aryan had ordered.

Darius still got the impression that ever since their parents died she'd made Aryan the sole focus of her life, and that she felt deeply responsible for him.

They were almost at her flat when he asked, 'Have you tried taking Aryan to a doctor?'

'Several times,' Mallika said. 'Nothing's worked. You see, he needs to be interested in getting better. Right now, he doesn't want that. He seems happy as he is.'

Darius wished he could ask her if *she* was happy, but it was too personal a question, so he contented himself with giving her a light hug before she got out of the car. Her hair smelt of orange blossom and bergamot, and her slim arms were warm and strong around his neck as she hugged him back.

'Thanks,' she said as she straightened up. 'For dropping me home, and for listening to me chatter about things.'

She turned and went into her apartment block quickly, and she heard him start the car and drive away as she got into the lift. The lift man was off duty and the lift was empty—Mallika got in and pulled the old-fashioned door shut behind her before sagging onto the lift man's chair.

It had been a long while since she'd last talked about her family, and the conversation with Darius had brought the memories flooding back. For perhaps the hundredth time she wished she'd gone with her family to Alibagh that weekend.

It had been one of those totally pointless accidents—the kind that could have been avoided easily if only someone had been around at the right time. The cylinder of cooking gas had probably been leaking slowly for a while, but her mother hadn't smelt it because she'd had a cold. She'd picked up the lighter and clicked it on to light the gas stove, the way she did every evening—only this time there'd been a swooshing sound as the petroleum gas pervading the air had caught fire.

Her mother had screamed once, and the scream had brought her father rushing to the kitchen.

They hadn't stood a chance.

The wall of flame had hit the leaking cylinder, and the spare one next to it, and in the next second both cylinders had exploded, turning the kitchen into a blazing inferno. Aryan had been outside in the garden, but he hadn't been able to get anywhere near his parents. And Alibagh was a small, sleepy seaside town—it had been almost twenty minutes before a fire engine reached the house.

It had been in time to save the rest of the house, but far too late to save Mallika's parents. The firemen had told her later that both of them must have died within a few minutes of the explosion, and her only consolation was that at least it must have been quick.

She'd been in shock, but she'd managed to hold herself together long enough to let her relatives know, organise the funeral, and get her brother back to Mumbai. Then, when everything was done, and she'd been about ready to fall apart in private, she'd realised that something was seriously wrong with her brother.

CHAPTER FOUR

MALLIKA KNEW SHE was going to be at work late the next day. A neighbour had complained about Aryan's habit of taking photographs from the windows using a telescopic lens—apparently she thought he was spying on her. It had taken some time to soothe her ruffled feathers, and now Mallika had spent almost an hour trying to explain to Aryan that he couldn't go around peering into other people's houses.

'I was trying to take a picture of a crow on her windowsill,' he said. 'I mean, look at her—d'you think it's likely I'd want a picture of *her* taking up disk space?'

'She doesn't know that,' Mallika said, as patiently as she could. 'And that was *my* camera you were using without asking me. Aryan, look…things are tough enough without you trying to make them tougher. Be a little more considerate, will you? Please?'

He didn't reply, and she almost gave up. Another woman in her place might have lost her temper, or created a scene, but Mallika had had years of training from her mother. However upset she'd been, she'd always concealed her true feelings from the men of the family and soldiered on. For years she'd watched her mother deal with her grandfather and father, and with Aryan as he grew up—the other two men were gone now, and so was her mother, but Mallika found it difficult to shake old habits.

'I'll see you this evening, then,' she said. 'Make sure you eat your lunch, okay?'

He mumbled something that she couldn't catch.

'I didn't get that,' she said.

'I'm sorry,' he whispered, without looking up. 'I didn't mean to upset you.'

Mallika felt her heart twist painfully within her. Aryan was demanding, and sometimes troublesome, but he was very different from her father—and he was the only part of her family left to her.

She went across to him and patted his shoulder awkwardly. 'It's all right,' she said. 'Just be a little careful, *baba*. We can't afford to antagonise the neighbours.'

'I'll be careful,' he said, and looked up, his eyes pleading. 'Do you *have* to go to work?' he asked. 'Can't you work from home today?'

Mallika hesitated. She *could* work from home, but the last time she'd spoken to Aryan's doctor he'd told her that she should try and gently wean him from his excessive dependence on her. She hated leaving him when he'd asked her to stay—it filled her with guilt and worry. But she knew she had to do what was best for Aryan, to try and help him. He was her responsibility.

'I'll come back early,' she promised. 'Why don't

you go downstairs and sit in the garden for a bit? Then when I come back we can try going for a drive. Wouldn't that be fun?'

Aryan's face clouded over and he shook his head. 'No,' he said.

Mallika sighed. She'd been trying for months to get Aryan to step out of the flat with absolutely zero success. 'Why, Aryan?' she asked. 'I know you're finding it tough without Mum and Dad, but you need to try and get back to normal. I'll be with you—we don't even need to go anywhere far...'

His grip on her hand tightened painfully. 'I just... can't,' he said, and she had to be content with that.

She couldn't push him any further. If he didn't want to get better she couldn't make him. Something had broken in Aryan when their parents died, and all her love didn't seem enough to set it right.

HER PHONE WAS ringing as she let herself into her room at work an hour later.

'Nidas Investments, Mallika speaking,' she said automatically as she picked up the phone without looking at the caller ID.

'Very businesslike,' a familiar voice said approvingly, and her mood was immediately lifted by several notches.

The scene with Aryan had left her feeling drained and helpless, but just the sound of Darius's voice made the world seem like a better place.

'I've called to ask you for some help,' he said. 'I'm looking for a flat to rent, and I'm kind of desperate now. Since you know the real estate business inside out…'

'Don't you have a flat of your own already?'

'It's a long story,' he said. 'I have a flat in the same building as my parents. My sister's moving back to India, and I offered it to her when I thought I'd be leaving Nidas this month. But now that the board's asked me to stay on for another three months I need a place to stay. Only it's difficult to get somewhere for three months—I'm okay with paying rent for six, but not too many people offer leases that short. I really liked a condo in Parel, but it got snapped up by the time I got around to making an offer.'

'That's a pity,' Mallika said, wondering what kind of flat Darius would like. You could tell a lot about a person from the type of home they chose, and she thought she could picture the kind he'd go for. Big, airy and luxurious, but in an understated way. 'Which building?'

He told her, and added, 'It was a great flat—really large living room, with a massive balcony and two bedrooms. But there are only a few flats in the building with that plan. The rest have normal-sized living rooms.'

'Yes, it's only the flats next to the fire refuge areas that have that layout,' Mallika said, chewing her lip thoughtfully. 'I know the building pretty well.'

She was silent for a few seconds, and Darius could hear her slow, careful breathing over the phone line.

'If you're really keen on a flat like that I might be able to get you one for three months,' she said. 'Reasonable rent, and you won't have to pay brokerage. But you'd need to keep the flat in good condition, be careful not to upset the neighbours and all that.'

'I'm keen,' he said, smiling slightly at her tone. 'And I'm housetrained.'

'Hmm…' she said, as if she was only partially convinced. 'Meet me in the parking lot at lunch-time—say at around one—and I can take you to see the flat. It won't take more than half an hour.'

'You mean today?'

'You were the one who said you were keen!'

'So I did.' Darius got to his feet. 'We'll take my car. See you downstairs at one.'

THE BUILDING WAS only a couple of kilometres away, and Darius crossed his fingers as they drove through the gate. He'd been trying to make the best of it, but living with his parents again after a gap of fourteen years was far more stressful than he'd anticipated. So far he'd found only that one place to rent that he'd liked, and he'd been seriously considering choosing one at random from the row of sub-par flats and service apartments his agent had lined up for him.

Mallika's suggestion was a godsend—even if the flat wasn't precisely the same layout as the one he'd initially chosen he was inclined to take it.

He glanced across at her. She was more casu-ally dressed than usual—perhaps because she had no meetings to attend. A black top in some silky material clung lovingly to her curves, and he could see a tantalising hint of cleavage. Her trousers were well cut, and her shoes as sensible as always—the only dash of colour in her outfit was provided by a turquoise blue stole that matched her leather tote.

'You always carry a funky handbag,' he said suddenly as a security guard waved the car to a stop just inside the gate. 'But you wear sensible-looking shoes. Not seen too many girls do that—it's usually neither or both.'

She gave him a quick smile. 'I can't wear heels,' she said. 'Always trip and fall over. But I love bags, and I buy a new one almost every month. I'm surprised you noticed.'

She wasn't just surprised, she was also flattered he'd paid that much attention. Most men didn't notice anything about women's fashions beyond necklines and hemlines.

'I've grown up with a shopaholic sister,' he said, laughing. 'And every girlfriend I've ever had has been crazy about shoes and bags.'

Mallika wrinkled her nose a little at the thought of his girlfriends—she was sure he'd had several, and she found herself thinking negative thoughts about all of them.

The security guard came up to the car and Mallika had to get out and talk to him. Darius tapped the wheel idly as he looked out across the sprawling private garden that was one of the most attractive features of the building.

A tall man came out of the main entrance, and Mallika smiled at him, driving all thoughts of property prices out of Darius's head. The man put an arm around Mallika and gave her a hug that was halfway between friendly and proprietorial, and Darius felt an unfamiliar surge of jealousy as Mallika hugged him back. He knew that Mallika wasn't in a relationship, and it hadn't occurred to him that she might have close male friends. The thought was surprisingly unsettling.

'I have the keys,' Mallika said, sliding back into the passenger seat. 'There's parking for visitors at the back of the building. Take a left after the ramp… Left, Darius—*this* is your left.'

She tugged at his arm as he narrowly missed driving into a flowerbed and Darius grinned as he swung the wheel to the left. 'Sorry, I'm a bit directionally challenged,' he said. 'Especially when bossy women bark into my ear.'

'I'm not bossy!' Mallika protested. She'd let her hand linger on his arm a bit longer than strictly necessary, and now she squeezed it hard. 'Park by the wall. No, not behind the truck—there's more space behind that little red car.'

'Not bossy in the least,' Darius murmured, and she made a face as she got out of the car.

'I'm bossy only when the situation demands it,' she said, linking her arm through his. 'Come on, let's go see the flat.'

'Who was the man you were talking to outside?' he asked as they walked towards the building. 'The guy who gave you the keys? You seemed to know him pretty well.'

He sounded faintly jealous, and Mallika felt her mood improve even further.

'He's an old friend,' she said. 'We were at college together, and he worked with my mother for a while. He and his wife bought a place here last year, and they've been keeping an eye on the flat I'm taking you to.'

Darius nodded. It was ridiculous—it shouldn't matter to him in the least—but he felt a lot better now that he knew the man was married.

The lift man saluted when they got into the lift, and Mallika gave him a quick smile.

'Twentieth floor,' she said, and the man nodded.

'*Sahib* is going to stay here?' he asked.

'*Sahib* is going to figure out first if he likes it or not,' Mallika said. 'What do you think, Shinde? Will he like it?'

'*Sahib* will like it definitely,' Shinde said.

His expression suggested that *sahib* would have to be a blithering idiot not to like it, and Darius suppressed a smile. Mallika had an automatic air of command that Shinde was clearly not immune to—if she'd said that she was taking Darius up to the twentieth floor to persuade him to jump off it she would probably still have had Shinde's wholehearted support.

'It's a beautiful flat, madam,' Shinde added, giving Darius a disapproving look as the lift doors opened at the twentieth floor.

Shinde was right—the flat *was* beautiful. The layout, of course, was excellent, with a living room

that was huge by Mumbai standards, two respect-
able-sized bedrooms and a compact but very well-
designed kitchen. Unlike the stark, unfurnished flat
Darius had seen the last time he'd come to the building, this one was fully furnished—right down to elegant white leather sofas and sheer silver curtains
with a blue thread running through them.

The colour scheme was predominantly blue and
white, but lampshades and rugs made little splashes
of vibrant colour. There were a couple of framed vin-
tage Bollywood posters on one wall, while another
had a collection of masks from across the country.
The overall effect was one of laid-back luxury, and
Darius could imagine a high-end interior designer
working very hard to produce it.

'You can get rid of the posters and the masks, if
you like,' Mallika said as she walked across the room
to open the large French windows leading onto the
balcony. 'And if you have furniture of your own we
can get this put in storage.'

Darius followed her out onto the balcony. The flat
overlooked a racecourse and the view was amazing.
It was an unusually clear day, and the sea shimmered
in the distance, the steel girders of the Bandra-Worli
sea link providing a counterpoint to the expanse of
blue water. The cars crossing the sea link were so far
away that they looked like toys, but Mallika seemed
unusually fascinated by them.

'Think of all those people driving from one place
to another, feeling ever so busy and important,' she
said as Darius came to stand next to her. 'From here

they look just like ants—completely insignificant. And if they look at us we'll look like ants to them too.'

Darius turned to face her, leaning his back against the balcony railing. There was a slight breeze ruffling her curls, and her eyes sparkled beguilingly as she smiled up at him.

'It seems to please you,' he said, laughing as he lifted a hand to tuck a stray curl neatly behind her ear. 'The insignificance of humanity in general and the two of us in particular.'

Mallika laughed, and her dimples deepened. Darius's fingers trailed to her cheek and he traced the line of her jaw, his thumb rubbing very close to her mouth. She went very still, but her large eyes held not even a hint of alarm as he bent down to brush his lips lightly against hers.

Her lips were soft and tempting, and they parted very slightly against his. He deepened the kiss, his arms going around her to pull her closer to him. She came willingly, her arms twining eagerly around his neck and her slim body fitting perfectly against his. Kissing her felt completely natural and wildly erotic at the same time, and it took a huge effort of will to finally stop.

He hadn't wanted to—it had been a last remnant of sanity that had prevailed before he could get completely carried away. It was too soon, he hardly knew her, and he was going away in three months. There were all kinds of things wrong with the situation. But the feel of her in his arms had been so right that stopping the kiss had been almost physically wrenching.

Mallika swayed slightly as he raised his head, and he put his hands on her arms to steady her.

'Wow,' she said softly, her eyes still slightly unfocussed. Then a sudden realisation of her surroundings seemed to hit her and she stepped back, running a slightly shaky hand through her hair. 'So, anyway,' she said, rushing into speech before he could say anything. 'You should probably look at the flat and…um…make up your mind. Whether you want to rent it or not. I'll wait here for you.'

'Or you could come and look at it with me?' he suggested, reaching out and taking her hand. She looked uncharacteristically flustered, and he could feel her pulse beating wildly in her wrist.

'Yes, of course,' she said, but she disengaged her hand from his before following him into the flat.

For a few seconds Darius wondered if he should ask her what was going on. The kiss had definitely not been unwelcome—he'd felt the desire surging through her body, and the urgency with which she'd returned it. Even afterwards, the way she'd looked at him had made him think that she wanted to take things further.

The change in her had been sudden—maybe she was just more conservative than she'd initially seemed and was trying to cover up her embarrassment. The temptation to repeat the kiss was huge, but Darius didn't want to crowd her.

It didn't take long for him to look the flat over,

and he'd come to a decision by the time they were back in the living room.

'I'll take it,' he said. 'Any idea what rent the landlord's asking?'

She quoted a number that was around fifteen per cent lower than what his broker had quoted for the unfurnished flat he'd seen the week before.

'Are you sure?' he asked. 'Not that I'm complaining, but I was told that rents have gone up in the last few months.'

'There's been a market correction,' Mallika acknowledged. 'Not very major, though, and this building was overpriced to begin with. The landlord will be okay with the rent—she's…um…a little particular about the kind of person she gives the flat to.'

Darius looked around the flat. 'Whose is it?'

'Mine,' she said, and as he turned to look at her in surprise, she said, 'My mum bought up some flats in this building when it was still under construction.'

'When you say "bought up some flats"…?'

'Two,' Mallika said hastily. 'She bought two flats—one each for Aryan and me. The rates were lower when the project was first floated.'

Darius's eyebrows flew up. *His* family was reasonably wealthy, but buying a single flat in this building would use up at least half their life's savings. Buying two at a time was as inconceivable as sauntering off and buying a sack full of diamonds because you were getting them at a discount.

'Did she…um…do this kind of thing often?' he asked.

'Not really,' Mallika said, her voice guarded. 'Real estate is expensive.'

But between Aryan and her, they owned six flats in Mumbai, three in Bangalore and a farmhouse in Alibagh. It was a fact she usually tried to keep hidden—this was the first time she had voluntarily told anyone even about the flat they were standing in.

'Did the previous tenants leave just recently?' Darius asked, instinctively changing the topic. 'The flat looks as if someone was living in it until yesterday.'

Mallika shook her head. 'I got it furnished a year ago,' she said. 'Sometimes I just need a place to… to think in.'

'Most people do their thinking in the bathroom,' Darius said drily.

She flushed, wishing she'd kept her mouth shut. It was too much, expecting him to understand when he didn't know the first thing about her.

'I meant to rent it out eventually,' she muttered. 'I guess I got a little carried away, doing up the place.'

'Clearly you have more money than you know what to do with,' he said, sounding amused. 'Why d'you need a job?'

'To keep myself from going crazy,' she said.

And her voice was so serious that Darius felt she actually meant it.

CHAPTER FIVE

'THIS IS SO typical of a government office,' Darius said, glancing at his watch in annoyance. They were waiting in the property office to register his rent agreement—the appointment had been for seven in the morning, but it was already seven-thirty and the clerks hadn't yet turned up.

'It's always like this,' Mallika said, shrugging. 'Do you have morning meetings?'

He shook his head. 'No, but there's a ton of work I need to get done. And I thought I'd get started on the paperwork for my Schengen visa.'

'Stop thinking about it,' Mallika said, sliding down in her uncomfortable-looking moulded plastic chair and leaning her head against the back to look at the ceiling. 'We're here now. Let's talk about stuff until the clerks turn up.'

'What kind of stuff?' Darius asked, giving her an amused look.

Since the kiss in the flat they hadn't seen each other alone—Darius had been travelling, and after he'd come back Mallika had worked from home for a week. They'd agreed on the rental terms over email and, sensing that she needed some space, Darius hadn't suggested that they meet.

He glanced around the rather seedy office, with its broken furniture and *paan* stains on the walls where it had been chewed and spat out. It wasn't exactly romantic, but at least he was with Mallika, and she looked relaxed and pleased to be spending time with him.

"'Of shoes and ships and sealing wax,'" she said dreamily. "'Of cabbages and kings.'"

'*Alice in Wonderland*,' Darius said. 'It's from The Walrus and The Carpenter poem, isn't it?'

'Is it?' she asked. 'My dad used to keep saying it whenever I asked him what he was thinking about. I didn't realise it was a quotation.'

It was the first time she'd spoken about her father, though her mother figured prominently in her conversation, and Darius took it as a good sign. She was still looking up at the ceiling, as if she found something particularly fascinating in the stains and cracks.

"'*Paisa toh haath ka mail hai,*'" she said after a pause. 'My dad used to keep saying that too. "Money is like dirt on one's palms. Here one moment, washed away the next."'

'He piled up one huge mound of it all the same, though, didn't he?' Darius said without thinking.

Luckily Mallika didn't seem offended. 'Actually, he lost money as fast as he made it,' she said, her mouth curving up into a wry grin. 'It was my mum who was the careful one.'

From her tone, it sounded as if she wished she could admire her mum for it, but couldn't quite bring herself to do so.

Sensing his enquiry, even though Darius hadn't said anything, she went on.

'She was into real estate,' she said. 'My mum. She started off as a real estate agent, but when the markets improved and my dad got back some of his capital she started investing in property herself.'

'Impressive,' he said.

She shrugged. 'I don't think she had much of a choice. My dad couldn't think of any way of making money other than the stock market. If she hadn't taken charge we'd have been out on the streets. Aryan and I were little kids when the stock market crash happened.'

'The Harshad Mehta one?' Darius remembered the crash, but it hadn't affected his life at all. His parents' money was all in fixed deposits and blue chip stocks, so the crash had made good dinnertime conversation—nothing else.

'Yes. My dad lost pretty much all the money we had. Not just his own money but his parents' as well. We used to live in my grandmother's flat in Malabar Hill, but she had to sell it and we moved to a tiny place in Kandivali. Even there, he could barely afford to pay the rent.'

'Must have been tough.'

She shook her head. 'It wasn't. When you're kids it doesn't matter, not living at a good address or having a car and a driver. My dad had more time to spend with us, and he made the whole thing seem like an adventure. He'd take us on bus rides to the zoo and to parks, and he'd invent games for the three of us to play… When I look back, it feels like the best time of my life. It was hell for my mum, though.'

It had been years later when she'd realised that her father had had a mild case of bipolar disorder. The wacky, fun Dad she remembered was the persona he'd taken on during his manic phases. When he'd been going through a depressive episode her mother had concealed it from Aryan and her, telling them that their father was busy at work when he'd locked himself up in a room for hours on end.

'Was that when your mum started up with the real estate thing?'

Mallika nodded. 'She'd been brought up in a rich family, but the dowry she brought with her went with everything else during the crash. And she was too proud to ask her parents for anything more.'

'Why real estate?'

'I guess because that was the only business she understood. Her father was a builder in Gujarat, and she knew how the industry worked. In those days there were very few women property brokers, and she was one of the first to figure out that wives play a huge role in deciding on a house. Most brokers ignored them, but whenever my mom met a couple who was trying to buy a house she went out of her way to understand what kind of layouts the woman liked, how big she wanted the kitchen to be. And kids—no one had heard of pester power, but she made sure she told them about the great play area downstairs and the guy who sold cotton candy across the street...'

'She sounds smart,' Darius said, thinking of his own mother. She was smart too, but she'd been a schoolteacher—selling anything at all was completely alien to her character.

'Yes...' Mallika sounded a little sad. 'But along the line she forgot to have fun or spend time with her family or relax. All she did was work hard and make money. And every rupee she made had to either go into the bank or into property or gold. I probably have more gold jewellery than the Queen of Oman, even though I hate every piece of it.'

Darius gave her a quick smile. 'It sounds like a problem lots of women would love to have,' he said.

Mallika immediately wondered if she'd sounded too self-obsessed, too demanding and needy. It was difficult to explain the various things that had gone wrong in her family without mentioning stuff that she'd rather not talk about. Which begged the question—why the heck had she started moaning about her parents in the first place?

Giving herself a rapid mental slap, she straightened up.

'You're right,' she said. 'Perhaps some day I'll melt all the stuff down and make a dinner set out of it. I've always wanted to eat off a gold plate.'

'Or give it away to charity?' he suggested.

Mallika shook her head with a laugh. 'There's too much of my mum in me to actually give it *all* away.

I do the usual annual donations to charities, and to a couple of religious trusts, but not much more.'

Used to people who claimed to do a lot more for society than they actually did, Darius found Mallika refreshingly upfront. He did a fair amount of volunteering, and he supported a small NGO financially as well, but it wasn't something he talked about much. He was beginning to understand the differences between them. Mallika craved stability, structure and security, whereas he longed for adventure, risk and new experiences that pushed boundaries and frontiers.

'What about *your* family?' Mallika was asking. 'What are *they* like?'

Darius grinned. 'They're a bunch of lunatics,' he said. 'Each one's nuttier than the next. Look—I think someone's actually arrived to open up the office.'

He was right—a surly clerk in a bright magenta sari was making a big show of opening a counter and ignoring the people who'd been queuing up for over forty-five minutes waiting for her.

Registering the agreement took around forty minutes—the last step involved putting their thumbprints onto the documents before signing them, and Darius grimaced as the clerk held out a stamp pad with purple ink to him.

'I thought you just took an electronic thumbprint?' he asked.

The clerk gave him a steely look. 'It's part of the procedure, sir,' she said severely.

Mallika suppressed a little giggle. Darius's thumb

was now covered with bright purple ink, and he was looking at it with the kind of horror people usually reserved for maggots and slugs.

'Here, let me help,' she said, taking a pack of cleansing tissues out of her bag.

Darius eyed the packet. 'What're those?' he asked, clearly deeply suspicious of anything in pink packaging.

'Make-up-removing tissues,' Mallika said, taking his hand and beginning to rub the ink off his thumb.

They were out of the office and halfway down the dingy stairs, and there was a curious intimacy in the situation. Mallika took her time, her mouth puckering as she concentrated on getting the ink off. Darius stood still and watched her. The temptation to pull her close and kiss her was immense, but they were in a very public place—and already they'd attracted curious looks from a couple of people.

'Thanks,' he said, once she was done with scrubbing his hand. 'Mallika, the other day in the flat...'

Mallika cringed inwardly. She'd behaved stupidly at the flat, and she knew it. She was very thankful Darius had left the topic alone so far—the reason for her behaviour was solid enough, only it was so incredibly embarrassing that she didn't want to talk about it.

'Yes?' she said.

'Did I upset you? Because you've been a little... different ever since.'

'I wasn't expecting it,' she said. 'And I've been feeling a little awkward—I'm sorry.'

She looked up at him, and for a second Darius forgot what he'd been going to say as he looked into her lovely brown eyes.

'I'm sorry if you think I crossed a professional line,' he said after a bit. 'I kissed you on impulse—I wasn't thinking straight.'

'I'm told that the best kisses happen on impulse,' she said, so solemnly that he burst out laughing.

'Really? Who told you that?'

Mallika shrugged. 'I've forgotten,' she said. 'Anyway, whoever it was, they definitely would know more about it than me.'

Darius gave her a curious look. She didn't come across as being prudish or inexperienced—maybe she meant that her previous lovers hadn't been impulsive.

There was a little pause as they walked out of the building. Mallika was looking straight ahead, her lips pressed tightly together. Embarrassing or not, she'd have to tell him if she didn't want a repeat of what had happened in the flat.

They'd agreed to go back to the office together in Darius's car, and Mallika waited till they were safely inside before she said, 'It was the first time.'

He looked puzzled, as well he might—there had been enough of a pause for him to start thinking of something totally different—like national debt, or the future of the economy. Still, Mallika couldn't help feeling peeved at his not understanding immediately. She'd had to muster up a fair bit of courage to say it the first time, and having to repeat it was just piling on the embarrassment.

'It was the first time anyone had kissed me,' she announced, adding firmly, 'I'm warning you—if you laugh I'm going to have to kill you.'

It didn't look as if there was any danger of his laughing—his eyes widened slightly, and he switched the car engine off.

'You mean—ever?'

'Ever,' she said, wishing he wouldn't stare at her as if she was an alien with three heads and a beak. India was still pretty conservative—surely even in Mumbai it wasn't that unusual to have reached the age of twenty-nine without having been kissed?

Except clearly it was, because Darius looked completely gobsmacked. It took him a few seconds to find his voice, and when he did all he said was, 'Does that mean that you're…a…?'

'A virgin?' Feeling really cross now, Mallika said, 'Yes, it does. And I'm surprised you're asking. What kind of person would have sex and not kiss the person that they're…um…'

'Having sex with?' Darius supplied helpfully.

She glared at him, though that was exactly what she'd wanted to say. 'Anyway, so that was why I was feeling awkward,' she said. 'Can we go now?'

'In a minute,' Darius said, and then he leaned across and kissed her again.

Given that this was the second time it had happened, she should have been better prepared. But the kiss was so different from the first that she was left completely stunned. His lips barely grazed hers, and there was something tender, almost reverential in his touch. Unfortunately her long-dormant hormones weren't in the mood to be treated reverentially, and before she knew it her hands had come up to bunch in his shirt and pull him closer.

The kiss suddenly became a lot less tender and a lot more exciting. *Yessss!* her hormones said happily. *Got it right this time. Don't stop!*

She'd have probably gone with the flow, but catching sight of a large and interested audience of street children outside the car had a sudden dampening effect on Mallika. She pulled away abruptly, straightening her hair with unsteady fingers.

'Sorry,' she muttered. 'I got a bit carried away.'

'So did I,' Darius said, his voice amused. 'You have that effect on me.' Then her suddenly horrified expression registered, and he said, 'Are you okay?'

'Your shirt!' Mallika squeaked, and he looked down to survey his once spotless white shirtfront. Not only was it creased where Mallika had grabbed at it, the top button had popped off and her thumb had left purple ink stains all over it.

'I forgot to use the make-up remover on my own hands,' she said ruefully.

He laughed. 'I have a wardrobe full of white shirts,' he said. 'I won't miss this one.'

'I'll get you a new one,' she said. 'I'm so sorry— I'm a complete klutz when I get carried away.'

'Your getting carried away is worth ruining a shirt

for,' he said, his smile warm and sexy as he put out a hand to lightly brush her curls back from her face.

She smiled back, though her heart was thumping at twice its normal rate.

'You're pretty amazing—you know that, right?' he said as he leaned across to kiss her again.

The second kiss was less explosive, but it made her feel cherished and incredibly desirable, and it was like stepping out into the sunlight after months of being locked in a cellar. The sensible part of her mind knew perfectly well that Darius was leaving in a few months, and that they had no future together. But somehow it didn't matter—what mattered was the feel of his strong arms around her and his firm lips moving against hers.

When he finally drew away she gave a little moan of protest.

'I know. I feel that way too,' he said regretfully, though his eyes were dancing with amusement. 'But we need to go—we're providing free entertainment to half the street population of Mumbai.'

He was right—the children had gathered closer to the car and were peering in curiously, and Mallika gave a little sigh.

'All right,' she said, though it felt as if she'd been pulled back to earth with a thump.

'There's a bike parked right in front of the car— I'll have to move it,' Darius said, opening the car door and getting out before Mallika could stop him.

The children followed to watch him, offering their help in shrill voices as he wrestled the locked motorcycle a couple of metres down the road. Mallika got out as well. This was the first time she'd seen Darius do anything…well…*physical*, and he was a treat to watch. He must work out often, she thought, admiring the muscles in his back and shoulders as he lifted the bike. And he was strong—the bike weighed a lot more than he did, and he made moving it seem absolutely effortless.

'Today's not my day,' he remarked as he handed the children a handful of loose change and walked back towards the car. 'First ink and then grease.'

Sure enough, his shirt now had a black grease stain on it.

'Give an old woman something…I haven't had a proper meal since yesterday,' a beggar woman whined from the kerb, and Darius gave her the rest of his change before sliding behind the wheel.

'Blessings on you and your pretty one,' the woman called out after them in Hindi. 'May you have a hundred handsome sons!'

'I like the sound of my "pretty one",' Darius said, sounding amused as Mallika spluttered in annoyance. 'Though having a hundred sons sounds a little impractical.'

'I thought you didn't understand Hindi,' she said crossly.

'Oh, I can get by,' he replied. 'Where to now? I need to get out of this shirt before I show up at work, but I can drop you there before going home to change.'

'You could come to my place,' Mallika suggested

impulsively. 'It's nearby, and one of Aryan's shirts would fit you.'

Her body was still tingling in the aftermath of the kiss, and she wanted to keep Darius by her side for as long as she could. It was completely out of character for her to suggest such a thing, and it was reckless and spontaneous, but Darius's kiss had opened a door inside her that could not now be closed. She felt free, and she didn't want that feeling to end.

'Are you sure?' Darius asked.

Going to her place implied taking their kiss further, and he wasn't sure at all if that was a good idea. Kissing her had been on his mind for weeks now, and he hadn't been able to resist any longer. But he should have stopped once she'd told him she was a virgin. He had no intention of getting into any kind of long-term relationship—not at this stage in his life—and he couldn't imagine that Mallika was up for a casual fling.

'Sure that the shirt will fit?' Mallika asked, purposely misunderstanding him. 'It will—Aryan's skinnier than you, but he wears his shirts loose.'

She wasn't sure how Aryan would react to her bringing a man home—either he wouldn't even notice or he'd withdraw even further into his shell—but she found she didn't care. Her home had begun to seem like a prison to her. She loved Aryan to bits, and she felt responsible for him, but he seemed to be getting worse, becoming increasingly difficult to manage, and demanding more and more of her time.

The thought of taking Darius home was strangely

liberating. She'd spent the last two years of her life mourning her parents and helplessly watching Aryan get worse. Her friends had gone through the usual ups and downs of relationships and heartbreak before settling down, but she'd listened to her ultraconservative mother and steered clear of men. And after the accident she had been so wrapped up in Aryan that she'd had no time for anyone else.

If she hadn't met Darius she probably wouldn't even have realised that she was living a half-life, and every instinct told her to make the most of the time she had with him. With her mother gone, her links with her conservative extended family had weakened, and she didn't really care what they thought of what she did. And right now she wanted to be with Darius more than anything else.

It took them less than ten minutes to reach her apartment complex, and Darius parked in a free spot outside the compound wall.

'Should I wait here?' he asked in a last-ditch attempt to keep his distance.

She shook her head. 'Better come with me,' she said. 'You'll need to try on the shirt. And I'll give you the keys to your flat too. Now that the paperwork's done, and everything, you'll probably want to move in this weekend.'

A neighbour coming out of the building looked a little surprised to see Darius, but Mallika gave her a sweet smile and swept him into the lift without stopping to talk. The neighbour had known her for years and was a notorious gossip. Mallika would bet her last rupee that she'd make an excuse to call or come over in the evening, with the sole purpose of finding out who Darius was.

The lift stopped on the third floor and Darius followed her to the door of her flat. She dug around in her bright blue tote for the keys—while Aryan was at home, there was only around a ten per cent chance of him opening the door if she rang the bell. Mostly, unless he'd ordered something for himself on the internet and was expecting it to be delivered, he didn't bother answering the door. Mallika used her own keys to let herself in and out, and she'd got duplicates made for the cook and the cleaner.

Darius's clear, warm gaze on her made her fumble a little, but she finally got the door open, flushing a little as she ushered him in. He stopped as he stepped in, looking around the flat in surprise. He'd expected it to be done up in the same way as the flat he was renting—clean lines, lots of light and space. This flat, however, was crammed full of heavy furniture in some kind of dark wood. The upholstery was in shades of brown and maroon, and the oil paintings on the walls were depressing landscapes in dingy colours. Mallika herself seemed to have shrunk a little after stepping into the flat.

'We…um…usually take our shoes off before going into the house,' she said as she pushed the door open, slipping her own flat-soled pumps off and putting them on a rack just inside the door.

It was a common enough rule in conservative households, and Darius gave her an impish wink as he sat down on a bench next to the shoe rack and pulled off his shoes and socks.

'Sorry,' she said. 'My mum used to be very fussy about shoes in the house, and we've stuck to the rule even without her being around to yell at us.'

'It's a sensible rule,' he said, suddenly understanding why the house looked the way it did. She'd probably changed nothing after her parents had died.

He knew how much she hated any kind of pitying overture, so he didn't say anything, but his heart went out to her.

'I'll get the shirt—give me a minute,' she said, and went into a little corridor and knocked on Aryan's door. There was no response, and after a minute she gave an exasperated little huff and went into the kitchen.

There was a little service area beyond the kitchen, and a pile of ironed clothes was lying on top of the washing machine. She took two shirts out of the heap and went back to the living room. Darius was still standing, and she held the shirts out to him.

'Here—one of these should fit,' she said. 'You can change in my room.'

Her room turned out to be at the end of the corridor, and unlike the intensely depressing living room it was painted a bright, clean white, with blue curtains and a turquoise bedspread. It was a cheerful room, and Darius felt a lot better as soon as he stepped into it.

'I'll find you a bag to carry your messed-up shirt in,' Mallika said as she shut the door behind her, and she went across to the small dressing table that occupied one corner of the room. 'Here you go.'

She handed him a medium-sized plastic bag and then went to sit on the bed, her eyes on him. The kiss earlier in the car had left her in a confused, half-aroused state so that she could hardly think straight. All she knew was that she wanted to kiss him again, and his suddenly formal attitude was making her feel so frustrated she could scream.

Darius caught her eye and started undoing the top button of his shirt.

Mallika was mesmerised. She couldn't move. 'Uh…maybe I should leave?' she eventually managed to say, but he laughed mischievously.

Darius continued to unbutton his shirt, a gently teasing smile on his lips, and Mallika knew she couldn't leave now. With a boldness that surprised her she slipped off the bed in one fluid movement and came up to him.

'I can help if you want,' she said softly, her hands going to the buttons of his stained shirt.

In the back of her mind Mallika was aware of a lifetime of duty, responsibility and conservative values. But faced with Darius, this beautiful man with his quiet strength, who challenged her but never tried to control her, she found herself responding with an uncharacteristically coy smile. This wasn't her, but it was the person she wanted to be—even if only for a little while. And it felt good…really good.

Darius stood very still as she undid the first two buttons, her hand slipping under the cloth to slide over his bare chest. Inexperienced she might be, but Mallika was very aware of what she was doing and the effect she was having on him. The height difference between them was only a few inches, and she leaned up to press her lips against his, her hands still busy with the buttons. Her tongue lightly teased his mouth, and finally that proved too much for Darius's self-control.

With a muttered oath, he pulled her into his arms, his mouth hard and demanding against hers. His shirt had fallen open, all buttons finally undone, and Mallika could feel his heart pounding under velvety hair-roughened skin.

Without quite knowing how she'd got there Mallika found herself lying on the bed, pinned under his heavy body as he began to kiss his way down her throat. Her hands knotted in his hair and she arched her body to get as close to his as she could without actually breaking skin. Her own clothes were in disarray, her top having ridden up to expose most of her torso, and the feel of his bare skin against hers was indescribably good.

They were probably a nanosecond away from having hot, messy sex on the bed when the sound of a door closing in another part of the flat made Darius jerk away from her.

'Damn, I'm so sorry,' he said.

His eyes were still hooded and a little unfocused as he groaned under his breath and wrapped his arms around Mallika to hold her tightly against his body.

'Bad timing,' he said softly as he dropped a kiss

onto her forehead. 'I wish I'd met you a couple of years earlier, Mallika, before I decided to leave India.'

'You could delay going a little,' Mallika said, but she stopped trying to get the rest of his clothes off. She could feel the moment slipping away and she couldn't bear it. 'Or we could just be together until you leave.'

'It's not fair to you,' he said gently. 'Not that I wouldn't love to take this to…to a logical conclusion. I shouldn't have kissed you to begin with, and what happened right now was pretty inexcusable.'

Feeling frustrated, and a little hurt, Mallika sighed. He was right about their timing being completely off, and Mallika wished desperately that she *had* met him a few years earlier. Not that she was in the market for a serious relationship either, but at least they'd have had time to work something out. At least she could have explored all the new sensations and desires that were currently flooding her system. But it looked as if she was going to have to imagine where they might take her instead.

'Go latch the door and put on one of the shirts,' she said, pushing him lightly away.

He groaned reluctantly but got up, giving her an opportunity to admire his perfectly toned torso as he shrugged off the shirt and put on a clean one. She'd been right—Darius was broader built and more muscular than Aryan, but the shirt fitted perfectly. And the colour suited him. So far, she'd seen Darius only in white or cream formal shirts. This one was a dark blue, and set off his golden skin and jet-black hair perfectly.

'Looking good, Mr Mistry,' she said as he bundled up his old shirt and shoved it into the plastic bag. 'Time for a cup of coffee before you go?'

Darius nodded and Mallika slid off the bed and headed for the kitchen, hastily rearranging her clothes into some semblance of normal.

'Black or with milk?' she asked.

'Black, but with plenty of sugar,' he said.

He took a minute before following her out—his body had reacted with indecent haste to her kisses and he wanted to be sure he was fit to be seen before he left the room. Once he was sure he had everything under control, he tucked the shirt in, gave himself a cursory look in the mirror and strode out.

Mallika was tapping a foot nervously on the floor as she spooned instant coffee powder into two mugs. Her frustration at having to stop was turning into an irritation with everything around her—especially Aryan, who'd disturbed them by slamming his door shut.

'D'you want to grab something to eat before we leave?' she asked Darius when he walked into the kitchen.

It wasn't food he was thinking about just then, but he shrugged. 'A sandwich or something,' he said. 'I'm not particularly hungry.'

She handed him his coffee and went to the fridge. 'I'm sure I can figure something out. The cook will have made lunch for Aryan…I'll just need to see if there's enough for all of us.'

'MALLY, DO YOU know where my camera is?'

Darius had built up a mental picture of Aryan, and the reality was so different from the weedy, sallow-looking youth he'd imagined that he blinked in surprise. The resemblance between brother and sister was so close that they could have been twins if not for the obvious differences of gender and age. If anything, Aryan was better-looking than Mallika, and other than his skin being a little pale there was nothing to indicate that he hadn't been out of doors in months.

Mallika had turned at the sound of his voice, and she said curtly, 'It's in my room. And you're not getting it back until you promise to stop taking photos from your window.'

'I promise,' he said. 'Can I have it back now?'

'I'll tell you in the evening,' she said. 'Say hello to Darius, Aryan.'

Aryan's brow furrowed a little as he turned.

'Hello, Darius,' he said slowly, and it was difficult to tell if he was being sarcastic or not. His brown eyes, disconcertingly like Mallika's, flicked over Darius, stopping a little to take in the shirt.

'I lent him one of your shirts,' Mallika said. 'His got ruined by ink and grease—long story. Have you had lunch?'

'Fruit and some milk,' Aryan said. 'There were only oily *parathas* for lunch.'

'Those'll do for us,' Mallika said, locating the *parathas* and sliding them onto two plates with a little heap of pickle on each. 'Here you go, Darius.'

Darius took the plate. Their hands touched briefly, and a slight blush suffused Mallika's face. Aryan gave her a thoughtful look, but he didn't say anything.

Mallika looked up at him. 'Did you get any work done today, Aryan?' she asked.

'Lots,' he said, stretching like a cat, his mouth curving into a boyish smile that was surprisingly charming. 'The market's very active today.'

'Hmm, I saw the alerts,' Mallika said as she finished her last *paratha*. 'Be careful, though, it'll be very volatile until the elections. Shall we go, Darius? Venkat's probably tearing his hair out—I was supposed to submit a report to him before lunch.'

Aryan watched them leave, an indefinable expression in his eyes. There was clearly a lot going on beneath the surface with Mallika's brother that Darius could only guess at.

'See you around,' Darius said as he brushed past him to get to the door. 'I'll get the shirt cleaned and sent back to you in a couple of days.'

'See you,' he echoed.

His voice was perfectly cordial, though Darius got the impression that Aryan was happy to see him go. It was an odd set-up, and he felt desperately sorry for Mallika, living in that depressing flat with only her reclusive brother for company.

'Aryan works?' Darius asked as they got into the

car. He didn't want to talk about what had just happened between them, and felt that Mallika was thinking the same.

'Stock-trading,' Mallika said. 'He inherited the knack from my father and he's doing quite well. Unlike my dad, he knows how to take calculated risks, so he makes money.'

'And your dad?' Darius said eventually.

She shrugged. 'Made a fortune one day—lost it the next. He let his gambling instincts take over too often.'

There hadn't been any photos in the house, Darius realised suddenly. That was what had seemed out of place. The flat was like a museum—all that expensive heavy furniture and dark draperies—with no personal touches at all. No photographs, no tacky souvenirs from foreign trips, no sign that anyone actually *lived* there.

'What did you think of him?' Mallika was asking. 'Aryan, I mean. It's been a while since he met anyone. He doesn't go out, and the only people who visit us have known him for years. I was wondering how he comes across to someone who's met him for the first time.'

'He didn't talk much,' Darius said cautiously. 'It's not that uncommon to be a bit of a hermit at that age, is it?'

'"A bit of a hermit"?' she repeated, and laughed shortly. 'That's a good description.'

He got the sense that she wanted to say more, but she seemed to think better of it and began talking about work instead. Darius felt a strange sense of frustration—not all of it physical. There was something elusive about Mallika…a quicksilver quality that made him feel he was never quite sure of where he was with her.

The admission that he was the first man she'd ever kissed had shaken him up—it was the first indication he'd got that she felt more for him than she'd shown. As for his own feelings—he knew he was already in way too deep to walk away at this point. In addition to wanting her so badly that it hurt, he needed to talk to her, find out what made her tick.

CHAPTER SIX

'NOT THIS WEEKEND. Aryan needs me around,' Mallika said.

She'd tried talking to Aryan again about getting help—it was eight months now since he'd last stepped out of the flat—but she hadn't got anywhere. And he'd been even more distant since he'd met Darius, talking even less than usual and not coming out of his room except for meals. She was really worried about him—afraid he would become so reclusive that she would lose him completely.

'I really want to see you,' Darius said, his voice dropping an octave.

She felt a pleasurable heat curling through her body. And this was in reaction to just his *voice*. A mental image of him shirtless and super-hot intruded, and she squirmed.

'I want to see you too,' she whispered back. 'It's just that this weekend is a bit...tough. I need to figure a few things out.'

As she put the phone down she noticed Aryan at the door, looking at her. It was impossible to gauge how much he'd overheard, and he didn't say anything—just walked off to the dining table.

A surge of annoyance left her cheeks warm and her pulse racing—she badly wanted to meet Darius, and Aryan was one of the main reasons she'd said no. But it seemed a rather pointless sacrifice when it didn't seem to be helping him.

She obsessed over it for a while, before she came to a decision. Her aunt wouldn't mind coming down and being with Aryan for a bit—heaven knew she deserved to have a life of her own. For a minute she wondered what her mother would have thought of her decision and her nerve almost failed her. Her mother had been courageous and independent, but she'd also been rigidly conventional—which was partly why she'd ended up being deeply unhappy all her life. She'd have hated the thought of what Mallika was about to do. But she was gone anyway, and Mallika had her own life to live and her own choices to make.

Picking up her phone, she typed out a quick text.

Are you still free this weekend? Might be able to meet you on Saturday.

Her text arrived in the nick of time—Darius was just about to promise an elderly aunt that he'd drive her to visit a friend who lived around thirty kilo-metres away.

'Next Saturday instead,' he told his aunt firmly.

The last time he'd driven Auntie Freny to meet a friend she'd insisted on leaving home at nine in the morning, and had subsequently proceeded to party till three the *next* morning.

'*Dikra*, this time you can have a drink too,' Auntie Freny said cajolingly.

Darius promptly felt as if he was six again, being promised a chocolate if he was good.

'Last time, *ni*, you had to drive, no? This time we can stay overnight—just pack some clothes.'

'Next Saturday,' Darius said, and gave his aunt an affectionate hug.

'Some girl you're going to meet—don't think I don't know.'

His aunt made a surprisingly nimble grab for his phone, and Darius managed to whisk it away only just in time.

Balked of her fun, Freny shook her head at him sorrowfully. 'Never do I get to meet these girls. Get married and settle down, *dikra*, this is no time for flirting and having fun. Our race is dying out! I went to the Parsi *panchayat* last week and...'

'And they told you that unless I got married and fathered fifteen children I'd be responsible for the end of the Parsis?'

Aunt Freny gave him an exasperated look. 'No, I met an old friend with a really nice daughter who'd be perfect for you. If you just met her once you'd give up this crazy idea of travelling around in all kinds of strange places, away from your family. Should I call my friend?'

'Thanks, but no thanks,' Darius said firmly. 'I'm perfectly capable of finding a girlfriend of my own if I want one.'

'Freny, he doesn't *want* to marry and settle down,'

his mother said tartly as she walked into the room. 'If he did, he wouldn't want to go traipsing across the world like this.' She caught Darius's suddenly stricken look and added in a gentler tone, 'Relax, I'm not trying to make you feel guilty. You've done everything you can for this family, and you deserve a few adventures for yourself.'

FINDING SOMETHING TO wear for a date when you possessed a sum total of zero remotely suitable outfits shouldn't have been difficult, but it was.

Mallika grimaced as she surveyed her clothes. She had several shelves of cotton tunics that she teamed with jeans when she went out to indulge her photography hobby, two formal business suits, a couple of silk *churidaar kameez* and half a dozen saris. Dozens of loose cotton T-shirts…

Even the 'remotely suitable' outfits were beginning to look unusable—one of the tops had a mark on it, and the other two hung loose on her slim frame. Evidently she'd lost weight and not realised it.

Beginning to feel a little desperate, she took everything out of the wardrobe, in the hope that something suitable would surface. Buying new clothes to go out with Darius would be taking the concept of trying too hard to a completely different level…

Perhaps she could wear a silk *kameez* over jeans and pretend that she was going for an arty look.

At the back of the wardrobe, a little patch of flame-coloured matt silk caught her eye. *Ah, right.* That was the dress that an old college friend had given her, evidently not realising that Mallika never wore dresses or skirts.

Tugging the dress from its cellophane wrapping, she shook it out and held it against herself. There was a reason why she avoided anything that showed her legs—there was a narrow, but very visible scar from a bicycle accident that ran up her left leg from mid-calf to knee.

'If it scares him off it's probably a good thing,' she muttered to herself as she pulled the dress on and smoothed it over her hips.

It should have looked hideous. The colour was anything but subtle, and it was a while since she'd last worn a dress. But the fabric clung softly to her curves, outlining the soft swell of her breasts and emphasising her perfect waist. The hem was asymmetrical, and it hid part of the scar—but she found the scar itself was nowhere as scary as she remembered it being. Her legs were long and shapely, and the scar was barely noticeable.

The dress was probably not suitable for a simple date, but once she'd seen how she looked she didn't feel like taking it off.

'You're looking nice,' Aryan informed her as she stepped out of her room.

Her eyes flew up to his in surprise. She hadn't expected him to come out of his room to see her off. Still less had she expected him to notice what she was wearing.

Feeling the excitement drain out of her, she said

tentatively, 'Thanks. Um…are you sure you'll be okay with *mausiji*?'

He nodded, and when she didn't look convinced gave her a crooked smile. 'I'm alone at home when you go to work,' he reminded her. 'Go ahead—I'll be fine today.'

Aryan probably hadn't intended it, but she felt inordinately guilty as she stepped out of the flat. She did her best to work from home whenever she could, but she did end up having to go to the office at least two, sometimes three days a week. Aryan never liked being left alone in the flat, and ever since she'd changed jobs he'd been more on edge—staying in his room and skipping meals if she wasn't around to force him to eat.

Darius was waiting in his car at the end of the lane, and she half ran the rest of the way to reach him.

He leaned across and unlocked the door, giving her a quizzical smile as she slid in, half out of breath. 'Are the Feds after you?' he asked.

She laughed. 'No—worse, I have the snoopiest neighbours in the universe. So, what are we doing today?'

He'd planned lunch and a movie, but one look at Mallika in her flame-coloured dress had driven everything out of his head—all he could think of was taking her home and making slow, delicious love to her.

'Whatever you want,' he said slowly. 'I've booked tickets for a movie, and a table at a restaurant. But most of all I want to talk to you. We left a lot of things unfinished the last time we met.'

His eyes met hers, and it was as if she could read what he'd been thinking a second ago.

'You've moved into the Parel flat, haven't you?' she asked, and he nodded. 'And have you managed to set up your home theatre system yet?'

He nodded again, and she broke into a smile so bright and alluring that he could hardly tear his eyes away from her face.

'Let's go there then,' she said. 'Watch an old movie, order takeaway…talk.'

'Right,' he said, his throat suddenly dry. 'Sounds like a plan.'

PREDICTABLY, WATCHING A movie was the last thing on their minds as they tumbled into the flat fifteen minutes later. Darius had pretty much broken every speed limit in town, getting them there, and they were barely inside the flat before Mallika was in his arms, kissing him so eagerly that it took his breath away.

'Slow down,' he said softly, smoothing her hair away from her face. 'We have all the time in the world. And I really do think we should talk.'

It took everything he had not to whisk her straight into the bedroom, but it was important that they laid some ground rules before taking things further.

She sighed and pulled away from him. 'What's there to talk about?' she asked. 'You're leaving in a few months and I'm stuck here.'

'I know,' he said. 'Logically, we should stay away from each other—but that's not happening, is it?' It looked as if she wanted to interrupt, but he went on, 'It's mostly my fault—I've been trying to convince you to meet me. If you want me to, I'll stop.'

'I don't want you to stop,' Mallika said, her voice low. 'Look, I can't commit to a long-term thing either, but I haven't felt like this about anyone ever before. I haven't wanted to do this with anyone before. Maybe it's just physical attraction, but I…I dream about you. And when I'm with you I can't seem to stop myself from…from…'

Touching you, she wanted to say. *Kissing you and wanting to make love to you all night long.* The words didn't come, though—and already she'd said more than she'd meant to.

Darius's expression had changed. Maybe he thought she was throwing herself at him. She quickly tried to dispel the thought.

'I can't marry while I still have Aryan to look after,' she said. 'Until I met you I used to stay away from men and concentrate on work. It was much easier that way. Only with you I've not been able to stick to the rules I made for myself.'

Mallika took a deep breath. She'd never had such a conversation with a man before, and she had to screw up her courage to get the next words out.

'So I was thinking—maybe I should just forget about the rules for a bit. Do what *I* want for once—with someone who wants it just as much as I do.'

Darius leaned closer to her, capturing both her

hands in his. 'Mallika, I don't want to take advantage,' he said. 'I'm crazy for you, but the last thing I want to do is hurt you in any way.'

'You won't,' she said, her eyes meeting his steadily. 'I know you'll leave, and I'm okay with it. I just…' Her voice quivered a bit, but she steadied it with a visible effort. 'I haven't really been able to let go and do what I want. *Ever.* When I was in school and college I was studying hard all the time, because that was the way my mother wanted it. Even when I started working I stayed away from parties and men. She was trying to protect me because she'd had such a tough life herself. By the time I figured out that the world wasn't that bad after all, she was dead. And I had Aryan to look after.'

Darius's eyes were sympathetic now, and she felt she couldn't bear it.

'While you're here, let's be together,' she said, making her voice as upbeat and cheerful as possible. 'And once you need to go we'll separate—with no regrets. How does that sound?'

'Like the last bit's going to be damn tough,' Darius said honestly. 'I'm finding it difficult enough to be objective right now. I don't know what it'll be like three months from now.'

'If we're lucky it'll wear off by then,' she said.

He had to laugh. 'If we're lucky,' he repeated, tracing a line down the side of her face with one hand and watching her quiver in response. 'But—just so that you know—even if we're perfect together I'm not going to stay. I need a clean break from my current life, and that's important for me. More important than anything else.'

'Relax, I get that,' she murmured. 'If you like we'll get the legal team to draft a set of disclaimers for you! I'm not looking for a happy ending, here— just a few weeks of fun.'

'Right,' he said.

There was an awkward moment while they stared at each other, both unsure of what to do next, then Darius muttered something and swept her into his arms, his lips hot and insistent against hers. Mallika melted against him, but a few minutes later, as his hands went to the zip on her dress, she made a little sound of protest and Darius pulled back.

'Are you okay?' he asked, his mouth against her throat.

She nodded her head. 'Yes,' she said decisively. 'Just go a little slower. I'm…nervous.'

The admission shook him more than he would have cared to admit and he changed his touch, skimming his hands over her skin as gently as if she was made of spun glass.

It was only when she made a little sound in her throat and pressed her hips hard against his that he let his lips become a little more urgent, his hands more demanding…

MUCH LATER, MALLIKA raised her head lazily from Darius's shoulder and surveyed the room. Her dress lay in a tangled heap near the foot of the bed, next to his jeans, and the rest of their clothing was strewn around the room. It was a miracle that they'd made it to the bed and not ended up making love on the living room sofa or on the floor.

'That was good,' she said.

'Just *good*? I must be losing my touch,' he murmured, running a finger lightly down her arm. She shivered in reaction and he grinned, twisting her around to kiss her. 'Did I hurt you?' he asked, more seriously.

She shook her head. 'I'm a little sore, but I guess that's to be expected. And I hate to spoil the mood, but I'm starving after all that exercise. Any chance of getting something to eat?'

'We'll have to order in,' Darius said. 'The sum total of food available in this house is one apple and a box of biscuits.'

'I'll take the apple,' she said, turning and burrowing closer to him.

'I have some takeaway menus in the kitchen,' Darius said. What do you feel like eating?'

'I'm not sure,' Mallika said with a sigh. Lying in Darius's arms felt so good she wouldn't move at all if her stomach weren't rumbling.

'Did you live here ever, Mallika?' he asked. 'Before you decided to rent the flat out?'

The place had a sense of having been lived in, despite its pristine state.

'I wanted to move here when my parents died,' she said. 'Our old place reminds me of them every minute I'm in the flat. But Aryan wasn't keen, and now I can't leave him there by himself.'

'That's understandable,' he said.

There was a brief pause as Mallika cuddled up closer to him and nibbled playfully at his shoulder. She responded enthusiastically when he pulled her in for a hard kiss, but after a bit twisted away from him.

'I'm really, really hungry,' she said. 'Can we order food first?'

Darius groaned and picked up the first of the menus. 'Here you go,' he said. 'I can see I'm much lower in your priority list than lunch.'

Mallika took the menu and gave him a conciliatory little kiss. 'You're *much* more important than lunch,' she assured him. 'I just want to get lunch out of the way so that I can concentrate on you.'

The thought of her concentrating only on him made it difficult for Darius to think straight, but he leaned back and watched Mallika as she went through the menu.

'*Tandoori roti, daal tadka* and *aloo jeera*,' she said. 'What about you?'

'I think I'll have the chicken *sagawala*,' he said, mentioning the first thing he'd noticed on the menu. 'Or, no—you're vegetarian. I'll have the same stuff you're having.'

'I'm okay with you ordering chicken as long as I don't have to eat it,' Mallika said. 'But it's *saagwala*—not *sagawala*.'

Darius frowned. 'What's the difference?'

'*Saagwala* means that it's made in a spinach sauce,' she explained patiently. '*Sagawala* means that the chicken is a blood relative.'

'Seriously?'

'Seriously.'

He looked impressed. 'There's more to this speaking Hindi thing than meets the eye,' he said. 'Maybe you should give me Hindi lessons.'

'Maybe I should,' she said, dimpling as she tossed the menu back to him and went to get a glass of water.

Darius used his cell phone to order lunch, and once he was done wandered back to the bedroom. He lay down and stared at the ceiling. In spite of it being Mallika's first time, the sex had been mindblowing, and he could hardly stop a goofy grin from spreading across his face at the thought of how good it had been.

Mallika came back into the room a few minutes later, still swathed in the bed sheet. She perched on his side of the bed and looked at him thoughtfully. Darius was sitting up now, his bare chest on display as he gave her a slow smile—and he looked so heartbreakingly perfect that for an instant she forgot the lines she'd been rehearsing in the kitchen.

Impulsively, she leaned across and kissed him, but pulled away when he tried to take her into her arms. Losing her head once a day was enough—it had been amazing, unforgettable, but now she needed to be sensible.

'This is going to be complicated,' she said. 'We should talk.'

CHAPTER SEVEN

'I AGREE,' DARIUS SAID. 'I think ground rules are a very good idea.'

'So that we don't end up making a mess of things,' Mallika continued. 'I mean, you'll be going away, so it doesn't matter so much for you, but I don't want to have to deal with unnecessary gossip.' She thought for a moment, and went on, 'Plus it'll be difficult for me if Aryan finds out. He's very fragile right now—even more so than usual.'

'We don't need to tell him,' Darius said, reacting to the last sentence first. Her expression changed and he added hastily, 'Or anyone else. What's next?'

He looked so tempting, standing there with his shirt still partly unbuttoned and his hair rumpled after making love, that Mallika felt like abandoning the list of rules and going back to bed with him.

Sighing, she turned away and walked to the window. 'Gossip is only part of it,' she said. 'We should probably be careful not to…um…get too close—like talk about our lives too much and all that. Keep it limited to the physical stuff.'

Darius nodded again, a little more slowly this time. What she said made sense, but it made him think that she was perhaps more emotionally affected than she said she was. It sounded as if she was trying to build up walls so that she didn't get hurt when he left.

'What else?' he asked, beginning to wonder if this had all been a huge mistake.

He was a lot more experienced than her, and he should have foreseen the complications that would occur if they slept together. He couldn't get tangled up in something that would make him question his travels. He needed this...he *deserved* this—it had been his goal for so many years and now it was within touching distance. He wouldn't give it up— not again.

'We should...um...be together only in the evenings,' she said. 'I'll come to you.'

That would set some boundaries, she thought. Ensure that she didn't throw herself at him at all hours. And she'd make sure she went to him only on the days that she'd been working from home, so Aryan wasn't alone for more than a few hours.

He nodded again, and she said, 'Just one more thing. I have a lot of stuff going on right now, so while I'd love to meet you as often as you want to it probably won't be possible.'

This was beginning to sound a bit clinical, thought Darius. He understood that Mallika was only trying to protect herself, and goodness knew the rules certainly worked in his favour, but it made him feel concerned that she had already got in over her head.

'Problems with Aryan?' Darius asked, and his

voice was so gentle that Mallika felt suddenly very close to tears.

'Yes,' she said. 'He doesn't like me leaving him at home and going out.'

Darius moved to stand behind her, his arms coming around her to pull her gently against him. He would agree to the rules, of course, but he would have to stay on his guard. After all, rules could always be broken.

'Maybe I could help?' he suggested. 'If nothing else, I could take your mind off everything that's bothering you.'

Mallika turned abruptly and buried her face in his chest. 'It isn't so simple,' she said, her voice muffled against his shirt.

'It could be,' he said, his breath stirring her hair. 'Think about it.'

'I should go now,' she said, without looking up. It's getting late and Aryan's alone. My aunt will have left by now.'

For a few seconds Darius felt like telling her that Aryan was a grown man and capable of taking care of himself for a few hours. But he bit the words back. Mallika clearly felt responsible for her brother, and making snide remarks about him wouldn't help matters. Also, he trusted her judgement—if she said her brother wasn't fit to be left alone for long periods she was probably right.

But he was feeling incredibly frustrated—Mallika had got to him in a way no woman had before, and her determination to stay emotionally unattached bothered him more than he would have expected.

'I'll drop you home,' he said, but she shook her head again.

'I'll take a cab.'

'Stop being stubborn about it,' he said. 'Even if someone sees us, we can tell them you're my land-lady.'

She nodded obediently, and Darius tipped her face up so that she was forced to look right into his laughing eyes.

'Come on, landlady,' he said teasingly. 'Let's get you home.'

PERHAPS IT WOULD have been easier if Darius had taken her rules at face value, Mallika thought a few weeks later. She slipped into Darius's flat almost every alternate evening, and the sex was as hot and passionate as it had been the first time. But Darius didn't seem content with that—she'd expected that he would stay away from her when they weren't ac-tually sleeping together, but he was doing quite the opposite.

'People know that we're friends,' he said. 'It'll seem far more suspicious if I stop talking to you at work than if we continue to hang out together.'

And so, in public, he'd assumed the role of a friend—one who wanted to spend as much time with her as possible. Every couple of days he'd call to suggest meeting up for coffee or a movie—if she said no he'd laugh and suggest an alternative date.

Or he'd bully her into admitting she needed a break and take her out anyway.

Once he'd bought tickets for a stand-up comedy show and told Venkat that she needed to leave work early to participate in a personality development exercise.

Venkat had asked suspiciously, 'What's wrong with her personality?'

He'd said, 'Her sense of humour could do with some work—she takes life way too seriously.'

And Venkat, who wouldn't have recognised a joke if it had walked up and hit him on the nose, had agreed with him and forced her to go.

Another time he'd booked both of them onto a heritage walk across the old parts of South Mumbai, which had ended at an open-air music festival at the Gateway of India. The music had been a crazy jumble of jazz, blues, fusion and rock, and Mallika had had the time of her life.

Afterwards, they'd wandered through Colaba and had dinner at a little tucked-away Lebanese café. They'd talked for hours and hours about music and travel and books, and hadn't realised how late it was until they'd been the last people in the café, with the owner waiting patiently for them to pay their bill and leave.

When she'd got home Aryan had been waiting for her, his eyes large and accusing in his pale face, and she'd resolved never to stay out so late again.

The next few times Darius had asked her out she'd made excuses and stayed at home, playing Scrabble with Aryan, or just sitting in his room with a book while he pored over his laptop screen.

Today, Darius was on the phone insisting she get up at this unearthly hour in the morning to go with him to Sewri. A flock of migratory flamingos stopped at the Sewri mudflats for a few weeks every year on their way from Siberia, and Darius was appalled to hear that she'd lived in Mumbai for her entire life and never seen them.

'Darius, I can't,' she protested. 'I've just woken up, and I need to get breakfast for Aryan. And I need to go to my Alibagh house for a few hours in the afternoon. I can't come.'

And I can't be with you and pretend to be friends without wanting much more, she said silently to herself. It was time she put her foot down and made sure they stuck to the rules. She was new at this, and she could feel herself starting to fall for him, to rely on him being a part of her life. She didn't want to get hurt, and of course there was Aryan to consider.

'I'll stop at a café and fetch something for Aryan's breakfast,' Darius said easily. 'And we'll be done with the flamingos by ten—I'll drop you to the ferry after that.'

'I don't want to leave Aryan alone for that long,' she said. 'My aunt can't come over today—she's got a *puja* prayer ritual to go to. And I'm a little tired.'

She'd woken up with a bad headache, and the thought of the Alibagh trip was depressing. The little beach villa was where her parents had died—she'd not been able to bring herself either to sell it or rent it out, and it had been lying vacant for the last two years. It had been repainted after the accident, and there was a caretaker who kept the house clean and tended the lawn, but she'd visited it only four times in the last two years. Now there was a leakage problem and she had to go.

'We can go tomorrow, then,' Darius said. 'Or next week, if you like.'

Mallika sighed, and then said abruptly, 'Darius, why are you doing this?'

'Doing what?' he asked innocently.

'You know what I mean,' Mallika said.

She got up and closed the door to her room, to make sure that Aryan couldn't overhear her.

'Look, we're doing what we said we would—having a fling before you go to Alaska or Mongolia or wherever. But you're also doing this "just good friends" routine. I'm not sure if it's fooling anyone, and it's definitely confusing the hell out of *me*. It just…doesn't make sense.'

'It does to me,' he said. 'I really like you. I like being with you—in bed and out of it. And, maybe I'm wrong, but it feels like you don't have any close friends—not people you can be yourself with.'

'So you feel *sorry* for me?'

She probably hadn't meant to sound bitter, but it came out that way and Darius winced. He hadn't wanted to have this conversation so soon—and definitely not over the phone. What she'd said about never having had a chance to have fun and do what she wanted had struck a chord with him. He'd never had the kind of problems she had, but he understood the need to break loose and he'd been doing his best to help.

Quite apart from that was the fact that he actually loved every minute he spent with her—but he tried not to think about that too much. He knew that their spending time together like this was dancing on the edge of what their rules allowed, but somehow he couldn't stop himself.

'Not sorry, exactly,' he said. 'I just think that you're young and you have your whole life ahead of you—it's a little early to be cooping yourself up at home and only coming out when you need to go to work. You said it yourself—you want to go out and have fun, do all the things you missed doing when you were younger.'

'I might have said it, but it's not practical to think only about myself,' she said. 'I have a brother with problems, remember?'

'I know,' Darius said.

She didn't mention Aryan often, but he had now got a fair idea of what she was dealing with there. He gritted his teeth before plunging ahead.

'But I don't think you can solve his problems by locking yourself away as well. He needs professional help, and the sooner you get it for him the better it'll be for both of you.'

'Perhaps *I* need professional help as well, then,' Mallika said. 'Because I can't see my way to dragging him to a doctor when he refuses to go. And I can't stop caring about him or looking after him.'

'There's always a way out,' Darius said. 'It's just not obvious because you're so closely involved.'

'Maybe I don't want a way out,' she said softly, the hopelessness of the entire situation striking her anew. 'I'm not like you, Darius—I can't just walk away from my family without a backward glance.'

There was a long pause, and then Darius asked, 'Is that what you think I'm doing?'

'Well, isn't it?' she countered hotly. He had pressed her buttons and now her blood was up. She was spoiling for a fight. 'Your parents are old, and there's your grandmother, and your aunt—you're just leaving them to fend for themselves, aren't you?'

'My sister's here,' he said, wondering why he was even bothering to justify himself.

He hadn't talked to Mallika about his family much—their rules forbade it, after all—so it wasn't surprising that she was jumping to all the wrong conclusions. Still, her words stung, and he couldn't help thinking they'd been right about keeping their relationship superficial. Their approach to life was so different that they didn't have a hope of ever fully understanding each other.

'That's not the same thing,' Mallika was saying. 'She's got kids and a husband, hasn't she?'

Shirin was in the process of divorcing her husband. That was another thing Darius had never told Mallika, and this was definitely not the right time. Suddenly his plans for a glorious morning with Mallika had turned into an ugly argument and he coulnd't wait for it to be over.

'Mallika—' he said, but she interrupted him.

'I'm sorry,' she said. 'This isn't any of my business, and I'm getting a bit too emotional about it. I miss my own parents and I can't understand you leaving yours behind while you go off to discover yourself, or whatever. So I'm not being rational, and I've probably said a bunch of things I shouldn't have.'

Her voice was shaking a little, and Darius felt his anger dissipate as quickly as it had flared up.

'It's all right,' he said. 'You're right, in a way. But my family and my decisions don't have anything to do with the situation you and Aryan are in. I really do want to help, Mallika. Don't keep pushing me away.'

'I'm not,' she said. 'It's just...very tough talking about him with anyone. Even you. It feels like I'm betraying him. And I love spending time with you, but I feel guilty every minute because I know he needs me more than you do.'

There was a longish pause, after which Darius spoke. 'I can understand that,' he said slowly. 'But what about what *you* need?'

'I don't know, Darius, but I do know that I have to put him first. That's what you do when it comes to family—you don't just go off and leave them to it.'

Family would always be her priority, but as she began to calm down she realised how harsh that must have sounded to Darius. It had been a long and tiring week, and Aryan's moods and ingratitude had pushed her over the edge. A weak, but insistent part of her kept saying that she should apologise and do whatever he wanted, but she squashed it firmly.

Luckily, before she could say anything, he said, 'All right, then. I guess I'll see you around the office next week.'

His voice was remote and expressionless, and Mallika just got to say a brief goodbye before he cut the call.

She put the phone on her bedside table and flopped back into bed to stare at the ceiling. It was all very well to tell herself that she'd get over Darius in a bit—right now she felt as if she'd succeeded in cutting her heart out with a rusty knife. He had been genuinely trying to help her, to connect with her better, and she'd said some unforgivable things to him. No wonder he'd sounded as if he never wanted to see her again.

She tried to focus on Aryan instead. Darius wasn't the first person to say that he needed professional help, though he'd said it far more bluntly than most. Mallika had done her best to shield her younger brother from the aftermath of their parents' death, but he'd actually been there when the accident had happened. He'd escaped completely unharmed, but since then he'd been a shell of his former self.

Mallika and he had been close when they were growing up, but despite her best efforts she hadn't been able to get him to talk to her about what was wrong. And the more she tried to draw him out, the more silent he became.

The only time Aryan seemed really happy was when he was in front of his laptop, staring at the flickering screen as he traded stocks and moved money around from one set of investments to another. He had inherited just the right mix of talents from his father and mother to be a formidable trader, and he had almost doubled the money they had inherited from their parents over the last year.

Aryan lived most of his life online—he worked online and bought everything he needed on various websites and had it delivered to the flat. They had a cook and a cleaner, and of course he had Mallika for anything else. He no longer needed to go out at all.

After a while, she had stopped pushing him to talk, and that had had the result of making him more and more dependent on her. He tried to stick as close to her as he could whenever she was at home, and messaged her constantly when she was at work. Mallika sometimes found herself wishing he'd leave her alone—he was as demanding as he'd been when he was three and had toddled behind her everywhere like a pudgy little shadow.

Mallika sighed as she got out of bed. There were little sounds coming from the kitchen that indicated that Aryan was awake and foraging for breakfast. She'd forgotten to order groceries the day before, and there wasn't any ready stuff that he could eat. She'd need to make him some *upma* or something before she got ready and left to catch the eleven o'clock ferry to Alibagh.

THERE WAS A long queue for the ferry at the Gateway of India and Mallika joined it, cradling her bright green tote in her arms. The sun was beating down uncomfortably on her head and she wished she'd thought to wear a hat in addition to the sunglasses that she'd perched on her nose.

The glasses served the dual purpose of saving her eyes from the sun as well as concealing quite how puffy they were. Post-breakfast, with a morose and monosyllabic brother, she'd gone to her room and had a good cry. It hadn't done much for her looks, but at least she felt a lot calmer than she had in the morning.

'Excuse me, would you mind keeping my place for me in the queue for a few minutes?' the woman in front of her said. 'My son wants an ice cream, and if I don't get it for him right now he'll whine for the entire hour that we're on the ferry.'

'No, I won't,' the pudgy youngster standing next to her said indignantly.

He had a pronounced accent which Mallika couldn't quite place—it wasn't American, but it was close.

'You promised me an ice cream last week and I didn't whine when you didn't buy it, did I?'

'Of course you did,' his slightly older sister chimed in.

Their mother groaned. 'Can it, both of you,' she said. 'Do you want ice cream or not?'

'Want ice cream,' both of them said firmly.

The woman turned back to Mallika. 'Sorry,' she said. 'They're at a terribly argumentative stage. So— is it okay if I leave the queue for a minute?'

'Yes, of course,' Mallika said.

'Of course it's okay if you *leave*,' the girl said scornfully. 'The point is, will she let you back in the line when you come back?'

'I will,' Mallika promised, her lips twitching slightly. The girl was around nine, dignified, knob-bly-kneed and totally adorable.

'Thank you so much,' the mother said with evident relief, grabbing her children's hands. 'Come on, people.'

Mallika gazed after her as she walked towards the ice cream vendor, holding a child's hand in each of her own. She had a slight twang to her accent as well, and there was something about her that was vaguely familiar.

The queue had moved quite a bit before the woman came back, breathless and clutching ice cream bars in each hand.

'Oh, thanks,' she said in relief as Mallika waved to her. 'Here—I forgot to ask you which flavour you'd like. So I got chocolate and vanilla both—you take the one you like and I'll have the other.'

'You shouldn't have,' Mallika said, taking the chocolate bar gratefully. 'But thank you so much— it's so hot I feel like I'm about to melt.'

'It'll be more pleasant on the boat,' the woman said. 'Come on, now, kids—be careful on the stairs or you'll slip and fall in the water.'

'Papa would have carried us if he was here,' the boy grumbled.

His sister glared at him. 'Well, he isn't, so *manage*,' she said fiercely. 'Whine-pot.'

'Cry-baby,' the boy retorted. 'Mud-face.'

'*Muuuummm...*' the girl said.

'Be *nice*, people!' the woman snapped.

'I can carry you, if you like,' Mallika offered. 'Your mum's got too many bags to handle.'

The boy looked as if he wasn't sure which was worse—being carried in public by a *girl*, or having to walk down the stairs on his own. His evident fear of heights won over, and he held his chubby arms up to Mallika.

'I wish Papa was here,' the boy said defiantly once she'd picked him up, and Mallika wondered where their father was.

'He divorced us,' the girl said in a fierce whisper to her brother. 'Stop whining or I'll punch you in the face.'

Their mother sighed. 'So much for being dignified and discreet,' she said, and gave Mallika an artificially bright smile. 'I'm so sorry you're being subjected to this.' In a whisper, she continued, 'My husband ran away with his secretary a few months ago and we're still trying to deal with it.'

Under the smile she looked tired and defeated, and Mallika's heart went out to her. 'Men can be pigs,' she said quietly once they were all on the ferry. 'I'm sorry—it must be tough for you.'

'I'm thrilled to be rid of the cheating bastard, actually,' the woman replied in an undertone as they climbed to the upper deck behind the kids. 'But it's tough on the kids. If he'd given me a choice I might have actually stayed with him to keep them happy.

As it turned out he didn't, so here we are—back in India.'

'Where were you before this?'

'Canada,' she said. 'But I'm happy to be back with my family.' They had reached the upper deck, and the woman looked around. 'Are you in the A/C section as well?' she asked.

Mallika shook her head. 'I prefer the sea breeze,' she said. 'See you in a bit.'

She took a seat towards the front of the ferry, where she didn't have to look at other people, and leaned her head gratefully against the cold guard rail. She'd loved these ferry rides to Alibagh when she was a teenager. Aryan had still been a kid then, and he'd used to run around madly while Mallika stood near the railing, soaking in the sun and the sea breeze.

Even in those days she'd been more of an outdoor person than Aryan was—he'd preferred the lower deck, and after a few arguments their mother had started buying two tickets for the upper deck and two for the lower, so that they didn't fight.

Mallika cast a glance towards the air-conditioned cabin where the woman and her kids had gone. *'I might have actually stayed with him to keep them happy...'* It sounded so terribly sad, when the woman was clearly happier without her husband.

Mallika wondered whether her own mother would have been happier without her father. She'd definitely been more than capable of taking care of herself, but their extended family was extremely conservative.

Maybe she'd stayed so that she didn't have to be cut off from them. Or maybe she'd not wanted to separate Aryan and Mallika from their father.

She still felt guilty when she thought of how much trouble they'd given their mother during their growing up years. It had only been when she was in her late teens that Mallika had begun to understand why her mother worked so hard and was so grim and serious most of the time. And even then she'd not known the full story.

As she'd told Darius, her father had lost most of his money in the stock market crash of the eighties—what she hadn't realised for many years was that her mother had been supporting the family ever since. When she'd found out she'd been more sympathetic, but she still hadn't been able to understand why her mother couldn't loosen up a little…be a little more fun.

Her attention was attracted by the girl and her mother coming out of the air-conditioned cabin. The girl's face was distinctly green.

'I'll be all right on my own,' she was telling her harassed mother. 'You go inside and be with Rehaan.'

'I'm not leaving you here on your own,' the mother said. 'Are you still feeling pukey?'

'Not that much,' the girl said, pushing her way through the crowded deck to come and stand next to Mallika by the railing. 'It's better in the breeze.'

'Seasick?' Mallika asked, and the woman nodded.

'The sea's really choppy, and it's a bit disorientating inside the cabin. Rehaan's refusing to come out.

I should have just stayed home instead of trying to take these two out for a weekend break.'

'I'll be okay on my own,' the girl insisted.

'I can keep an eye on her, if you like,' Mallika offered.

The woman laughed. 'You know, this is the part I love about being back in India,' she said. 'It feels like being part of one big family. I'm Shirin, by the way, and this is Ava.'

'Pleased to meet you,' Mallika said, grinning back at her. 'So, if you like, you can leave Ava with me and go be with Rehaan.'

'He'll be all right on his own for a bit,' Shirin said, and lowered her voice a little. 'It's Ava I worry about—it's not as safe for a girl as it is for a boy, and I don't know how to explain that to her. And I'd die before I admit it to her, but I'm feeling a bit seasick as well.'

They were both silent for a while, watching Ava as she waved to a flock of seagulls following the ferry.

Ava was too engrossed in the seagulls to hear them, and Mallika said impulsively, 'I don't mean to be intrusive, but you said that you'd have stayed with your husband for the sake of the kids—it's not worth it. You'll be much happier on your own.'

Shirin turned to look at her, raising her brows a little. 'Sounds like you're speaking from personal experience.'

'Sort of,' Mallika admitted.

She'd never spoken about this before, and confiding in a stranger wasn't the kind of thing she normally went in for. Still, there was something about Shirin that made Mallika want to talk to her.

'My dad had affairs,' she said. 'Many of them. My mum put up with them—I guess she didn't have much of a choice—but me and my brother didn't understand why she was unhappy most of the time and we tended to blame her a little. My dad was fun, only he wasn't around much—it was only when I was in my teens that I figured out that he was a pathetic excuse for a husband.'

'No wonder you don't have a high opinion of men,' Shirin said. 'Is your dad still like that?'

'He died in an accident,' Mallika said. 'Along with my mum.'

'Oh, my…' Shirin said sympathetically. 'That sucks.'

Mallika nodded. There was something oddly familiar about Shirin's reaction, but she couldn't put her finger on who she reminded her of.

'Anyway, what I was trying to say is that your kids might be a bit upset now, but it's better for them to be growing up with you.'

'That's good to hear,' Shirin said. 'Most of the time I'm sure I'm doing the right thing, but sometimes I wonder. The kids miss their dad, and they miss Canada, and I'm not really sure how I'm going to manage.'

'Where do you work?' Mallika asked.

'I don't,' Shirin said with a sigh. 'I sponge off my brother. But I'm planning to start once I get the kids settled in school.'

Mallika wondered for an instant what it would be like to have a brother she didn't have to worry about, then shook herself. Aryan might be a bit of a liability, but she wouldn't swap her own life for Shirin's for anything.

'Older brother?' she asked, for the sake of something to say.

'No—younger,' Shirin said. 'I used to make his life hell when he was a kid, but he's—without exaggeration—the best brother a girl could have.'

There was a little pause, and then she went on.

'My parents offered me a place in their flat, but it was impossible to manage. They're old, and set in their ways, and the kids drove them crazy. My brother had a flat in the same building and he's turning it over to me.'

'Has he moved out already?' Mallika asked, though she already knew the answer.

It had taken a while for the penny to drop, but she'd finally realised why Shirin seemed so familiar. She didn't look much like Darius—she was petite and sharp-featured—but some of her mannerisms were just like his, and their smiles were identical.

'Yes, he's rented a hideously expensive place in Parel,' she was saying now. 'He says he's enjoying being on his own, but I still feel terribly guilty. Anyway, he's going overseas in a few months—some complicated "finding himself" kind of journey. I'm happy for him, but I'll miss him like crazy.'

And so will I, Mallika thought to herself, feeling suddenly very shallow and stupid.

It hadn't even occurred to her to ask Darius *why* he'd given his flat to his sister. All this while she'd thought Darius was being callous about Aryan, not realising that he took his responsibilities as a sibling quite as seriously as she did.

'Are your parents okay with your brother going away?' she asked, the words slipping out before she could help herself.

Shirin nodded. 'He's wanted to do it for as long as I can remember, and he planned his trip a couple of years ago,' she said. 'He's had to cancel it twice already—once because Dad had a heart attack, and a second time because I'd come back to India to have my second baby. Our grandmother fell down and broke pretty much every bone in her hip around the same time, and poor Darius was saddled with looking after all of us *and* paying the medical bills. Luckily he was minting money by then, so the bills weren't a problem, but he went crazy trying to look after everyone at the same time. It doesn't help that we're a bit of an eccentric family too… Anyway, this time hopefully he'll get away before one of us does something stupid.'

Rehaan stuck his head out of the cabin, and Shirin hurried towards him while Mallika tried to get her disordered thoughts back on track. This didn't really change things. If anything, it underlined the fact that she wasn't suited to be with a man like Darius even if he had been ready for a relationship.

Any other woman would have tried to find out about his family—*she* was so hung up about her own that she'd avoided the subject of his completely. From what Shirin had said, Darius was as unlike her father as he could be—he was responsible and trustworthy. And she'd made all kinds of assumptions about him that were totally untrue. Worse, she'd accused him of not caring for his family—and he hadn't even defended himself.

Shirin waved to her as they got off at the jetty, and Mallika saw them get into a car that had the logo of an expensive resort printed on the side. Alibagh had been a sleepy little seaside town during her growing up years, but in the last decade high-end hotels and villas had gone up all around the place. Property prices had rocketed as well, and her mother's decision to buy a bungalow there had been more than vindicated.

IT TOOK HER most of the day to get a contractor to commit on the money and the time it would take him to get the leakage in the Alibagh house fixed. It didn't turn out to be as expensive as she'd feared, but she'd need to make a few more trips to the house over the next few weeks.

She grimaced at the thought. Even now she couldn't bring herself to go into the kitchen and cook a meal for herself, and she ended up sitting in the living room and eating the packed lunch she'd brought with her.

It was ironic, she thought—after all the grief and heartache he'd caused her mother, her father had finally died trying to save her from the fire. If there was an afterlife, perhaps her mother had forgiven him. Mallika still couldn't bring herself to do so.

The weeks after her parents' death would have been horrific enough without having to deal with her father's mistress. She was a virago of a woman, out for all that she could get, and finally Mallika's father's impecuniousness made sense—all this while he'd been supporting her on the side.

Mallika's mother had known, and she'd been careful to make sure that all her investments and the property she'd bought were either in her own name or in her children's. Even so, there had been a bitter battle to hold on to Mallika's grandparents' flat, which her father had inherited, and his mistress had done all she could to claim a share of it. Finally, when she hadn't been able to take any more, Mallika had paid her off—she didn't regret the money, but the experience had left her very bitter.

Once she'd sorted everything out with the contractor and the caretaker, and made advance payments to the workers, Mallika headed back to the jetty. There was just about time for her to catch the last ferry out, and she settled herself into a corner seat with a sigh. She hadn't been able to stop thinking about Darius all day, and impulsively she pulled out her phone and dialled his number.

The phone rang a few times, but Darius didn't pick up and she dropped it back into her bag. Calling him had been a stupid idea anyway—he was probably out partying with his friends.

Feeling suddenly very lost and alone, she shut

her eyes and tried not to think about him. The images kept coming, though, and she had to blink very hard to stop tears from welling into her eyes. Damn Darius—he was proving far more difficult to forget about than she'd thought.

CHAPTER EIGHT

IT WAS PAST eleven when Darius finally got back home. He'd gone to the tennis court in his building to see if he could catch a game, and he'd run into an ex-colleague who was now a neighbour. They'd played a couple of gruelling sets, after which they'd walked down to a nearby bar to watch a football match over beer and chicken wings. His ex-colleague was a cheerful, sporty sort of man who didn't go in for deep thinking—he was the perfect companion to take Darius's mind off Mallika.

Once he was back in the flat, though, the morning's conversation replayed itself in his head. He was able to be a little more objective now, and he could see things from Mallika's point of view. She was going through a tough time with Aryan, and she wasn't yet over her parents' death—she couldn't be blamed for not wanting to complicate her life by getting into a relationship with a man who was about to go away for who knew how long.

He'd left his phone in the flat, and picked it up now to see three messages from his sister. Shirin had taken the kids out for a weekend on the beach, and while she said it had got off to a rocky start they seemed to be fine now.

He smiled as he read through her quirky messages about the kids' reactions to the hotel and the pool—and the last message read: Hired a babysitter and am now off to the spa!!!

He was still smiling as he scrolled through the list of calls he'd missed, and his expression stilled as he saw the call from Mallika. Damn, she'd called over four hours ago—she must have thought he was purposely avoiding talking to her.

He glanced at the time—too late to call her back, but he could text her. They both used the same mobile chat app, and he checked her status. It said she was last on at ten twenty-five p.m., which wasn't that long ago.

Hey—sorry I missed your call, he typed. Had forgotten my phone was at home.

MALLIKA REACHED OUT for her phone as it pinged. She still kept in touch with a few school friends through mobile chat—most of them lived overseas now, and she was used to getting texts at odd hours from them. But this time it wasn't Naina or Kirti messaging about their latest boyfriends…

No worries, she typed. I just wanted to apologise for being so rude when we spoke in the morning.

The reply was almost instantaneous.

I'm sorry too. I shot my mouth off a bit.

Cool, so we're quits.

Mallika thought a bit and added a smiley.

How was Alibagh?

Not bad. I got most of my work done. Guess what—
I met your sister on the ferry on the way out.

She took the ferry? I thought she was taking the
speedboat!

Must have changed her mind. She's really nice, by
the way. And so are the kids.

She didn't mention meeting you! I saw her messages a minute ago.

We just had a random conversation. I figured out
she was your sister from something she said.

You didn't introduce yourself?

No L wasn't sure if she'd know who I was.

I've talked about you. No details, though.

Thank heaven no details.

Mallika typed the words, even though she felt
flattered that he'd spoken about her at home.

She's my older sister—what d'you expect?

The text was quickly followed by another.

Can you talk? Texting feels a bit teenagerish...

Teenagers don't type full words. Can't talk L A's a light sleeper and his room's right next to mine.

There was a pause of a couple of minutes, as if Darius was deciding how to respond.

OK, got it.

Will the flamingos still be there tomorrow?

Guess so.

Can we go?

Guess so.

Mallika stared at the phone in frustration. The problem with texting was that she couldn't figure out whether he wanted to see her or not—*Guess so* was as vague as it got. She was about to type a message when his chat window popped up again.

Should I pick you up?

Can meet you there. But no pressure, seriously, if you don't want to go.

Isn't that my line?

It was—this time I'm the one who's asking you to come!

I want to see you. The flamingos are incidental.

They agreed on a time, and Mallika put her phone back on her bedside table, feeling strangely euphoric.

MALLIKA TOOK A cab to Sewri the next morning. She'd arranged to meet Darius at the path that led to the mudflats, and her body was thrumming with nervous energy—she had to take several deep breaths to calm herself before she got out of the cab.

The cabbie gave her a jaundiced look as she fumbled in her wallet for change. 'Should I wait?' he asked. 'You won't get a cab back from here.'

Mallika shook her head and handed him the fare. 'No, I have a ride back.'

'I can wait anyway,' the man said. 'In case whoever you're meeting doesn't turn up.'

Goodness, she hadn't even thought of that! What if Darius didn't come?

She spotted him as soon as she'd dismissed the thought as ridiculous, and her breath caught in her throat. He looked achingly familiar and wildly desirable at the same time.

'He's here—you don't need to wait,' she muttered to the cabbie, and got out of the cab, standing stock-still as Darius came up to meet her.

He was wearing a dark blue open-necked T-shirt over jeans, and he looked good enough to eat. It took a significant effort of will not to throw her arms around him.

'Hello,' she said shyly—but she didn't get any further. Darius put an arm around her and pulled her against his side in a surprisingly fierce hug.

'Good morning,' he said. 'Come on, let's go.'

There was an ancient shipwreck at the beginning of the mudflats that gave the best view of the flamingos. There were people milling around, and Darius took his arm away from her shoulders to help her up the rickety ladder.

'I can manage,' Mallika said, but just at that instant her foot slipped a little and she had to cling onto him for support.

'I'm sure you can,' he said soothingly. 'I just feel like holding your hand for a bit.'

Put like that, she could hardly say no, and the ladder *was* rickety…with a thirty-foot drop to the mud below.

The flamingos were amazing—flocks and flocks of them, perched among the mangroves that grew out of the sludgy mud. They were a bright salmon-pink, and they were showing off a little—taking off and swooping back onto their perches in little groups. Some of them were busy looking for food, and a guide nearby was explaining their migratory habits to a bunch of serious-looking kids.

'Did you ever bring Ava and Rehaan here?' Mallika asked, cuddling in a little closer to Darius. Public displays of affection weren't normally her thing, but she could hardly bear to keep her hands off him.

He nodded. 'Last week,' he said. 'I hear Shirin confided in you quite a bit on the ferry yesterday?'

Mallika looked up in surprise. 'Is she back?' she asked. 'I thought they were away for the weekend?'

'She called this morning,' Darius said. 'Thanks for pepping her up. She's going through a bit of a guilt trip, keeping the kids away from their dad.'

'I figured that,' Mallika said slowly.

If Shirin had relayed their conversation to him, she'd probably told him what Mallika had said about her own family.

Feeling suddenly a little vulnerable, she leaned her head against his arm and said, 'When you told me she'd moved back to India I didn't realise she was going through a divorce.'

'I guess we didn't talk about her much,' he said, even though he'd consciously *not* told her. She had enough problems of her own without him moaning about his family to her as well, and they had agreed not to talk too much about personal family matters.

'I'm sorry about all I said yesterday,' Mallika said. 'I made a lot of assumptions about you that were completely wrong.'

'It doesn't matter,' he said quietly. 'It was as much

my fault as yours—it was natural that you jumped to a few wrong conclusions.'

'*Very* wrong conclusions,' she said, her mouth twisting into a wry smile. 'From what Shirin said, you've done far more for your family than I've ever done for mine.'

'And I'm now escaping from them,' he said, holding up a hand when she began to protest. 'It's true,' he said. 'Not exactly the way you thought it was, but it's true all the same. They've come to depend on me a lot over the last few years. My mother says she's fine with me leaving, but I know what she'd really like is for me to marry a nice Parsi girl and settle down in Mumbai for the rest of my life. Shirin would like me to hang around and be a father figure for my niece and nephew. And my father would like me to join his golf club and start taking an interest in fine wines.'

It was the most Mallika had ever heard him say about his family, and it took her a few seconds to absorb it fully. 'It all sounds rather overwhelming,' she admitted.

'It is,' he said. 'I love my family a lot, and if they really needed me I'd cancel my travels for a third time without a single regret. But with Shirin around I think they'll be fine.'

'I'm sure they will,' Mallika said, wanting more than anything to remove the slight uncertainty lurking in his eyes. 'You should go—especially since it's something you've wanted to do for so long.'

'It's bigger than me, in a way,' he said, and

laughed slightly. 'This whole need to go out and see the world. Shirin says it's inherited—some ancient Persian wanderlust gene that's skipped a few generations.'

'Maybe she's right,' Mallika said, reaching out to take his hand.

There was a tinge of sadness in her voice as she thought of how different the two of them were. His family sounded like the kind she'd always longed for and, while she understood his motivations a lot better now, she knew that she wouldn't have taken the same decisions in his place. She craved stability and was comfortable with the conservative values of a traditional family, whereas Darius wanted to break out, challenge himself and push boundaries.

He helped her down the ladder, and once they were on dry land again turned her to face him.

'Want to come over?' he asked, and she nodded, her throat suddenly dry.

There was no mistaking his meaning—and there was also no point bringing up the rules again. Their attraction was too strong to fight, and the most she could hope for was that it would die away after a while without doing too much damage.

Neither of them spoke during the short drive to his flat, their heightened anticipation too intense to allow for casual conversation. Mallika found that her knees were trembling just a bit as Darius unlocked the flat and let her in.

She had barely stepped inside when he bolted the door and turned to take her into his arms.

'Welcome back,' he murmured against her mouth, and then there was no room to talk any more as a tide of pure unadulterated desire overtook both of them.

'WHAT NEXT?' DARIUS asked many hours later. 'I guess a few of the rules just went out of the window.'

'I guess,' she said, trailing her hand slowly down his chest.

She didn't want to think about practical stuff right now, and Darius's question had brought her back to reality with a bump.

'We can take each day as it comes, can't we?' she asked. 'I mean, some of those rules I made were downright silly.'

'I agree,' Darius said, and it sounded so heartfelt that both of them burst out laughing.

Mallika pressed herself closer to him. With her slim, pliant body and sparkling, naughty eyes, Mallika was almost impossible to resist, and Darius bent his head to capture her lips under his.

'You know, Shirin really liked you,' he said.

'I liked her too,' Mallika said, feeling absurdly flattered.

Darius reached out and tucked a stray strand of hair behind her ear.

'I think it's time for you to meet the family,' he said musingly.

Mallika looked up in alarm. 'Whose family?' she asked.

'The Prime Minister's,' Darius said. 'Whose do you think? Mine.'

'I thought we'd agreed not to tell them!' Mallika said.

'We did. You're going to be my scary colleague-cum-landlady. Shirin's guessed, but to my parents you'll be just one more among my many admirers. Come on, I'd like you to meet them—they're a little crazy, but they're fun.'

Mallika couldn't bring herself to say no—she still didn't know *why* Darius would want to take her home, though.

'Aunt Freny's going to be there as well,' he told her. 'You'll like her.'

'What should I wear?' she asked.

'I've no idea,' Darius said. 'We'll be going from work, so regular office gear should be fine. My parents aren't particular.'

PARTICULAR OR NOT, Mallika felt devoutly grateful that she'd dressed up a little when she met Darius's perfectly groomed mother the next day. All of five feet tall, she was like a Dresden figurine with her pink cheeks and carefully styled snow-white hair. She gave Mallika a polite kiss on the cheek, her flowery perfume enveloping them as she ushered Mallika and Darius into the room.

'Papa Mistry, this is Darius's landlady,' she announced, and Darius's father peered short-sightedly at her.

'She looks too young and too pretty to be a landlady,' he said firmly. '*Now* I know why Darius didn't want to live here any more.'

'He didn't want to live here because this place is like a mausoleum,' Aunt Freny grumbled. 'Or a madhouse when those kids of Shirin's turn up. Little devils.'

'Don't you dare call my grandchildren names,' Mrs Mistry said, her eyes narrowing dangerously. 'They're perfectly angelic if you know how to handle them.'

'With a pair of long-handled tongs,' Aunt Freny muttered.

Mrs Mistry pretended not to hear her. 'Do sit down, child,' she said to Mallika. 'How do you take your tea? One cube of sugar? And milk?'

The tea tray had a tea cosy on it with a fat little teapot inside, and a tiny jug of milk with a bowl full of sugar cubes next to it. Mallika looked curiously at Mrs Mistry as she poured the tea. She'd seen tea served so elaborately only in British period movies on TV—real, live people drinking it this way was a novelty. Her own mother had always just boiled everything together and then strained it into cups.

'So you met Darius at work?' Mr Mistry asked, leaning forward curiously. 'This is the first time he's brought a girl home.'

'The first time this month,' Aunt Freny said promptly, and Mallika dissolved into laughter.

Aunt Freny was adorable—Mallika's own relatives tended towards the stiff and formal, and she wished she'd had someone like Aunt Freny around when she was going up.

'Freny is our *enfant terrible*,' Mr Mistry said indulgently. 'Tell us about what you do, Mallika. Darius said you work in real estate investments? How did you end up there?'

He seemed genuinely interested, and he knew far more about real estate than most people did.

Shirin trooped in with her children when they were halfway through the conversation, and Rehaan promptly clambered onto his grandfather's lap.

'Where's Great-Granny?' he demanded.

Mr Mistry turned to his wife. 'Is Mummy still asleep?' he enquired.

'No, I'll go and call her,' Mrs Mistry said, and a few minutes later a tiny, very frail-looking old lady emerged from somewhere inside the house.

Darius got up to help her to a chair. 'Meet my grandmother,' he said to Mallika. 'She was an army nurse during the Second World War.'

The elder Mrs Mistry was alert and very garrulous. But with the children running around, and Shirin keeping up a parallel conversation on school admissions, poor Mallika could hardly understand what she was saying, and after a while she gave Darius an appealing look.

'Darius, you should take Mallika out dancing instead of making her sit with us old folks,' Aunt Freny said.

'I used to love dancing when I was a girl,' Darius's grandmother said wistfully. 'My Rustom used to waltz so well.'

'He used to step on everyone's toes,' the irrepressible Aunt Freny said. 'And sometimes he got the steps wrong. But he looked good—I'll give you that.'

'Darius, I'm coming to your building on Saturday,' Ava announced. 'To swim in the pool.'

'You're very welcome,' Darius said. 'I won't be there, but don't let that stop you.'

'Why can't you swim in the club, *dikra*?' Mrs Mistry asked, shooting a quelling look at Darius.

'Because the club pool is full of old hairy men,' Ava said. 'Can I just say—*ewwwww*?'

'Men *should* be hairy,' Mrs Mistry said. 'Not too much, but all these models and actors nowadays with waxed chests—they look terrible. What do you think, Mallika?'

Completely thrown by the sudden appeal for her opinion, Mallika floundered. 'I…uh…I guess it's fashionable nowadays.'

'Darius doesn't wax his chest,' Rehaan volunteered. 'I saw him in the pool last week and he's got hair. Not the orangutan kind—just normal.'

'Thank you, Rehaan,' Darius said, getting to his feet. 'And on that note I think we should leave. People who aren't used to our family can handle us only in small doses.'

'If you mean Mallika, I think she's made of sterner stuff,' Shirin said, giving Mallika a friendly smile.

'Do you like orchids?' Aunt Freny asked abruptly.

Mallika nodded, and Freny reached behind her chair and produced a flowering orchid in a small ceramic pot.

'This is for you,' she said, handing it to Mallika

with a firm little nod. 'Don't overwater it, and make sure it's not in the sun.'

Mallika took the orchid, and as Darius looked all set to leave she stood up as well, and followed him to the door.

'It was really nice meeting all of you,' she said, giving the four generations in the room a comprehensive sort of smile.

'It was lovely meeting you too, *dikra*,' Mrs Mistry said warmly. 'Darius, you must bring her again.'

'Yes, sure,' he said drily, but he was smiling as he bent down to kiss his mother.

He waited till they were in the car before turning to her and raising his eyebrows.

'Well? Did they scare you?'

She laughed and shook her head. 'They were fun,' she said.

And so they were—but she wasn't sure why Darius had decided that it was the right time to introduce her to his family. After all, he was going away, so what they had couldn't go anywhere.

Back at Darius's flat, she shut the front door behind her and leaned against it, her eyes dancing as she looked at him.

'I need to refresh my memory,' she said. 'Exactly *how* hairy is that chest of yours?'

CHAPTER NINE

'ONE OF MY schoolfriends is coming from the US this Friday,' Darius said a few days later. 'We haven't met in years, so I've invited him to stay with me over the weekend. Shirin and a few other people are coming over for dinner on Saturday. Would you like to come?'

Mallika hesitated. She'd insisted that Darius still did not tell his parents the truth about them, the way she'd not told Aryan or any of *her* relatives, but Shirin had guessed anyway—and meeting a few people for dinner trumped not seeing Darius at all for the entire weekend.

'Okay,' she said. 'D'you need help planning the dinner?'

'No, I'll outsource everything,' he said. 'There's a friend of mine who does catering for Parsi weddings. I'll just ask her to manage it.'

'Catering… Exactly how many people are you inviting?'

'Around twenty-five or so, I thought,' Darius said, not noticing Mallika's horrified expression. 'The living room's big enough to hold that many, and if it isn't they can go and stand on the balcony.'

The intercom rang and he went to answer it, leaving Mallika to deal with her panicky reaction to meeting twenty-five of Darius's friends all at once. She always felt shy in large groups—while not agoraphobic, like Aryan, she still preferred meeting a maximum of three or four people at a time.

Darius came back after a short conversation—presumably with the security guard who screened visitors at the main gate.

'I bought a painting last week and it's on its way upstairs now,' he said. 'I was hoping I'd get a chance to show it to you before I left for Delhi again.'

Nidas had recently taken over a smaller firm, and Darius was travelling to Delhi almost every week to manage the merger of the two companies' assets. It was stressful, and Mallika knew he didn't enjoy the trips. She hoped it was because they took him away from her and the small amount of time they had left together...

'I didn't realise you had to go this week as well,' she said. 'When's the takeover going to be complete?'

'At least another two months,' Darius said, sighing as he pulled her close. 'It's crazy. There's so much to do. But it's a big acquisition for Nidas, and in the long term it will make a big difference to our share value. It's just a difficult process right now—especially since the need for greater efficiencies means some of their staff are being let go.'

He was silent for a while, and Mallika hugged him back without saying anything either. It was the first time he had touched her seeking comfort, she realised—so far everything had been about sex. In a way she felt closer to him this way than when they were making love, and it was an odd sensation.

The doorbell rang, and he let her go to open the door. The painting was carefully packaged in layers of bubble wrap, and Darius had to use a knife to get it out.

'What d'you think?' he asked as he knelt to prop the painting against the nearest wall.

The painting had appealed to him the minute he'd seen it, tucked away in the corner of a little art gallery he patronised. A mass of swirling colours, it managed to capture exactly the feel of an Indian market—you could almost smell the spices and feel the dust and the heat.

Mallika looked at the signature at the bottom right-hand corner. 'This is a good example of the artist's work,' she said, sounding impressed. 'It would have been a brilliant investment if you'd bought it a few years ago.'

'I bought it because I like it,' Darius said, a puzzled look on his face. 'It isn't an *investment*.'

'That's a good reason as well,' Mallika said, sounding amused. 'I'm sorry—I guess I've been working on investments too long to remember that people sometimes buy expensive things just because they like them.'

'Different perspectives,' he said, laughing as he got back to his feet.

He came closer and slid his hands around her waist, making her shiver with longing.

'Stay for dinner?' he asked, nuzzling the most sensitive part of her neck.

'I can't,' she said regretfully. 'I need to get back home.'

'Stay this once,' he said, pulling her closer, and they kissed once more—a long, drugging kiss that left her with trembling knees and a blind desire to tug his clothes off and spend the rest of the day making love on the living room floor.

'Aryan...' she said.

Darius groaned. 'He'll be okay just this once,' he said. 'We've never spent a night together, Mallika, and I'm leaving soon—we mightn't get another chance.'

Put like that, she found it almost impossible to say no, and after another half-hearted protest she messaged Aryan to let him know that she was staying over at a friend's home.

IT WAS AROUND four in the morning when Mallika woke up with a start. She didn't know what exactly had woken her, but her pulse was pounding as if she'd just finished a gruelling race. Next to her, Darius muttered something in his sleep and put a heavy arm around her, pulling her close to his magnificent chest.

Gingerly, Mallika stretched a hand out to the bedside table to pick up her phone. Perhaps the message tone had woken her—she wouldn't put it past Aryan to be messaging her to come home quickly, or perhaps to pick up some exotic computer accessory on her way home.

The screen was blank, however, and there were no messages at all other than one from her bank offering her 'never before' rates on a loan. Puzzled, she checked the signal—it was at full strength, so that meant Aryan hadn't messaged her at all.

'Darius,' she whispered, and he woke up, blinking a little as the light from the mobile phone display hit his eyes.

'Something wrong?' he asked, sitting up as he took in her expression.

'There's not a single message from Aryan,' she said weakly, realising how stupid she sounded as soon as the words were out of her mouth.

Thankfully, Darius immediately understood what she was trying to say.

'Have you tried calling him?'

'He might be asleep,' she said, and to his eternal credit Darius reached across and put his arms around her.

'Do you want me to take you home?' he asked softly, and she nodded.

There were very few cars on the road, and it took less than ten minutes to drive to her flat. The watchman was asleep, and the lift had been switched off, so they had to climb the stairs to her flat. Mallika's knees were trembling by the time she got to the right floor and unlocked the door.

'Should I wait outside?' Darius asked.

She shook her head. 'Stay in the living room,' she said. 'I'll just check on Aryan—hopefully he's fine and I've dragged you all this way for nothing.'

But he wasn't fine.

When Mallika tiptoed into his room she found him lying stock-still in bed, his eyes wide open and feverish. For a few seconds he didn't seem to recognise her, and she sagged onto her knees in relief when he blinked and said, 'Mally...'

'Are you okay?' she asked.

He shook his head. 'I have a headache,' he offered.

She reached out to touch his brow. 'You're burning up,' she said, trying to keep the worry out of her voice. 'I'll get you a paracetamol...maybe you'll feel better after that, okay? Why didn't you call me?'

'I fell in the bathroom and hit my head. I'm not sure where my phone is.'

Mallika clicked on the light—sure enough, there was a huge purpling bruise on his forehead.

'Is he all right?' Darius asked softly as she came out.

She shook her head. 'I don't think he's eaten a single meal since yesterday,' she said. 'And he's got a raging fever. He's also fallen down and hurt his head.'

'I'm so sorry,' he said quietly. 'I shouldn't have pushed you to stay. Is there anything I can do?'

She shook her head angrily. 'It's not your fault,' she said, almost to herself. 'It's mine—for even imagining that I could have a life of my own. Will you get me some biscuits from the kitchen, Darius? I need to make sure he eats something before I give him a paracetamol.'

He nodded, and she went to the medicine cabinet

to try and locate the pills. There were only three left in the blister pack, and she popped one out. Darius came back with the biscuits and a glass of water, and she carried them into Aryan's room.

'Eat these first, and then swallow the medicine with the water,' she said.

'I'm not hungry,' Aryan whispered.

Suddenly her control snapped. 'I don't *care*!' she said. 'I stay away for one night and you don't even take care of yourself! Sit up right now and eat—if you don't want me to call an ambulance and get you put in hospital.'

It was the first time she'd ever shouted at him and Aryan sat up in shock, blinking woozily as he took the biscuits from her. Mallika felt horribly guilty, but at least he ate them silently before swallowing the medicine.

'Try and sleep now,' she said, tucking him back into bed. 'I'll call Dr Shetty as soon as it's morning.'

'Stay with me,' Aryan mumbled, reaching for her hand as she got up, but she pulled away.

'I'll be back in a minute,' she said, and went out to Darius.

'I'm so sorry I dragged you out like this,' she said wearily. 'I should have just come home last night.'

'Do you need me to go and fetch a doctor?' he asked.

She shook her head. 'I'll call our family doctor in the morning,' she said. 'I think he'll be okay till then.'

'Right,' Darius said. 'I'll see you when I'm back from Delhi, then—okay?'

She nodded, and he dropped a quick kiss on her forehead before letting himself out.

'HE'S GOT AN INFECTION. His immunity levels have dropped, staying indoors like this,' the doctor said as he prescribed a course of antibiotics over the phone. 'I'll try to come and see him in a couple of hours, but if he doesn't start leading a normal life this is going to happen more and more often.'

'How's he catching an infection, then, if he isn't going out?'

'From *you*,' he said. 'You work, don't you? *You're* carrying the infections home, but because your immunity levels are normal you're not catching them yourself.'

SHE SPENT THE next two days nursing Aryan. The doctor visited him, as he'd promised—he'd known both Mallika and Aryan since they were children, and he was as worried about him as Mallika was.

Aryan didn't react as the doctor spoke to him—he'd slipped back into silent mode, and he stared passively at the ceiling while the doctor tried to explain the harm he was doing himself by his self-imposed house arrest.

'The quicker you get him to a good psychiatrist, the better,' Dr Shetty told Mallika when she took him aside to ask what she should do. 'I can treat his physical symptoms, but I can't do much about his mental state. And you're just making it worse by humouring him.'

Perhaps he was right, Mallika thought wearily as she went back inside to persuade her brother to eat something and take his medicine. Perhaps she *was* making her brother worse. Only there was little she could do if he refused to see a psychiatrist— it had been difficult enough persuading him to see Dr Shetty.

She tried to get a psychiatrist to come and meet Aryan, perhaps by pretending to be a friend of hers, but that wasn't the way they operated, apparently. Or at least the reputable ones didn't, and she didn't want to trust Aryan to a quack.

'I mightn't be able to come for dinner on Saturday,' she told Darius when he called one evening.

'Won't Aryan be okay by then?'

'He's over the worst, but he's still a little weak— and he's still not eating properly.'

'Can't one of your relatives stay with him? That aunt of yours who lives nearby?'

'He doesn't want anyone else around,' Mallika said. 'I'm so sorry, Darius.' She was very tired, and her voice shook a little.

Darius immediately softened.

'I'm sorry too,' he said gently. 'Take care. I'll be back from Delhi tonight, and I'll come across and see you on Sunday.'

Mallika was too exhausted to tell him not to come—anyway, Aryan had probably figured out by now that she was dating him. And she wanted to see Darius badly. He'd become the one sane, stable thing in her world, and she knew she was growing horribly dependent on him.

'Are you going out?' Aryan asked on Sunday morning.

It was obvious why he'd asked—Mallika had changed the ancient T-shirt and tracks she normally wore at home for a peasant blouse and Capri pants, and she'd brushed her hair into some semblance of order.

'No,' Mallika said shortly. 'A friend's coming over, and I don't want to look like something from a refugee camp.'

'Is it that Parsi friend of yours? Cyrus, or something?'

'Darius,' she said.

Aryan didn't reply, and she felt a surge of annoyance sweep over her. She'd spent the last few days waiting on him hand and foot—he hadn't bothered to thank her, even once, and now he was behaving as if she didn't have the right to invite a friend over.

Hot words bubbled up to her lips, and she was about to say something when Aryan spoke again.

'Your hair looks just like Mum's when you tie it back like that,' he said, and suddenly Mallika felt tears start to her eyes.

She'd inherited her riotously curly hair from their mother, but while her mum had always carefully brushed her curls into a tight bun, she'd always kept hers short.

DARIUS GAVE HER a brief kiss, full on the mouth, as he strode into the flat. 'For you,' he said, handing her a box of expensive-looking chocolates. 'How's Aryan doing?'

'He's much better,' she said, taking the chocolates from him. 'Thank you so much.'

He grinned at her. 'You don't need to be so formal,' he said. 'We missed you yesterday—especially Shirin. She's been dying to meet you again.'

'I wish I could have come,' Mallika said regretfully. 'I couldn't leave Aryan alone, though.'

'I'd have been all right on my own,' Aryan said petulantly, walking into the room, his eyes hostile as he looked at Darius. 'Hello,' he said, nodding briefly at him before sitting down on the sofa.

'She was worried about you,' Darius said as he settled his tall frame into the chair opposite Aryan. 'You were quite ill, weren't you?'

The boy looked a little thinner than the last time Darius had seen him, but otherwise he seemed perfectly healthy. And more than capable of looking after himself for one evening.

'I'm better now,' he said, his eyes dark and resentful. 'I can manage on my own if I have to. Anyway, she's hardly at home—whenever she can, she goes away without telling me where she's going.'

The unfairness of it took Mallika's breath away, and she could only stare at Aryan speechlessly.

Darius took one look at her, and took over the conversation. 'I think your sister stays with you for as much time as she can,' he said. 'She can't work from home *every* day, can she?'

Aryan bit his lip, but didn't reply.

Mallika jumped in to dispel the suddenly awkward silence. 'Which would you prefer? Tea or coffee?'

'Tea's good, thanks,' Darius said, and she got up to make it.

'Aryan…?'

'You should know by now that I don't drink the stuff,' he muttered.

Darius frowned.

'Did you have an argument with your sister?' he asked quietly once Mallika had left the room.

Aryan said nothing, but his eyes widened a fraction.

Darius leaned forward. 'I don't think that's the way you normally speak to her,' he said. 'She's completely devoted to you, and she wouldn't be if you were that rude all the time.'

For a second it looked as if Aryan would burst into speech, but then he got to his feet and left the room without a word. A door shut somewhere inside the house, and Darius assumed that he'd gone back to his room. He exhaled slowly, standing up and running a hand through his hair. He very rarely lost his temper, and the sudden surge of anger he'd felt had surprised him as much as it had upset Aryan.

He made his way to the kitchen, where Mallika was pouring tea into two delicate china cups. She looked up at him and smiled, and he felt immediately guilty.

'Sorry—did Aryan leave you alone?' she asked. 'His social skills are a bit basic.'

'I think I sent him away,' he admitted, leaning against the doorway. 'I didn't like the way he spoke to you and I called him out on it. It's not the kind of thing I normally do, but he got under my skin.'

He'd expected Mallika to be annoyed, but she just handed him his teacup, her brow furrowed in thought.

'What did you say to him?' she asked.

He told her, and she shrugged.

'That's pretty mild,' she said. 'Our family doctor spoke to him for a good fifteen minutes yesterday—I'm not sure Aryan even registered what he was saying.'

'How long are you going to manage like this?' Darius asked softly, his hand going out to caress her cheek. 'You need to have a proper life of your own—it just isn't fair to you.'

Mallika went into his arms, burying her face in his chest. 'I don't know,' she said. 'I need to sit down and have a proper talk with Aryan—maybe I'm reading him all wrong, hovering over him when he could do with some space.'

'It's worth a try,' Darius said, bending down and brushing his lips lightly against hers, making her quiver with need. 'Will you be able to get away for a while in the afternoon? Varun really wanted to meet you.'

For a few seconds Mallika couldn't remember who Varun was. Then she realised he meant the schoolfriend who'd come over from the US.

'At your place?' she asked.

'Yes,' Darius said. 'I'm going down to his hotel to collect him—I'll see you in a couple of hours, okay?'

AFTER DARIUS LEFT, Mallika went and knocked tentatively on Aryan's door. There was no reply, and she knocked once more before pushing the door open. Aryan was in bed, his face turned towards the wall, and she went in and sat next to him.

'Are you feeling okay?' she asked, putting a gentle hand on his shoulder.

He flipped over onto his back—an abrupt movement that threw her hand off.

'Are you going to marry that guy?' he demanded.

Mallika took a deep breath. Clearly she'd been wrong about the conversation with Darius having had no effect on her brother.

'He's just a friend, Aryan,' she said. 'I'm not planning to get married for a long, long while. Perhaps never.'

Aryan stared at her, his eyes stormy. 'Because of me?' he asked.

She shook her head. She couldn't lay all the blame at his door, however much she wanted to. 'Because I think I'd make a rotten wife,' she said, a little sadly. 'Don't worry about it, Aryan. Concentrate on getting better. Once you're back on your feet, maybe we could try going out together. Maybe for a walk to Hanging Gardens. Remember how much you used to love going there as a kid?'

'I don't want to go out,' he said, sounding like a truculent kid. 'You don't need to fuss over me, Mally. I'll go when I want to.'

'When will that be? You heard what the doctor said. You're making yourself ill like this.'

'I don't care,' he said, turning away from her again. 'And if I do get ill you can leave me here and go wherever you want. I'm not forcing you to hang around and look after me.'

'You're not,' Mallika said calmly. 'I feel like looking after you because you're my brother and I love you, even though you're perfectly obnoxious at times.'

Aryan didn't react, but when she got up to go he stretched out a hand and held her back without turning around.

Mallika sat down again, reaching across to smooth his hair off his brow.

'I do too,' he muttered under his breath.

She leaned closer. 'You do too, what?' she asked.

'I love you too,' he said, the words so indistinct that she had to strain to hear them. 'And I'm sorry if I'm obnoxious. It's just so hard without Mom.'

His breath hitched in his throat, and Mallika's heart went out to him. They had never been a very demonstrative family, and this was probably the first time she'd told her brother that she loved him since they'd both reached adulthood. Maybe that was part of the reason he was this way—he'd been only twenty-two when their parents had died, and it had to have been tougher on him than her.

'I miss her too,' she said softly.

Aryan said something under his breath that she couldn't hear at all.

'What was that, *baba*?' she asked.

He said in a whisper, 'It was my fault.'

'What was your fault?'

'The accident,' he said. 'I smelt the gas leak when I went into the kitchen to fetch some water. But I forgot about it and I didn't tell Mom.'

'You *knew* about the leak?' Mallika said blankly.

This had never occurred to her. She'd berated herself so many times for not having gone down to Alibagh with the rest of the family—if she'd been around she'd have gone into the kitchen with her mother and smelled the leak. The only reason her mother hadn't noticed was because she'd had a bad head cold and had completely lost her sense of smell. Her father, of course, never stepped into the kitchen, and normally neither did Aryan.

'I've been wanting to tell you ever since,' he said. 'I can't stop thinking about it.'

'Why didn't you tell me?' she demanded, but deep, dry sobs were racking his body now and he couldn't answer.

Mallika got up from the bed, too worked up to stay still. The last two years had been hellish. She still wasn't over the shock and grief of losing both parents together. Almost every day she wished she could have done something to make her mother's life easier—if she'd known about her father's unfaith-fulness she'd at least have been more understanding with her mum. Every teenage tantrum she'd thrown had come back to haunt her, and every time she'd taken her father's side in an argument now seemed like a betrayal of her mother.

She looked at Aryan, huddled up on the bed. Aryan had always been petted and spoilt. Her mother had expected Mallika to grow up fast and shoulder responsibilities as soon as she could, but she'd been far more indulgent with Aryan. Her father had been equally indulgent with both, but it had been quite evident that he had valued his son over his daughter.

'Did you tell Dad about the leak?' she asked sud-denly, but Aryan was already shaking his head.

'I didn't realise it was serious,' he said in a flat little voice. 'It was only when I heard her scream-ing... And by then it was too late to do anything.'

He'd been in the garden, Mallika remembered, studying for his college exams. She'd always felt terrible for him—actually being there and unable to help. A lot of her subsequent indulgence towards him had been because she'd thought he was dealing with the trauma still.

'I'm sorry,' Aryan said, his eyes pleading with her. 'I'd do anything to undo what happened...but I can't.'

'I know,' Mallika said. 'I know. I just wish...'

There were so many things she wished—that Aryan had raised the alarm, that he'd at least told their father... The accident hadn't been his fault, but the fact that he could have prevented it made it seem even more tragic than it had before.

Aryan bit his lip, tears welling in his eyes, and Mallika suddenly remembered him as a child, toddling around the kitchen one day and getting underfoot until her mother had picked him up and sat him on the kitchen counter. Mallika had protested at the unfair treatment—*she* never got to sit there—but her mother had laughed and picked her up as well, dancing around the kitchen with her to the tune of an old Bollywood song playing on the radio while Aryan laughed and clapped his hands.

It was one of the very few memories of her childhood she had where her mum was happy and smiling.

'Mum wouldn't have wanted you to torture yourself like this,' she said, going to Aryan. 'It was an accident, and we can't undo any of it. Come here.'

She held out her arms and Aryan crawled into them, hugging her back surprisingly fiercely.

'I'll try to be less of a pain from now on,' he said. 'I wish I'd told you earlier…but, Mally—you don't know how difficult it's been.'

'I can imagine,' she said. 'But it's behind us now. Let's try and get you sorted out.'

For the first time Aryan seemed amenable to the thought of getting help, and Mallika used the opportunity as best as she could. After an hour of coaxing and cajoling she'd managed to get him to agree to going with her to a psychiatrist, and she heaved a sigh of relief. Hopefully things would take a turn for the better now that she knew exactly what was bothering Aryan.

It was only when she went to fetch her phone to make an appointment that she noticed all the messages and missed calls from Darius. Her mouth dropped open in dismay—it was past six, and she'd agreed to meet him and Varun at four.

Fingers trembling a little, she dialled his number. 'I'm so sorry—' she said when he picked up.

'It's all right, Mallika, you don't need to apologise,' he said, sounding resigned. 'Is Aryan okay?'

'Yes,' she said. 'I should have called. I'll explain when we meet, but I really couldn't have come.'

'I understand,' he said. 'I'll see you around at work tomorrow, then.'

DARIUS WAS FROWNING as he put the phone down, and Varun raised his eyebrows. 'You've got it bad, haven't you?' he said.

Darius smiled reluctantly. 'Is it that obvious?'

'Pretty obvious,' Varun said lightly. There was a brief pause, and then Varun said, 'So what are you going to do about it?'

Darius shrugged. 'Nothing,' he said. 'I'm out of here in a few weeks, and I don't know when I'll be back. There's no point trying to do anything about it. In any case, she isn't interested in anything serious either.'

'You could be wrong about that,' Varun murmured.

Darius shook his head. 'I'm not,' he said, but he wondered if it was true.

There were times when he'd thought Mallika was close to admitting that she cared for him, but something seemed to hold her back. Perhaps the same thing that held him back—the realisation that they wanted very different things from life. He was going away, and for Mallika Aryan would always be her first priority.

'If you really care about her there's always a way,' Varun said.

Darius laughed. 'You sound like a soppy women's magazine,' he said lightly, trying not to show how much the words had affected him.

He *did* care about Mallika—in fact, there was a real risk of his being completely besotted by her. But he couldn't give up his adventures—not when he was finally free to go.

Maybe there *was* a way, and all he had to do was convince her that it would work.

CHAPTER TEN

'I'M SORRY ABOUT YESTERDAY,' Mallika said guiltily. 'Aryan was very upset, and I completely lost track of the time.'

'Don't worry about it,' he said. 'I understand. Is Aryan okay now?'

'Yes,' she said, and before she knew it she was telling him what had happened. 'I think he'll be better now,' she said. 'The guilt was eating him up, and he hadn't told anyone.'

'Poor chap.' Darius's expression was sympathetic. 'That's one hell of a burden to be carrying around. But you're right—if he's talking about it, it's a turn for the better.'

'Let's see how it goes,' Mallika said.

She was being careful not to sound too optimistic, but it was clear to Darius that she was much happier than she'd been in weeks.

'In any case, I'm feeling a lot better about leaving him on his own now. There was a time when I was scared he'd actually harm himself...he was behaving so oddly. Anyway, let's not talk about Aryan—how was your weekend with Varun? Did you guys have a good time?'

'The best,' Darius said, thinking back to his last conversation with Varun. This was probably a good time to bring it up with Mallika, only he wasn't sure how to begin.

'You look very serious,' Mallika said teasingly. 'What are you thinking about so deeply?'

'Not thinking, really. Just…wondering.' He'd meant to lead up to the subject slowly, but his naturally forthright nature made it difficult.

'Wondering about what,' she asked. 'Global warming? Cloud computing? How to save the euro?'

He grinned in spite of himself—Mallika was so often serious that she was irresistible in a lighter mood.

'Nothing quite so earth-shattering,' he said. 'I was thinking about us.'

Her smile faltered a little, and she said, 'Oh…' before making a quick recovery. 'Serious stuff?'

'Well, kind of.' He reached across and took her hands in his. 'Mallika, I know you've had a lot to deal with since your parents died, and I don't want to put you under pressure. But I was thinking—perhaps we don't necessarily need to split up when I leave.'

'Not split up?' she repeated stupidly.

He leaned forward, his expression serious and intense. 'Come with me,' he said. 'If not for the whole trip, at least for part of it.'

Mallika stared at him as if he had suddenly gone crazy. 'What about my job?' she said. 'Aryan?'

'We'll work that out,' he said. 'You can take some time off—I'll square it with Venkat. And Aryan will be fine for a while—especially since it sounds like he might be on the mend now. I'm not asking you to come immediately, if that doesn't work for you. Take some time to settle him properly…maybe ask a relative to be with him. But you need to get away perhaps even more than I do.'

It was an incredibly tempting thought. Being alone with Darius, far away from the problems and complications of her day-to-day life.

Darius meant a lot to her, and if she'd been a little less cynical about life and relationships she'd have fancied herself in love with him. He was committed and caring, and so incredibly hot that she could hardly keep her hands off him. Any other woman would have kidnapped him by now and forced him to marry her—she must be certifiably insane to let the thought of splitting up even cross her mind.

He was still looking at her, the appeal in his eyes almost irresistible, but she slowly shook her head.

'I don't think it would work,' she said slowly. 'I'm not saying I don't want to, but it just makes more sense to end this before it gets too complicated.'

'Mallika…' He took a deep breath. 'How d'you *really* feel about me?'

'I like you,' she said, stumbling over the words a little. 'You make me laugh when I want to cry. You're honest and straightforward, and I can trust you with every secret I have. When you look at me I feel like I'm the most beautiful girl in the world—you're probably the best thing that ever happened to me.'

'I can sense a *but*,' he said softly, though he gripped her hands a little harder.

'But I'm not sure I'm the best thing that ever happened to *you*,' she said in a rush. 'I'm not good for you, Darius. We shouldn't drag this out.'

'And what made you arrive at that conclusion?' he asked.

'We're completely different,' she said. 'You're a straightforward guy—everything's simple for you— you know exactly what you want. If you feel like doing something, you go ahead and do it. If you like someone, you tell them. If you don't understand what they want, you ask. Things are a lot more complicated for me. Especially when it comes to love and relationships. My parents had the most messed-up marriage ever, and the thought of anything serious or long-term makes me want to run.'

It was probably the most direct conversation they'd ever had, but Darius was beginning to have a bad feeling about the way it was going.

'So we're different?' he said. 'That doesn't mean it can't work. And we're not in the same situation as your parents—we're not even planning to get married.'

Mallika sighed. 'I know,' she said. 'But it isn't just about us being different, or about my parents, Darius. Aryan's better, but I don't think I can leave him for a long while. And I'm not sure if I believe in long-distance relationships. It'll be torture for me, and it might end up being a drag on you. What if you meet someone else? For that matter, what if *I* meet someone else when you're away?'

Darius took a deep breath. 'I'm just saying that we have a good thing going and we don't have to split up when I leave. If either of us meets someone we like better, we can deal with it when it happens.'

'It won't work,' she said unhappily. 'It might be years before you come back—what's the point of trying to drag things out? We'll just make each other unhappy, and when we do split up we'll hate each other. I don't think I could bear that.'

Darius took her by the shoulders and turned her to face him.

'Mallika, do you know how many reasons you've given for not coming with me?'

Mallika shook her head.

'Five,' he said. 'Or maybe six—I lost count after a while. Sweetheart, no one needs five reasons not to do something. One or two are usually enough. Maybe you're overthinking this? For once you should just go with what your heart tells you.'

'I stopped listening to my heart years ago,' she said wryly.

She hadn't been making up the reasons—they were all there, buzzing around like angry bees in her head, and the more she thought about them, the more confused she got.

'Okay, so let's do something less drastic,' Darius said.

He was still holding her by the shoulders, and he

pressed on them lightly to make her sit down opposite him.

'Why don't you take a couple of weeks off and come with me for the first leg of my trip at least? We could spend some more time together. Aryan should be fine.'

But she was already shaking her head. 'I don't want to,' she said flatly.

Darius just didn't seem to understand, and she was done with trying to explain herself.

'I left Aryan for one night, and you saw what happened to him.'

'Yes—he had a breakthrough! Maybe the start of his recovery,' Darius countered.

Mallika clenched her teeth. He just wasn't getting it.

'If you want to spend more time with me, shouldn't you stay here, instead of asking me to go with you? I have a perfectly good reason to want to stay here. Why should I leave my brother to traipse around after you just because you've got some quixotic notion in your head?'

Darius inhaled sharply as a whole lot of things suddenly fell into place for him.

'So *that's* the reason,' he said quietly. 'You're scared because I'm doing something that's a little unconventional and you don't know how to deal with it. All this stuff about not wanting to get into anything long-term is hogwash.'

'I'm not a risk-taker,' she said. 'So you're right—it

bothers me. And if we're still in a relationship when you leave I'm not sure I'll be able to handle it.'

'Right,' he said, his expression tight and angry. 'So we stick to the original plan, then? It's over when I leave?'

'That would be best, I think,' she said.

She was so close to falling in love with him that she couldn't bear the thought of dragging out the end—pretending that they could sustain a long-distance relationship. There was only heartbreak at the end of it, but she couldn't bear to see him so upset either.

'Darius?' she said. 'I know you've tried to explain it many times, but *why* do you need to go?'

His expression relaxed a little and he said, 'I thought I *had* explained it. There's just so much more to life than this—so much to learn, so many places to explore, so many things to do... I don't want to wake up one day and discover that I've wasted most of my life. The world is such a big place, and I've only seen one small corner of it. I want to explore, have adventures, challenge myself—really see what I'm made of.'

'Right,' she said. 'I hear what you're saying, but I guess my brain's just wired differently. I like the comfort of what's familiar...of doing what's expected of me.'

'It's wired just fine,' he said, reaching out to twine a lock of her hair around his fingers. 'I suppose I'm the one being unreasonable, asking you to stick with me when I'm not offering anything concrete in return.'

'It's not that,' Mallika said, and when he didn't reply, she added, 'I can't handle uncertainty, that's all. If it helps, I'm crazy about you.'

Darius's eyes darkened in response.

'How crazy?' he asked, and she pressed her body against his, nibbling at his throat and tugging his shirt out of his jeans to slide her hands over his hot bare skin.

'Moderately crazy,' she whispered. 'Actually, make that extremely crazy.'

He was moving against her now, lifting her so that her body fitted more snugly against his, and unbuttoning her top to get access to her pert, full breasts.

'I guess crazy will have to do for now,' he said, and she gasped as he finally got rid of her top and laid her down carefully on the nearest sofa. 'But I'm not going to give up on you.'

'I'LL BE MOVING out of the flat in a couple of days,' Darius said over lunch a few weeks later. 'The board's agreed to let me leave Nidas a little early.'

Mallika stared at him in dismay. While she was sticking to her decision, she hadn't realised how much it would hurt when he actually left. Unconsciously, she'd got addicted to him—to seeing him every day, hearing him laugh, running her hands over his skin and putting her lips to his incredibly sexy mouth.

Sometimes she thought that agreeing to go with

him for part of his trip would be worth the inevitable heartache—then all her old demons would came
back to haunt her and she'd change her mind again.

'When are you leaving Mumbai?' she asked.

'Four weeks from now,' he said. 'But I thought
I'd spend the last month or so with my parents and
Shirin—just to make sure everything's settled for
taking care of them while I'm away.'

Who's going to take care of me? Mallika felt like
yelling at him, but she knew there was no point, so
she tried to look as unconcerned as possible.

'Do you need help with moving?'

He hesitated. 'Not really. It's mainly clothes and
some kitchen things—I'll be leaving most of it with
Shirin anyway.'

'Finished packing?'

'No, I'll start tomorrow,' Darius said, wondering
if he was being a colossal idiot.

He knew Mallika cared for him, and that if he
pushed just a little harder he'd be able to break
through her defences. But he'd planned for years to
take this time off just for himself, with no work or
family responsibilities, and he knew he'd regret it
all his life if he stayed. And Mallika hadn't even
tried to understand why he felt the way he did. If
he stayed for her he knew he'd resent it—and her—
after a while, and that would be the end of any kind
of relationship.

HE WAS HALFWAY through packing the next day when
the doorbell rang. Straightening up from the carton

he was taping shut, he wiped a hand across his fore-head. It was a hot day, and the number of cartons was growing alarmingly—he seemed to have col-lected a fair amount of junk in the few months that he'd lived in the flat.

'Oh, good, you're here,' Mallika said when he opened the door. 'I was worried you'd have already packed up and left.'

She was wearing skin-tight jeans and a peasant-style top that showed off her slender neck and shoul-ders, and Darius stood staring at her for a minute, his mouth growing dry with longing. Over the last few days he'd told himself over and over again that their relationship no longer made sense. He'd more or less bullied Mallika into giving it a shot, but now that his departure was imminent keeping the pres-sure on just wasn't fair. To either of them.

Wordlessly, he stood aside to let her into the flat. A whiff of her citrusy perfume teased his nostrils as she walked past and he bit his lip. Good resolutions were all very well, but he was only human.

Mallika stopped in the middle of the living room. 'Oh…' was all she said as she took in the cartons neatly lined up in rows and filling more than half the room.

'Shouldn't you have hired professional packers?' she asked. 'Do you have any help at all? Or are you trying to handle this on your own?'

'On my own,' he said. 'A lot of these are books and CDs—they take up more space than you'd think.'

But she wasn't listening to him any longer—her

mouth was turning down at the corners and she put her arms around him abruptly, burying her face in his shoulder. 'I wish you didn't have to go,' she said, her voice muffled against his shirt. 'I'll miss you.'

'I'm leaving the country, not dying,' he said drily, though all he wanted to do was tip her face up and kiss her and kiss her, until there was no space for conversation or thought.

'Yes,' she said. 'But we won't have a place to be together for the next month. Unless....' She looked at him, her face lighting up. 'Oh, how silly—why didn't I think of it before? This flat'll be empty, won't it? I won't rent it out, and we can meet here whenever we want.'

Darius shut his eyes for a second. Mallika probably had no idea of what she was doing to him. All his life he'd prided himself on his decisiveness and self-control—it was only when he was with Mallika that he turned to putty.

'DON'T LEAVE INDIA right away,' she said, stretching languorously on the bed a couple of hours later. 'Stay on in Mumbai for a few more weeks. You can start your self-discovery thing here just as well as in any other country.'

He shook his head, smiling at her. 'It won't work.'

She cuddled a little closer to him, pulling the sheet up to her chin. 'Don't move all your things, then,' she said. 'I'll cancel the lease agreement, so you won't need to pay rent, but you could come back to stay here whenever you want.'

Darius caught her close, pressing his lips to her forehead. 'Sweetheart, I need to do this *my* way,' he said. 'I need to work some things out, and I need a little space.'

The words stung far more than he'd meant them to, and he saw Mallika bite her lip to keep it steady.

'That's odd,' she managed finally, her tone as light as she could make it. 'I didn't have you pegged as someone who really got the concept of space.'

He gave her a wry grin. She had him there, and he knew it. 'Perhaps you were right,' he said. 'Perhaps I never should have pressured you in the beginning.'

Mallika stared at him, a nasty, icy feeling gripping her heart. She'd been so close to telling him that she'd changed her mind—that she'd found she cared for him and wanted to give a long-distance relationship a shot. The last thing she'd expected was Darius himself having a change of heart.

'So you're saying that this is it?' she said, her voice still deceptively light. 'We don't stay in touch after today?'

'Something like that,' he said, and she nodded, not trusting herself to speak any more.

After a few seconds she slid out of bed, keeping the sheet wrapped around her as she collected her clothes from the floor.

'Be back in a minute,' she said, and slid into the bathroom.

For a few minutes she could only stare at her face in the mirror, feeling mildly surprised that it looked just as it usually did. Then, after splashing some water on her face, she quickly put on her clothes and flushed the toilet to account for the time she'd spent.

When she came out of the bathroom she looked as if she didn't a have a care in the world. Unfortunately Darius wasn't around to notice, and her lips trembled a little as she saw that he was already dressed and back to his packing.

'Got a lot to finish?' she asked, after watching him dump a big pile of clothes into a suitcase.

He shook his head. 'Another fifteen minutes or so. I'm sorry—I need to get this stuff done and then get back home. My mother has organised a family gathering and I promised I'd be there.'

She sat down on the bed, looking at him thoughtfully. One of the things *her* mother had repeatedly dinned into her head was to act with dignity. *'Apni izzat apne haath*—your dignity is in your own hands.' That had been one of her favourite sayings, along with, 'No one will respect you unless you respect yourself.'

'You should head off soon, then,' she said, getting to her feet with a brightly artificial smile on her lips.

It cost her every last ounce of willpower, but she walked across to him and leaned up to kiss him lightly on the lips.

'It was really good while it lasted,' she said. 'Thanks for putting up with all my whims and *na-khras*. Have a good life.'

'Mallika...' he said, and something indefinable flickered in his eyes.

She stepped back quickly, before he could touch her.

'I'll see you, then,' she said. 'Some time. Deposit the keys with the watchman, will you?'

And, leaving him standing in the bedroom, she hurried out of the flat, waiting till she was in her car before allowing a few hastily wiped away tears to escape.

CHAPTER ELEVEN

'I'M GOING OUT,' Aryan said.

He sounded oddly defiant—as if he expected Mallika to object.

It was almost a month since she'd broken up with Darius, and it had been tough. She missed him so badly that it hurt, and only the highest levels of self-control had stopped her from calling him.

Aryan hadn't said anything, but he'd been unusually well-behaved—probably sensing that she was very close to breaking point.

'Out?' she asked. 'Where?'

'Um…I thought I'd get a haircut. And maybe buy a couple of shirts.'

She should have felt pleased—Aryan was a lot better, but except for his trips to the doctor he'd stepped out of doors only once, for a walk around the garden with her. Wanting to go somewhere on his own was a first. He still ordered his clothes on the internet, and paid a local barber to come to their home and trim his hair once a month, and she couldn't figure out what had prompted the sudden decision to go to the shops on his own.

'D'you need the car?' she asked, trying to stall for time while she gauged his mood.

Aryan shook his head. 'Not today,' he said. 'I'll walk down Warden Road and get what I need. But if you could spare it for some time on Saturday that would be great?'

Feeling completely at sea, Mallika nodded. 'Yes, of course. You can have it for the full day, if you like.'

'I'm meeting someone,' Aryan volunteered after a brief silence. 'A…um…a girl. She's from Bangalore, and she's going to be here for a few days. I got to know her online,' he added a tad defensively as Mallika gaped at him.

'Figures,' Mallika muttered, once she'd got her breath back.

While she'd been obsessing about her little brother's lack of social interaction he'd gone right ahead and acquired an online girlfriend. Served her right for being so presumptuous, thinking he needed her help to get back to a normal life.

An unpleasant thought struck her, and she said, 'Aryan…?'

'Yes?'

'This girl—just checking—she's real, right? Not computer-generated or a…a…fake persona or something?'

Aryan laughed—a full-bodied, boyish laugh that made him look years younger. 'She's real, all right,' he said. 'I've video called her a few times, and I've done basic checks on her online profile. She's a computer engineer, and she's training to be a hacker. An *ethical* hacker,' he added hastily as Mallika choked on her tea. 'She's hired by corporates and governments to identify possible security breaches in their systems.'

'She sounds lovely,' Mallika said, wondering what kind of 'basic checks' one did on a prospective girlfriend. Finishing her tea, she got to her feet. 'Are you inviting her home?'

'I might,' Aryan said cautiously.

Mallika knew she had been a bit on edge ever since she'd broken up with Darius and Aryan was probably testing her mood. She turned her back to him now, and rinsed her tea cup with unnecessary vigour.

'You okay with me meeting her?' he asked.

'Yes, of course,' Mallika said, turning towards him with an overly bright smile on her lips. 'It's a good thing—you getting to know more people.'

She kept the smile plastered on her face until he left the flat, and then let out a huge sigh and flopped down onto the nearest sofa.

It was a relief, having the place all to herself to be miserable in. Aryan wasn't an intrusive presence, but he was around all the time, and sometimes she wanted to give full rein to her misery. Maybe scream and throw a few things, dignity be damned. She'd thought of going to the flat that Darius had vacated, being by herself for a few days, but it was too closely linked to him.

She'd gone back once, to get it cleaned and cover up the furniture, and the first thing she'd seen on walking in was the huge painting of a spice market that Darius had bought. He hadn't taken it with him, and it was still occupying pride of place on the living room wall. Walking closer to it, she'd noticed a little note stuck to the frame. *'Leaving this for you,'* it had said. *'Love, Darius.'*

It was the *'Love, Darius'* that had done it—she'd burst into tears, standing right there in front of the painting, and the skilfully etched heaps of nutmeg and chillies and cardamom had blurred into random blotches of colour. Once she'd stopped sobbing she'd locked up the flat and never gone back.

Sighing, Mallika buried her face in her hands. She'd finally admitted to herself that she loved Darius, and that letting him go had been one of the stupidest things she'd ever done. She should have worked harder at their relationship instead of endlessly obsessing about her own troubles. But it was too late now—Darius had made it quite clear that he wanted a clean break.

After a while she pulled herself together and went out for a jog in a park near the sea. It had been a while since she'd last run, and she found the rhythm soothing—the steady pounding of her feet on the track helping her push everything to the back of her mind at least for a little while.

She stopped only when she was completely exhausted and the sun had begun to set. And when she got home she was so tired that she flopped into bed and sank into a blessedly dreamless sleep.

'IT'S THE *ANNUAL party*!' Venkat said, in much the same tones that an ardent royalist might say, *It's the coronation*!

Strongly tempted to say *So...?* Mallika raised her eyebrows.

'You can't *not* come,' he said, looking outraged. '*Everyone* will be there.' He brightened up at a sudden thought. 'Darius will be there—he's still in town, and he's made an exception. We haven't told him, but we're holding a little surprise farewell for him at the end.'

Which was exactly the reason why she didn't want to go—but she could hardly tell Venkat that.

'I'll come,' she said. 'But I'll need to leave early. I have some relatives over.'

Well, Aryan *was* a relative, so technically she wasn't lying. And she could think of several things she would rather be doing that evening.

As it turned out, Darius was the first person she ran into when she walked into the party. *Of course*, she thought, giving herself a swift mental kick. She should have landed up there after nine, when the party would have been in full swing, said hello to Venkat and slipped out. Now she was terribly visible among the twenty or so people dotting the ballroom.

Darius found himself unable to take his eyes off Mallika. She was simply, even conservatively dressed, in a full-sleeved grey top and flared palazzo pants. The top, however, clung lovingly to her curves—and it didn't help that he knew exactly what was under it.

'Looking good,' he said, and her lips curved into a tiny smile.

'Thank you,' she said primly, hating the way her heart was pounding in her chest.

The people around them had melted away as soon as they saw Darius and Mallika together—even a blind man would have sensed the strong undercurrents to their conversation.

'Not too bad yourself,' Mallika added, just to prove that she wasn't shaken by his proximity.

It was true—in jeans and a casual jacket worn over a midnight-blue shirt Darius was breathtakingly gorgeous. His hair was brushed straight back from his forehead, and his hooded eyes and hawklike features gave him a slightly predatory look. He'd lost weight in the last month, and his perfectly sculpted cheekbones stood out a little.

'Venkat said you mightn't come,' he said.

She shrugged. 'I don't like formal parties,' she said. 'But he made a bit of a point about it. So I thought I'd hang around until a quarter past eight and then push off.'

Darius glanced at his watch—it was barely eight, and most of the Nidas staff hadn't even arrived yet. In previous years the party had continued till three in the morning. While a few people had left earlier, even then, an eight-fifteen exit would set a new record.

'Do you really need to leave?' he asked. 'Dinner won't be served before ten.'

'I'll eat at home,' she said, giving him a quick smile. 'I'm not too keen on hotel food in any case.'

There was a brief pause, and then they both started speaking together. Somehow that broke the awkwardness, and when Darius laughed Mallika smiled back at him.

'You go first,' he offered.

'I was just asking how your parents are,' she said. 'And Shirin and the kids.'

'They're fine,' Darius said. 'Though my mum's taken to bursting into tears every time we talk about me leaving. It's driving my dad nuts.' His smile was indulgent, as if he was talking about a child and not a sixty-year-old woman. 'And Shirin's doing well. Her divorce hasn't come through yet, but we're hoping it'll happen by the end of the year. She's coping, the kids have settled and she's started looking for a job.'

'That's all good news, then,' Mallika said, smiling warmly at him.

He felt his heart do a sudden flip-flop in his chest.

'Yes,' he said stiltedly. It was tough enough, having to pretend that she was just like any other colleague. Having to actually stand here and carry on a superficial conversation was proving to be incredibly difficult.

'I'll…um…circulate a bit, then,' she said, indicating the half-full room. 'Now that I'm here I should say hello to as many people as I can before slipping out.'

He nodded, about to tell her that he'd like to see her before she left when the lights went out quite suddenly. A loud popping sound followed by the smell of burning plastic indicated a short-circuit.

Mallika stopped in her tracks as people around her gasped and exclaimed. A few women giggled nervously and Darius came to stand next to her, his features barely discernible in the dim light.

He took her arm and swivelled her around a little. 'Maybe you should wait till the lights are back on before you walk around and talk to people.'

'No, I'll just go now,' she said. She hated the dark, and the people milling around were making her nervous. 'I have a torch on my cell phone—hang on, let me put it on.'

The light from the torch was surprisingly strong, and he could see her quite clearly now, her brow furrowed in thought.

'Damn,' she said. 'This thing's running out of charge. I must have taken dozens of calls during the day, and I forgot to charge it before I left.'

'I'll walk you to the exit,' Darius said, taking her arm.

She thought of protesting, but her whole body seemed to turn nerveless at his touch—following him obediently seemed to be the sensible option.

'Shouldn't they put on a back-up generator or something?'

'They won't if it's a short-circuit,' he said. 'There's a risk of fire. Here—I think this is a shorter way out.'

He led her down a corridor that to Mallika looked exactly like the one she'd been in earlier. This was deserted, though, and it opened into a little *faux* Mughal courtyard with a small fountain in the centre. The fountain wasn't playing, but the pool of water around it shimmered in the faint light coming from the streetlights outside the hotel.

At that point the light coming from her phone flickered and the battery died. Mallika made a frustrated sound and shoved it into her bag. 'I can't call my driver now,' she said.

'D'you want to use my phone?'

'That would be very helpful,' she said drily. 'If only I remembered his number.'

'We'll page the car, then,' he said. 'Do you remember the car's number?

'Sort of,' she said. 'It has a nine and a one in it.'

'That helps,' he said gravely. 'Driver's name?'

'Bablu,' she said, so triumphantly that he laughed.

'We can page Bablu, then,' he said. 'That's assuming the paging system is working.'

She grimaced. 'I didn't think of that,' she said. 'Which way's the exit, anyway?'

He pointed to some glass doors opposite the ones they'd used to enter the courtyard.

'That way,' he said. 'Though we might as well sit here for a while. There's a bench over there, and it'll more pleasant outside than inside the hotel with no air-conditioning.'

She followed him to the bench, and he brushed a few leaves off it before they sat down. 'It's so quiet here,' she said. 'You'd hardly think we were in the middle of Mumbai.'

'The walls cut off the noise,' he said. 'But you can

tell you're in Mumbai, all right. Look up—you can't see a single star because of the pollution.'

Mallika laughed. 'You're right, I can't,' she said. 'I should have known you'd burst my little fantasy.'

Darius went very still next to her. 'Why d'you say that?' he asked finally.

She flushed, thankful he couldn't see her in the dark. The words had slipped out, but she *had* been thinking of the happy bubble she'd been living in when they were still dating.

'It was just a stray remark,' she said, wishing he wasn't so perceptive. 'I didn't mean anything by it.'

'I think you did.'

'And I'm telling you I didn't!' Her voice rose slightly. 'Can't you just leave things alone, instead of digging around and trying to make me say more than I want to?'

'I'm sorry,' he said quietly, putting a hand over hers. 'I'm not trying to upset you.'

Mallika jerked her hand away. It was a childish gesture, but she was very near tears, and soon a few drops did escape and roll down her cheeks. She didn't wipe them off, hoping he wouldn't notice in the dark.

Of course she should have known better—Darius immediately leaned closer.

'Are you crying?' he asked, sounding so worried and concerned that her tears rolled faster.

'Of course not,' she said, trying to sound dignified and totally in control.

Unfortunately a little sniffle escaped, and Darius muttered something violent under his breath and swept her abruptly into his arms.

'Mallika—don't,' he said, trying to kiss the tears off her cheeks while simultaneously smoothing her curls away from her face. 'What's wrong? Is it something I did?'

Mallika fought for control and jerked away from him finally, scrubbing at her cheeks with her hands.

'It's all right,' she said. 'Moment of weakness. All better now.' She was feeling hideously embarrassed—crying all over an ex-boyfriend was the ultimate dumped woman cliché.

'It's *not* all right,' he said firmly. 'I know we're not together now, but I care about you still, and I'm not going away until you explain what's wrong.'

'*What* did you say?' Mallika asked, so stunned that she could hardly get the words out coherently.

'I'm not going away until I find out why you were crying,' he said.

'Before that, you dimwit!'

'We're not together now?'

'No, no—*after* that!' Mallika said, sounding outraged.

'I care about you still?' he asked, puzzled and amused in equal parts now.

'Yes, that's it,' she said, relieved that he'd finally got it right. 'Did you mean it?'

'Yes,' he said slowly. 'But you already know that.'

'You never told me!' Mallika said through gritted teeth. 'How the *hell* was I supposed to know?'

It was still dark, and Darius couldn't see her face,

but he could sense the anger coming off her in waves. For the first time since he'd met her that evening he began to think that there might be some hope after all.

'Why else do you think I kept on trying to make it work for us?' he asked gently. 'Even when you kept sending me away?'

'I don't know!' she said. 'I thought it was general cussedness or something! And you lost interest as soon as your travel visas came in!'

He should have been annoyed at that, but right now what she was *not* saying was more important than what she was.

'I *do* care,' he said gently. 'In fact, I think I've been in love with you for a while now—only I kept trying to make myself believe that I was confusing attraction and affection with love. It was only after we split up that I realised how much I love you, and by then it was too late to do anything about it.

'You utter *idiot*,' she breathed.

He frowned. 'Does that mean…?'

'Of course it does,' she said, grabbing him by the shoulders and managing to shake him in spite of his bulk. 'I've been in love with you ever since you took me to meet your family that day. But after that you started to back off, and I didn't know what to think! I wanted to—'

What she'd wanted was lost as his arms came around her, crushing her against his chest.

'I've missed you,' he said, his lips hot and urgent against hers. 'God, so much.'

Mallika kissed him back just as hungrily, her hands gripping his shoulders as if she'd never let him go again. It felt so *right*, being back in his arms—she felt completely alive for the first time since he'd left.

'I missed you too,' she said, when she was able to speak. 'I'd think of calling you every single day, and then I wouldn't because I didn't want to seem desperate.'

'You couldn't have been more desperate than me,' he said wryly. 'I've been an idiot, Mallika. I was so sure I was doing the right thing.'

'By breaking up with me?' She shook her head, sounding confused. 'If you were in love with me, how could it possibly be the right thing?'

'I didn't know you cared for me too,' he said, tracing the delicate line of her jaw with one finger. 'It felt like I was forcing myself on you sometimes. Not physically,' he added as she made a sudden movement of protest. 'But you wanted to keep things light—and there I was, talking about long-distance relationships and making it work, when you clearly didn't want to listen... And you were obviously so uncomfortable with me giving up my job and leaving Mumbai that I thought the best thing to do would be to call a halt.'

'I've thought a lot about that,' Mallika said, sliding a hand up his chest to rest right against his heart. 'I think I finally do understand why you want to get away from the rat race—why you need to break away from what's expected of you.'

'So will you come with me?' he asked, capturing

her hand in both of his and dipping his head to kiss it. 'At least for a while?'

The hidden lighting in the courtyard came on as if on cue, and he could see that her lovely lips were curled up slightly in a smile.

'I'd love to,' she said. 'Not right away—you should have the first few months to yourself, to do what you originally planned, and Aryan still needs me around—but I'll spend every bit of leave I get with you. And once you're back we can figure out what we should do.'

'Get married,' Darius said, and when she instinctively pulled back he didn't let her go. 'I know all the reasons you have for not marrying,' he said. 'But if you think about it none of them hold if we're in love with each other.'

'I'm scared of marriage,' she admitted. 'Scared that things will go wrong and we'll end up being unhappy like my parents were. Even if we love each other now.'

'We'll be fine,' Darius said. 'Trust me.'

And suddenly Mallika knew that she did. She trusted Darius completely and absolutely, and she wanted to spend the rest of her life with him. Marriage still scared her, but she'd have plenty of time to get used to the idea.

'I love you,' she said softly. 'And you're right. We can make it work. Together.'

EPILOGUE

'A GHAR JAMAI—that's what these Hindustanis call men who marry their girls and move in with them,' Aunt Freny said with relish. 'That's what you're going to be. Not that we're not happy you're back. This gypsy-type living for a year might have been fun for you, but it drove all of us mad with worry. Hopefully once you marry you'll stay put. And as you've had your honeymoon before the wedding...'

'Freny!' Mrs Mistry said in awful tones.

Darius had been back for a month, tanned and leaner than he'd been when he left, but otherwise unchanged. Mallika had left Nidas and spent the last three months with him, travelling around Europe. After the wedding they would move into Mallika's flat in Parel, and then they had plans to set up a small company to aid NGOs with improving the infrastructure in rural areas.

'We're still going for a honeymoon, Aunt Freny,' Darius said mildly. 'It's just that it'll be in the villages around Mumbai.'

'It's his wedding day—you leave him alone, Freny,' Mrs Mistry said warningly as Freny geared up to retort. 'Come here, *dikra*, your collar's just a little crooked.'

Darius ignored her. 'Mallika's here,' he said, his eyes lighting up.

Aunt Freny snorted. 'Your son's a son until he gets a wife, et cetera, et cetera,' she said to Mrs Mistry. 'Though in your case your daughter really does seem set to be with you all her life!'

Luckily Mrs Mistry wasn't paying attention either, and she didn't hear Aunt Freny.

Mallika was walking in on Aryan's arm, dressed in a perfectly lovely red brocade sari with a heavily embroidered deep-red veil draped over her head. Her arms were loaded with gold bangles, and she wore a heavy gold *kundan* necklace around her slender neck. For the first time in years her curly hair was parted in the middle and tied back in a demure chignon, and she wore a red *bindi* in the centre of her forehead.

Darius was still gazing at her, spellbound, when she stumbled a little. She was quite close to him now, and he caught her by the shoulders to steady her.

'High heels,' she said, making a little face and laughing up at him. 'My aunt insisted.'

'You look lovely,' he said, meaning it.

She blushed a little. 'I don't feel like myself,' she said. 'If I could, I'd get married in my work clothes.'

'You'd look just as lovely,' he said, bending down to kiss her.

There was a collective indrawn breath from Mallika's side of the family, while Darius's smiled indulgently.

'Come on—let's get this show on the road,' Aryan said. 'Stop looking into each other's eyes, people.' His newly acquired, now *off* line girlfriend elbowed him, and he said, 'What? They'll miss the *muhurat* and Auntie Sarita will have a fit!'

It was a simple registered wedding, in spite of Mallika's interfering aunt's insistence on a traditional wedding sari and the actual signing happening at an auspicious time. Once they were done, both bride and groom heaved a sigh of relief.

'Any chance of us being allowed to skip the reception?' Darius asked hopefully.

His mother glared at him. 'Absolutely not,' she said firmly. 'How can you even suggest it, Darius?'

'Because I want to be alone with my wife,' he said in an undertone.

Mallika smiled up at him. 'We have the rest of our lives together,' she said, and he smiled back, putting an arm around her and pressing his lips to the top of her head.

'So we do,' he said softly as she slipped an arm around his waist and leaned in closer. 'Did I happen to mention how much I love you, Mrs Mistry?'

'You did say something about it,' Mallika said thoughtfully. 'But it wasn't all that clear. Could you explain it a little more clearly, please?'

* * * * *

We hope you enjoyed reading this
special collection from Harlequin® books.

If you liked reading these stories,
then you will love
Harlequin® Blaze® books!

You like it hot!
Harlequin Blaze stories sizzle with strong
heroines and irresistible heroes playing the
game of modern love and lust. They're fun,
sexy and always steamy.

Enjoy four *new* stories from
Harlequin Blaze every month!

Available wherever books and
ebooks are sold.

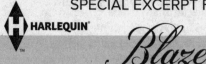
Sailor boy didn't look up. Not because he didn't notice
the other woman's departure—something about the way
he held himself warned her he was aware of everyone
and everything around him—but because polite clearly
wasn't part of his daily repertoire.

Fine. She wasn't all that civilized herself.

The blonde made a face, her ponytail bobbing as she
started hoofing it along the beach. "Good luck with that
one," she muttered as she passed Mia.

Oookay. Maybe this *was* mission impossible. Still,
she'd never failed when she'd been out in the field, and
all her gals wanted was intel. She padded into the water,
grateful for the cool soaking into her burning soles. The
little things mattered so much more now.

"I'm not interested." Sailor boy didn't look up from
the motor when she approached, a look of fierce concentration creasing his forehead. Having worked on more
than one Apache helicopter during her two tours of duty,
she knew the repair work wasn't rocket science.

HBEXP0315

She also knew the mechanic and…holy hotness.

Mentally, she ran through every curse word she'd learned. Tag Johnson hadn't changed much in five years. He'd acquired a few more fine lines around the corners of his eyes, possibly from laughing. Or from squinting into the sun since rescue swimmers spent plenty of time out at sea. The white scar on his forearm was as new as the lines, but otherwise he was just as gorgeous and every bit as annoying as he'd been the night she'd picked him up at the Star Bar in San Diego. He was also still out of her league, a military bad boy who was strong, silent, deadly…and always headed out the door.

For a brief second, she considered retreating. Unfortunately, the bridal party was watching her intently, clearly hoping she was about to score on their behalf. Disappointing them would be a shame.

"Funny," she drawled. "You could have fooled me."

Tag's head turned slowly toward her. Mia had hoped for drama. Possibly even his butt planting in the ocean from the surprise of her reappearance. No such luck.

"Sergeant Dominatrix," he drawled back.

Don't miss
WICKED SECRETS
by New York Times *bestselling author Anne Marsh,*
available April 2015 wherever
Harlequin® Blaze® books and ebooks are sold.

www.Harlequin.com

Love the Harlequin book you just read?

Your opinion matters.

Review this book on your favorite book site, review site, blog or your own social media properties and share your opinion with other readers!

Be sure to connect with us at:
Harlequin.com/Newsletters
Facebook.com/HarlequinBooks
Twitter.com/HarlequinBooks